STONE COL

A ROCK SHOP MYSTERY

STONE COLD DEAD

CATHERINE DILTS

FIVE STAR
A part of Gale, Cengage Learning

GALE
CENGAGE Learning®

Detroit • New York • San Francisco • New Haven, Conn • Waterville, Maine • London

LIBRARY OF CONGRESS CATALOGING-IN-PUBLICATION DATA

Dilts, Catherine.
   Stone cold dead : A Rock Shop mystery Catherine Dilts— First edition.
    pages cm
   ISBN-13: 978-1-4328-2743-4 (hardcover)
   ISBN-10: 1-4328-2743-X (hardcover)
   1. Women-owned business enterprises—Fiction. 2. Rocks—Fiction. 3. Teenagers—Crimes against—Fiction. 4. Murder—Investigation—Fiction. 5. Donkeys—Fiction. I. Title.
PS3604.I4633S76 2014
813'.6—dc23   2013031774

First Edition. First Printing: December 2013
Find us on Facebook– https://www.facebook.com/FiveStarCengage
Visit our website– http://www.gale.cengage.com/fivestar/
Contact Five Star™ Publishing at FiveStar@cengage.com

Printed in Mexico
1 2 3 4 5 6 7 17 16 15 14 13

To my husband, Leonard.

ACKNOWLEDGMENTS

An afternoon in Lin Ottinger's Moab Rock Shop in Moab, Utah, provided the inspiration for this story. Kyle answered my many questions about the business, and sold us a fossilized fish. I give credit for the legal and procedural scenes in this book that are correct to the El Paso County Fourth Judicial District Citizen's Academy presented by District Attorney Dan May.

CHAPTER ONE

When Morgan Iverson pushed open the rock shop door, a cowbell clanged loud enough to raise the dead. There were plenty of candidates for resurrection in the shop, starting with the massive T. Rex skull.

"Anybody here?" she called.

The shop faded into gloom as the winter sun dropped behind the mountains. Morgan felt her way through the maze of dusty specimen tables, cluttered with fossilized fish and dinosaur bones. The living quarters butted against the back of the building, separated only by a door with a "Private—Do Not Enter" sign thumbtacked to its center. As Morgan tapped lightly, the unlatched door swung open.

"Hello?"

A fire crackled in the wood-burning stove in a corner of the kitchen. Faded linoleum creaked under Morgan's shoes. Straight ahead, the door to the back pasture stood ajar. She stepped outside, where a van idled with staccato hiccups, spewing exhaust into the chilly air. Morgan watched her brother stuff a suitcase into the back of the van while his wife supervised. They wore baggy, faded jeans, sweatshirts, and hiking boots, not the sandals and camelhair robes Morgan had expected.

"I'm here," Morgan said.

Allie turned, brushing straw-blond hair back from her forehead. "Morgan! You were supposed to be here hours ago." Worry lines creased her fair skin.

"I should have called. My car doesn't like the mountains. I crawled the last hundred miles."

As Allie rushed toward her, Morgan opened her arms, expecting a hug. Instead, Allie splashed through the slushy snow and ran past her into the house.

"It looks like you're leaving already," Morgan said to her brother. "I thought you were going to show me the ropes before you took off."

"Slight change of plans," Kendall said.

Allie lugged a suitcase to the van, brushing past Morgan.

"I'm so grateful you can take over for us," she said.

"This will be like a vacation for me," Morgan said. "Two weeks in the Colorado mountains is a treat, even in the middle of January."

"Two weeks?" Allie frowned and looked up at Kendall. "Didn't you tell your sister?"

He took the suitcase from Allie. "I thought you were going to," he mumbled.

"Tell me what?" Morgan asked.

"Kendall." There was a threat in Allie's voice.

A gust of wind tossed Kendall's wild mane of gray-streaked hair. Scraggly whiskers hid his face. Six years had passed since Morgan had last visited Colorado, but something beyond age had etched deep lines in her brother's face. The part of his face she could see, anyway. Morgan had been so caught up in her own crisis that she hadn't considered her brother and sister-in-law might have faced troubles of their own.

"The thing is, we're not coming back."

"What do you mean?"

Kendall glanced down at his hiking boots. "Our trip has kind of been extended into forever."

Morgan shoved her hands into her coat pockets, and drew in a slow breath. "But I'm only supposed to watch the shop for two weeks."

Kendall finally looked her in the eyes. "How can I make it any clearer?" He placed his hands on his hips and leaned toward Morgan, like he used to when they were kids, squabbling over the rules to a board game. "Are you listening? Not. Coming. Back."

His words echoed off the mountain and bounced back at Morgan like a slap across the face.

"Be nice to your sister," Allie said. "She just drove all the way from South Dakota. She must be exhausted." Allie grasped Morgan's hand. "I thought Kendall told you."

And then he did, explaining with precious few details that their two-week mission trip had morphed into a scheme to establish a group of like-minded religious folks in the Central American jungle. Lately, Kendall and Allie had been speaking of their faith with a zeal that didn't fit the sleepy little church they attended. Morgan tried to banish television news images of failed cults that had ended badly, this time starring her brother and sister-in-law.

Kendall slammed the rear door of the van. "That's it. We're ready."

Morgan wanted to scream that she wasn't ready, that everything was moving too fast, that she needed time to adjust to the curve ball Kendall had just lobbed off the side of her head. Instead, she felt frozen to the walkway, a chill creeping up from the ground, coiling around her legs and working its way under her winter coat.

"You've lost your mind." Morgan turned to Allie. "You're not going along with this, are you?"

"We've been called by the Lord to go on this mission," Allie said.

Morgan tried unsuccessfully to wrap her head around what that phone call must have been like.

"We're leaving," Kendall said. "Just walking away. And if you won't take over, so be it."

He dangled a fistful of keys in front of Morgan.

"Can't you wait another day or two?" she asked. "We need to talk this over. You can't throw away the shop. The land."

"Allie and I have been managing the Rock of Ages for the past twenty years. You used your family as an excuse to dump it on me. Well, that excuse is gone now."

"Kendall." Allie grabbed his arm. "You're out of line."

He shrugged off her hand. Morgan tried to return his glare, but her eyes filled with tears. She was too tired to fight. Kendall balled his hand into a fist and pulled his arm back, preparing to pitch the keys across the pasture.

"Wait." Morgan snatched the keys away from Kendall. "I said I'd stay for two weeks, and that's how long I'm staying."

The next morning, Morgan heard thudding noises through the thin wall. For a moment, she imagined she was back in Sioux Falls, and Sam and the kids were rattling around the kitchen. Then she opened her eyes to a view of a mountain through southwest-patterned curtains, and remembered she was at the Rock of Ages, alone. She pulled on jeans and a sweatshirt and opened the door dividing the living quarters from the shop.

An old cowboy helped himself to coffee from a carafe on the checkout counter, then settled onto an aspen-wood bench.

"Del!" Morgan rushed down the aisle between two long tables covered with dusty rocks.

Delano Addison rose from his seat, his cowboy boots clomping across the pine floor. A tooled leather belt cinched blue jeans to his lean frame, and a worn cowhide vest covered his pressed western shirt.

He thrust out his knobby hand. "Glad you made it in one piece."

Morgan grasped his hand for a moment before Del pulled her into a quick bear hug, then held her at arm's length.

"How you doin', kid?"

Del towered over her. A few more wrinkles creased his weathered face, and his gray hair had thinned out some, but it was the same old Del, bristly mustache and all.

"It's been two years," Morgan said, "and I still miss Sam."

"It don't get any easier, despite what folks try to tell you."

Morgan turned from Del to survey the shop. "I don't have a clue about running a rock shop."

"No problem at all. Kendall's been preoccupied with his church group the past few months. I know the ropes pretty well."

So, Kendall had apparently dumped responsibility for managing the shop onto Del, before dropping his bomb on Morgan. She struggled to smile and nod.

"I'm glad you agreed to take over," Del continued. "I'd be at loose ends if the Rock of Ages closed. Jobs are hard to come by in Golden Springs."

"Kendall wasn't clear about his plans. I came to fill in for two weeks. After that, I'm not sure what's going to happen."

Del's smile collapsed. He tugged at his mustache.

"After I get a cup of coffee," Morgan said, breaking the uncomfortable silence, "how about you show me around?"

"This doesn't have anything to do with running the shop, but it appears you just woke up. Maybe the place to start is the barn."

"The donkeys." Morgan slapped her palm against her forehead. "I forgot all about them. My first day on the job, and I'm late with their breakfast."

In past trips, the smell of hay, manure, and aged wood in the solid old barn had been soothing. This time, Morgan felt the burden of being responsible for its residents, for the next two weeks, anyway.

A stall door stood open to the elements in all but the worst weather. Houdini and Adelaide could enter the barn as they pleased, but Del told her they preferred to wander around the pasture behind the rock shop. Except, of course, at mealtime.

"So where are they?" Morgan asked.

"Maybe they got tired of waiting for breakfast."

Morgan followed Del outside.

"Shoot. The back gate is open. Guess we'll have an old-fashioned roundup your first day here."

Houdini and Adelaide apparently lived up to their escape-artist namesakes. Morgan didn't think all-terrain vehicles were standard equipment in the Old West, but she didn't argue when Del insisted they needed an ATV to retrieve the donkeys. She zipped up her thick blue coat, well suited to South Dakota winters, but too bulky for cowgirl work. Morgan climbed onto the ATV behind Del, gripping the handholds with her mittens as the noisy machine bounced across a pasture soggy with melting snow. Del parked beside the fence and turned off the ATV.

"Get your oats. Rattle the can a little. They should come right to us."

The donkeys grazed on the far side of the fence. Morgan shook her coffee can. Houdini stretched out his neck, his nostrils flared and his brown eyes riveted on the tin can as Morgan approached the open gate. Mud caked the donkeys' gray legs from hoof to knee. Their thick winter coats looked impervious to the chilly wind, and their stubby manes stood at attention, stiff as bristle brushes.

Morgan wondered what would become of the donkeys if she sold the Rock of Ages. Would their final home be a glue factory?

"Houdini." Del rattled his can of oats. "Adelaide. Come get your oats."

Instead of enticing them back into the pasture, Del's offer seemed to alarm them. The donkeys spun around, parting ways where the trail branched in three different directions. Houdini followed the fence line to the left, while Adelaide headed straight uphill.

"What do we do now?" Morgan asked.

"Follow them." Del sighed. "On foot. If we go after them with the ATV, they'll just run faster. I don't want to take a chance on them getting injured. It's gonna be a long morning."

Morgan's sneakers filled with cold mud as soon as she walked through the gate.

"I'll go after Houdini," Del said. "He's harder to catch. You get Adelaide."

"What if I can't catch her?"

"They'll tire out after a while. Do you have a cell phone on you?"

Morgan patted her jeans pocket. "Yes."

"Not that you always get a signal out here, but it's best to be prepared." Del lifted a daypack off his ATV. "There's water, granola bars, and a first-aid kit in here. If you don't make it back to the shop in an hour, give me a call."

"It could take that long?"

"With these two, you never know. Put this on."

He helped Morgan pull the pack on over her winter coat. The straps dug into her shoulders.

"This weighs a ton. I'm just chasing a donkey. What could happen?"

"You hear about it every winter," Del said. "Some flatlander heads out unprepared. They don't get found until a hiker sees their frozen body in a snowbank come springtime."

"You have quite the way with words."

Del tugged his bushy gray mustache. "I'm just saying."

★ ★ ★ ★ ★

"Adelaide," Morgan called. "Come back. The mountain lions will get you."

The threat used to work on the kids, when she and Sam hiked with them on summer visits. The donkey ignored her warning, disappearing over the top of the hill. Morgan clenched her hands into fists inside her wool mittens.

"Stupid donkey. I'm not acclimated."

Coming from low altitude prairie to the mountains was a difficult transition. It was best to ease into strenuous activity. Instead, Morgan was chasing a donkey up a mountain her first full day in Colorado.

The crisp January air puffed out of her lungs in humid clouds. Like the steam locomotive in the children's story, Morgan told herself. *I think I can, I think I can, I think I can.* It hadn't been this hard six years ago. Halfway up the hill, she paused. No bird song. Pale sunlight filtered through high thin clouds. Sodden brown grasses and naked branches poked through the last of a week-old snow.

Not exactly a picture postcard.

She shrugged out of the heavy daypack. She could pick it up on the way back. Right now, it was just slowing her down. At the top of the hill, Morgan pressed her hands to her knees and leaned over, gasping for breath. Adelaide stood at the bottom, drinking from the creek that ran across the trail. Morgan hurried downhill, her worn sneakers slipping. The donkey lifted her head, water dripping from her muzzle. She waited until Morgan was nearly close enough to grab her halter, then trotted up the next hill.

The path ended at the intersection with a wider, well-groomed trail. Adelaide seemed to know where she was going, taking the trail branching to the right. When Morgan reached the intersection, she read the wooden trail sign. They had reached the Columbine Trail.

"I should just go back," Morgan said aloud. "Leave you to fend for yourself."

She waited until her racing heart slowed, then continued her pursuit. At the top of the next hill, the trail leveled out. A meadow stretched from the railroad tracks on the right to the creek on the left. Across the creek, at the top of a cliff, Morgan could see four log cabins peeking through pine trees.

Adelaide strolled past the meadow, following the trail as it plunged into a grove of cottonwood trees. Morgan hurried to catch up. Bare limbs arched over the trail. The dim January sun cast mottled shadows onto a carpet of decomposing leaves.

Morgan walked swiftly, anxious to escape the short section of tunnel-like trail. A shiver ran up her spine, and not from the chill wind. She tried to catalog the discordant symphony of sounds, connecting each to a harmless source. Wind gusted through the brush, rattling dried leaves. The creek gurgled over rocks and under sheets of ice. Birds cried warnings to each other. Morgan wouldn't have called it song.

An abrupt crashing instantly drowned out the subtler sounds of the forest. Morgan stopped and held her breath. An unseen creature thrashed its way through the brush, parallel to the trail. She searched the shadows, hoping she had caught up with Adelaide at last.

She thought she glimpsed dark wings fluttering like a curtain blown by the wind. The racket faded as it moved away from Morgan. She started walking again, debating the wisdom of continuing her chase. It had to be a deer, she told herself. A clumsy deer.

Morgan rounded a curve, then skidded to a halt. She squinted, straining to identify the dark object sprawled half on the trail, half in the brush. For one instant, she feared it was Adelaide, the victim of a mountain lion after all.

17

But it was a darker color than Adelaide's muddy gray. Maybe some other animal. Morgan struggled to remember whether to stand her ground and act ferocious, or drop and play dead. That depended on whether it was a bear or a mountain lion.

It moved.

Backing up, Morgan stepped on a dry branch. The branch snapped, the sound loud as a gunshot. The creature raised itself out of the brush. Morgan pressed her mitten against her mouth, stifling a scream.

She turned to run, but tripped over her own feet. Scrambling on hands and knees, she struggled to put distance between herself and the creature. Morgan turned to look back, her arms raised protectively in front of her.

Feathers burst into motion with a raucous cry. Morgan lowered her arms. It was just a magpie. The black and white bird hopped on top of a dark mound. It stabbed with its beak, gave a violent jerk, and flew toward the top of a cottonwood. A glittering chain dangled from its beak.

Morgan rose and dared take a few steps closer. If her imagination could turn a magpie into a monster, what was the object on the trail? A trash sack? An abandoned sleeping bag?

As she neared, she noticed a pale hand extending from a fold of fabric. A human hand.

CHAPTER TWO

Morgan's legs felt unsteady as she moved closer. There was no mistake. A small, pale hand extended from the dark cloth. A person, presuming the hand was attached to an arm, a shoulder, and all the rest.

"Del!" Morgan yelled. She listened for a moment. "Del!"

She jerked her mittens off and pulled her cell phone out of her pocket. No signal. Morgan fought nausea as she forced herself to kneel by the hand. She played back the steps she had learned in her first-aid training class.

"Hello?"

No answer.

Check the safety of the surroundings. Glancing around, Morgan saw no reason to move the person. *Personal protective equipment.* A stranger might be infected with a communicable disease. Del's daypack had a first-aid kit. It probably had the latex gloves and face shield she needed, but she'd left it several hills back. *Call nine-one-one.*

She flipped open her phone again, somehow expecting it to work now. Still no signal.

"What next?" Morgan whispered to herself. "What next? Check the victim. Injuries or illness."

The body—the person—was cloaked in a long black garment similar to a trench coat, but too lightweight to be useful as a winter coat. Morgan reached out, tugging the black cloth away from the mound.

She faced the back of the person's head. The short, raggedly trimmed black hair had blond roots. Morgan took a deep breath to steady herself, and stepped over the person.

It was a young girl. A teenager. Her bloodshot eyes stared at nothing. Black lipstick coated her open mouth. Pale skin stretched across gaunt cheeks. Piercings marred one eyebrow, her right nostril, and her lower lip.

A tattoo of dark wings peeked above the collar of the black coat. They might have been the wings of the monster Morgan had imagined. Or maybe it was a magpie.

"Miss? Miss? Are you okay?"

Morgan grasped the girl's shoulder and gave a gentle shake.

No response.

She watched the girl's chest for any rise or fall indicating that she was breathing. She was as still as she was silent. Morgan pressed her fingers to the girl's wrist. She couldn't feel a pulse.

This would be the point at which to begin CPR. But her instructor had cautioned repeatedly about the dangers of performing CPR on a stranger. Tattoos and piercings increased the likelihood that a person carried blood-borne pathogens.

Morgan cursed herself for leaving Del's daypack on the trail. She wasn't sure how far she had come, chasing after Adelaide, or when she would reach cell phone range. Surely the cabins she had seen before reaching the cottonwood grove had cell signal.

Keeping one eye on the signal bars on her phone, Morgan ran up the trail. She glanced behind once, imprinting the location in her memory. Then the trail dipped and turned, and the girl was out of view.

Climbing another hill, her already racing heart screamed for oxygen. Morgan slowed to a brisk walk, then a slow walk, then a painful plodding. Finally, she found signal.

"Nine-one-one." A calm, efficient voice.

"Y—yes. Hello?" Morgan gasped for breath.

"What's your emergency?"

"There's a girl. She's hurt."

"What's your address?"

"I'm on a hiking trail."

"Can you tell me which trail?"

"The Columbine Trail."

"Are you with the girl now?"

"No," Morgan said. "I had to leave her to get in cell phone range."

"Is the girl breathing?"

"I don't think so."

"Did you try CPR?"

"I didn't have a CPR kit with me. She has tattoos and piercings and I was afraid she might be on drugs or have hepatitis or something, so I didn't try." Morgan's words came out in a sob. "I'm sorry. Should I go back?"

"No. Stay where you are. We're dispatching a crew right now. Hang on. Can you tell me your name?"

"Morgan Iverson."

"Okay Morgan. Stay calm. Pine County Search and Rescue is on the way."

The dispatcher kept a conversation going. An agonizingly long time passed before Morgan heard squawking walkie-talkies, the clanking of gear, and heavy boots crunching in the gravel.

Two men and one woman trotted up the trail, unmistakable in white helmets and black and yellow jackets, and loaded down with huge backpacks. The men carried an aluminum-framed stretcher. Even their hiking slacks looked heavy, the many pockets bulging.

"Where's the victim?" the woman on the rescue team asked.

"That way." Morgan pointed.

The crew trotted up the trail. She managed to keep up until

they neared the spot where she had found the girl. The crew broke into a full gallop, leaving Morgan behind. She slowed to a walk, trying unsuccessfully to catch her breath.

The woman jogged back to Morgan. "Where's the victim?"

Morgan hurried to the arching cottonwood trees. She stared at the crushed grasses at the side of the trail.

"She's gone."

Morgan watched with dismay as the Pine County Search and Rescue crew stomped through the thick brush hunting for the young woman, destroying any sign that a body had been there.

Rolf, a large man with sandy hair, mangled a sapling pulling himself back onto the trail.

"You're sure you saw something?" he asked.

"I'm not crazy." Morgan neglected to mention the creature she had seen just before finding the girl, which might contradict her claim to sanity. Was it possible the girl hadn't been there? She shook her head. "I'm certain. I touched her. She was real."

"No one else came by?" Judy, an athletic blonde, had jogged down the trail "a mile or so" just to be sure.

"No. I didn't see anyone." Morgan placed her mitten-covered hands on her hips. "Maybe you should call the police."

"We're under the authority of the county sheriff," Lonnie said. "I phoned in, but they're responding to an incident."

"The entire police department?" Morgan asked.

"Sheriff's department," Lonnie corrected. He pulled off his battered white helmet and pushed thick black hair out of his eyes.

Rolf held his hands out to his sides. "There's no evidence there was anyone here."

"You saw the impression in the grass," Morgan said, pointing toward the brush.

"That's exactly what it looks like when deer lie down in the grass," Rolf said. "If there was a girl here, maybe she left."

"Or maybe it was that donkey you were chasing," Lonnie said.

Morgan remembered the crashing sound in the brush. If she told Rolf about it, he would be convinced Morgan was a city slicker who couldn't tell the difference between a human and a deer.

"There was a girl." Morgan shook her head. "She wasn't in any condition to leave. I'm not even sure she was alive."

"Lacking a body," Lonnie said, "and considering it could have been a deer, I don't see the point of bringing in the sheriff."

Judy's walkie-talkie squawked. "Judy here. Yeah, we're with her now. Who? Hang on." She waved the device at Morgan. "A Mr. Addison wants to talk to you."

Morgan grabbed the walkie-talkie, pressing the talk button. "Del?" She released the button.

"I tried calling your cell phone," Del said. "When you didn't answer, I called search and rescue. What's going on?"

Morgan gave Del a quick rundown of her situation. Finding the girl. The nine-one-one call. Losing the girl.

"We're still looking for her," Morgan said. "Del, I didn't find Adelaide."

"She came back on her own. Must have circled around you."

By the time the crew convinced Morgan they needed to call off the search, the sun had dipped behind the mountains. The air turned frigid as the shadow of the mountain range fell across the trail. Morgan shivered. Her wet sneakers felt stiff with cold.

The search and rescue trio escorted Morgan to the trailhead on the highway. She filled out paperwork, even though she feared it would be filed in a "crazy lady sees things" folder. Morgan's hands shook and her stomach churned as they drove toward town. Judy cranked up the SUV's heater, but it couldn't dispel the chill that sent tremors through Morgan's body.

The rock shop sat uphill from the small tourist town of Golden Springs. The SUV roared up the gravel road to the shop. The sign at the entrance to the Rock of Ages, painted in black block letters on a green wooden T. Rex, had faded badly. As they pulled into the parking lot, Houdini brayed in greeting. Adelaide ignored them, concentrating on reaching a clump of dried grass through the pasture fence.

"Are you sure you're okay?" Judy asked.

"I'm fine. Thanks for the ride."

The door to the Rock of Ages opened as Morgan climbed out of the SUV. A pregnant stranger ushered Morgan inside, her fringed denim skirt revealing cowgirl boots as red as the hair pinned up in a bun on top of her head.

"You gave us a scare. Del told us search and rescue had to come after you." She steered Morgan to the aspen bench facing the checkout register.

"They didn't come after me." Morgan plopped down on the bench. "We were looking for a body."

"A body?" Another woman sat next to Morgan, her slender legs too long for the low bench. She didn't look much older than Morgan's daughter, her olive skin smooth across high cheekbones. Morgan envied the woman's hiking boots. Her feet were two frozen lumps.

"I'm Lucy Geary." She extended a hand. "You must be Kendall's sister."

"Morgan Iverson." Morgan returned Lucy's firm handshake.

"Lucy makes the Native American jewelry," the redhead said. "I'm Cindy. I've been working for Allie and Kendall for the past two years. Part-time." She patted her pioneer-style maternity blouse, cascading over an advanced pregnancy.

Del stepped out of the restroom with a coffee carafe full of water. "I didn't tell them much." He poured the water into the coffeemaker's reservoir. "You might as well start at the beginning."

Morgan wrapped her coat tightly around her. She wasn't sure if she was shivering from the cold, or from shock.

"I don't know that there's much to tell. Del and I were trying to round up the donkeys. When they went different directions, I followed Adelaide." She paused. "I saw a body. I called nine-one-one."

"A real body?" Cindy's green eyes seemed to contain more curiosity than fear.

Morgan pulled her wool cap off and ran her fingers through her shoulder-length curls, brushing them away from her face. "I saw something." She paused, unsure whether she should mention hallucinating a monster. "When I figured out it was a girl, I don't know. I panicked."

Cindy pressed a hand against the front of her maternity blouse. "A girl?"

"A young woman," Morgan said. "Maybe a teenager. I didn't have cell phone signal where she was. I don't know if she was dead or not when I found her, but by the time the search and rescue crew got there, she was gone."

"If she moved," Lucy said, "she couldn't have been dead."

Morgan twisted the wool cap in her hands. "I should have tried CPR. Then I'd know."

Del folded his arms across his cowhide vest. "Eighty percent of the time, CPR won't revive a person. And dead people don't walk away. So she must have been okay."

"Maybe she was drunk," Cindy said. "Passed out on the trail. When you found her, she woke up."

"What did she look like?" Lucy asked. "This is a small town. Maybe we've seen her around."

Morgan took a deep breath and blew it out quickly. "Okay. You'd remember if you've seen her. She was white. Really pale.

Her hair was coal black, but the roots were blond, and it was choppy, like a child had cut it with safety scissors. She had piercings in her nose, eyebrow, and lip. And she had black lipstick."

"She sounds goth," Cindy said.

"What's that?" Del asked.

"Some kids fall into witchcraft." Cindy waved her hands around. "They wear black to reflect the darkness of their souls. It's like they're imitating death."

"Sounds like she did a pretty good job of that," Del said.

"There's a big difference between a kid playing Harry Potter, and someone actually practicing witchcraft," Lucy said.

"Less difference than you think, my friend," Cindy said.

"Is there anything else about her that was distinctive?" Lucy asked.

"She was wrapped in a black coat or robe," Morgan said. "She had a tattoo on her neck, but it was mostly covered by her collar."

"It's a good thing you didn't try to do CPR," Cindy said. "Tattoos? Piercings? She could have had AIDS."

"My first-aid instructor warned us that tattooed victims can carry blood-borne pathogens."

"Do you know how to do CPR?" Lucy asked.

"I've taken the class," Morgan said. "The first-aid training has come in handy, but I've never had to use the CPR. This would have been the first time. And I blew it."

"If the girl was taking drugs," Del said, "and you started doing CPR on her, she might have attacked you."

"She didn't look like she was alive, much less ready to attack. Del, please don't tell my daughter, Sarah, about this, if she calls. Or my son. I don't want them to worry about me."

"Did you have any pepper spray?" Lucy asked.

"No."

"You've got to be prepared for emergencies when you go hiking," Del said. "The mountains aren't like the big city you came from. You had your survival pack, right?"

Del looked Morgan over like he was taking inventory.

"I took the pack off, Del. I left it on the trail. I'm sorry. I'll go get it."

Morgan started to rise. Del shook his head.

"Don't worry about it. I need to fix the latch on the gate. I'll get it then."

"Golden Springs is really a safe area," Lucy said. "Don't let this experience stop you from hiking."

"I could barely jog up that hill to get in cell phone range," Morgan said. She rested her elbows on her knees and buried her face in her hands. "Maybe if I'd been faster, the rescue people would have found the girl."

Lucy rested a hand on Morgan's shoulder. "A new running club is starting up. We'll help you get in shape. Then you can run up a hill when you need to."

Morgan didn't want to think about future emergencies. She'd had a chance to save a life, and she had failed.

CHAPTER THREE

The alarm clock buzzed. Morgan pulled the pillow over her head. The mystery of the missing goth girl had given her a nearly sleepless night, the teen's empty eyes haunting her restless dreams. Now that she had finally fallen into a deep sleep, the alarm sounded. Morgan remembered Lucy's statement that Golden Springs was a small town, and her own hope that Kendall and Allie's congregation was still Gossip Central. By dropping in on the Golden Springs Community Church, she might find out if anyone was missing a teenage girl. Morgan groaned and sat up.

The queen-sized pillow-top bed was heavenly. The larger of the two small bedrooms, the cramped room contained a nightstand, a lamp, and a wardrobe. Morgan rummaged through her suitcase, looking for something appropriate to wear to church services. She settled on gray wool slacks and a matching blazer, with a pink blouse. The slacks were snug.

That's the problem with wool, Morgan thought. *It shrinks.*

She sucked in her stomach and fastened the slacks. Maybe she did need to join Lucy's running club. Morgan attended to her top priority first, feeding the donkeys and making sure their water hadn't frozen overnight.

Then she hurried across the driveway to the garage. Long ago it had been a carriage house, and not much had been done to modernize it. Morgan tugged open the heavy wooden doors and stepped between her car and the two ATVs taking up the

28

other half of the garage. The Buick started reluctantly and chugged down the hill to Golden Springs.

The church sat on a generous plot of land a block south of Main Street. The lawn that stretched from the curb to the flower beds was brown in the January cold. To the right of the front entrance, a stand of aspens huddled together, skeletal branches grasping at the sky.

The church occupied a building that looked much older than it was, by design. The stonework, wood shingle roof, and stained-glass windows gave the impression that it had stood on that spot since the founding of the town in 1876. The cornerstone stated the foundation had been laid a mere twenty-five years ago. It was a gentle deception, in Morgan's opinion.

Morgan's low-heeled ankle boots crunched on ice-melting granules scattered across the sidewalk. The entrance doors opened into a narrow foyer. Stepping into the social hall, warm coffee-scented air enveloped her.

Morgan timed her arrival to avoid the new-visitor-greeting routine. She had attended the church twice every summer for many years. She and Sam brought the kids for their annual stay with Kendall and Allie, picking them up two or three weeks later. Six years had passed since her last visit. She doubted anyone remembered her.

The couple guarding the sanctuary doors stuffed an order of service into her hand and scooted her inside.

Wood pews with maroon cushions lined the oak-floored sanctuary. Morgan slipped into a seat as far to the rear as she could find. She had barely gotten settled when the introit music ended and the choir started a song. Morgan stood with the rest of the congregation and shuffled through the hymnal to the correct page.

She went through the motions, struggling to keep her attention on the sermon. Pastor James Filbury had not changed his preaching style. His voice was soothing, his message comforting.

The congregation was solidly mainstream. How it had inspired Kendall with the crazy idea to move to Central America to establish a cult baffled Morgan. The kindly old gentleman behind the podium hardly seemed the type to spawn zealots.

The crisp white collar of Pastor Filbury's dress shirt and the knot of his blue tie peeked above the solid black of his clerical robe. Silver hair groomed short and neat was losing the battle with a growing patch of scalp. The oversized silver frames of his eyeglasses were a couple decades out of date, but they suited him.

A closing hymn ended the service. Feeling a bit like an undercover agent, Morgan moved with the crowd into the social hall. She stood by the windows, a white ceramic mug of steaming coffee in her hand, murmuring "good morning" to strangers, and mulling over the polite way to strike up a conversation about a missing body.

Cindy Lyons waved at Morgan. She towed a tall, red-haired lumberjack of a man to the windows. Morgan was surprised to see her employee in Golden Springs Community Church. After her pronouncements about goth kids and witchcraft, Cindy seemed more a candidate for the hellfire-and-brimstone type church.

"Herb, this is my new boss lady. Mrs. Iverson, this is my husband, Herb." Cindy looked up at Herb, a good head and a half taller than she, although Cindy was not short. "She's the gal who found the body and then lost it."

Herb shifted the toddler he was holding from one arm to the other. He held out a large, calloused hand and crushed Morgan's fingers briefly. "Nice to meet you, ma'am," he mumbled.

"Please call me Morgan."

"And these are the kids." Cindy placed a hand on top of the red heads of children with uniform upturned noses and freckled cheeks. "Jacob, a year and a half. Isaac, three. Rebekah, six. Ruth, eight. And Matthew, nine." The boys wore blue jeans, cowboy shirts, and sneakers. The girls wore jumpers over long-sleeved blouses, cable tights, and Mary Janes. Cindy's outfit matched the girls', except for her ever-present red cowgirl boots.

Morgan surveyed the children. "What a beautiful family. And another on the way!"

"We believe in big families." She glanced up at Herb with an adoring smile. "Right, honey?"

"Yup," Herb grunted. The three-year-old boy grabbed Herb's hand and led him to the cookie table.

Morgan decided to cut to the chase. "Cindy, I wondered if you've heard whether anyone here's missing a teenager?"

"You mean the body you lost?" Cindy didn't wait for a reply. "You need to meet Beatrice. If anything happens in Golden Springs, Beatrice knows."

Cindy grabbed Morgan's arm and pulled her to the church kitchen. The room was designed to prepare food for a crowd, with two refrigerators, a restaurant-style stove and oven, and cupboards lining walls painted industrial white. The humid air smelled faintly of bleach and lemon-scented dishwashing soap.

Three women, aprons tied around their waists, bustled around cleaning and putting away dishes.

"Ladies," Cindy announced, "this is Kendall's sister, Morgan Iverson."

A stout woman with short, steel-gray hair stuck out her hand. "I'm Beatrice," she said in a no-nonsense tone. "Welcome to Golden Springs." A white cotton apron covered her navy-blue sweater. Polyester slacks and thick-soled shoes completed a look that screamed "sensible." Beatrice's handshake was as solid and assured as her words.

"I remember you." A tiny lady held out a delicate hand. Her soft words carried a hint of a Japanese accent. "You are Kendall's sister. You came every summer."

Morgan was careful not to squeeze her hand too tight, for fear of breaking bones.

"Mrs. McCormick," Morgan said. "I'm so happy to see you."

The Irish name might seem incongruous with her refined Japanese features, but Mrs. McCormick was a WWII war bride. Her Irish-American husband had passed away over a decade ago. A cream jacket and mid-calf skirt accented her thin figure, and a cotton puff of white hair cradled her pale face.

"Please call me Teruko," Mrs. McCormick said. "I feel as though we are old friends. How are your children? I remember they were so polite and well-behaved."

"Thank you," Morgan said. "Dave's at college studying engineering, and Sarah's married and has a baby on the way."

"I'm so happy for you."

The third woman was somewhere between Morgan's age and Beatrice's. Tall and lean, she had the tanned face of a lifetime outdoorswoman.

"Anna Heiden." She climbed off a step stool and held out her hand. The frilly apron tied around her waist covered a safari jacket and khaki slacks. "I work for the newspaper."

She clasped Morgan's hand, her grip firm.

"I understand you're here to stay," Beatrice said.

"I agreed to fill in temporarily for Kendall and Allie," Morgan said. "Two weeks."

"Allie told me they're not coming back," Cindy said.

"Someone's got to run the Rock of Ages," Anna said.

"You bet," Cindy said. "Or else I'm out of a job, and Del loses his job and his home."

"The first time I heard about this crazy plan to move to Central America permanently was when I arrived Friday night.

I don't know what I'm going to do about the rock shop. I haven't even unpacked my suitcase yet."

"Whatever you do," Beatrice said, "don't let Piers Townsend get his hands on your property."

Morgan held up both hands in a gesture of surrender. "Please, slow down. You're throwing too much at me. I've got a lot of unexpected changes to adjust to."

"Like finding a body?" Beatrice asked.

News traveled even faster than Morgan had anticipated.

"I told the ladies," Cindy said. "At the shop you said you wanted to find out who the girl was."

Beatrice settled her weight onto the padded seat of a four-legged wooden stool.

"Sit down, Morgan."

The ladies joined her, perching on mismatched chairs and stools.

"I'm not sure how much I'm supposed to say." Morgan met Anna's eyes. "This is off the record."

Anna shook her head. "I'm the administrative staff, not a reporter."

All business, Beatrice asked, "Did the police tell you to keep quiet?"

"The police didn't show up. Search and rescue looked for the girl, but they couldn't find her."

Beatrice frowned. "Maybe you'd better start at the beginning."

Morgan recited a condensed version of her story. She was getting better with every retelling of her misadventure. Instead of the jumble she had spilled out for search and rescue, or the emotional account she had dumped on Del, Cindy, and Lucy, the story was coherent.

"Huh," Beatrice said. "No body. Nothing to investigate."

"From Morgan's description, I'd say she's goth," Cindy said.

"Goth?" Teruko asked.

Cindy delivered her colorful explanation again.

"You're sure you saw the girl?" Beatrice asked.

"I touched it. Her." Morgan wiped her hands down her gray slacks, then stopped herself. "You can't feel something you imagine."

"Moving is very stressful," Anna said.

Beatrice nodded. "Search and rescue wouldn't overlook a body. You must be mistaken."

Teruko patted Morgan's knee with a trembling hand. "I believe you."

"We would have heard if she was a Golden Springs girl," Anna said. "I'll bet she's from the city."

"I agree," Beatrice said. "Doesn't sound like a local kid. But I'll see what I can find out."

"You're both fooling yourselves." Cindy leaned forward, speaking in a hoarse whisper. "Golden Springs is infested with New Agers and devil worshippers. We need to clean up this town, before it's too late!"

Morgan hoped she didn't look as startled as she felt. She wondered how Cindy proposed cleaning up, and whether it involved burning at the stake.

Downtown Golden Springs was a protected historic district. Shops might change, but the outward appearance still exuded Old West. Brick facades, hitching posts, and streetlights designed to look like old-fashioned wrought-iron gas lamps lined the six blocks.

Morgan pulled in to the first empty parking space, a half a block from the bakery. A pink and white striped awning shaded the front bay window. Silk banners decorated with bright flowers flapped from flagpoles on either side of the glass-paned front door. The name had changed from Hindersman's Baked

Goods to Bibi's Bakery, in loopy pink script across the bay window.

A gentle bell tinkled when Morgan pushed the door open. She doubted the owner could hear it above the conversations of the half dozen people waiting in line at the counter. Another dozen sat at bistro tables covered with pink and white striped cloths.

Morgan inhaled deeply the yeasty smell of fresh baked goods. When she reached the counter, a teenage girl took her order: a latte, a blueberry scone, and a loaf of whole grain bread to take home.

The young woman behind the counter wore her wavy strawberry-blond hair pulled back with a pink hair clip. Her cheeks were flushed the same shade of pink as her apron. While not overweight, she looked like she was not averse to sampling a few of the pastries.

No piercings. No tattoos. Definitely not goth.

Another girl filled the orders. Thinner, and with straight brown hair cut in a bob, she exuded a girl-next-door wholesomeness. She moved with efficient energy, placing pastries in bags or on plates.

On the wall behind the cash register hung an embroidered sign in a Victorian-style picture frame: "Never trust a skinny cook." The woman running the cash register was definitely to be trusted. She wore a chef's jacket in the same shade of pink as everything else in the bakery, tailored to her generous figure. Her name badge identified her as Bernie.

"Are you visiting Golden Springs?" Bernie smiled as she took Morgan's debit card and swiped it through the reader.

"I'm managing the Rock of Ages, temporarily," Morgan said.

"You're Kendall's sister?" She handed Morgan her card and receipt.

"Yes." In Golden Springs, it seemed her identity would always be tied to Kendall.

Bernie waved her hands in excitement. Her green eyes sparkled. "I've been dying to meet you. Can you stay for a bit? The after-church rush will be over soon."

"I have to clean the barn," Morgan said, "but it's not going anywhere."

"Good!" Bernie clapped her plump hands together. "Grab a table, and I'll be over as soon as I can take a break."

Morgan picked up a newspaper and sat at a small, round table by the window. The *Golden Springs Gazetteer* had an old-fashioned appearance, but the pages contained modern issues.

"Big Box Goliath Defeated, But No Victory for David," screamed the above-the-fold headline. Morgan started reading, wondering if the local newspaper had a religious slant.

"The Golden Springs City Council voted down an ordinance that would have allowed a corporation to develop meadowland on the south end of town. While many of us are grateful that the desecration of our fair town with a behemoth retailer has been halted, we face another development issue of equal magnitude. The big box Goliath has been defeated, but what will become of the Mom and Pop shops, the Davids of retail, if you will."

Only in a small-town, weekly newspaper could someone get away with writing anything so over the top. Morgan continued reading.

"City Council, in yet another shortsighted move, voted down a rezoning proposal that would open up much needed land for a residential development."

First development was bad. Now it was good.

"Rezoning would increase the tax base, draw more year-round business, and change the very complexion of Golden Springs. The undue influence of certain factions of our city is delaying needed change."

Morgan wondered who stood to profit from rezoning.

"I can take a break now." Bernie stood beside Morgan's table. "Find something interesting?"

Morgan folded the paper. "I thought I was reading an article, but I think it's an editorial."

Bernie eased her large frame onto a bistro chair. "Kurt owns the newspaper, and I can tell you, he's thoroughly opinionated." She held out her hand. "I'm Bernadette Belmont, thus the name of the bakery, Bibi's. My friends call me Bernie. Welcome to Golden Springs."

Morgan grasped her hand. "Morgan Iverson."

"How are Kendall and Allie? Have they gotten settled in?"

"They haven't called yet," Morgan said, "but Kendall promised he would as soon as he could."

"I had Kendall and Allie over for dinner a couple nights before they left town. They were so excited about moving."

Her brother had apparently told everyone in town his plans, and yet lied to her. Probably because he knew she wouldn't have agreed to move to Golden Springs. Not permanently.

"Yes," Morgan said, "they were certainly anxious to leave." She broke a piece off her blueberry scone. "I can see why your bakery is so popular. This is delicious."

Bernie patted her ample tummy. "I don't cook anything I won't eat." Bernie laughed and pulled off her chef's hat, setting it on the table. She brushed a strand of straight brown hair that had strayed from her stubby ponytail away from her face. "I worry about Kendall and Allie, but they insist the Lord directed them to make this move."

"Do you attend the Golden Springs Community Church?"

"No, I'm a confirmed Catholic, in spite of your brother's best efforts," Bernie said with a laugh. "And he's still a Protestant, in spite of mine."

"The bakery wasn't called Bibi's the last time I was in Golden

Springs. Did you take over recently?"

"I've been here for over five years."

"My last visit was six years ago. The kids got older and busier, and we just couldn't find the time to make it out here. Then my husband became ill, and we couldn't manage the trip again."

"I watched the donkeys for Kendall and Allie when they went to the funeral. I'm so sorry." Bernie's concern seemed genuine.

"That was two years ago." Morgan wadded a paper napkin in her fist, ready to staunch the tears that usually erupted when she spoke about Sam. "You'd think that was long enough to get over it."

Bernie covered Morgan's hand with hers and gave a gentle squeeze. "Not at all. That just shows what a wonderful man he must have been."

"Excuse me, Miss Yates?"

Morgan glanced up. She tried not to gape at the handsome stranger standing beside the table. Wavy blond hair brushed his shoulders, and short whiskers dusted his square jaw. A pale green natural fiber tunic and matching trousers draped his athletic frame.

"My name is Iverson."

"She's Kendall's sister," Bernie said. "Morgan, this is Piers. He owns a shop on Main Street, a few doors down."

"Ah," Piers said. "Then your name was Yates, at one time."

"That was my maiden name, yes."

"You're married?" Piers asked.

Morgan answered his blunt question with equal directness. "I'm widowed."

He motioned to the chair beside Morgan. "May I?"

38

CHAPTER FOUR

"Sit down, Piers," Bernie said. "I'll get your bread."

Bernie headed behind the counter as Piers pulled out the chair and sat next to Morgan.

"I own Faerie Tales," Piers said.

"The metaphysical store," Morgan said.

"The same." Piers seemed to wait for a reaction, leaning forward slightly on his chair. He held her gaze with blue eyes the color of a summer sky. She wondered if he wore tinted contact lenses. If so, they were worth whatever he paid for them.

"It's nice to meet another shop owner," Morgan said.

Piers relaxed, leaning back. "I had heard Mr. and Mrs. Yates left town, but I had no idea their replacement would be so approachable."

"I don't know if 'replacement' is the right word," Morgan said. "I was just supposed to fill in for two weeks."

Piers leaned forward. "And after the two weeks, what happens?"

"I don't know. Kendall seems to have lost interest in the Rock of Ages. I have a home in Sioux Falls. I wasn't planning to stay."

"If you should decide to sell, please let me know. I have expressed my interest in the land to your brother numerous times."

Beatrice, the church kitchen lady, had just warned Morgan not to let Piers get his hands on the property. But Morgan

39

couldn't afford to let local politics sway her decision. If she decided to sell, the highest bidder would own the Rock of Ages.

Piers lowered his voice. "Excuse me for expressing myself so freely when we've just met, but your brother and I have not enjoyed the most amicable relationship. He has a dark aura."

"Excuse me?" One of Morgan's Sioux Falls friends went to a metaphysical healer to have her aura read, but Morgan had only a vague idea of what that meant.

"Your brother has a sadness that saps him of joy."

If Kendall was sad about anything, Morgan knew it was because he and Allie had not been able to have children. But that had not diminished his joy of living.

"I'm afraid you don't know my brother very well."

"It is my gift to know a person's inmost emotions. I am an empath." Piers narrowed his eyes and seemed to look through Morgan. "I can see that you have sustained a heavy blow."

Morgan supposed that was an easy call. She had just told Piers she was a widow. Unless news of her finding a body had already circulated around town.

"Come by the shop," he said. "I can realign your chakras."

Morgan watched Bernie return with relief.

"Here's your bread," Bernie said.

Piers stood, pressed his hands together, and bobbed a little bow. "Many thanks."

He took the loaf from Bernie and held it in a careful embrace. The brown bread was mottled with dark bumps.

"I didn't see that in the display case," Morgan said.

"It's a special order," Bernie said. "Extra high fiber whole grain and flax seed bread."

"My own recipe," Piers said. "It's impossible to find decent bread in Golden Springs. Even our little health food store doesn't stock bread with adequate fiber."

"You're a vegetarian, Piers," Bernie said, resting one hand on her well-padded hip. "Everything you eat has fiber."

"It's important to maintain a healthy colon," he said.

Bernie pressed her lips together, but her eyes betrayed repressed laughter.

"I must open my shop," Piers said. "Please add this purchase to my tab, Miss Belmont."

"It was nice meeting you." Morgan extended her hand. "I hope we can chat another time."

Piers clutched the bread to his chest. "I never shake hands. As a healer, I could contaminate myself with negative energy, and pass it on to my clients."

Morgan was not sure how to react to being equated with a contaminant.

Piers glanced toward the door as the bell tinkled. His jaw tightened.

"I must go."

He passed Lucy as she entered the bakery. Apparently she was a source of contaminants, too. Piers went to great effort to step around her and the two children she had in tow. He avoided looking at Lucy, which was good, because Morgan thought Lucy had a rather nasty scowl on her face. Her expression softened to a smile as she turned to her children.

"Pick out one pastry each," Lucy told them, handing the girl a twenty, "and get Daddy a bear claw, and Mommy a cinnamon twist." Lucy sat at the table. Her buckskin skirt hit her long legs mid-calf, and a plain beige sweater displayed her turquoise necklace nicely. "Good morning."

Bernie leaned forward on her chair. "Piers offered to realign Morgan's chakra." She giggled.

"That has to be a record," Lucy said.

"That's his profession," Morgan said. "I'm sure he didn't mean anything by it."

"Don't be taken in by his good looks." Lucy flipped her long, black braid over her shoulder. "So how are you doing, Morgan? After yesterday and all."

Bernie leaned forward. "I knew it. You're the one who found the body, aren't you?"

News did travel fast.

"Yes," Morgan said with resignation. "And lost it."

Lucy saved Morgan yet another retelling by giving her own condensed version of Morgan's story.

"Wow," Bernie said. "Instead of a cup of coffee, I should have offered you a shot of Jack Daniel's."

"Mommy, we're done." A kindergarten-aged girl with Lucy's long, straight hair stood by the table. A smaller boy with a dark, round face clutched the pastry bag with his fist.

"Okay, honey." Lucy stood. "Paul's waiting in the truck," Lucy told Bernie and Morgan, "so I can't stay and visit, but I wanted to remind you both about the new running club Tuesday night. We'll meet in downtown Granite Junction, run a five K," Lucy pumped her arms, "then hang out at the pub."

"What's a five K?" Bernie asked.

"It's only three point one miles," Lucy said. "Paul's walking with Kimmie and pushing Danny in the stroller."

"I can walk," Danny declared. "I not a baby."

Kimmie rolled her eyes. "You have it easy, Danny. I have to walk and walk and walk."

"There'll be other walkers," Lucy said. "You don't have to run. Come on, ladies. It'll be fun."

"I'm not doing anything Tuesday night," Morgan said.

Bernie bit her lower lip.

"Morgan, work on Bernie."

Lucy hustled her kids out the door. Morgan watched through the bakery window as she loaded Kimmie and Danny into the full rear passenger seat of a huge truck. Her husband sat in the driver's seat, a serious expression creasing his face. A worn felt cowboy hat sat on his raven black hair. Even seated in a truck, Morgan could tell he was tall and broad-shouldered.

Bernie set her elbow on the small table and rested her chin in the palm of her hand. "I made the mistake of telling Lucy I needed to start walking, and now she won't leave me alone."

"I'm definitely a walker," Morgan said, "not a runner. I need to get in shape, too. Maybe we should try it."

"I can't possibly keep up with Lucy," Bernie said, "but if you promise not to leave me behind, I might consider going."

"Leave you behind?" Morgan exclaimed. "I couldn't run three miles to save my life."

Or someone else's, she thought.

Cleaning the barn was more time-consuming and strenuous than Morgan expected, even with Del doing the lion's share of the labor. The barn hadn't received proper attention in the weeks before Kendall and Allie left, Del assured her. It would be easier to clean from now on.

Morgan hoped he was right. When the alarm woke her Monday morning, she groaned as every overworked muscle made its presence known. Soaking in a tub full of Epsom salts and hot water would have been the preferred method to begin the day. Instead, she prepared to spend her time in the shop, hoping she'd learn something that would help her make the right decision about the rock shop's future.

Her business clothes from her days as an executive administrative assistant for a Sioux Falls engineering firm hardly seemed appropriate. She didn't have the western fashions so many folks in Golden Springs seemed to favor. She pulled on a pair of comfortable blue jeans and a Washington Warriors sweatshirt.

After starting a pot of coffee, Morgan unlocked the door connecting the living quarters to the shop. Whether she kept or sold the place, it needed a cleaning. The office seemed a good place to start. She opened the door and hit the light switch.

Her aching shoulders slumped.

Stacks of dust-coated papers tottered in disorderly piles on every horizontal surface. Morgan pulled open the top drawer of the ancient metal filing cabinet. The drawer was empty. Everything that should have been filed was strewn around the small office, including on top of the cabinet.

Kendall had told her there was a computer, but she couldn't reach it. Her brother never emailed. Was it because the computer was broken, Morgan wondered, or had he abandoned it because he couldn't find it in the clutter?

Deciding that the place to begin was organizing the piles of papers, Morgan pulled open the middle filing cabinet drawer. No file folders. But there was a stack of papers. They must have been important if Kendall and Allie had actually put them inside the cabinet. Morgan thumbed through vaguely legal-looking documents. They had something to do with zoning. She would have to wait to read them until she had the top of the desk cleared. So far, Morgan had only managed to make a bigger mess and let her coffee go cold.

She took a break, nuked the coffee, and toasted a slice of Bernie's bread.

As she sipped coffee in a stoneware mug, she wondered when her employees would make it in. She didn't want to barge in and establish a bunch of rules, but the place was in serious need of organizing. A work schedule had to go on the list.

Morgan finished her toast and grabbed a clipboard and pen. She started with the office.

"File folders," she said aloud, scribbling on the pad of paper. "File folder labels."

A trip to an office supply store went on her agenda, but she couldn't leave the shop unattended. She would have to wait for one of her employees to arrive, and hope that would be today.

In the meantime, she could take a closer look at the rock shop.

She flipped on the shop lights, a series of fluorescent lights in rectangular metal casings suspended from the low ceiling on short chains. She shook her head slowly.

"Kendall, how have you been spending your time?" Morgan placed her hands on her hips and released a tired sigh.

Now that she could really examine the shop with no distractions, it was apparent that it was in worse condition than the barn. Someone had planned to do spring cleaning once upon a time, if the broom, dustpan, mop, and liquid cleaners hidden away in a small utility closet were any indication.

Morgan hunted down a step stool. She found the rusty relic behind a cabinet crammed with dinosaur bones, plaster castings of footprints, and fossilized dinosaur excrement with the unlikely name "coprolite."

She settled the step stool in front of one of the large windows. Three shelves nested flush to the window frame. The bottom shelf extended from the windowsill. The next two divided the window in thirds. Morgan emptied the shelves, piling the rocks and curios on the display table across the aisle. Each item had a price-tag sticker or tag on a string, handwritten.

She tackled the shelves, armed with a bucket of warm sudsy water. They reluctantly relinquished grime to her scrub brush. The aching in her muscles eased as she worked, but every movement reminded her that she was out of shape.

Next, she attacked the filmy window inside and out with a spray bottle of glass cleaner and wadded up newspapers. The transformation was startling. The weak winter sun shone through the window, making the dingy little shop seem almost cheerful.

Finally, she dusted the rocks. Each was a marvel, some featureless, some glittering with crystals, others streaked with surprisingly vibrant colors. Morgan resisted the impulse to study the rocks as she placed them back on the clean shelves.

The bottom shelf had held rusty farm implements. A long-handled nipper for trimming horses' hooves, well-worn pliers, a hammer with a splintered wooden handle, assorted bits of wire, nuts and bolts, and items Morgan could not identify.

It would be a shame to place the dirty items back on her clean shelves. There had to be rust remover in the shop.

Morgan headed for the utility closet when the cowbell clanged.

"Mornin'!" Del called.

"I wondered when someone would get here," Morgan said. "Or if. I couldn't find a work schedule."

Del clomped across the pine floor in his cowboy boots. "It's pretty much verbal," he said. "Cindy works Tuesday and Thursday afternoons, and Friday mornings, except when her kids are sick or have some event planned. I'm around most of the time, but Kendall pays me for full days Monday, Wednesday, and Saturday. My trailer is just up above the shop." He pointed vaguely northeast. "So when things are slow at my place, I drop by to help out."

"I'll need to write down the schedule." Morgan grabbed her shopping list and jotted down "dry erase board."

"Sure," Del said. "Kendall kept me and Cindy on a pretty loose rein. We can adjust if you need to switch things around some."

"It's not that," Morgan said. "I didn't know this morning whether anyone was coming in, or if I'd be able to leave the shop to run errands."

Del stepped behind the counter and picked up the glass carafe from the coffeemaker. "In cases like that, you just use the be-back-in sign."

"The what?"

Del walked to the front door, carrying the empty carafe.

"This." He flipped around a sign with a clock face. "Set the hands to when you'll be back."

"Oh."

"And I'll be back after I get some water." Del carried the carafe into the one-seater restroom.

Morgan slouched on the aspen bench in front of the checkout counter. Del strolled back, water sloshing in the carafe, and busied himself preparing a pot of coffee.

Her job in Sioux Falls had required punctuality. Often, her phone was ringing before she hung up her coat in the morning. Running the rock shop was going to take some adjusting.

Switching mental gears, she asked, "Do we have any rust cleaner?"

"Why do you want to clean rust?" Del asked, a smile quirking his mustache up on one side.

"You know what I mean," Morgan said. "Rust remover."

The coffeemaker gurgled and sputtered.

"Maybe out in the barn? What do you need it for?"

Morgan pushed herself up off the bench and walked to the display table. She brought back the hoof nippers.

Del seemed to notice the clean window for the first time. "You've been busy."

"And there's so much more to do," Morgan said. "I want to clean up this stuff before I put it back on the shelf."

"And ruin the resale value?" Del appeared genuinely alarmed.

She turned the nippers in her hand. The blades were worn to rounded nubs. "They're useless."

"That's the way our customers want them." Del took the nippers from Morgan's hand and placed them back on the shelf. "When somebody cleans out their barn or workshed, and brings us a pile of rusty old tools, it's like finding a treasure chest."

"People buy this stuff?"

"Sure. They decorate their houses or vacation cabins. Old

47

West charm, I guess."

Morgan sat on the bench as Del poured coffee into a chipped ceramic mug.

"There can't be much money in selling other people's trash," Morgan said. "And who buys rocks and bones?"

"You'd be surprised." Del slurped the steaming coffee. He pulled a blue and white bandana from the back pocket of his jeans and pressed it against his mustache.

"Kendall and Allie actually made a living at this?" Morgan waved a hand in the air.

Del shrugged. "I never pry into my bosses' financial situation, as long as I get paid."

Morgan and Kendall had inherited the rock shop and the seventy-five acres it sat on from their great-uncle Caleb. Morgan had been happy to let Kendall manage the property back when she had a life of her own in Sioux Falls. If Kendall had tried to take out a loan against the land, he would have needed her signature. He had never asked.

"I've got a lot to do." Cleaning the window had only made the rest of the shop more dismal in comparison. Morgan sighed. "I'd better get back to work."

Del set his mug on the counter. "I'm not opposed to cleaning. Just so long as we don't damage the merchandise in the process."

Morgan stood. "Whatever the future holds for the Rock of Ages, we've got to clean this place up."

CHAPTER FIVE

Washing the rest of the windows and shelves took all morning.

"We can tackle the display case next," Morgan said. "You can't even see what's inside."

She opened the cash register drawer and fished out the display case key. The lock opened, but the sliding glass door hadn't been budged in a while. Del helped Morgan work it open.

They gently removed dozens of petrified bone and eggshell fragments, and a glorious mound of dinosaur dung. Coprolite, Morgan reminded herself. Each had a price attached. Some of the dinosaur dung was more expensive than dinosaur teeth.

Morgan grabbed what looked like a large horn carved out of rock. It was heavier than she expected. The two-foot object, tapering on one end to a point, nearly slipped from her hands.

Del's mouth fell open. He jumped forward and snatched the horn from Morgan, cradling it against his chest.

"This is the showpiece of the Rock of Ages." Del rested it gently on top of the display case. "Possibly the most expensive fossil in the entire shop."

"Not the T. Rex skull?"

"That's a replica."

"I don't see a price tag." Morgan peered at the object from all angles.

"Our better fossils have their pertinent info typed up on cards." Del poked around inside the display case. "Here it is."

He handed the yellowed file card to Morgan.

" 'Species: Triceratops horridus,' " she read. " 'This Triceratops brow horn is from the Cretaceous Period, approximately 70–66 million years ago.' Oh, no. You have to be kidding me." Morgan squinted as she read the price. "Would someone really pay over three thousand dollars for this?"

"No one has yet," Del said, "but that is a fair price."

Morgan turned her attention back to the display case. She and Del had not accomplished much but stirring up dust. She sneezed three times in rapid succession.

"I'm going to get clean water," she sniffled.

While Morgan filled the bucket with clean water and soap, the cowbell above the door clanged. The college-aged man who entered seemed to know exactly what he wanted. He browsed the shelves and specimen tables quickly, stopping at a coprolite display.

"My roommate's turning twenty-one," he said, turning the coprolite over in his hands. "This will make the best gag gift."

Del winced. "Gag gift? That's authentic coprolite. A scientific treasure." Del took his dinosaur dung seriously.

"Oh, he'll treasure it," the young man said. "He's a geology major."

Del bagged the coprolite and accepted the young man's twenty.

"As long as it's going to a good home," Del said.

"I had a hard time finding your shop." The young man accepted his change from Del. "You guys need a sign."

"We have a sign," Del said. "The big green dinosaur. Can't miss it."

"No, I mean downtown. At the turnoff."

When the college student left, they finished cleaning the display case. No amount of scrubbing could restore the well-worn fixture to its original condition, but it was still a huge improvement. Morgan envisioned the shelves covered with a southwest print material. Something with turquoise, earth tones, and a splash of red.

By the time they had placed all the fossils back in the case, the sun slanted through the west-facing windows.

"We've been working all day," Morgan said, "and we've only had one customer. Is it always like this?"

Del sat on the bench. "It's the off season. We might get a few tourists heading to the ski resorts, but we're off the beaten path. Business is better in the summer."

"That young man suggested we needed a sign," Morgan said.

"There's a problem with that idea."

"What?" Morgan rubbed the aching muscles in her left bicep with her right hand.

"The best spot to put a sign is at the bottom of the hill where our road intersects with Main Street."

"Sure," Morgan said.

"But Piers Townsend has buildings on both corners."

"I met him," Morgan said. "He owns that metaphysical shop."

"He and your brother don't exactly see eye to eye."

Morgan laughed. "I can only imagine." She remembered Piers's comment about her brother's dark aura. "He doesn't own the sidewalk. Wouldn't the town clerk or someone in charge of city code enforcement decide whether I could put up a sign?"

"Piers has a lot of influence," Del said. "He's blocked every one of Kendall's attempts to put up a sign."

"Maybe I can talk him into it."

It was Del's turn to laugh. "You can give it a try."

"I'll put that on my list." Morgan scribbled on her notepad.

A car crunched across the gravel in front of the shop.

"Two customers in one day," Morgan said. "Business is picking up."

51

"I don't think this is a customer." Del tugged at his mustache. "Looks like a police cruiser to me."

"I filed a report with search and rescue," Morgan told the two Granite Junction police officers. "The sheriff's department was too busy."

Officer MacKenzie jotted in a notepad with a cheap mechanical pencil dwarfed by his huge hand. After brief introductions, he had not said another word.

"We understand," Officer Alicia Sanchez said for the fifth time. "We're not questioning their response to the incident, considering the circumstances. We're trying to determine whether a missing person's report might be related to the young woman you think you saw."

Morgan bristled at the implication. "I did see a woman."

Officer Sanchez raised her hands, palms facing Morgan. "We understand."

Morgan was getting frustrated with the depth of the officer's understanding. Sanchez struck Morgan as a just-the-facts style investigator, with dark brown hair slicked back in a ponytail, and dressed in a crisply pressed uniform.

"Can you describe the person you thought you saw?" Sanchez asked.

"That I did see. I've already given that information to search and rescue. Didn't someone write it down?"

"We understand how stressful this is," Sanchez said.

Morgan bit her lower lip and glanced at Del. He concentrated on starting another pot of coffee, but Morgan thought she detected an amused smile hiding under his mustache.

Measuring out her words, Morgan spoke with exaggerated clarity. "I did see a woman on the trail. She was in her late teens or early twenties. She was white, very pale, and very thin."

Her stomach didn't churn quite as much, or her heart race as fast, as she repeated the details for the fourth time in three days. She left out the part about a monster transforming into a magpie. When she stopped speaking, MacKenzie's pencil stopped scribbling. Morgan felt drained.

Del poured Morgan a mug of coffee, then offered Styrofoam cups to the two officers. Sanchez shook her head.

"Do you have cream?" MacKenzie asked.

It was dark by the time Officer Sanchez seemed satisfied that she had obtained all the information available from Morgan. She handed Morgan her business card.

"Call me if you think of anything else."

MacKenzie ducked under the low shop door and headed for the cruiser. Sanchez followed.

"Wait," Morgan said.

Sanchez paused in the doorway.

"Search and rescue didn't believe I saw a girl. You sound pretty skeptical. Why take a report from me now?"

"Your description matches that of a young woman who was recently reported missing."

Sanchez closed the door behind her before Morgan could ask more questions. Apparently, there was no reciprocity when it came to interrogation.

"More coffee?" Del waved the nearly empty pot.

"Thanks, Del, but I'll have a hard enough time sleeping tonight. How many times am I going to have to tell that story?"

"I'd think you'd be happy that someone in an official capacity finally takes your story seriously."

Morgan rubbed her temples with both hands. "I'd rather I had imagined it all, for that girl's sake."

"If she's mixed up with drugs, maybe they can find her and get her straightened out."

"If it's not already too late."

Del stayed to close the shop for the night. Morgan had the

distinct feeling that he was stalling around, not wanting to leave her alone after the police interview.

"Are any office supply stores open this late?" Morgan asked.

"There aren't any in Golden Springs. But there are in Granite Junction. You have an urgent need for pencils?"

"I want to start cleaning the office tomorrow morning. I need file folders, labels, things to get organized."

"Sounds like you're settling in."

Morgan didn't want to build false hope.

"I'm not sure what's going to happen yet, but if I sell the property, the financial records will need to be in order."

Del ducked behind the counter and pulled a battered phone book out from under the cash register. "Better call ahead and find out what's open. You don't want to drive all that way for nothing." Del thumbed through the yellow pages, then looked up. "You want me to ride with you?"

"Sure, Del. Maybe we could grab a bite to eat while we're out."

Granite Junction was a curvy ten miles down Topaz Pass from Golden Springs. Del kept a conversation going about local history, the weather, and the merits or lack thereof of every vehicle they encountered.

Morgan recalled that Del was a widower. She wondered if his offer to accompany her was due to loneliness. And now she was talking about selling his home out from under him.

"Do you have any family here?" Morgan asked.

"My son and his wife live in Denver. The grandkids make it down this way every so often. Which reminds me, I was hoping to repair the donkey cart before their next visit."

"I didn't know we had a donkey cart," Morgan said.

They stopped at a family-owned restaurant. The service was fast, and the food was good. Just as important, it was cheap.

Morgan still had money in a savings account. She had used

some to compensate for the pay she lost taking time off from work to be with Sam. She didn't regret her choice. The life insurance money went faster than expected, paying medical bills the health insurance didn't cover. Her 401K was strictly off limits, unless the direst of emergencies arose.

"A penny for your thoughts," Del said through a mouthful of taco.

"If only," Morgan said. "I could use a few more pennies."

"After the office supply place," Del said, "do you mind if we stop at the grocery store?"

Granite Junction was nearly twice the size of Sioux Falls. Morgan was reminded of shopping trips to the big city of Minneapolis as they drove to different shopping centers. They stopped at the hardware store, and a fabric store, where Morgan found material to line the display case.

Heading home, Del commented on a particularly desirable half-ton pickup truck. Morgan asked the question she'd been debating since the grocery store stop.

"Are you shopping for a new car, Del?"

"The truck's not running too well." His cheeks flushed red, and he glanced out the passenger window into the darkness. "I sure hope you didn't mind running me around tonight."

"I'm glad you showed me around," Morgan said. "Now I know where the good places to shop are."

The Buick sputtered as they pulled in to the Rock of Ages parking lot.

"Apparently, my car is running about as well as your truck." The engine light flashed red. "It overheated the last hundred miles of my trip here."

"The garage in Golden Springs is honest," Del said. "I know the owner."

"I suppose I need to find out what's wrong, before the old girl blows up completely. I can't afford to buy a new car." She glanced at Del. "What about your truck?"

Del sighed. "I've been trying to decide whether to sink more money into it, or to start looking for a good used truck."

"Until you do," Morgan said, "feel free to borrow the car."

"I couldn't—" Del began, but Morgan held up her hand before he could finish.

"I might ask you to run errands for the shop," she said. "Consider it the company car."

It was the only running vehicle at Rock of Ages. Kendall had given his rust bucket of a van to a single mom in exchange for driving them to the Denver airport. The woman might not have gotten a good deal.

"Then you have to let me help with the repairs," Del said.

"It's a deal."

Morgan started cleaning the office the next morning, clearing a path to the computer. It did run, but using pencil and paper might have been faster. She had trouble making sense out of her brother's antiquated accounting system. Records ended in August of the previous year.

When Kendall had told Morgan he was leaving his computer, she'd made the wild assumption that the rock shop was up to speed with technology. Morgan wasn't sure she could survive the next week and a half without the Internet.

She rested her elbows on the desk and lowered her face into her hands.

"Fella from the newspaper wants to talk to you," Del said.

Before Morgan could insist that she was too busy, Del escaped.

The husky man standing in the office doorway could have walked off the set of a 1940s era film. He wore a rumpled white shirt under a brown leather trench coat. A jaunty brown fedora, complete with a press card tucked into the hatband, perched on his short brown hair. Morgan wondered if costumes were required attire in Golden Springs.

"Welcome to the neighborhood." The man beamed a smile that was as sincere as a politician's. His broad cheeks were candy-apple red, and his teeth brilliantly white. Morgan decided he might have possessed boyish good looks forty pounds and a decade or so ago. "Kurt Willard, owner and editor-in-chief of the *Golden Springs Gazetteer* at your service."

Kurt stepped over a stack of papers and held out a hand as big and thick as a bear's paw. Apparently, he didn't share Piers's aversion to human touch. Morgan stood to grasp his hand briefly.

"Morgan Iverson," she said. "Nice to meet you, Mr. Willard." She sat back in the wobbly office chair. "I've seen your paper."

The article she had read in the bakery had seemed like one big editorial.

"Oh, good." Kurt beamed. "Then you've noticed how valuable advertising in such a high-quality publication could be."

Morgan gave him credit for getting to the point quickly.

"I'm afraid I can't discuss advertising right now," Morgan said. "I'm in the middle of cleaning up." She waved a hand around, hoping the desperate condition of the office would deter Kurt from further sales pitches.

"And you have no doubt already noticed how slow business is," Kurt said.

"I suspect that has more to do with not having a sign on Main Street. Right now, I think that would be the most cost-effective use of our advertising dollars."

Kurt smiled his best used-car-salesman smile. "Are you aware of the history behind your absent sign?"

Morgan leaned back in the office chair. "I understand it has something to do with Piers Townsend."

"Precisely!" Kurt looked pleased. "Piers and your brother

hold opposing views on nearly every subject under the sun."

"I don't see what their personal differences have to do with putting up a sign on Main Street. Why should one shop owner be able to dictate what another does?"

Kurt shoved his hands deep into the pockets of his trench coat. "I hear you came from Sioux Falls. You'll soon discover that small towns operate differently than the big city."

"You seem to know a lot about this disagreement."

Kurt shrugged. "What can I say? Reporting is in my blood. Anything I happen across in the course of the week is potential fodder for my newspaper."

Morgan sighed. She really needed to get back to work straightening out the office.

"Say, we've gone far afield from my original purpose," Kurt offered in a friendly tone.

"Which was?" Morgan asked.

"I understand one of your first days in Golden Springs was quite eventful."

CHAPTER SIX

Morgan could see what was coming. She decided to head it off at the pass. "You mean the incident on the hiking trail?"

"Everyone in town is talking about it," Kurt said, "but no one seems to know what really happened."

Every detail she had shared with the church ladies had no doubt traveled through all the information channels in town by now.

"I'm not sure myself what happened," Morgan said. "So I'm afraid I won't be much help."

"Correct me if I'm wrong," Kurt said, "but my sources tell me you found an unconscious woman on the Columbine Trail."

"That's what I thought. But when search and rescue arrived, the woman was gone." Morgan shrugged.

"What did you see, exactly?" Kurt asked.

"Apparently nothing."

Kurt pulled off his fedora and brushed a hand through his brown hair. "Can you describe what you saw?"

"How can I describe what wasn't there?"

Kurt turned the fedora around in his hands, fussing with the brim of the felt hat.

"Can you describe what you *thought* you saw?"

"I don't see the point," Morgan said. "It's all speculation."

"My readers would find it interesting," Kurt said. "In a town this small, there are rare few unsolved mysteries."

"As you pointed out," Morgan said, "I'm woefully unschooled

in the ways of small towns. I can't take the chance of appearing to be a person who imagines bodies on hiking trails."

Kurt leaned back, an "I give up" expression on his face. He settled his fedora onto his head.

"If you change your mind about the story, or about purchasing advertising, please give me a call." Kurt retrieved a business card from an inside pocket of his brown leather trench coat and flipped it onto the cluttered desk.

He left the office with much less flair than he'd had when he entered.

Del stuck his head in the door. "Cindy's here. I'm gonna go to the barn and pull the donkey cart out."

"You abandoned me," Morgan said.

"I figured you could hold your own, and I was right. Kurt tore out of here like his tail was on fire."

"We've got to get that sign up on Main Street." Morgan stood. "I'm going to have a talk with Mr. Townsend. Make him listen to reason."

Del laughed.

"You don't think I can?" Morgan asked.

"I think a man who runs a shop called Faerie Tales doesn't have much to reason with."

Del moved out of the doorway, letting Morgan pass.

"I met him at Bernie's Sunday," Morgan said. "I think I can talk to him."

"You're as stubborn as your brother."

"Nobody's as stubborn as Kendall." Cindy stood behind the checkout counter, a roll of paper towels in her hand.

"I agree with Cindy," Morgan said.

"You spill something back there?" Del asked.

"I haven't seen the windows clean in the two years I've worked here," Cindy said. "It's kind of inspiring. I'd like to start cleaning out those dirty old rock tables."

Three narrow rows of tables in the center of the shop held dozens of rough-hewn open cases full of rocks and assorted junk. Shoppers had mixed shark teeth with trilobites, polished quartz had spilled into the turquoise nuggets, and dust, dirt, and crud malingered in the corners of the wooden cases.

"You have my full support for any cleaning project you want to tackle," Morgan said.

"Can you manage by yourself?" Del asked Cindy. "I'm going out to the barn, and Morgan's running a fool's errand."

"Thanks for the vote of confidence, Del," Morgan said.

Del headed out the front door of the shop. Morgan went through the back, and the attached living quarters. She stopped in the kitchen to get her coat and car keys, then headed for the garage.

Kendall had often called to brag about the good weather they enjoyed in the Colorado Rockies, while Morgan and Sam suffered through a South Dakota blizzard. She thought her brother was prone to hyperbole. Yet here she was, pulling off her wool cap and gloves. She stuffed them in the top of the canvas bag slung over her shoulder, and unzipped her quilted blue coat.

Walking down Hill Street wouldn't take much longer than pulling the car out of the carriage house garage. She changed direction. Morgan was still learning the layout of the rock shop property. Fences, driveways, and paddocks seemed scattered over the seventy-five acres without any sense of order.

One thing she did have etched into her brain—always leave gates the way you found them. It was an inviolable law of the West. Morgan made sure the paddock gate was latched before she walked through the perpetually open front gate and headed down Hill Street.

Halfway down the gravel road, a black SUV with tinted windows passed her going up. It looked like a cross between a Humvee and a jeep. She thought she saw a Mercedes Benz logo on the hood, but that didn't seem right. Maybe Mercedes was in the SUV market now. If so, the driver surely wasn't a customer for the Rock of Ages, Morgan thought. Unless the driver was in need of a Triceratops brow horn.

Morgan turned and watched the vehicle, trailed by a cloud of dust. It slowed as it passed the rock shop's dinosaur sign, then sped up.

They had to be visiting one of the neighbors farther up the hill, where the road dead-ended. Morgan continued her trek to town, walking carefully down the steeper sections of road where her slick-soled sneakers refused to grip the gravel.

She ran through the argument she would present to Piers, to convince him to let the Rock of Ages put a sign on the corner of Main and Hill Streets. Morgan might have to smooth over past offenses delivered by her opinionated brother, but she would not apologize for him. She might think her brother was crazy, but family stuck together.

When Morgan neared the bottom of Hill Street, she heard a car behind her, engine racing, tires scattering gravel. She looked over her shoulder. The black SUV already took up more than its share of the narrow road, but it seemed determined to crowd into Morgan's space, too.

Or run her down.

For a brief moment, she debated crossing to the other side of the road. The vehicle was coming too fast. Maybe the driver hadn't seen her. Through the windshield, Morgan glimpsed dark glasses and a shaggy goatee. She waved her arms. Instead of correcting its course, it veered closer to her side of the road.

The wide tires scrabbled on loose gravel. Morgan teetered on the edge of the ditch. She flailed with her arms, struggling to keep her balance. The SUV barreled past her. Morgan's feet slipped. She pitched down the steep bank and fell, landing in the slushy, ankle-deep water on her hands and knees.

Furious, she scrambled up the bank. The SUV raced past the pockmarked stop sign at the bottom of Hill Street without slowing. Morgan tried to read the license plate. It was a Colorado plate, green and white, but the cloud of dust kicked up by the SUV obscured the letters.

Morgan retrieved her bag from the ditch. She debated continuing to town, or heading back to the shop. Town was closer, and downhill. Her shoes squished with every step.

Piers's be-back-in sign, the clock framed with glittery fairy stickers, said he would return in an hour. More time than Morgan had intended to spend in town.

Standing in front of his store, her jeans soaked from her knees to her sneakers, she regretted her decision to walk to town. Then she noticed the traffic rolling up and down Main Street. If she could put up a sign, some of those customers might drive the few blocks up the hill to the Rock of Ages.

She walked west on Main Street, smelling the bakery before she saw the pink and white striped awning. The teenage girls were not behind the counter today, but it didn't look like Bernie needed help. Only two customers sat near the large bay window, sharing a bistro table.

"Hi, Bernie," Morgan said.

"What happened to you? You're all wet."

"I walked from the rock shop. A car ran me into the irrigation ditch."

Bernie's mouth fell open. "You're kidding. Are you hurt?"

"No, just wet."

"You need to call the police."

Morgan shrugged. "I didn't get the license plate number. It was probably a case of someone changing a CD or lighting a cigarette."

Bernie shook her head, making her pink striped chef's hat wobble on her head. She looked more like an old-fashioned ice cream vendor than a baker today.

"Or drunk. You really should report this." Bernie picked up the phone receiver from the wall-mounted phone behind the counter. "I'll call Bill."

Golden Springs had a two-man police department that resided in a small office inside City Hall.

"Okay," Morgan said, "but I'd rather call Officer Sanchez in Granite Junction. She already knows me."

"You've been here less than a week, and you have your own personal police officer?"

Morgan shrugged. "They came by yesterday to ask about my report to search and rescue." She dug the business card and her cell phone out of her bag.

The two customers left as Morgan settled at a table by the window. Officer Sanchez asked several questions that Morgan couldn't answer, such as the license plate number. The description of the driver, wearing sunglasses and sporting a goatee, was probably no help. At least Officer Sanchez seemed to take Morgan seriously.

Bernie brought a tray with two teacups, a teapot, and two plates with lemon squares to the window table. She poured steaming water into the cups.

"Now tell me about the car." She passed a container of tea bags to Morgan.

As she described the incident to Bernie, Morgan considered that it might be easier to start a blog than to keep repeating every Golden Springs experience ten times.

"I'm already the lady who imagines bodies on trails. I'm afraid people will think I'm a paranoid lunatic."

"I believe you," Bernie said. "I'll keep an eye out for that SUV."

"It looks like business is as slow for you today as it is for us," Morgan said, hoping to change the subject. "We're at a complete standstill. How do you survive the off season?"

"I'm fortunate to have a loyal following of local customers." Bernie dunked a tea bag in her cup. "I work like the dickens during tourist season, and save for that rainy day. Or around here, that snowy day. Businesses are more likely to go under during the winter. That's when Piers snaps them up. In Golden Springs, it's not so much keeping the wolf from the door as keeping Piers from the door."

Morgan tried to imagine the handsome metaphysical shop owner as a ruthless businessman. The image didn't fit. Even if it was true, if other Golden Springs business owners ran their shops as lackadaisically as Kendall, maybe they deserved to go under.

"I've had time to do some serious cleaning," Morgan said. "There's no end to the to-do list."

"It's hard work, but there are so many perks to being your own boss."

The bell over the door tinkled. Lucy entered, dressed in New West style, with jeans and western boots, a pale green silk blouse, and a black jacket. Morgan felt plain and dumpy in her baggy jeans and faded Washington Warriors sweatshirt.

"What happened to you?" Lucy asked, pointing to Morgan's wet jeans and soaked sneakers.

As Morgan retold the incident, she tried to remember every detail. It had happened so fast.

"Do you suppose this has anything to do with the missing body?" Lucy asked.

"Why would someone try to run me down just because I saw a body?"

"There must be a dozen reasons," Bernie said. "Maybe they thought you stole the body."

"I just came from the rock shop," Lucy said. "I brought some new jewelry to show you, but Cindy said you were in town. I didn't see a black SUV." Lucy sold her handmade jewelry on consignment at the rock shop. It was one of the few displays not gathering dust.

"Do I need to come back to the shop?"

"Cindy took care of me." Lucy pointed at Morgan's lemon square. "I might get one of those."

"They turned out really nice," Bernie said. She slid open the display case and retrieved a lemon square with a pair of tongs. "But you can tell me what you think."

"Are we on for tonight?" Lucy asked as she took a bite of lemon square. "Mmm, this is good."

"Tonight?" Bernie asked.

"O'Reily's Runners." Morgan must have looked as lost as Bernie, because Lucy added, "The running club."

Morgan and Bernie spoke at the same time. "Oh."

"It's supposed to be a nice night," Lucy said. "Clear skies, temps in the thirties. Great for your first time."

"First time?" Bernie asked. "That implies there'll be another."

"I'll give it a try," Morgan said, "if you will, Bernie."

"Okay. I guess it won't kill me. But I'm not running."

"Great," Lucy said. "It'll be fun."

"Only someone as young, thin, and healthy as you," Bernie said to Lucy, "would consider running around Granite Junction in the dark fun."

Lucy laughed, apparently thinking that Bernie was kidding. Morgan was sure she was not. Lucy stood and turned to leave. She froze, her eyes glued on the window.

"Uh-oh."

Morgan followed her gaze.

"Houdini and Adelaide!" Morgan cried.

The two donkeys trotted up the middle of Main Street.

Chapter Seven

Vehicles slowed for the donkeys, who negotiated traffic with a remarkable lack of concern. Their hooves tapped on the asphalt in an easy rhythm.

"I'd better get Del." Morgan flipped open her cell phone and hit speed dial for the Rock of Ages. The signal dropped before anyone picked up.

"Use my phone," Bernie said.

Morgan stepped behind the bakery counter and dialed, but got a busy signal.

"The phones are always going out on the hill," Bernie said. "It used to drive Allie crazy."

"We can round them up," Lucy said.

The donkeys had different ideas.

The three women followed Houdini and Adelaide up Main Street, always three paces behind the donkeys. Morgan's cold, wet sneakers squished as they crossed the bridge to the park, and cut through the open-air penny arcade. They surrounded the donkeys in front of the Winston House, a historic hotel that had been converted into a retirement home. Several seniors relaxed on the wraparound porch soaking up the unseasonably warm sun. Undeterred, Houdini climbed the stone steps. Adelaide followed, her hooves click-clacking across the oak planks.

"What have we got here?" one gentleman asked, a delighted smile creasing his wrinkled face.

He held out a cookie. As Adelaide stopped to accept the

treat, Morgan reached for her halter. The donkey snatched the cookie and jerked her head away. She trotted after Houdini, across the porch and down the far steps.

When they headed back to Main Street, several shopkeepers joined the round up. Kurt Willard stepped out of the *Golden Springs Gazetteer* to snap photos. Morgan considered the humorous scene they made, two donkeys leading a parade of citizens headed by Bernie in her pink and white striped chef's coat and hat. If she hadn't been so annoyed, Morgan might have laughed.

"Hey, I think they're heading home."

Lucy pointed to Hill Street. It did seem that the donkeys were finally going the right direction. They climbed onto the boardwalk and stopped in front of Faerie Tales. Bernie grabbed Adelaide's rope halter. Morgan threw her arm around Houdini's neck. After applauding the successful capture of the donkeys, people hurried back to their shops.

"Where'd Lucy go?" Bernie asked. "I thought she was helping."

Houdini shook himself from head to toe, nearly breaking Morgan's hold. Adelaide stuck her muzzle in a wooden half-barrel planter and snuffled her lips across the bare dirt. The smell of sweaty donkey mingled with the sweet incense permeating the air around Faerie Tales.

Piers stepped outside. He shook his head and cast a sad glance at Houdini, then Adelaide.

"You ate those flowers last summer," he told the donkeys. "There are no more." Piers pushed his hands inside opposite sleeves of his loose gray tunic. "Your efforts are in vain."

"She's not hurting anything," Bernie said.

"There's nothing left to hurt." Piers raised his hands. "They ate my columbines, right before the storefront decoration contest. The flowers had just reached perfection when they were mowed down by your brother's livestock."

"I can replace the flowers this spring," Morgan said.

Houdini stretched his neck, trying to reach the planter. Morgan held tight to his rope halter.

"It was my karma," Piers said. "I had become full of pride about my beautiful storefront." He stepped closer to Adelaide, the breeze stirring his wavy blond hair. Adelaide stomped her hoof dangerously close to Piers's sandal. "I thank you for your generous offer, but I would rather wait until the donkeys are gone before attempting to replant."

"These donkeys aren't going anywhere," Morgan said.

"Livestock is banned under the new city ordinance," Piers said.

"The donkeys are illegal?" Morgan asked.

"They were grandfathered in," Bernie said. "Kendall told City Council the donkeys were family pets, and couldn't be moved from the property without great distress."

Piers pointed at Morgan's wet and dirty sneakers. "Did those creatures drag you through the mud?"

If he had the psychic powers he claimed, it seemed to Morgan that Piers should know what happened. Unless he was covering up. Morgan wondered if Piers owned a black SUV.

"No," she said. "They're gentle animals. I don't see what you have against donkeys."

"I hold no grudge against these two," Piers said. "They and their offspring may remain at the rock shop, but no new livestock may be introduced within city limits."

"They don't have any offspring," Morgan said.

"Thus they will be the last donkeys in Golden Springs."

Houdini turned his mournful expression from Piers to Morgan, his big brown eyes nearly brimming with donkey tears. She wondered how much the donkey understood.

"I don't know how they got out," Morgan said. "I checked the gates before I left."

"They run freely in the streets on a frequent basis," Piers said.

Morgan looked to Bernie for confirmation. The baker shrugged.

"This is the second time in the past year," Bernie said. "I don't see what the problem is. When tourists come here, they're looking for Old West charm, and what's more charming than Houdini and Adelaide?"

"Speaking of tourists," Morgan said, "people would slow down if they saw a sign pointing them toward the donkeys. They'd notice your shop, too. Maybe this is a bad time, but can I talk to you about a sign?"

"An omen?" Piers asked, a glint of humor in his summer blue eyes. "Or a premonition?"

"Ha ha," Bernie said without enthusiasm.

"You know what I mean." Morgan waved a hand at the corner. "A sign, to let people know our shop is up the hill."

"Kendall's proposals did not meet my criteria." Piers crossed his arms. "We have been unable to reach an agreement."

Houdini lifted his tail. He deposited a gift on the boardwalk. It splattered onto the wood in a glorious alfalfa-green pile.

Piers raised his hands. A strangled sound caught in his throat.

"I'd save that if I were you," Bernie said. "It'll be good for your flower planters."

"And on that note," Morgan said, "I'd better get them home."

Morgan and Bernie tugged on the donkeys' halters, leading them off the boardwalk and away from Faerie Tales. When they reached Hill Street, Lucy joined them.

"You've got customers," she told Bernie. "I can help Morgan."

"Gladly!" Bernie relinquished Adelaide's halter to Lucy and hurried to her shop.

"I can't wait to tell my friends in Sioux Falls about the

donkey roundup on Main Street," Morgan told Lucy. She grasped Houdini's halter. "It would be a shame if Houdini and Adelaide are the last donkeys in Golden Springs."

"You have Piers to thank for that ordinance," Lucy said.

"Ordinances can be changed," Morgan said.

"Trying to negotiate with Piers is pointless. There's only one way, and that's his way."

Houdini jerked his halter out of Morgan's grip and snatched a mouthful of dried grass alongside the ditch. Morgan wrapped her fist tightly around the rope halter and dragged him up the road.

"Piers seems like a nice enough guy."

Lucy rubbed Adelaide's neck with her free hand as she walked. "Piers wants you to think he's just a harmless guy selling crystals and hoodoo to gullible people, but he has an agenda."

"Agenda?" Morgan couldn't keep the smile out of her reply.

"He's buying up property in Golden Springs."

"I've heard something about that." Morgan didn't mention his interest in the Rock of Ages. "But if people are selling, he's got the right to buy, doesn't he?"

"Legally, I suppose so. But just because something is legal doesn't make it right. I don't know if Kendall and Allie told you, but he's after the rock shop."

"The Rock of Ages isn't exactly a moneymaker."

"It sits on a lot of land. Close to town. Golden Springs doesn't have much room for expansion. We're surrounded by national forest. And Piers usually gets what he wants. It's like he's cast a spell over City Council."

Adelaide stopped, pulling Lucy to a halt. Morgan almost thanked the donkey for the chance to catch her breath.

"Adelaide must be out of shape," Lucy said. "She's sure moving slow."

"She's old," Morgan said. "It's sad to think they'll be the last donkeys in Golden Springs."

"Thanks to Piers's ordinance," Lucy said.

Morgan hesitated. "It keeps coming back to Piers."

"Do you think I'm being unfair?" Lucy asked. When Morgan didn't reply, Lucy continued. "I can see that it might look that way. I used to sell jewelry at Faerie Tales, until Piers started offering to align my chakras or give me a massage. I quit selling jewelry at his shop, but every time he saw me, he asked me to come back. It was a business relationship—nothing more—but he made me feel as though something inappropriate had taken place." Lucy shook her head, sending her long black braid swinging across her back like a pendulum. "Or could, if I'd just cooperate. Paul warned Piers to leave me alone or else."

Lucy walked faster as she talked, until Adelaide pulled her to a halt again. Morgan remembered Paul's grim expression when she'd seen him through the bakery window. She imagined he could be quite intimidating. Not that Piers wouldn't have deserved it.

Now she understood Lucy and Bernie's amusement when Piers had offered to align her chakras. He was a garden-variety skirt chaser in a New Age package.

"I know you need to form your own opinion of Piers, but please take me seriously when I say you shouldn't let your guard down around him."

They reached the open gate to the rock shop parking lot.

"I'm used to dealing with challenging men," Morgan said. "I can handle Piers."

"What did you do in Sioux Falls?" Lucy asked.

"I was an admin for an engineering firm," Morgan said, relieved with the change of subject. "I ran the office, dealt with contractors, engineers, suppliers, customers. It was a good job, and I enjoyed it, but when the economy tanked, they had to lay off all the peripheral employees. That was me. Peripheral. They said they'd call me back when business picked up again."

"You're not staying here, are you?"

Morgan shrugged. "I have a home and family in Sioux Falls. Maybe a job."

"Sioux Falls is bigger than Golden Springs?"

"Yes. It's about half the size of Granite Junction." Morgan laughed. "I thought it was funny when Kurt Willard told me I didn't understand about small towns. I never thought of Sioux Falls as the big city."

"Like he's an expert?" Lucy led Adelaide across the rock shop parking lot. "Kurt moved here from San Francisco four years ago."

"I was under the impression he's lived in Golden Springs his whole life."

Houdini snorted, and pulled Morgan toward the paddock gate.

"Kurt is big on impressions," Lucy said.

Del met them at the gate.

"Have these two been running wild again?" he asked.

"They might be front page news," Lucy said. "Kurt was taking pictures of the roundup."

"Famous once again," Del said.

"Or infamous," Morgan said. "Not everyone was happy about it."

"You left the paddock gate open," Del said. "Gerda called the shop to let us know the donkeys were loose. I was headed to town just now to get them."

"I didn't leave the gate open. I checked before I left."

"I'll take the escapees." Del snapped ropes onto their halters. "What happened to you, Morgan? Did these two drag you through the creek?"

Morgan looked down at her wet pant legs and filthy sneakers.

"This happened before I even made it to town. An SUV ran me into the irrigation ditch."

Del raised one bushy eyebrow. "You have more than your fair share of disasters."

"My thoughts exactly. I called Officer Sanchez. She was really happy to hear from me again. Did you notice a black SUV after I left?"

"I was in the barn," Del said, "until Cindy came to tell me about the donkeys. I wouldn't have heard anyone on the road."

"Maybe someone opened the gate after I left."

"Why would they do that?" Lucy asked. "You just don't mess with other peoples' gates."

Morgan watched Del lead the donkeys back to the paddock.

"When I was here earlier," Lucy said, "I noticed that fabric you put in the display case. I could cover my jewelry board with matching fabric."

"That's a great idea," Morgan said. "I got it at the fabric store in Granite Junction."

"I hope they have enough left to cover my display." Lucy glanced at her watch. "I've got to go. I'll see you later tonight, at the pub, right?"

Del closed the paddock gate, checking the latch before walking up to Morgan and Lucy.

"Six o'clock?" Morgan asked.

"That's when we start," Lucy said, "but get there earlier to sign up."

Lucy waved as she jogged across the parking lot.

"Where are you going?" Del asked.

"A running club in Granite Junction," Morgan said.

Del followed her into the rock shop. He rummaged under the checkout counter for a notepad and pencil.

"Did anyone pull up here after I left?" Morgan asked Cindy.

"No customers today," Cindy said.

"I saw a black SUV drive up the hill when I was walking to town," Morgan said.

"It tried to run her down," Del said.

Cindy gasped. "You're kidding. Run you down?"

"I fell in the irrigation ditch," Morgan said. "I thought maybe the same person opened the gate after I left."

Cindy shook her head. "I didn't see anyone. But I was cleaning, so I might not have noticed."

Del mumbled, and scribbled on the notepad.

"Del, what are you doing?" Morgan asked.

"You said you're going running," Del said.

"Bernie and I will more likely walk," Morgan said. "There's a new running club," she told Cindy. "It meets in downtown Granite Junction."

"What time?" Del asked.

"The run starts at six," Morgan said. "But Lucy said to get there earlier. Bernie is picking me up at five."

"Good," Del said. "That'll give me time to prepare."

"Prepare for what?" Morgan asked.

"You'll need equipment," Del said.

"I think shoes and a jacket are all that's required," Morgan said. "Maybe a flashlight."

"For downtown Granite Junction?" Del shook his head. "The city's not safe for a couple of women walking at night. Especially considering that someone's out to get you."

CHAPTER EIGHT

Cindy helped Morgan close the shop for the night. Before they locked the front door, Del walked in with an enormous olive-green camouflage fanny pack. He set it on the glass display counter.

"Going camping?" Cindy asked.

"Very funny," Del said.

"What is that?" Morgan asked.

"A survival pack for your trip to Granite Junction tonight."

"I'm going to a running club with Bernie and Lucy," Morgan said. "We're not hunting bear."

Headlights shone through the front windows.

"Herb's here," Cindy said. "I'll see you Thursday."

Cindy waddled out the door, a hand pressed to her lower back.

Morgan grabbed the strap of the fanny pack with one hand and lifted it an inch above the counter. She dropped it back on the glass.

"Careful!"

"Del, I can't carry this for three miles. I can barely lift it."

Morgan unzipped the pack and started pulling out gear. A Buck knife, a roll of duct tape, granola bars, pepper spray.

"Pepper spray?" Morgan asked. "I'll be in a crowd."

"I'm guessing you won't be in the middle of the pack," Del said. "The pepper spray stays."

"Thanks for the vote of confidence."

Morgan haggled with Del about what stayed in the pack and what she refused to carry. They had finally reached an agreement when the headlights of Bernie's vehicle shone through the shop windows.

"My ride's here," Morgan said.

"Call me when you get home," Del said.

Morgan might have argued with the old cowboy, but she knew he would worry.

"Okay, I'll call. If the phone's working."

"I'll lock up the shop," Del said. "You go have fun. And be careful."

Bernie drove an older model SUV that was, like her, of grand proportions. Morgan opened the passenger door and heaved Del's camouflage fanny pack up on the seat.

"Hi, Morgan. What's that?"

"Enough gear for us to live in the woods for a week." Morgan climbed into the SUV. "Del insisted I carry it." She buckled her seat belt. "He seems to think we're taking our lives in our hands going to downtown Granite Junction after dark."

"Maybe Del's on the right track. You were almost run down by the black SUV."

Bernie pulled through the rock shop gate and onto the gravel road. Her straight brown hair, unfettered by the chef's hat, brushed the shoulders of her heavy winter coat.

"Thanks for driving," Morgan said. "My car hasn't been running well lately."

"There's a good shop in town."

"Del recommended Gerda's," Morgan said.

"She's honest," Bernie said. "That's what's most important to me, as a single woman. Auto mechanics have been known to take advantage of us girls."

"I haven't had to deal much with car repairs," Morgan said. "Sam used to take care of our vehicles. Then my son, Dave, helped, until he went off to college."

The drive to downtown Granite Junction went quickly as they chatted about Morgan's children, Bernie's cat, and whether or not they could walk three miles. In the dark.

A crowd of runners stood outside O'Reily's Pub, looking chilled in their shorts and thin T-shirts. Some had earbuds and MP3 players. Others had small packs with water bottles strapped to their waists. Morgan did not feel quite so conspicuous wearing Del's suitcase of a fanny pack.

The pub looked like it had been lifted from a street in Dublin and nestled into the eclectic Granite Junction downtown. The red brick exterior was trimmed with dark wood window frames and a heavy wooden door. A low, wrought-iron fence marked off a small patio area on the wide concrete sidewalk.

Lucy stood in the doorway of the pub, a clipboard in one hand. She fit in with the crowd, dressed in black running slacks, bright yellow and white sneakers, and a thin turquoise windbreaker. She spotted Morgan and Bernie, and waved.

"Come on in and get signed up."

Morgan pushed through the crowd, Bernie following on her heels. Lucy led them to a tall, round, wooden table just large enough for the clipboard and a stack of papers.

"Here's the waiver." She handed Morgan and Bernie each a sheet of paper and a pen.

"Waiver?" Morgan asked.

"It just says that if anything happens to you, you won't sue the running club or the pub."

"How dangerous is this?" Bernie asked.

"Any physical activity carries a certain risk," Lucy said. "Waivers are standard for running clubs."

Bernie glanced at Morgan, a trace of fear in her green eyes.

"Let's do it." Morgan put pen to paper, signing with a flourish.

"Here's a map." Lucy handed Morgan a sheet of paper. "There are a couple turnaround points, if you don't want to walk the whole five K. If you run with us ten times"—Lucy reached into a cardboard box under the table—"you get one of these, for free."

She held up a white T-shirt emblazoned with the running club mascot: a bear dressed like a leprechaun, stealing a beer from a picnic basket.

Bernie clasped her hands together. "I've got to have one of those shirts." She turned to Morgan. "You have to stay in Golden Springs. At least nine more weeks, so you can get your shirt."

Kimmie tugged on Lucy's running slacks. "Mommy, I hafta go." The five-year-old's outfit was a smaller version of Lucy's, with a heavier jacket.

"I'll see you ladies out front." Lucy took her daughter's hand. "You can leave your coats here," she told Morgan and Bernie. "They'll be too hot."

They walked outside. Morgan glanced at the runners, hardly dressed for the chilly January evening. She shivered.

"I'm keeping my coat," she told Bernie.

Bernie wrapped her arms around herself. "Me, too."

A man climbed onto a chair in the small patio area. A breeze flapped the legs of his running shorts.

"Okay runners. Listen up."

He shouted out the rules of engagement, warning people to be careful crossing streets, and to obey traffic lights and stop signs. Headlamps or flashlights were required. The pub owner announced two-dollar beers for club members after the run, which brought a rousing cheer from the runners.

"All set?" the man asked. "Let's go!"

The runners surged forward, bumping against Morgan and Bernie. They funneled from the front of the pub to the sidewalk.

"See you later," Lucy called. She disappeared into the crowd of churning arms and legs.

Glowing headlamps sent shafts of light in advance of the runners. They looked like crazed miners, each determined to find the vein of gold before the others. Traffic lights and the crowded conditions kept even the fleet of foot from going faster than a swift walk. Morgan struggled to keep up for all of a block and a half. Finally Bernie grabbed her sleeve.

"I can't keep this up," Bernie wheezed.

"Me neither."

They slowed, allowing people to rush past them. Lucy's husband, Paul, trotted by on their left, grunting a greeting as he pushed Danny in the jogging stroller. A long black braid hung down his back, bouncing with every stride. Shorts revealed muscled runner's legs. He was a big man, but apparently, it was more muscle than fat.

"Look," Bernie puffed. "Even Kimmie, on her short little legs, is faster than us."

"She's a kid," Morgan said. "She's supposed to be faster than us."

The family disappeared down a street illuminated with feeble streetlights.

"If I had remembered we were running tonight," Bernie said, "I would have let someone else chase those silly donkeys."

"We're not running," Morgan said. "We're walking."

Bobbing headlamps showed the route of the runners, charging across the street, then flying onto a graveled trail through the city park.

Bernie stopped when they reached the trail.

"Through the park?" she asked. "Alone?"

"We're not alone," Morgan said. "We have each other."

"You have Del's backpack," Bernie said. "You'll have to defend me."

They walked along the gravel trail, their sneakers crunching loudly in the silence.

"It's really weird being here in the dark," Bernie said.

"Look." Morgan pointed to the crescent moon peeking through clouds silvered by its reflected light.

Bernie stopped. "Wow."

They watched the clouds drift to cover the moon, then resumed walking.

"That was worth the trip," Bernie said.

Morgan unbuttoned her coat. "I should have listened to Lucy. I'm sweating."

"Me, too." Bernie unzipped her coat. "Oh, Morgan."

She pointed to a bench. A homeless man curled on his side under a tattered sleeping bag.

"We're complaining about being too warm."

While Bernie seemed moved with compassion for the sleeping man, Morgan's heart beat faster with fear. The entire park could be crawling with drunks, derelicts, and drug addicts.

"How far do we go?" Bernie asked.

Morgan slowed as she unzipped her pack and fumbled through Del's idea of what was required for a walk in the park. "Here's the map." She handed the paper to Bernie, clicking on her flashlight. The little circle of light was reassuring.

"Where are we?" Bernie asked.

"Good question." The street names were meaningless to Morgan. "Can you tell?"

Bernie traced a finger along the route. "We came down here. Then this is the park. That's the bridge we passed. We must be here." She jabbed her finger at the paper.

"The first turnaround is close," Morgan said. "I thought I wanted to walk the entire five K, but I'm okay with just walking half."

"Just," Bernie exclaimed. "This might be the first time in my life I've walked a whole mile."

They walked with more confidence as they neared a street-light.

"Pavement," Bernie exclaimed. "Civilization."

They had to stop twice to breathe as they climbed the steep street out of the park.

"We should get back before everyone else," Bernie said. "Won't it be funny when we're sitting at the pub and Lucy and her family walk in?"

But running three miles apparently took less time than walk-ing one. When they reached Oak Street, runners dashed past them.

"Hi, ladies." Lucy blew past Morgan and Bernie. "I'll get us a table."

"She wasn't even breathing hard," Bernie said.

After another two blocks, Paul trotted by, pushing the stroller. Kimmie had squeezed in next to Danny.

"I would have felt really bad if a five year old had beaten us," Bernie said.

Morgan laughed. "I had no idea you were in this to win."

"It kind of fires up the competitive spirit."

By the time they trudged into the pub, it was obvious that Morgan and Bernie were dead last.

"Over here." Lucy waved. Her family sat at a long wooden table surrounded by laughing people. "I saved you seats."

Lucy introduced them to the other runners.

"We were getting ready to send search and rescue after you," Chuck, a thirty-something businessman in top-of-the-line run-ning attire, said with a grin.

"You are so bad." His trim wife, Vonne, makeup and hair un-fazed by the run, slapped him lightly on the shoulder. "We've only been here a few minutes."

"Minutes and minutes," Danny said.

Kimmie rolled her eyes at her little brother, and resumed coloring the kid's menu.

"I think I need better shoes," Bernie said. "My feet are killing me."

"What are you wearing?" Lucy asked.

Bernie held her foot to the side. "Just plain old sneakers."

"What have you got?" Lucy asked Morgan.

She moved her leg from under the table, showing Lucy the same worn sneaker she'd chased the donkeys in.

"You'll both do better with decent shoes," Lucy said.

As the conversation at the table of runners turned to stories of past victories, and plans for future adventures, Morgan tried to concentrate on the menu. She doubted that good athletic shoes would be cheap. The running club was free, but eating and drinking afterwards was not. Then there was parking.

"Morgan," Bernie called from her side of the table. "What beer are you drinking? Guinness or Smithwick's?"

Morgan looked up from her menu. She stared at the waitress. The young woman had the same chopped off, poorly dyed hair as the girl on the trail. Piercings marred her china-doll skin, and a rash of inartistic tattoos covered her shoulders, bare under the spaghetti straps of a tight tank top. Maybe it was the same girl.

The waitress boldly returned Morgan's stare, while working over a wad of moist gum. Morgan turned her attention to the menu, but she couldn't focus on the drink list.

"I don't know," Morgan said.

"I suppose beer negates the walking we just did."

"A Guinness is actually quite low in carbs," the waitress said, "for a beer."

"Guinness it is," Bernie said.

Corny jokes and clean limericks ran around the table several times before the fish and chips arrived.

Morgan relaxed. It had been a long time since she'd been

among people who didn't tiptoe around her widowhood. She had gotten off to a bad start in Golden Springs, finding a body, and then losing it, being run into a ditch, and chasing donkeys.

She watched the waitress move between the heavy wooden tables. There was a resemblance, but she didn't have the winged monster tattoo on her neck. The waitress wasn't the girl on the trail. Which meant the girl was still missing.

CHAPTER NINE

Morgan might have slept in, if her big toe hadn't started throbbing. She sat up in bed and examined her foot.

"Blister," she muttered. "Ugh."

Crawling out of bed, Morgan moved in slow motion. Surely one beer couldn't have given her a hangover.

"Altitude," she said aloud. "I'm still adjusting to the altitude."

Coffee helped dispel her lethargy. Her muscles loosened up as she went through the morning routine of feeding the donkeys and opening the shop. When she turned around the "open" sign, Morgan felt ready to face whatever adventures the new day chose to present.

Del arrived, and puttered around fixing dozens of things that needed fixing. He and Cindy seemed determined to maintain the momentum of Morgan's cleaning frenzy. As she watched Del oiling door hinges, Morgan again wondered at Kendall's lack of attention to the shop.

A customer browsed, studying every fossil in the shop, but buying nothing. Another purchased two dozen shark teeth for a Boy Scout project.

Morgan left Del in charge, and closed herself up in the office. She had no idea whether the shop was making or losing money. She wanted a clear picture of the property's worth before contacting a real-estate agent. And then there was the IRS. They wouldn't understand that in his haste to start his Central American cult, little things like the shop financial records had slipped Kendall's mind.

Close to noon, Del rapped on the office door.

"Come on in," Morgan said.

"I called Gerda at the auto repair shop," Del said. "You can take your car in today. She'll look at it for no charge."

"I do need a break." Morgan saved her file and shut down the dinosaur of a computer.

"I'll hold down the fort here," Del said.

Morgan tugged on her coat. It was a chilly day, the sky gray and cloudy. She pulled the gate to the driveway closed, making sure it was securely latched, before she drove out of the Rock of Ages parking lot.

Kruger's Auto Repair squatted a block off Main Street on the west edge of Golden Springs, between a coin laundry and boarded-up cabins sitting in a lot overrun with weeds. A rack of tires, a chain looped through their centers, marked the division between the laundry parking and Kruger's. Morgan pulled onto the crowded asphalt lot.

The two raised bay doors revealed a tidy work area. A thin young man with a crew cut and a heavier man with short gray whiskers wore matching dark-blue jumpsuits. They consulted under the open hood of a passenger car.

The older man looked up. "Can I help you?"

"I'm looking for Gerda," Morgan said.

The man jerked a thumb toward the office. "She's in there."

The shop windows needed scrubbing. Faded fliers taped to the inside of the glass advertised events dating back three years. The wood framing the scratched glass door badly needed paint. Inside, a cash register sat on a pitted glass display case.

"Are you Kendall's sister?" A short, stout woman filled the office doorway, a German accent making her words heavy and terse.

"Yes," Morgan said. "Del sent me."

"I'm Gerda."

Morgan winced as Gerda clasped her hand in a calloused, iron grip. Gerda wore the same dark-blue jumpsuit as the men. It accented her roundness, making Morgan think of an eggplant. A shock of white hair stuck up at odd angles from her round, flushed face.

"You come in here." Gerda waddled ahead of Morgan, leading her inside a small office. She sat behind a gray metal desk. "What's wrong with your car?"

"I don't know." Morgan resisted the urge to tell Gerda that was her job—finding out what was wrong. The frown lines etched deep in Gerda's face told Morgan the woman might not have a well-developed sense of humor. "It's been overheating ever since I drove here from South Dakota last week."

"I have my boys take a look at it," Gerda said. "No charge since you're a friend of Del. Then we decide what to do. Right?"

How could I disagree? thought Morgan. "That sounds fine," she said aloud.

"Good." Gerda stood. "We'll take good care of your car."

Morgan followed Gerda out of the office. She noticed an empty bourbon bottle in the trash can by the door. Morgan wondered if it was Gerda's, or one of the mechanic's.

"Do you know how long it will take?" Morgan asked. "It's the only vehicle we have at the rock shop right now."

"Maybe tomorrow we'll know what's what."

Gerda held out her hand. Morgan obediently handed over her keys.

"You got a ride?" Gerda asked. "I can have one of my boys take you home."

"I can walk," Morgan said, thinking of the liquor bottle.

Morgan headed to Main Street. The chilly breeze pushed down the neck of her coat. She wished she'd remembered a scarf. The blister on her toe throbbed with every step. Morgan hobbled into the pharmacy and bought blister bandages.

When she came out, a magpie landed on the hitching post in front of the newspaper office. Snow-white feathers on its underside and the shoulders of its wings contrasted sharply with its iridescent black head, back, and tail. It hopped down the rail, turning its head to watch Morgan as she passed. Morgan shuddered. She wondered if she would forever think of the girl on the trail when she saw magpies.

As she passed the bakery, the smell of baked goods and soup lured her closer. Morgan resisted the urge to drop in. As long as she was already in town, she might be able to solve one little mystery.

She hurried to Hill Street, turning at Faerie Tales. Piers stood with his back to the window. Wavy blond hair brushed the shoulders of his green silk tunic.

Piers had been worked up about the donkeys eating his flowers last summer. Could he have been angry enough to let the donkeys loose, in the hopes of getting them banned from Golden Springs? Angry enough to try to run her down, regardless of the karmic consequences? She needed to see what kind of vehicle he drove.

A wooden fence enclosed the small parking area behind Piers's shop. Morgan glanced around to see whether anyone was watching. She stepped down the alley and inside the parking area. A tiny lime-green hybrid car with a sparkly Faerie Tales bumper sticker perched near the back stoop. A late model silver two-door compact sat next to it.

No black SUV.

Morgan chided herself. Houdini and Adelaide could have been hit by a truck, or had any of a hundred mishaps. She couldn't imagine the gentle vegetarian Piers exposing them to harm by letting them out, even if they had eaten his flowers. It was even less believable that he would try to kill a human.

By the time Morgan walked in the door of the rock shop, she was limping. The blister on her big toe distracted her from further paranoid fantasies.

Thursday morning Morgan sat at the cash register, writing the work schedule on her new dry erase board. She looked up as a Granite Junction police cruiser pulled into the Rock of Ages parking lot.

Officer Sanchez walked in, followed by Officer MacKenzie, who had to duck under the low doorway. Their polished shoes and pressed uniform slacks were mud spattered.

"I don't suppose you're here to buy rocks," Morgan said.

"A hiker found a body," Sanchez said. "It was several hundred feet off the trail, but close enough to the spot where you led search and rescue that it could be the same girl."

"You said 'body.' Does that mean she's dead?"

MacKenzie nodded. Morgan felt like someone had knocked the wind out of her.

Del ducked through the shop door. He yanked the cowboy hat off his head and clomped across the pine floor. He glanced at the police officers, then focused on Morgan. "What's going on?"

"Officer Sanchez thinks they might have found the missing girl."

"We'd like you to come with us," Sanchez said.

"Why?" Del asked.

"We don't need you, Mr. Addison," MacKenzie said.

"If you're taking Mrs. Iverson anywhere, I'm going, too." Del planted his hat back on his head.

"Look, Mr. Addison," Sanchez said, "we really don't need any help here. The more people we have at the scene, the more danger there is that evidence will be compromised."

"Evidence?" Morgan's heart skipped a beat. "Was she murdered?"

"We don't know how she died yet," Sanchez said. "We'd like you to see the scene before we remove the body."

"My car is in the shop," Morgan said.

"We'll take you," Sanchez said.

Morgan glanced at Del. "I'd really like Del to go with me, if that's okay."

"Only if he promises to stay out of the way," Officer Sanchez said, frowning at Del.

Officer MacKenzie parked at the Columbine trailhead. Sanchez got out, pulling on a heavy winter jacket covered with Granite Junction Police Department patches. Another police cruiser, a Pine County Search and Rescue truck and trailer, and two other cars crowded the small parking lot.

Rolf sat in the driver's seat of a large ATV. He gripped the steering wheel with leather-gloved hands. A white search and rescue helmet covered his sandy hair.

"Hello Morgan," he said. "I guess we weren't looking in the right spot. Hop on. I'm driving you to the site."

The ATV seemed more like a golf cart than the traditional all-terrain vehicles they had at the rock shop. Roll bars encased the two narrow, padded seats. She climbed inside, sitting behind Rolf. Del climbed into the back seat with her, his long legs scrunched up nearly to his chin. His hunter's green and brown camouflage jacket, covered with pockets, seemed appropriate for the trek through the winter woods. Officer Sanchez squeezed in next to Rolf.

Morgan gripped the roll bar with one hand. She was glad she'd remembered mittens and a scarf. The wind whipped through the open vehicle as it bounced down the trail.

The trip was fast in the ATV. Rolf slowed when they reached

the spot where Morgan had found the girl. They continued past the cottonwoods and turned into a meadow. Rolf followed muddy tire tracks through the dried grass and scrubby bushes. Morgan watched a magpie fly toward the cottonwood trees. It might have been cawing, but Morgan couldn't hear it over the ATV's engine. Rolf stopped where the meadow dropped off at a creek. Officer Sanchez climbed out.

"We have to walk from here," she said.

Del followed Morgan down a steep bank through knee-high brush. She struggled to keep the police officer's dark-blue jacket in sight. Her blistered toe throbbed.

The narrow creek etched a curving bed at the base of a pink sandstone cliff mottled with mud dauber nests. Pine trees rose from thick brush at the base of the cliff, their upper branches rising above its flat top. Morgan would not have guessed the low cliff was just yards off the well-traveled trail.

Unseen things could happen in pockets of Colorado wilderness and never be discovered. Treasures preserved. Secrets hidden.

Sanchez slowed her march. Morgan stopped beside the police officer. Two search and rescue personnel stood to one side, holding an aluminum-framed stretcher. A skinny police officer who looked too young to be in uniform stared at the ground, looking like he wanted to be anywhere but here. A tall, barrel-chested black man in a suit coat and jeans stood to the other side. In the center of their semicircle, a balding man wearing blue nitrile gloves crouched over a still form.

Morgan's stomach clenched at the sight of the familiar black cloak. Del put his hand on her arm.

The man in the gloves looked up. "Good," he said in a nasal tone. "You made it." He stood. "We're ready to move the body."

Quick introductions identified the man in the gloves as the coroner, and the one in the suit coat as a detective. A dark-haired man in cowboy attire, complete with chaps and a shiny sheriff's-style badge grasped Morgan's hand and gave it a vigorous shake.

"Chief Bill Sharp. My job is to serve and protect Golden Springs citizens," Bill said, emphasis on Golden Springs. "Feel free to call on me." He jabbed a thumb at his chest.

Morgan had the distinct feeling that jurisdictional toes had been stepped on. She wanted to explain to Chief Sharp that she wasn't responsible for the chain of events her call had set in motion, including the Granite Junction police department taking the case as their own. The Columbine Trail wasn't within either Golden Springs or Granite Junction city limits.

Detective Roland Parker interrupted before she could speak. "Is this the person you reported seeing Saturday?" His voice was a commanding baritone.

Morgan walked around the still form, stopping next to the coroner. Del followed, his hand gently holding her arm just below the elbow, as though she might faint at any moment.

The girl lay in a heap, her limbs twisted at awkward angles. The same pale face Morgan has seen before peeked out from under the black cloak. Morgan recognized the piercings, and the raggedly cut short hair with the bad dye job.

Morgan clutched Del's arm and leaned closer. She could see more of the tattoo on the girl's neck. Bat wings sprouted from the hunched shoulders of a creature that would have been at home perched on a medieval cathedral.

"Her face wasn't puffy when I saw her." Morgan nodded. "But that's her. I'm sure of it. She was back there." Morgan pointed in the direction they had come from. "But that's the same girl."

"The weather has been cold," the coroner said. "There hasn't been much decomposition."

Morgan backed away, bile rising in her throat.

"So she came down that?" Del pointed to the top of the sandstone cliff.

"That's what it looks like," the coroner said. "At first glance, anyway."

"Listen, Mr. Addison," Officer Sanchez said, "I know you like to be helpful, but I'd really appreciate it if you'd keep what you saw here to yourself. You, too, Mrs. Iverson."

Morgan watched the search and rescue team lift the body onto the stretcher, her vision blurry through the tears filling her eyes.

"If I could have gotten in cell phone range quicker to call for help, or if I'd tried CPR, she might not be here now." Morgan swallowed hard. "Was she alive when I saw her Saturday?"

"We won't know until after the autopsy," the coroner said.

CHAPTER TEN

Officer MacKenzie pulled the police cruiser to the curb in front of the newspaper office. Morgan stared out the window, only half-aware of the streets of Golden Springs. The image of the girl's pale white face would not fade.

"Detective Parker's not a bad guy," Officer Sanchez said.

The detective had been unsympathetic to Morgan's tears, and had insisted on reviewing her report to Pine County Search and Rescue and Officer Sanchez, before allowing Morgan and Del to leave.

"I know," Morgan said. "He was just doing his job."

"You sure you don't want a ride back up the hill?" Officer Sanchez asked, half turning in the passenger seat.

"I need to take care of some business in town," Del said.

Morgan nodded her head. "Me, too."

"We understand you've had a shock," Sanchez said. "It might be better for us to drive you home, Mrs. Iverson."

Maybe Officer Sanchez did understand.

"Thank you, but I'd rather walk," Morgan said.

Del waved at the cruiser as it pulled away from the curb. A gust of wind tumbled a crumpled paper bag across the boardwalk.

"I'm going to Gerda's," Del told Morgan. He zipped up his hunter's jacket. "See if your car's been checked yet. Unless you want me to walk with you?"

Morgan couldn't face the empty rock shop just yet. She

tugged her wool cap down on her wind-whipped curls.

"I might stay in town a little while."

"I'll call your cell phone when I leave Gerda's." Del headed west, his cowboy boots loud on the wooden walkway.

The detective had asked Del and Morgan to keep what they'd seen to themselves. Surely she could confide the trauma of the experience with her new friend without giving away potential evidence. But a be-back-in sign hung in the bakery window. Morgan checked her watch. Bernie would be gone for another thirty minutes.

Morgan turned around. As she walked past Faerie Tales, she considered marching in to have a talk with Piers about a sign. There was plenty of room for a rock shop sign on either corner of Hill and Main.

Seeing the dead girl had taken the fight out of Morgan. What was the point, anyway? If Kendall didn't come back, she would be selling the property. She'd only been in Golden Springs a few days, and she already had enough bad memories for a lifetime. She took a deep breath and prepared herself for the climb up Hill Street.

The door to Faerie Tales opened, and Piers stepped out on the boardwalk. The wind tousled his blond hair. The sleeves of his brown tunic flapped against his arms.

"Hello, Morgan. Is everything okay?"

"I'm fine." Morgan wondered if Piers had seen her dropped off by the police. While she was confident Bernie would not pump her for details, she was afraid she might spill everything to Piers. "I'm waiting for Del."

Piers studied Morgan for a moment. She was certain he was reading her aura, or doing something to her chakras. Morgan tugged her quilted coat tighter around her.

"Would you like a cup of tea?" Piers opened the door to Faerie Tales, bracing it against the wind with his body. He motioned inside. "While you're waiting?"

"I wouldn't want to bother you," Morgan said.

"The wind is cold. Come in."

He pushed the door open wide. Morgan stepped across the threshold and into the warm, incense-scented shop. Soothing music played on hidden speakers. Tunics and drawstring yoga slacks like Piers wore hung on round racks. Bookshelves lined one wall. Birdbath-sized fountains clustered in front of the checkout counter, the water trickling musically over glass globes and sculpted objects.

Piers led Morgan to a cozy sitting area. A half dozen upholstered chairs grouped around two low, round tables. In the center of one sat a jade-green ceramic teapot painted with golden bamboo stalks. Piers poured tea into a small round cup with no handle and presented it to Morgan.

She cradled the cup in her hands and held it under her chin, letting the steam warm her face.

"This smells nice," she said. "What kind of tea is it?"

"Chamomile flowers, a touch of peppermint, and a dash of cinnamon. It's my own recipe." He turned a box toward Morgan so she could see the silver-and-green-foil label, embossed with faeries.

Morgan sipped the tea. The chamomile gave it a distinct apple favor.

"Delicious," Morgan said.

"It will help you calm down."

Morgan had the uncomfortable feeling that Piers could see more about her than she cared to reveal. She decided she'd better head the conversation in the direction she chose.

"Walking around town today," Morgan said, "I've noticed there are several shops on the side streets that have signs on Main Street pointing out their locations."

Piers poured himself a cup of tea. "You are persistent." A

smile tugged at his lips.

"I know I've been a pain about this," Morgan said. "Maybe you can explain to me. What would it hurt to let us put up a sign on one of your corners? Something that fits in with the rest of the downtown style."

"Have you changed your mind about selling your property?" Piers asked.

Morgan set her tea on the table. "I can't change my mind. I haven't made a decision yet."

"I would welcome either outcome." Piers flashed a genuine smile at Morgan. "I feel that you and I could be good neighbors. Even, perhaps, friends." He met Morgan's eyes with his icy-blue gaze.

A melodious doorbell sounded as the front door opened.

"Piers?" a raspy voice called.

"Back here," Piers said. "Sharing a pot of tea."

Morgan had seen the woman around town. She wore a long skirt, but not like Cindy's pioneer-style garb. Hers was vintage Woodstock, although the woman had obviously been born a few decades after the famed 1969 outdoor concert. The tattered hem of the denim skirt stopped below her knees, where it met the tops of rainbow-hued wool knee socks crammed into size twelve Birkenstocks. An overstuffed satchel hung on the woman's rounded shoulder from handwoven straps.

Piers stood and bowed slightly at the waist.

"Sparrow," Piers said, "I would like you to meet my new friend, Morgan. Sparrow owns the hemp store."

There was nothing birdlike about Sparrow. She was tall and large framed. Unlike Bernie, she carried her weight poorly, as though she had been formed from half-filled sandbags. She yanked a wool stocking cap off her head, revealing severely short green hair.

Morgan stood to shake hands. Sparrow held hers in a viselike grip for a moment too long. She eyed Morgan critically, as though assessing a rival, then flopped down onto one of the upholstered chairs.

"What brings you to Golden Springs?" Sparrow asked in a coarse smoker's voice. She fixed a smile on Morgan that had a sharpness to it.

"I'm managing the Rock of Ages."

Sparrow's smile vanished. She glanced from Morgan to Piers.

"I think you will find that Morgan has a refreshingly open attitude." Piers poured Sparrow a cup of tea.

Sparrow accepted the tea with a nod. "You're Kendall's sister?" She slurped from the cup, then set it on the table. "I never thought I'd see one of his family set foot inside Faerie Tales."

"That brother of mine." Morgan laughed nervously. "The whole family's not like that."

Piers practically beamed at Morgan.

Sparrow clasped her hands to her knees and leaned forward on her chair. "You should come to one of our meetings, then."

"What's the meeting about?" Morgan thought perhaps they belonged to a small business association of some sort.

"Our monthly interfaith potluck." Sparrow dug in her satchel and pulled out an orange flyer. "Golden Springs residents meet to discuss issues like tolerance."

Morgan accepted the sheet of paper. It contained a simple announcement of date, time, and location. The speaker was presenting photos from a recent tour of temples in Thailand.

"Interfaith?" Morgan asked.

"The group accepts people of all backgrounds and beliefs," Piers said.

"Or none at all," Sparrow said. "I'm atheist."

She watched Morgan, apparently waiting for a reaction.

"And you?" Sparrow asked in a challenging tone. "What do

you believe?"

Morgan sat up straight. She had always wondered how she would define her faith, if push came to shove.

"I'm attending Golden Springs Community Church," she blurted out.

Sparrow looked positively astonished. Morgan decided her declaration was worth the reaction.

"Certainly," Piers said. "The church is familiar. We often find comfort in tradition. As you meet new people, perhaps you will be encouraged to explore other faith communities."

"You're welcome to check out the potluck," Sparrow said, almost painfully holding back the "in spite of your beliefs" Morgan was certain she wanted to add. "The next one is Wednesday."

"It sounds very interesting." Morgan tried to hand the flier back to Sparrow. "But I'm overwhelmed with running the shop. I'm sure I won't have time."

"Keep it." Sparrow jabbed a finger at the paper. "That's my phone number." Sparrow struggled to get up out of the chair. "Piers, can I talk to you?"

Sparrow wrapped her arm through Piers's in a decidedly possessive gesture. She led him through the shop, talking in whispers. Morgan folded the flier and stuck it in her jeans pocket.

Between the strong incense and the strained conversation, Morgan felt a headache coming on. She wondered what was taking Del so long. Morgan checked her cell phone. She had signal.

The door chimed as Sparrow left the shop. She clambered into a beat-up VW bus parked in front. Morgan leaned back in her chair as Piers returned to the sitting area.

He perched on the edge of his chair. "Now, where were we?"

"Talking about a sign." Morgan sipped her tea.

Piers shook his head gently. "I suspect you are a woman accustomed to getting her way."

"If anything, I'm not used to getting what I want. I've had my share of disappointments."

"Ah," Piers said. "Then I begin to understand why this sign is so important to you."

"Oh, no," Morgan said. "I don't think you understand at all. I apologize for being so persistent, maybe even pushy, when I hardly know you."

Piers dazzled Morgan with a white-toothed smile. "Perhaps the solution is that we should get to know each other better, when we're not discussing a topic fraught with stress and conflict, as business inevitably is."

If Morgan was not mistaken, it seemed as though Piers had just expressed a desire to see her socially. Surely he wasn't hitting on her. She recalled Lucy's warning. An uncomfortable silence stretched across the table.

"I have to meet Del." Morgan jumped to her feet. "I'll just, uh . . ." She glanced at the table. "I'll buy some tea."

She hurried to the cash register. While Piers rang up the sale, Morgan glanced in the display case.

"Oh!" She leaned closer.

The creature she had seen perched on the girl's body, and tattooed on her neck, had been rendered in pewter and strung on a chain.

"Do you like my gargoyle?" Piers didn't wait for a reaction. "It came to me in a vision." He opened the back of the display case and lifted the necklace out of its nest of red silk. "Gargoyles were originally decorations for drain spouts."

He set the pewter creature on the display case. Two red, glittering gemstones glared out of a hideous face. Morgan tried to remember whether the monster she had seen perched on the dead girl had red eyes. But that monster had really been a magpie.

"I thought gargoyles were used to scare away evil spirits," Morgan said. "Or to scare reluctant parishioners into church pews."

Piers chuckled. "Actually, the poor gargoyle is, like most so-called monsters, a misunderstood creature. Its true nature is that of protector."

Morgan almost blurted out that she had seen the same creature on a corpse, but that would entail an explanation she wasn't prepared to give. Instead, she clutched the box of tea and backed away from the display case.

"I need to go," she said, forcing a smile.

She hurried out of Faerie Tales, and its cloyingly thick scent of incense. Morgan gulped deep breaths of fresh air as she rushed the two blocks down the wooden walkway to Bibi's.

She stepped inside the bakery, pulling the door closed against the wind. Bernie looked up from the table she was clearing.

"Morgan, you look like you've seen a ghost."

CHAPTER ELEVEN

"Are you okay?" Bernie asked.

Two customers looked up from their conversation. Morgan suspected she was already known as the crazy lady who imagined bodies on trails. She couldn't blurt out that she also hallucinated monsters, and that Piers had made hers into a necklace.

"My feet hurt," Morgan said. "I have a blister."

"Sit down," Bernie said. "My feet hurt, too. Thankfully I didn't get blisters."

Bernie hobbled behind the counter and filled a teapot with hot water.

"I haven't walked a mile in years." Bernie carried the teapot and mugs on a tray, setting it on the table. "Oh, who am I kidding? I haven't ever walked a mile."

Bernie sat across from Morgan and poured steaming water into the mugs. She wore a traditional white chef's coat today, but had livened it up with a pink silk neck scarf.

"I haven't hiked since the last time I visited Golden Springs." Morgan paused as the two customers gathered their coats and left. When the door closed, she turned to Bernie. "I came by earlier, but you were out."

"I had to take my kitty, Mr. Whiskers, to the vet for his annual checkup. What's up?"

Morgan glanced around the empty bakery, then leaned across the small round table. "Do you remember the girl I saw on the

102

trail? Who disappeared?"

"Yes."

"The police found her. She's dead."

Bernie's green eyes opened wide. "Oh, my. How could they have missed her before?"

"She wasn't where I found her."

"Does that mean she was alive when you saw her?" Bernie lowered her voice to a whisper. "Was she murdered?"

"I'm not supposed to say anything about the scene." Morgan twisted a paper napkin with her hands. "It could have been an accident. They can't tell yet."

The bell over the door tinkled. A customer stepped purposefully to the counter.

"I'll be right back," Bernie told Morgan.

She sold the customer a dozen croissants, then returned to the bistro table.

"This is not the sort of conversation that should be interrupted. Let's go upstairs."

Bernie turned around the be-back-in sign and led Morgan behind the counter and through the kitchen. A plain door opened to narrow, steep stairs. At the top was a bright apartment lined with tall windows, lacey curtains, and deeply cushioned furniture in a bright floral pattern.

Mr. Whiskers mewed a greeting. Bernie settled onto the loveseat and pulled the enormous gray cat onto her lap.

"Now tell me all about it," Bernie said. "At least the parts you can share."

Morgan related the story, leaving out the specifics of the scene where the young woman had been found.

"You don't suppose they think you had something to do with this girl's demise, do you?" Bernie asked.

"Why would they think that?"

Bernie shrugged. "You're new to town. Maybe they thought

if they took you to the scene of the crime, you'd crack and confess."

"It might not be a crime," Morgan said. "They don't know how she died yet. They just wanted me to see if it was the same person. And it was. She was worse. But I could tell it was the same girl."

"It's so strange that she wasn't in the same place," Bernie said. "She either had to be alive when you saw her, or somebody moved her, trying to hide her, or maybe animals moved her. That happens sometimes. A person dies in the woods, and body parts get dragged all over the place."

"The coroner said there hadn't been much decomposition because of the cool weather." Morgan watched Mr. Whiskers sitting regally on Bernie's lap. "I'm sure animals hadn't dragged her. If she was alive when I saw her, maybe she came to, and tried to get help. Why would anyone move her if she was already dead?" Morgan paused. "There's something else. Something I didn't mention to the police. When I first saw the girl, I thought she was a—I don't know how to explain this without sounding crazy—I thought I saw a monster. Like a gargoyle. A big black creature with wings." Morgan stopped herself from saying "with red eyes," because she didn't remember seeing its eyes. Her imagination might be embellishing what she saw. "But then a magpie flew away. So it must have been a magpie all along, and I hallucinated that it was a monster."

"Magpies are the most disgusting scavengers," Bernie said. "They're like buzzards."

"The odd thing is," Morgan continued, "when I was in Piers's shop just now, he had a pewter necklace in his display case that looked just like the thing I saw."

Bernie sat up straight. "You should tell the police about that."

"What would I tell them?" Morgan asked. "That I imagined a gargoyle, and then I saw the same monster in a New Age bookstore? Officer Sanchez already thinks I've got a screw loose, and now there's a detective on the case who's not exactly sympathetic."

Morgan's cell phone rang. She glanced at the caller ID.

"It's Del," she told Bernie, then flipped opened her phone. "Hey, what took you so long?"

"Where are you?" Del asked.

"At the bakery."

"I figured I'd find you here, but I'm standing outside. The bakery is closed."

"I'll be right down." Morgan hung up. "Boy, Del sounded stressed."

"After seeing a body," Bernie said, "I'm not surprised."

Del paced in front of the bakery door. He wore a grim expression, his mustache twitching.

"What's wrong?" Morgan asked.

"The be-back-in sign was up," Del said. "I thought something was wrong."

"We were just upstairs."

"Until we know whether that girl died of natural causes," Del said, "or was murdered, I'm gonna worry about you."

"The coroner said it looked like she fell off the cliff."

"No, he didn't say 'fell.' He didn't know whether she was alive or dead when you found her. There could be a killer out there. Someone who moved that body after you saw it."

"I've thought of that, too," Morgan said.

They walked a block in silence. Del shoved his hands in the deep pockets of his jacket.

"So what's the verdict on the car?" Morgan asked.

"The Buick's not terminal. That's the good news. I'll let Gerda fill you in on the rest."

Gerda sat behind her desk, looking authoritative in her dark-blue jumpsuit and short-cropped white hair. After a lecture in her clipped German accent about the importance of regular auto maintenance, Gerda handed Morgan an estimate. Morgan took the yellow sheet, focusing not so much on what needed repair as the total at the bottom.

"Six hundred?" Morgan squeaked.

"You are lucky you brought it to me when you did," Gerda said. "The water pump is going out. That's why your auto keeps overheating. If we replace the water pump, we should replace the timing belt, as well."

"Do I need to get it done right away?" Morgan asked.

"Are you planning any long trips?" Gerda asked.

"I'm driving back to Sioux Falls in a week," Morgan said.

Gerda shook her head. "Not in this car. I am amazed you made it here."

"I don't have the money to get it fixed right now."

"You may drive it around town," Gerda said, "but you need to check the radiator. If it goes dry, all is lost."

"How do I do that?" Morgan asked.

Gerda's round face puckered in a grimace.

"Hold on, now," Del said. "The girl's a widow. She didn't need to know about these things."

Gerda held up her hands. "Okay. Then the time is now."

She pushed herself up out of her chair. Morgan was again reminded of an eggplant as Gerda waddled around the desk and out the office door.

Gerda pushed "the boys" out of the way and led Morgan through the steps required to check the water in the radiator.

"Don't count on the water pump to give out at your convenience," Gerda warned. "It will most likely quit when you are in a hurry to go somewhere. If your engine starts to overheat, pull over! Do not keep driving! You can burn up your engine."

"I don't have six hundred dollars right now," Morgan said. "I guess I'll have to take my chances."

"Here is my card," Gerda said, "in case you need a tow. I also recommend you get a new battery. That battery is going to leave you stranded if the water pump does not."

She handed Morgan the keys to the Buick.

"I suppose I should be happy I don't have to walk up the hill." Morgan turned onto Hill Street. "Six hundred dollars," she grumbled. "Ouch!"

"That's a fair price," Del said.

"I just hadn't planned on spending that much on it right now." Morgan thought of her 401K money, and her resolve to not touch it except in an emergency. She sighed. "It'll have to be done before I can drive home."

"Is that still the plan?"

The question was too complicated for a simple answer.

"Maybe Kendall will change his mind and come home," Morgan said. "In the meantime, I'm stuck here."

"That's fine by me, kid." Del settled back into the seat, folding his arms across his chest. "I'm just getting used to having you around." Del closed his eyes.

Dust trailed behind the Buick as it crawled up the gravel road. Morgan clutched the steering wheel. The wind blasted against her car in ferocious gusts. She struggled to keep the car on the road and out of the ditch.

Dried leaves swirled up from the irrigation ditch, spilling across the gravel road. A blue grocery bag took flight. When a cloud of grit slapped against the windshield like hard rain, Morgan slowed. Her hands ached from gripping the steering wheel, and she wondered if conditions could possibly get worse.

Then the wind died abruptly. Morgan pressed on the accelerator, anxious to reach the rock shop before it started blowing again. Before they reached the gate, fluttering wings dropped into the tall, dried grass at the side of the road.

Morgan slammed on the brakes. The sudden stop, or maybe her shriek, woke Del. He threw his hands against the dashboard.

"What the—"

"Look!"

Morgan opened her door slowly. "That's it. The thing I saw." Then she remembered that she hadn't told anyone but Bernie about the creature she had seen on the trail.

She stood behind the open door, using it as a shield. Del climbed out of his seat and reached inside his vest. He drew a Smith and Wesson handgun out of the shoulder holster concealed under his western vest.

"Just what are we alarmed about?" Del asked.

"That—that thing. It's a monster! Maybe you should shoot it."

Del stepped cautiously toward the tall grass. Morgan followed him, ready to run if the gargoyle should take flight.

Flight. If it had wings, a person might not be able to outrun a gargoyle.

Black and white wings burst into motion. Morgan ducked. Two magpies went airborne. The muzzle of Del's handgun briefly followed, aimed at the birds, before he lowered his hand.

"Just what was all that about?"

"It was a—I saw it—there was a—"

Morgan tiptoed beside Del.

"It's a bunny," she murmured.

"And two magpies," Del snorted. "Nature's garbage disposal system."

Morgan shuddered.

"Is there something you haven't told me?" Del asked.

"Besides the fact that I'm prone to hallucinations?"

"You said 'the thing I saw,' like you'd seen it before."

"When I first saw the girl on the trail," Morgan said, "I saw something. A—a monster. It was perched on her, and then it turned into a magpie, just one that time, and flew away. She had a tattoo on her neck. You saw it. That's what the monster looked like."

Del nodded slowly. "I see."

Morgan walked back to the car. "I knew it would sound crazy. That's why I didn't tell anyone."

Del stood by the passenger door. He placed the gun back in his holster and snapped it closed.

"Do you always carry that?" Morgan asked. "You might have let me know."

"You should be glad I'm packing," Del answered, "seeing as how the hills are full of monsters."

CHAPTER TWELVE

Del opened the doors to the old carriage house. Morgan backed the Buick inside, avoiding the two ATVs. She climbed out and helped Del push the heavy doors closed.

"You know, when Cindy comes in to work tomorrow, we don't have to tell her about this."

"You don't think I should warn her?" Del smirked, his mustache twisting up on one side.

"I really thought I saw something," Morgan said. "And if it was absolutely nothing, explain why you pulled a gun on it."

"I had an instinctive reaction to the scream of a female. But don't worry. I won't tell Cindy. I'm going straight to the barn to work on the donkey cart."

"Thanks."

"Are you gonna be okay?" Del asked. "After this morning and all?"

"That girl wasn't the first dead person I've seen, Del. I'm at that age, you know. I should be getting used to people dying."

Del nodded. "I know what you mean."

Cindy called in Friday morning. Two of her children were sick, and she wasn't feeling all that well herself. Del borrowed the car to drive to Granite Junction to get parts to repair the donkey cart. Morgan sat in the office, filling in the lost months in the shop's financial records.

The Rock of Ages made a little money. Business was modest,

but Kendall and Allie were frugal. The previous years' property taxes had been paid. Morgan couldn't find an account or records specifically for money to pay the tax bill coming up, but she hadn't caught up on all the paperwork. She pushed her hands through her hair.

"Argh! What a mess."

It was like trying to untangle a big ball of yarn after a kitten had played with it. The accounts were full of knots and tangles.

Morgan's cell phone rang. She smiled when she saw the name on the caller ID.

"Hello, Sarah."

"Hi, Mom."

"I'm glad you called. I need a break." Morgan stood and stretched.

"How are things going?" Sarah asked.

"Fine." Morgan was not about to tell her pregnant daughter about the dead teenage girl, gargoyles, and homicidal SUVs. "Did you finish painting the baby's room?"

"You should see it, Mom. It turned out perfect. You remember the paint samples and fabric swatches you helped me pick before you left?"

"Yes."

"We went with the pastel green. Russ and I both thought we could live with those colors a lot longer than—oops! I almost told you."

"You know?" Morgan threaded her way around stacks of papers and walked through the shop, pacing up and down the center aisle. "Boy or girl?"

"Haven't you checked your email?" Sarah asked. "I sent you ultrasound pictures."

"Your Uncle Kendall's computer is a dinosaur," Morgan said. "It should be sitting in one of the fossil cases. I'll have to wait until I get home to see them."

"Mom, it'll be next week before you get to see the pictures."

"I'm not sure how long I'll be here now. According to the local mechanic, my car won't make it back to Sioux Falls without major repairs."

"Russ and I can send you the money."

"Thanks for the offer, but it's going to cost six hundred dollars."

"Ouch. Yeah, we might have trouble coming up with that much cash, especially after remodeling the bedroom for the baby. We could help you buy a plane ticket."

"Then I wouldn't have a car in Sioux Falls."

"You do have a car, Mom."

"I gave it to your brother. He needs it." Dave had formed an almost emotional attachment to Sam's pickup truck. He had taken his father's death hard, drifting away from Morgan and Sarah, hiding behind his college studies. "Have you heard from Dave lately?"

"Russ badgered him into coming over for dinner next week. We'll see if he shows up. So Mom, why don't you ask Uncle Kendall and Aunt Allie to drive you home, when they get back? I can't travel right now, but I'd sure love to see them."

"They've changed their plans. They're staying longer. Maybe forever."

Morgan filled Sarah in on Kendall's sudden change of plans.

"You can't sell the shop," Sarah said. "Russ and I will help, if we can."

"I'm hoping Kendall changes his mind."

They chatted for several more minutes. When Sarah hung up, the shop felt empty.

There had not been a customer all day. Morgan thought of the be-back-in signs everyone else seemed more than capable of using. She had to break the corporate mentality, and start enjoying the Colorado mountains before her two weeks were up.

Morgan walked to the front door. Both Del and Cindy had keys to the shop. She didn't need to be here. Morgan turned the deadbolt, and flipped the sign around. She nodded.

"Simple."

She unlocked the door with the "Private—Do Not Enter" sign, and entered the living quarters connected to the back of the shop. Morgan wished she still had her old hiking clothes. Loose jeans and a fleece sweater would have to do. She bandaged her blister and laced up her ratty sneakers. Coat, scarf, mittens. As she passed through the kitchen to the back door, she paused.

Morgan could almost hear Del warning her about the dangers of the Colorado wilderness. Not to mention monsters. She grabbed the olive-green camouflage fanny pack and strapped it around her waist.

When she closed the back door and walked into the back pasture, she felt like a kid slipping out of school to play hooky.

Houdini and Adelaide followed her halfway across the pasture before their curiosity gave way to their greater interest in a patch of grass. Morgan reached the back fence and the gate the donkeys had escaped through her first day. She untwisted the baling wire Del had added to prevent another escape.

The trail climbed steadily through dense pines and aspens. The vegetation thinned as the elevation increased. Hiking was strenuous, but soon she was above the height of the shop and the barn, and then she could no longer see the buildings below. The feeling of being utterly alone in the wilderness was invigorating and frightening at the same time.

The trail would eventually lead her to the Columbine Trail, and the final resting place of the teenage girl. She unzipped the fanny pack. The pepper spray rested on top.

A magpie burst out of a bush, cawing as it flew up into the trees. Morgan jumped backwards. She shook her mitten-covered fist at the bird.

"You darn bird. I'm really starting to dislike magpies."

The bird scolded her right back. Magpies seemed to have it in for her, since the day she found the girl. The day she first saw a monster. Piers had claimed that the true nature of gargoyles were as protectors. The one perched on the girl had not done a good job.

Morgan continued uphill, contemplating bungling gargoyles and persistent magpies.

"It came to me in a vision," Piers had said about his necklace.

The trail narrowed, tracing two straight lines along the side of the hill. The inner track hugged the hillside, while the outer track hung on the edge of a steep drop-off. It didn't seem possible that an ATV could negotiate the narrow trail, but she could see old tire tracks pressed into the dirt. Morgan stepped carefully in her worn sneakers. A fall might not be deadly, but rolling down the steep slope dotted with boulders would certainly cause some damage.

Maybe the girl had fallen to her death. But the trail was level where Morgan first saw her. And the cliff where the hiker found her hadn't been all that high.

What cycle of events could lead to a person lying dead on a trail, tattooed, tattered, and alone?

She wouldn't learn how the girl had died until after the autopsy. Until then, it was all speculation. Morgan frowned. She wanted an answer. She wanted closure.

Was there ever closure? she asked herself. She'd had plenty of warning with Sam's departure. The diagnosis—colon cancer. The treatment. The obvious futility of the treatment. A simple screening might have saved his life, but colonoscopies weren't typically performed before the age of fifty.

Sam had passed away in the hospice, in as much comfort as possible, surrounded by loving family and friends. He had a better passing than the girl on the trail, but it was the final departure nonetheless.

The wind gusted hard, pushing against Morgan. She shielded her face with her arm and looked up. Dirt stung her tear-dampened eyes. The sky darkened. Heavy clouds blotted out what little dim light had been offered by a reluctant sun.

A whirlwind of dry leaves roiled up the trail toward her. Morgan resisted her own imagination, willing herself to not see images in the whirling debris. She fumbled with the zipper on her fanny pack.

"Just a bunny." Morgan clutched the pepper spray. "Just magpies."

She turned, heading back to the shop, telling herself it was because Del would be upset that she hadn't left him a note. And there was a storm blowing in. Plus she had work to do. It wasn't her doubts about the effectiveness of pepper spray on monsters that sped up her steps to a near run.

Morgan slowed as she approached the dangerous stretch of trail clinging to the hillside, until the rhythmic crunching of feet on gravel sounded behind her. Morgan turned. Something was following her.

A blast of cold wind, grit, and dried leaves slapped Morgan's face. She tried to run, but blinded, she stumbled. One foot slipped off the edge of the trail. She flailed, reaching for anything to hold on to as she went down.

Something grabbed her arm, jerking her back. She preferred her chances falling downhill to being attacked by a gargoyle. Morgan aimed the pepper spray over her shoulder and blasted.

"Hey, I'm trying to help," a male voice yelled.

She struggled a moment longer before she noticed that the creature gripping her arm wore gloves.

"Oh." She turned slowly, facing a human male with a mountain-man beard, and clad in running clothes. "I thought you were . . ."

Morgan stopped herself.

"You were going way too fast on that stretch, considering your shoes," the man said. "You almost fell."

Morgan pulled away. He seemed harmless at first glance. A little wild around the edges, maybe. Gray streaked his bushy brown beard. His exposed skin was dark for winter, as though he spent a lot of time outdoors. His lean body suggested labor-intensive employment.

The man grabbed her wrist and pushed the hand clutching the pepper spray away from his face.

"You need to improve your aim," he said.

"I thought something was chasing me." Morgan couldn't admit she was running from a monster she didn't see. "A bear."

"I haven't seen any sign of bears around here. Maybe it was a raccoon."

"What are you doing here?" Morgan asked.

His gray eyes opened wide. "Running."

"Running from what?" Morgan asked.

"Just . . . running. Are you okay?"

"I'm fine, thank you." Morgan brushed her mittens down her sleeves.

"You need to get some decent shoes, if you're going to run the trails."

"I didn't intend to run," Morgan said. "Until the . . . whatever it was, started chasing me."

"A raccoon chased you?"

"I thought it was a bear. I wasn't going to take any chances."

The man gave her a you-must-be-from-the-city look.

"This is my hill, anyway," Morgan said.

A smile lifted the edges of his mustache. "You must be Kendall's sister." The man extended a gloved hand. "I'm Barton Potts."

"Morgan Iverson." She extended her own mitten-covered hand. "Pleased to meet you. Uh, thanks for catching me." She glanced down the hillside. "That probably would have hurt."

"No problem. I'll see you at the rock shop later. Well, gotta go." Barton nodded his head and ran across the narrow hillside trail.

Morgan knew she should be grateful that Barton Potts had saved her from a spill, but she couldn't shake the thought that he was running on the trail near where a girl had died. If he had been running that day, maybe he had seen something. She should have asked.

Morgan turned. He was long gone.

He had access to the trail, and he could move fast. For all Morgan knew, she just might have had an encounter with a killer.

And magpies were gargoyles, and whirling leaves were monsters.

CHAPTER THIRTEEN

Del was on the work schedule for Saturday, but he didn't arrive until noon.

"Sorry I'm late. I guess I didn't hear my alarm." He pulled off his camouflage hunter's jacket.

"I can't say I needed any help," Morgan said. "I gave directions to someone who was lost. He didn't buy anything. You might as well take the day off. You've already put in more than your scheduled hours this week."

Del's hands shook as he poured a cup of coffee from the pot on the display counter. He had dressed as though he was chilled, with a green down vest over a western-style flannel shirt.

"Do you mind if I borrow the car again?" he asked. "I need a few more things from the hardware store."

"Not at all," Morgan said. "Just keep an eye on the temperature gauge, like Gerda told us."

"Have you decided what to do about the car? My offer to pay half the repair bill is still good."

Morgan was tempted to accept, but she couldn't take the old cowboy's money if she was planning to drive the car back to Sioux Falls.

"Thanks, Del. Let me think about it."

Morgan had hung the Buick's extra key on a key-shaped pegboard on the office wall. Del stepped inside the office, returning a moment later.

"Can I get you anything from Granite Junction?"

"Actually, I'm thinking of taking a break at the bakery," Morgan said. "Until we get a sign up, I don't think we'll be missing out on many sales. You can drop me off in town."

"I might not be back for a while."

"That's okay," Morgan said. "I'll walk back."

"You're not afraid of running into monsters?"

"I'm getting used to them." Morgan had made a fool of herself in front of Del once. There was no holding back now. "I thought I saw another one yesterday. Hang on a minute and I'll tell you about it."

Morgan went through the door to the living area behind the shop. She grabbed her coat, purse, and a canvas bag. Del helped her lock up the cash register, not that there was any money in it, and front door, not that they expected anyone to drive up the hill and to their door.

She began her story about her hike on the trail behind the shop as Del pulled the car out of the garage. Halfway to Main Street, she reached the part about Barton Potts saving her from a tumble down the hill.

"Did he see the monster?" Del asked.

"Of course not," Morgan said. "I didn't see one either, this time."

"So you almost pepper-sprayed a guy, and he believed you that it was over a raccoon?"

"One more person in Golden Springs who thinks I'm crazy," Morgan said with a sigh. "But it wouldn't have happened if he hadn't been following me."

"Barton is a reclusive man, a little odd, I'll grant, but he's not a stalker." Del slowed at the stop sign on Hill Street and Main.

"What was he doing on my hill?" Morgan asked. "Who is that guy?"

"Barton is a real outdoorsman," Del said. "A kind of modern day mountain man. He spends a lot of time in the wilderness."

Bernie was busy with a small lunch crowd. Morgan enjoyed a sandwich and a cup of tea while she waited. When the customers were all tended to, Bernie joined her at a table, bringing a pot of hot water and more tea bags.

"What's new?" Bernie pulled off her pink and white striped chef's hat.

"I met a new person today," Morgan said. "On the trail behind the rock shop. It didn't go well."

"This sounds good." Bernie rested one elbow on the bistro table and placed her chin in her cupped hand. "Go on."

"I'll admit that my imagination was in overdrive again," Morgan said, "and I thought I saw something that wasn't there. But I had gotten a grip on myself until I realized I was being followed. So I ran."

"You ran?" Bernie asked. "Lucy would be proud of you."

"The trail was on the edge of a steep hill," Morgan said. "I might have fallen, but this man appeared out of nowhere and grabbed my arm."

"A stranger rescued you?" Bernie asked. "How exciting! Who was he?"

"Barton Potts," Morgan said. "Del told me he's a mountain man."

"I know him," Bernie said. "He's only a part-time mountain man. Barton started a computer software company that's become quite successful. They make electronic maps. GPS stuff."

"I nearly pepper-sprayed him," Morgan admitted.

Bernie slapped a hand on the table and laughed. "You tried to pepper-spray Barton Potts?"

Morgan cringed as every bakery patron turned to stare.

"It was confusing," Morgan whispered. "Everything happened at once. Del claims the guy isn't the stalker type, but how would I know? I'd never seen him before. Anyway, I didn't hit him with the pepper spray. Which might be a good thing under the circumstances, but it doesn't make me feel confident about my self-defense skills."

"That would be like the princess assaulting the knight in shining armor who rescued her from the fire-breathing dragon," Bernie said with a giggle.

"You make it sound so much better than it was," Morgan said, "and at the same time, so much worse." Morgan stirred a packet of sugar into her teacup and added more hot water from the ceramic pot. "So Barton spends a lot of time outdoors. He runs on the trail behind the shop. I wonder if he was hiking the day I found the girl?"

Bernie leaned across the small table. "You can't be thinking Barton had something to do with that poor girl's death," she whispered.

Morgan shook her head. "Until I know what happened to her, I'll suspect everyone. I'm getting so paranoid, I can't leave the shop without pepper spray in my pocket." She thumped her fist on the table. "But I refuse to give in to fear. I'm going to keep hiking."

Bernie leaned back. "Good for you. I'm still sore after the night with O'Reily's Runners. But I don't want to give up, either."

The bell over the bakery's front door chimed. Lucy negotiated the door, wrestling a stroller ahead of her. From somewhere inside a bundle of blankets, Danny sang a song involving the repetition of the phrase "bing bong."

Lucy wove the stroller between tables and pulled a chair beside Morgan. After liberating Danny from a few layers, she pulled a sheet of paper out of her canvas shopping bag. "Bernie, can I post a flier in your window?"

Bernie accepted the paper and studied it. Lucy handed one to Morgan. "Run for Amanda," curved across the top of the flier in bright pink. Beneath the words was a photo of a young woman seated in a wheelchair.

"I'm always happy to advertise for a good cause," Bernie said.

"Mommy!" Danny cried. "Out! Out! Out!"

Lucy reached into the stroller and unbuckled Danny's stroller harness. He scrambled out and ran across the wooden floor, trailing fleece blankets behind him.

Lucy turned to Morgan. "Amanda Palmquist is a Golden Springs high school student. She had just gotten her driver's license, and was going down the pass to Granite Junction. She was driving slowly during a snowstorm, when a gravel truck back-ended her."

"Is she still in the hospital?" Bernie asked.

"No," Lucy said. "She's out, but her mother took a leave of absence from work to take care of her. The family's been hit hard financially."

"Did they have insurance?" Morgan asked.

"Sure," Lucy said, "but there's always so much insurance doesn't cover, like the mother's lost wages. They aren't the kind of folks to sue the truck driver or the gravel company. No one did anything wrong. It was just an accident."

Bernie sighed. "Things happen."

"Mommy, Mommy!" Danny cried. He pressed his face against the pastry display case.

"Let me give him a cookie," Bernie said.

"You spoil him," Lucy said. "Just don't give him anything too sweet or he'll be bouncing off the walls all afternoon."

Bernie went behind the counter and retrieved a shortbread cookie for the toddler.

Morgan studied the flier again. All proceeds would go to the Palmquist family.

"Why not just take up donations for the family?" she asked. "Why have a race?"

"These fundraising runs do really well," Lucy said. "People feel like they're doing something to help others, and they get to enjoy a race."

"Is it here in town?" Bernie asked.

Lucy nodded, and pointed toward the bakery's bay window. "The race will start in Mineral Springs Park and follow the creek to a turnaround, then back to the park."

"That's just a couple blocks from here," Bernie said.

"Which brings me to another question," Lucy said. "Are you interested in participating?"

Bernie threw up her hands. "I barely survived O'Reily's."

"And we didn't even go the entire route," Morgan said.

"Lots of people walk in charity events," Lucy said.

"It's just a five K, right?" Bernie asked. "Three miles?"

"A little over three," Lucy said. "The same as the O'Reily's run. If you get tired, you can turn around early. But your time won't count."

"Count for what?" Bernie asked.

"Any of the age group prizes."

Morgan laughed. "I don't think we'll be in competition for any prizes."

Bernie turned to Morgan. "Will you still be here?"

Morgan gave them a quick rundown of her car problems.

"So I'll be stuck here until I can figure out what to do with my car."

"That's too bad," Bernie said, "although I'll admit I'm glad you'll be around longer. That will give us more time to convince you to stay."

"Great!" Lucy said, as though the discussion was settled.

"Fill out the entry form on the back, and get it to me in a couple days. The event is next Saturday." She stood. "The Run for Amanda came together so quickly, we're behind on getting announcements out. Can you help hand out fliers?"

Lucy pulled a stack of fliers out of her bag and handed half to Bernie and half to Morgan. She bundled up Danny and was gone before Morgan had a chance to react.

Bernie stared at the fliers in her hand. "What happened? One minute we're enjoying tea, and the next we're volunteers for a race."

Morgan stood. "I'd better head back to the shop."

"Be careful."

"Don't worry. I've got my pepper spray. I'm armed, but apparently not dangerous."

CHAPTER FOURTEEN

The deceptively bright winter sun did not warm the chilly air. Morgan wrapped her scarf around her neck. She clutched her canvas bag, now full of fliers and a loaf of bread, close to her side as she walked along the boardwalk. There was no pressing reason to return to the shop. Still, Morgan was supposed to be managing a retail operation.

She saw fliers posted in every shop window she passed.

Except Faerie Tales.

Morgan opened the door and stepped inside. The fountains in front of the checkout counter bubbled gently, adding moisture to the dry Colorado air. Piers stood at the cash register, huddled over an open book with a white-haired lady. He glanced up and nodded at Morgan.

"I'll be with you in a moment," he said.

"No hurry," Morgan replied.

She walked slowly alongside a bookcase, reading titles. Herb gardening. Drying herbs. Cooking herbs. Herbs for healing. Herbs for making amulets.

Morgan pulled out *Attracting Hummingbirds* and thumbed through photographs of the tiny iridescent birds hovering over colorful flowers.

Piers seemed to listen patiently as the elderly woman chattered about the empty space in her life since her husband passed away. Her expensive wool coat and stylish yet sensible snow boots spoke of a comfortable retirement, while her new interest in meditation spoke of a discontent with that life of leisure.

Piers concluded his explanation of a meditation book to his customer, and began ringing up the purchase.

"What an unusual piece of jewelry."

Morgan glanced up. The woman pointed at the display case. Her hand was weighted down with a large diamond ring that had to be worth more than the entire contents of the case.

"I designed it myself." Piers opened the back of the display case and pulled out a tray.

Morgan tried not to be obvious about listening.

"How much is it?" the woman asked.

"I don't sell my gargoyles," Piers said, with one of his dazzling smiles. "I present them to students who have achieved certain milestones in their studies."

Morgan thought about the gargoyle-turned-magpie, and how it had flown off the girl's body with something in its beak. A glittering chain, like the silver chains on Piers's gargoyle necklaces. Morgan gripped the hummingbird book tightly. She wondered if the dead girl had been his student.

"And what would that milestone be?" the older lady asked.

"Read this." Piers placed the meditation book inside a shopping bag and patted it. "Then perhaps you might be interested in joining our discussion group."

Morgan imagined the woman's attention would be pulled in some other direction long before she earned a necklace. But her curiosity about an object that could not be purchased might be strong enough to entice her into spending a lot of money in the shop first.

With effusive thanks, the woman exited the shop. Piers turned his attention to Morgan.

"How may I help you?"

He glanced at her hands, clutching the hummingbird book. Morgan had not intended to purchase the book, but she felt obligated now.

"I'll take this book," she said, approaching the checkout counter. "But I came to ask you about posting a flier."

While Piers rang up the book, Morgan pulled a sheet of paper out of the canvas bag hanging from her shoulder. She handed it to Piers.

He studied it for a moment, then set it on the counter with her change. Piers managed the entire transaction without touching Morgan's hands.

"Competition is contrary to my philosophy of cooperation."

"This isn't a competition," Morgan said. "It's a charity run. A fundraiser."

"There are prizes." He pointed at the flier. "It's competitive."

"Surely you can overlook the awards," Morgan said. "The main purpose of the run is to help this young woman and her family."

"I believe in karma," Piers said.

"I don't understand what that has to do with a charity race."

"Let me explain." Piers stepped from behind the checkout counter and headed for the cozy sitting area. He settled into a chair, and indicated that Morgan should sit to his right.

Morgan pulled off her heavy blue coat and tossed it across the back of the chair. Incense and soothing music filled the shop.

In a singsong voice, Piers presented his philosophy of life. It was much as Morgan had expected: a breezy blend of Buddhism, pop psychology, and New Age ideas such as might be spouted by a daytime television talk-show host.

"With the proper knowledge," he concluded, "the forces of the universe may be appealed to, even persuaded to act on our behalf. Imagine, Morgan. Power over the petty irritations in your life. No more fear. No more pain."

"Aren't those part and parcel of a normal life?" Morgan

thought of Sam, a good man taken too soon.

"Why do you think you were the person destined to find that girl on the trail?"

Morgan must have looked shocked, because Piers continued.

"That is not my intuition speaking." He leaned back in his chair. "The news is all over Golden Springs."

Morgan shrugged. "I was in the wrong place at the wrong time, I guess."

"There is no such thing as chance. You were placed there for a purpose." Piers poured two cups of tea from the round jade teapot. "Can you describe what you felt when you found the girl?" He handed Morgan a cup. "What you saw?"

"I'm not sure what I saw."

"The stress of the incident may have clouded your memory. I'm certified in hypnotic regression therapy. If you'd like, we could recapture those memories, and perhaps unlock the reason why you were the one destined to find her."

Morgan felt lulled by the incense, the music, the tea. She considered for one instant accepting his offer, then snapped to her senses. Detective Parker and Officer Sanchez would both be horrified if Morgan allowed Piers to tamper with her memories. She stood.

"Are you sure you won't post a flier?" Morgan asked.

"You are single-minded," Piers said. "If you could focus that energy in the right direction, no force could stop you from achieving your goals."

Piers escorted Morgan toward the front door.

The curtain behind the checkout counter caught her eye as it fluttered back into place. The movement reminded Morgan of the wings of the creature perched on top of the dead girl.

"Is someone back there?" she asked.

"One of my students," Piers said.

Morgan thought she had glimpsed Sparrow's green hair.

"I would like to continue this discussion," Piers said. "Perhaps over dinner?"

His invitation caught Morgan off guard.

"Dinner?"

"The Hot Tomato serves vegan dishes. Would Tuesday be convenient?"

"I have a previous commitment on Tuesdays."

"Ah, well." Piers opened the door. A chilly breeze swept into the shop. "Perhaps another time then."

Morgan was so far removed from the dating scene that she was halfway through the door before she fully realized she had been asked out.

"Another time," she stammered. "That would be nice."

The door closed behind her with finality. Morgan clutched her canvas bag to her side and headed for Hill Street. She had added a book to the loaf of bread and the fliers.

Another failed trip to Faerie Tales.

By the time Morgan returned to the rock shop, Del was test-driving the newly repaired donkey cart in the parking lot. Houdini and Adelaide seemed to enjoy pulling the cart in circles.

"I've still got to paint it," Del said, "but it's functional again. Want to give it a try?"

"Maybe another time," Morgan said. "I've got a quick errand to run."

She took a stack of Run for Amanda fliers and drove to the Golden Springs Community Church. Morgan fully expected someone to be around, preparing for the Sunday service. She didn't expect the crowd, the television news camera crew, and especially not the Granite Junction police cruiser.

The kitchen ladies clustered in front of the sink like a flock of frightened doves. Teruko clutched a dishcloth in her frail hands. Beatrice spoke in husky whispers while Anna shook her head.

"What's going on?" Morgan asked.

"You won't believe what's happened," Anna said. "It's a nightmare." She shoved her hands in the pockets of her safari jacket and shook her head sadly.

"A good man's name dragged through the dirt by trailer-park trash," Beatrice said. "It shouldn't be allowed."

"What happened?" Morgan asked.

"A girl made a horrible accusation against our Pastor Filbury," Teruko said. No need for her to whisper. Teruko's voice was soft as a whisper already.

"Then, before she could be questioned," Anna said, "before the whole thing could be cleared up, the girl died."

"Died?" Morgan squeaked.

Beatrice nodded. "Yes, Morgan, it was the same girl you found on the trail behind your shop."

Morgan groped for a chair and sat heavily.

"What kind of accusation did she make?" Morgan asked. She couldn't imagine the tattered girl coming anywhere near a church.

"The stuff that television docudramas are made of," Beatrice said. "Her family didn't attend our church, but she came to summer camp one year."

"The girl I saw was an older teen," Morgan said. "That must have been years ago."

"Yes," Anna said. "But that's the way of the world now. People go their entire lives minding their own business, and then, whoops!" She flung her hands in the air. "Suddenly they remember some terrible thing from their childhood."

"Repressed memories," Morgan mumbled, remembering Piers's offer of hypnotic regression therapy. She glanced up at Anna. "That can actually happen."

"In this case," Beatrice said, "it's not true."

Teruko shook her head. "Our pastor is not guilty. Of that I am certain." She folded her hands in her lap.

"Dawn Smith didn't have a father, and her mother is trailer-park trash," Beatrice huffed.

"Dawn?" Morgan asked. "That was her name?"

"Yes," Beatrice said. "Her mother was a drunk. The woman caused a lot of trouble in Golden Springs before she moved to Granite Junction. And now a police detective is in there questioning Pastor Filbury because of her wild-seed daughter."

Sarah and Dave had gone to the day camp when they spent summers with Kendall and Allie. If the mild-mannered pastor was being interrogated by Detective Parker, he would confess any wrongdoing, Morgan was certain. She scanned the faces of the three women. "You seem sure that he couldn't have done this."

They answered at once, their words overlapping.

"Absolutely not."

"Pastor Filbury is a good man."

"He is innocent."

Morgan certainly hoped so.

"If the girl is dead, why would the police question Pastor Filbury about the accusation? What's the point now?"

Beatrice placed her fists on her wide hips. "Maybe she was murdered, and they think Pastor Filbury killed her to shut her up."

"That's ridiculous," Anna said.

"In this day and age," Beatrice said, "I'm sad to say it's a plausible scenario."

Morgan hoped, for his sake, that the pastor had a good alibi.

"I guess there's not much I can do here." Morgan stood. "If the police need me, they know where to find me."

"What brought you to the church today?" Anna asked.

Morgan pulled fliers out of her canvas bag and handed one to each of the ladies. "A charity fundraiser for Amanda Palmquist."

"That's next Saturday," Beatrice said, studying a flier. "I thought you were only here for two weeks."

Morgan explained her car troubles.

"It sounds like *you* need a fundraiser," Anna said.

"I have options." Morgan didn't add that none of them were appealing. "I just have to decide which one to take."

"Bring your fliers to church tomorrow," Beatrice said. "I'm sure the pastor won't mind if you hand them out."

"I will speak to the elder who makes the announcements," Teruko said.

"Thanks," Morgan said. "I'd better get going. I need to clean out stalls."

"Be careful," Beatrice said.

Morgan held up her hands. "I'll wear gloves."

"I'm not talking about Houdini and Adelaide," Beatrice said. "This situation with Dawn Smith is turning ugly, and you're right in the middle of it."

CHAPTER FIFTEEN

The girl had a name now. Dawn Smith. Rather than resolving anything, that just made her seem more real, and the horror of discovering her body more personal.

The rest of Morgan's day was too full for her to linger on Beatrice's warning. After cleaning the barn, she helped Del pull a dead tree to the back of the house using an ATV. It was one more task Kendall had neglected: gathering enough firewood for the winter.

Sunday morning, Morgan joined the ladies in the church kitchen. Teruko took Morgan by the hand.

"Come with me," Teruko said. "Elder Mark Thompson offered to announce your charity race."

She led Morgan into the social hall. Elder Thompson towered over the diminutive war bride, and was a head taller than Morgan. His gray hair was short, and his suit crisply pressed.

"Mark, this is the young lady I was telling you about."

"I have your charity event on the announcement list," Elder Thompson said, tapping a clipboard. "After the service, I suggest you stand in the doorway to hand out fliers."

The introit music started, announcing the beginning of the service. Morgan and Teruko hurried to the seats Beatrice and Anna had saved for them.

"The pews haven't been this full since Christmas," Beatrice whispered. "Everyone comes out for a show."

The service began, following the program laid out in the

order of service. The hymns, the announcements, everything presented as though it was just another Sunday.

When Pastor Filbury stepped up to the podium, absolute silence fell over the congregation.

Ten minutes into his sermon, he stopped. Pastor Filbury looked out across the pews, a stricken expression creasing his face. Elder Thompson and another gentleman rose from their seats behind the podium and approached the pastor. He waved them back.

"I'm certain none of you can concentrate on my message," he told the congregation, "just as I can't concentrate on its delivery. What brought many of you here today is curiosity. You're wondering whether all this talk around town is true."

Elder Thompson jumped up. "James, you can't . . ."

"I understand what I can and can't say." Pastor Filbury pressed the knot in his tie with his fingertips. "I wish I could clear up this whole matter right now. Unfortunately I have been told that I may not speak on the subject you, as a congregation, most want to hear about."

He paused, taking a sip from the glass of water on the podium. Teruko wrapped her frail hands around Morgan's arm.

"When we hear of scandal on the television news, or from our neighbor, we have a tendency to assume an attitude of outrage, especially when there's a child involved."

Gasps and mumbling rolled across the pews.

"My friends," Pastor Filbury continued, "you will all have an opinion, based on reality or gossip or the newspaper headline. Stand by me or against me. It does not matter. Either way, this congregation will be divided. We don't know how long this investigation will take, but I do know, with certainty, that this process will be too disruptive for our congregation. I have discussed this with the Board, and while they do not agree with my decision, they have given me permission to step down—"

The low murmuring escalated to a roar.

"No!" Morgan heard behind her. "You have to fight this!"

Others expressed similar sentiments.

Pastor Filbury held up his hands. The crowd quieted.

"My plan is to step down temporarily. The elders will appoint a rotating schedule of guest speakers. I'll let Elder Thompson explain how this will work."

Thompson stepped up to the podium as Pastor Filbury left the chancel. The elder held up his hands, attempting unsuccessfully to quiet the congregation.

Morgan had time to consider which side she was on, the ardent supporters of the kindly old pastor or the ones willing to believe the worst about him. Her children had been in the very church camp the dead girl, Dawn Smith, had attended. If there was a danger, they had been exposed to it, while she was hundreds of miles away in Sioux Falls. But Sarah and Dave had never showed any signs of abuse. No sudden change of behavior, or reluctance to return to Golden Springs.

The crowd finally calmed enough for Elder Thompson to present the plan to request guest speakers from the district pool of semi-retired pastors, and pastors-in-training, to fill in for Filbury. He did not have the undivided attention of the audience.

The abbreviated order of service segued to the closing hymn. Morgan grabbed her stack of fliers, handing half to Teruko, and took her post at the door to the social hall.

People accepted the fliers she thrust at them. Some jotted their names and phone numbers on Morgan's clipboard.

"Are we going to walk together?" a woman asked.

"We'll meet up at the park the morning of the race," Morgan said.

Voices rose to shouts in the social hall. Morgan could see Cindy's redheaded husband, Herb, towering over the cluster of people surrounding him.

"This accusation came straight from the mouth of Satan," Herb yelled. "Our pastor is innocent!"

A man answered, in a voice not quite as loud, that he preferred not to place blind trust in a man who had access to his children.

"It's foolish not to investigate," the man said. "Our children are at stake here."

"Are you calling me a fool, Chris?" Herb asked.

"If the shoe—"

Herb swung his fist, but it glanced ineffectively off Chris's shoulder. Chris pushed Herb. They scuffled briefly, grappling and shoving more than exchanging blows, until cooler heads pulled them apart. Elder Thompson placed a hand on each man's shoulder.

"This is neither the time nor the place for strife," he said. "We have to stand together."

"How far do you expect to stretch our trust?" Chris asked. "Don't you think it's awfully strange, that girl dying right before she's supposed to talk to the police?"

"Yeah," another man said. "That was convenient."

Herb raised his hands, clenched into fists.

"Brothers," Elder Thompson said, "let's not forget we're in a house of worship."

He calmed the crowd, sending the men and their families on their way with no further violence.

Beatrice pulled Morgan toward the kitchen.

"I never thought I'd see the day," Beatrice said, shaking her head.

The ladies seemed as reluctant as Morgan to leave. They lingered over tea in the church kitchen, discussing the scenarios that could lead to a young woman falsely accusing Pastor Filbury of unspeakable crimes. Even more unimaginable to them was the willingness of people to believe the accusation.

No customers dropped in when Morgan opened for business that afternoon. Del and Cindy both had the day off. She grabbed the phone when it rang, desperate to hear a human voice.

"Hello?"

"Want to see a movie?" Bernie asked.

"What's playing?"

"One screen, no choices," Bernie said. "This week it's a comedy. I heard it's not bad."

"I can use a laugh."

"Tough day?" Bernie asked.

"I'll tell you all about it when I see you," Morgan said.

After the movie, they ate dinner at a Mexican restaurant, where Morgan filled Bernie in on the drama at Golden Springs Community Church.

By the time Morgan drove up the hill, it was late. Clouds darkened the sky. Morgan regretted not leaving any lights on at the shop. She almost missed the turn into the parking lot, despite the helpful dinosaur pointing to the rock shop. It was difficult to negotiate the driveway, until the motion sensor lights clicked on.

The converted carriage house filled with red light as Morgan backed in beside the ATVs. She closed the garage doors, and double-checked the latch on the gate.

Dry leaves clinging to the bushes rustled in the dark, although there was no breeze to stir them.

"Hello?"

Gravel crunched under feet other than her own. Probably deer, Morgan told herself. Del had told her there was a resident herd on the property. Or maybe the donkeys.

"Houdini?" Morgan called. "Is that you?"

There was no answer. The donkeys might be unusually

charming, but they couldn't talk. Morgan hurried across the empty parking lot, past the front of the rock shop, to the barn. She ducked inside the small door to the right of the double doors, and leaned against it, straining to hear above her own rapid breathing.

Whatever was lurking in the bushes, it hadn't been a donkey. Houdini and Adelaide stood in their stall, half asleep. They woke for their hay and oats, and let Morgan know with reproachful glares and indignant stamping of hooves that it was well past dinnertime.

She tried to atone for her tardiness with the currycomb. The brush curved around the female donkey's broad side.

"Adelaide, you didn't need dinner. You're getting fat."

Morgan lingered in the barn. She didn't look forward to the walk back to the dark shop.

Living alone in Sioux Falls, she had rarely been fearful. Her garage was connected to the house, the neighbors were right next door, and emergency services were a reliable phone call away.

Morgan peeked out the small barn door. She stepped outside, then took a deep breath and raced across the parking lot to the front door of the shop. She stumbled on something hard. It was a rock, not a body, but that realization didn't slow her pounding heart. She wished she had the pepper spray in hand right now. Not that it would help her any. Barton had assessed her skill with his comment, "You need to improve your aim."

The lid to a trash can crashed onto the stone walkway with a metallic clatter. It rolled across the gravel, slamming into an ore cart.

Morgan jammed her key into the lock. It wouldn't turn. Her hands trembled as she fumbled with the key, wondering whether she had enough time to make a run back to the barn. The key turned. The lock opened. Morgan stumbled inside, slamming the door closed behind her. She waited a moment, listening. The only sound was her own blood pounding through her veins.

Safe inside the shop, Morgan struggled less with the lock to the living quarters. She checked the latches on all the windows, then braced kitchen chairs under the doorknobs of the door to the shop and the door to the back pasture.

Inside the bedroom, she jammed another kitchen chair under the doorknob, and tugged the wardrobe in front of the window.

Huddled under the quilt, Morgan clutched her nearly useless cell phone in one hand, and Del's pepper spray in the other.

CHAPTER SIXTEEN

When Del arrived the next morning, Morgan was perched beside the cash register, guzzling coffee as though it were the nectar of life.

"Excuse me for noticing," Del said, "but you look like something the cat dragged in."

"I didn't sleep well. There was something outside."

"I saw the trash can knocked over," Del said. "Probably a raccoon."

"Another raccoon," Morgan mumbled. "Between magpies and raccoons, I'm going to have a heart attack."

"The gate was open, too." He reached for the coffee pot.

"The front gate?" she asked. "It's always open."

"No, the paddock gate." Del poured the half cup remaining into his mug. "Move out of the way, and I'll start another pot."

Morgan slouched over to the aspen bench, clutching her coffee mug in one hand. Del headed to the restroom.

"Houdini and Adelaide were about to make a break for it," he said. "An open gate is just an opportunity for those two."

"I did not leave the gate open." Morgan yawned. "It must have been the raccoon."

Del walked back to the counter. He poured water into the coffeemaker and filled the basket with ground coffee. The pot gurgled. The smell of coffee filled the shop. Morgan struggled to her feet and leaned on the counter, holding her empty mug out like a beggar seeking coins.

The phone rang. Del poured her a cup with one hand and picked up the telephone receiver with the other.

"Rock of Ages." Pause. *"Denver Post?"* Pause. "What's your business?" Del returned the carafe to the coffeemaker and put his hand over the phone receiver. "Do you want to talk to a reporter about the body? How's that related to the pastor of the Golden Springs Community Church? And when were you going to mention all this to me? The last question is mine."

"I don't want to talk to any reporters."

Del spoke into the phone. "Mrs. Iverson does not wish to speak to any reporters. No, not tomorrow or the next day either." He hung up. "So what's this about Pastor Filbury?"

Morgan blew on her coffee and took a quick sip. She set the mug on the counter. "Apparently, the girl I found, Dawn Smith, had accused Pastor Filbury of molesting her at the summer church camp when she was a child."

"Have they said yet how she died?"

"No," Morgan said. "They questioned the pastor, so maybe they suspect foul play."

The phone rang. Del answered. It was another newspaper. Then one of the Granite Junction television stations called.

"Someone must know something," Del told Morgan. "Or else the news people are just desperate for a scandal."

A battered truck pulled up in the Rock of Ages parking lot.

"The phone isn't good enough for them?" Morgan asked.

"That's not a reporter," Del said. "That's Barton."

"Great," Morgan groaned. "The guy I almost pepper-sprayed."

The shaggy-bearded runner entered the shop carrying a cardboard box that had seen better days.

"What ya got?" Del asked.

Barton set the box on the glass display case. "Tools. Cans. Wire. Some nails."

Morgan peeked in the box. More rusted junk.

"How much you want for it?" Del asked.

Barton scratched his beard and scrunched his face, making his whiskers bristle. "I dunno. Doesn't look like much, but I noticed the hikers have helped themselves to more every time I go up there."

"From your claim?" Del asked.

"Yup. There's an old cabin that attracts a lot of attention. People have no respect for another man's property."

An ironic statement, Morgan thought, considering she'd met Barton trespassing on her hill.

"Have they found the mine?" Del asked.

"Not yet," Barton said. "But hikers take everything that's not nailed down, and I've had poachers, too."

"That's a pity. Ruins the hunting, and on your own stomping grounds, too."

"What do you hunt?" Morgan asked.

"Elk, mostly," Barton said. "Some deer. Del, I dug this up." Barton reached into his front jeans pocket and pulled out a rock. "You can see why I need to keep quiet about the claim's location."

Del plucked the rock off Barton's palm and held it up to the light. He whistled.

"Nice topaz."

Del handed it to Morgan. It looked like a rock to her, with a brownish crystal embedded in the side.

"That doesn't look anything like what I've seen in jewelry stores," Morgan said.

"They clean up nice," Barton said.

"Any more like this one?" Del asked.

"Could be. It's slow going, though. Any time I spend digging, I have to spend that much time and then some covering it up and hiding my tracks."

"Why would you do that?" Morgan asked. "If it's your claim, can't you dig holes if you want to?"

"Claim jumpers," Del said. "You can't be too careful, or people swarm your mine like ants on a picnic the minute you're gone."

"Especially if they find out you're mining topaz," Barton said.

"Sounds like the Wild West." Morgan yawned as she handed the rock back to Barton. "Maybe you need to post a keep-out sign."

"And advertise my claim's location?" Barton said. "Even Del doesn't know where my mine is. If I told you, I'd have to shoot you. Ha ha."

Barton's comment was more effective than the three cups of coffee Morgan had consumed.

"You know I'm not a threat. I can't even aim straight." Morgan attempted a casual laugh. "But suppose somebody ran across your mine by accident. And they maybe found some topaz lying around. And maybe took it. Would you really shoot them?"

Barton stared at her. Del tugged at his mustache and frowned.

"What are you getting at, Morgan?" Del asked.

"Barton's the one who said he'd shoot somebody."

"I was just kidding," Barton said.

"Where were you last Saturday?" Morgan asked.

"On my claim."

Del held up a hand. "Morgan, you've either had too much coffee, or not enough."

"How close is your mine to where they found the dead girl?"

"What dead girl?" Barton asked.

"The girl I saw and then lost, and then the police found her again. How could you not know? It's been on the news."

"I don't keep up with the news." Barton looked confused.

"First you try to pepper-spray the man, and now this." Del shook his head.

"I just asked a simple question. Hang on. I've had a lot of fluids this morning."

Morgan ran to the restroom. When she came back, Barton was gone.

"Where'd he go?"

"You were obviously hot on his trail," Del said. "Maybe he figured he'd better flee before you made a citizen's arrest."

"It's not like I accused Barton of murder."

"Let's get this straight," Del said. "I've known Barton for years. He's a good guy."

"I just thought, well, he was in the area where they found the girl."

"So is anyone who was outdoors on the day you found her a suspect? You don't even know how she died. It could have been a drug overdose, or exposure."

"It's the not knowing that's driving me crazy." Morgan placed her elbows on the display case and rested her forehead in her cupped hands.

"Leave it to the police," Del said.

"I hope they figure it out soon," Morgan said. "Because I won't get a decent night's sleep until I know what happened." She looked up at Del. "Is Barton upset?"

"I smoothed it over with him. And he gave me a good deal on this." Del held a rock between his thumb and forefinger, admiring it at arm's length.

"Del!"

"What?"

"You bought a rock?" Morgan waved a hand around. "We have ten thousand rocks. I would have given you one for free."

"It's topaz." Del shook his head. "You'll see, once it's

144

polished. It's a beauty. You have a lot to learn about the rock business."

The phone rang.

"Don't answer it," Morgan said.

Del picked it up. "Rock of Ages." He frowned. "Hold your horses, gal." He put his hand over the receiver. "It's Bernie. She's going a mile a minute."

Morgan took the phone. "Hello?"

"You need to get down here right away," Bernie said.

"Are Houdini and Adelaide out again?" Morgan asked.

"No, it's the newspaper. A special edition. Kurt has written the most horrible article."

"I can't stop the free press," Morgan said.

"You've got to come now. Your name is in it." Bernie hung up.

Bernie shook a newspaper at Morgan the instant she entered the bakery.

"You won't believe what Kurt printed this time."

The three ladies sharing a pot of tea at a window table turned to watch for a moment, then returned to their conversation.

"Where does he get off?" Bernie frowned at Morgan, seeming to focus on her for the first time. "Morgan, you look like you were rode hard and put up wet."

"That colorful, huh?" Morgan yawned. "I didn't get much sleep."

"I'll get you a cup of espresso."

Morgan slumped down on the nearest chair. Bernie brought her a steaming cup. A timer went off in the kitchen. Bernie shoved the paper into Morgan's hands.

"Start reading. I'll be right back."

By the time Bernie returned, the window ladies had left, and Morgan had made it halfway through Kurt's front-page article.

She was ready to join Bernie in her paper-shaking tirade.

"Where did he get all these details?" Morgan asked. "I didn't let him interview me. Who could have given him this information? I don't think the search and rescue crew would compromise a potential criminal case."

"And he printed your name." Bernie jabbed a finger at the paper. "It almost sounds like you had something to do with it. He as much as calls Pastor Filbury a child molester."

Morgan folded the paper. She leaned back in the small chair. Bernie seemed anxious for her response.

"What are you going to do?" Bernie asked.

"What can I do?" Morgan asked. "If he's printed something he shouldn't have, I think the police will let him know. Kurt has the right to say what he wants. It's his newspaper."

"Freedom of speech," Bernie asked, "or freedom to lie? This is slander. He shouldn't get away with trashing your pastor."

"Bernie, calm down. Your face is bright red."

Bernie fanned herself with a paper napkin. "My blood pressure must be through the roof."

"Let's take a walk," Morgan said. "That'll help you calm down."

"You're right." Bernie flipped her be-back-in sign to face the sidewalk. "Let's go."

Bernie made a beeline to the newspaper office, towing Morgan in her wake.

"We're not going in there." Morgan held Bernie's arm.

"In the Old West," Bernie said, "we could have tarred and feathered Kurt Willard."

"Thank goodness some customs have gone the way of outhouses and kerosene lamps," Morgan said. "Let's keep moving."

Morgan struggled to keep up with Bernie as she marched to the end of downtown.

146

"Slow down," Morgan said. "You need to save something for O'Reily's tomorrow."

"I'm thinking of skipping O'Reily's," Bernie said. "We're walking a five K Saturday."

"You'll recover in time for the race," Morgan said.

"My feet still hurt."

"Mine, too," Morgan said. "We both need decent shoes."

"Let's get shoes today," Bernie said, "or we won't have time to break them in."

Morgan picked up Bernie at two-thirty and drove to Granite Junction to buy running shoes and socks. Morgan's heart nearly stopped when her total rang up on the cash register.

Her cell phone buzzed on the way home. The caller ID read "Rock of Ages."

Morgan flipped opened her cell phone. "Hello?"

"Good news," Del said. "Gerda said we can put a sign up at her garage."

"Her auto shop isn't on Main Street."

"I'm getting a lot of static. This phone's about to—"

Morgan lost signal. She frowned at her phone.

"So much for modern technology."

"What's up?" Bernie asked.

"Gerda said we can put up a sign for the rock shop at her place," Morgan said, "but I'm not sure that would help any."

"Let's check it out."

Morgan drove west, slowing as she neared Kruger's Auto Repair Shop. Main Street curved south, following a creek and the base of a hill on its way out of downtown Golden Springs. The shop sat at the intersection of Aspen and Palmer. Neither street crossed Main. An odd-shaped strip of dry, weedy land squatted between Kruger's and Main Street. Strategically placed in the narrow lot was the auto shop's sign.

"You can certainly see Gerda's sign from Main Street," Bernie said.

"If I can use large enough lettering, and maybe a simple map, it might work."

CHAPTER SEVENTEEN

At some point in the past, in a fit of industriousness, Kendall had started creating a sign. Del dug it out of the barn.

"The wood is sound," Del said. "But I need to do some sanding. It's gotten a little beat up."

"Finally," Morgan said, "I feel like we're making some progress."

Optimism spurred Morgan to clean another display cabinet, but her burst of energy faded quickly. She was glad when it was time to close the shop for the day. After a bowl of homemade soup from the slow cooker, Morgan settled into bed, snuggling under the quilt with a romance novel.

The phone in the kitchen rang.

"Just when I was comfortable," she grumbled.

The phone didn't have caller ID. Morgan had to take her chances answering calls.

"Hello?"

"Hello from paradise!"

Morgan sat at the kitchen table.

"Kendall? It's about time. You've been gone for over a week."

"Between the phone service in our village," Kendall said, his voice deep, his words crisp and clear, "and the phone service at the Rock of Ages, this is the first time I've been able to make the connection. I don't have much time. Let everyone know our trip was smooth. Allie had a reaction to the local water, even though we've been boiling it, but other than that, we're doing fine. How are things at the rock shop?"

Morgan considered unloading on Kendall about her entire experience. She opted for a single terse comment.

"You never told me Golden Springs was full of so many interesting characters."

Kendall rattled off something in Spanish. When had he learned another language? And fluently?

"En ingles, por favor," Morgan said in poorly accented Spanish remembered from her college days.

"Julio said I need to hurry," Kendall said. "The bus only runs to the jungle twice a week."

"Jungle?"

Kendall spoke again in Spanish, presumably to Julio, then switched to English. "I only have a minute. Give our love to everyone—"

"This conversation is not over," Morgan said. "You dumped the shop on me without any warning. Now my car is about to break down, and I'm stuck in Golden Springs. I have a pregnant daughter in Sioux Falls. I have to go home, and I can't, and it's your fault."

"Sarah has enough in-laws to fill a Viking longboat. She'll be fine."

"That's not the point. This is my first grandchild. I want to be with her. And another thing. I've been looking through the books and accounts. Have you saved any money for the property taxes, or did you pay them already?"

"Taxes?"

"Yes, taxes. You know. IRS. April fifteenth. All that fun stuff."

"Well . . ." Kendall sounded like a boy caught with his hand in the cookie jar. "Why would you need that information?"

"I'm half-owner, remember?" Morgan asked. "When I contact a real-estate agent, they'll want to know that kind of stuff."

"You're not selling the Rock of Ages."

"You threatened to throw the keys across the pasture. I think that means I can do what I want."

"Not without my signature," Kendall said.

"So now you want to keep the place?" Morgan asked. "Are you coming back?"

"No."

"Then what about the taxes?"

"We used part of the money for our plane tickets."

"Which part?" Morgan asked. "The big part? Let me get this straight. You dump the rock shop on me the year you decide to quit paying taxes?"

"Allie and I thought it was more important to establish our congregation," Kendall said in an authoritative televangelist voice. "If the Lord wills, the money will be returned tenfold. The bus is here. I have to go."

"Wait!"

The connection disengaged with a click.

Morgan stared at the receiver in her hand.

She had been prepared to slip into sound slumber, but now her pulse raced, and the rusty gears in her brain squealed into action. Morgan didn't have a job to go back to in Sioux Falls. Her daughter wanted the shop and land to stay in the family. Even if they had to sell the place, it would command a higher price if the rock shop was turning a profit.

Finally getting permission to erect a sign was a step in the right direction. Once the tourists could find them, the trick would be giving them a reason to leave their tourist dollars at the rock shop.

Morgan grabbed a notepad and pencil. She flipped to a new page. Across the top, she scribbled "rock shop money-making ideas."

★　★　★　★　★

The next morning Morgan worked for two hours updating the shop's financial records. When she couldn't stand typing any longer, she went back to composing her list of ideas.

"Mornin', cowgirl." The cowbell clanged as Cindy walked in the front door. "Or afternoon. I guess we're right in between the two."

Morgan sat on the aspen bench, her notepad and pencil in hand. "Kendall called."

Cindy placed a seat cushion on the stool behind the cash register. Between her pregnancy and her long denim skirt, she struggled to get seated.

"How are they doing?" Cindy asked.

"They made it there. They were waiting for a bus to the jungle when he called."

"Wow," Cindy said. "The jungle. What an adventure!"

Morgan didn't mention that Kendall and Allie's Great Adventure might cost Cindy her job and Morgan the rock shop.

"I've been coming up with a list of ideas to improve business," Morgan said. "Have you got any thoughts on how to get people to spend money?"

Cindy named two things Morgan had already thought of: expand Lucy's Native American jewelry display, and cleaning up the front of the shop so it looked more like a store and less like a junkyard.

"How about stocking more tourist items?" Cindy brushed a stray strand of red hair behind her ear. "Like coffee mugs with 'Colorado' printed on them?"

"That sounds good." Morgan scribbled on the notepad.

"People have asked about postcards, souvenirs, stuff like that. I think we have some catalogs around here somewhere."

Del arrived as Morgan and Cindy were studying a selection of western bandanas in a catalog.

"You're not scheduled to work today," Morgan said.

"I thought I'd get working on that sign. What are you gals doing?"

"Looking at souvenirs," Cindy said. "Morgan wants to expand what the rock shop sells."

"I'd like to attract more tourists, along with the rock hounds."

"We should have stuff for kids," Cindy said. "Cowboy and Indian toys, plastic horses and stuffed buffaloes."

"And donkeys." Del turned the catalog to face his side of the counter and thumbed through the already dog-eared pages. "They got any stuffed donkey toys?"

"We have to narrow this down," Morgan said. "I'm not sure how much we can afford to spend on stock, especially this early in the year."

"Kendall always keeps some money set aside for acquisitions," Del said.

"He hasn't told me where he keeps it." She didn't feel that now was the time to tell Del about the tax money. "Whatever we get has to be a sure seller."

"You never know what people are going to buy," Cindy said.

"Like the young fella who bought the coprolite for a gag gift," Del said.

It would take selling a truckload of dinosaur dung to dig the Rock of Ages out of its financial problems.

The shop door opened. Morgan, Del, and Cindy all looked up. Morgan wondered if they appeared as desperate as she felt.

Beatrice rushed through the door. She was dressed for action in stretch denim jeans and a puffy insulated car coat. Her thick-soled, sensible shoes squeaked across the pine floor. Morgan felt her shoulders slump. She suspected Beatrice had not come up the hill to buy petrified dinosaur dung.

"I have news." Beatrice swiveled her gray head around, checking the rock shop for eavesdroppers.

"Nobody's here but us," Del said.

Cindy placed her elbow on the display counter and rested her chin in the palm of her hand. "It's been deader than a doornail."

"How ironic you'd choose that phrase." Beatrice shrugged out of her winter coat and laid it across the back of the aspen bench. She took her time getting settled.

Morgan stepped around the display case and sat next to Beatrice.

"What do you mean?" Morgan asked.

"The girl you found on the trail?" Beatrice said. "Dawn Smith? The results of the autopsy won't be released until the toxicology results are in, but I learned the probable cause of death."

"And that is?" Del asked. "Or are you gonna keep us in suspense?"

Beatrice folded her hands in her lap. She looked prim and proper enough to be sitting in a church pew.

"Ligature strangulation."

The words rolled off her tongue with practiced ease. Beatrice might as well have said "angel food cake."

"I understand strangulation," Cindy said, "but what's ligature?"

"A rope," Beatrice said. "A necktie. Anything used to strangle a person. In this case, it was thin and strong."

Morgan's hand involuntarily went to her own throat.

"Like baling wire?" Cindy asked.

"They don't have the murder weapon," Beatrice said, "but yes, something along those lines."

"Murder," Morgan repeated.

"Cause of death is not being released to the family," Beatrice said, "so I trust you'll all keep this information under your hats, so to speak."

"Why won't they tell the family?" Morgan asked.

"The police don't want the killer to know they've discovered it was murder," Beatrice said.

"How do you know all this?" Morgan asked. "And don't tell me word gets around."

"My nephew works in the Metro Crime Lab," Beatrice said.

"Golden Springs has a crime lab?" Morgan asked. "I thought we barely had a police department."

"No, no," Beatrice said. "Everything is sent to Granite Junction. It's a county and city lab. We have to pool our resources."

"So she didn't die from falling off the cliff," Del said.

"The killer might have wanted it to look that way," Beatrice said, "but the victim was dead before she was thrown off the cliff."

"Was she," Cindy started, "you know . . ." She paused. "Raped?"

"No," Beatrice said. "My nephew said there was no evidence of sexual assault."

"Do you know if she was dead when I first saw her?" Morgan asked.

Beatrice pressed her fingers to her mouth and furrowed her brow. She lowered her hand. "I didn't think to ask specifically, but as I recall, they estimated her time of death right around the time you made your nine-one-one call."

"Could she have been alive when I found her?" Morgan asked.

Del placed a hand on Morgan's shoulder. "From everything you said, there were no signs of life. Quit beating yourself up, and accept that you couldn't save the girl."

Morgan desperately wanted to believe him.

"The murderer most likely threw her off the cliff in an attempt to cover up the crime. If the girl was under the influence of drugs, it might be reasonable to believe she fell off the cliff or committed suicide. Except that the coroner knows otherwise."

Beatrice stood and collected her coat. "I'm late for my ladies' prayer group."

Morgan helped Beatrice into her coat.

"With all the loose ends and unknowns," Beatrice said, "at least one mystery has been cleared up."

"What's that?" Cindy asked.

"Pastor Filbury didn't kill Dawn Smith," Beatrice said. "He was at a conference in Denver all that day. He couldn't have driven from Denver to Golden Springs to commit murder, then drive back. There are hundreds of witnesses who can testify that he was at the conference the entire time."

"That's a mixed blessing," Del said.

"How can you say that?" Cindy asked.

"If Pastor Filbury is off the suspect list," Del said, "that means the murderer is still running around somewhere."

"The more important question," Beatrice said, touching Morgan's arm lightly, "is whether the killer saw you."

"Saw me?"

"Think about it, dear. If someone strangled the girl on the trail, and then heard you coming, he or she knows you saw the victim before she was thrown off the cliff."

"Everyone in Golden Springs knows I saw the girl," Morgan said. "Kurt Willard wrote about it in his newspaper."

Beatrice patted Morgan's arm with her mitten-covered hand. "I'll make certain my ladies' group prays for you every day until the killer is found."

CHAPTER EIGHTEEN

Morgan invited Del to have a cup of homemade soup with her after they closed up the shop for the night. She told herself it wasn't because Beatrice's news had spooked her.

"I don't bother to cook much for myself," Del said. "Not from scratch. My soup's all from a can."

"I still tend to cook too much," Morgan said. "When Dave went to college, I had to cut back on portions, then Sarah moved out, and I had to reduce again. Then I lost Sam."

"I had to learn how to cook. My wife fixed all the meals, except for grilling. That was my territory. When she passed, it was kind of late in the game to get beyond the basics. I remember your daughter made brownies every summer she was here. That little gal could cook!"

"By the way, Del, I haven't mentioned to the kids about finding Dawn's body."

Del shook his head. "It's gonna hit the news. Especially now that the police say it was a murder."

"I hardly think the *Argus Leader* will run a story about a murder in Colorado. And I don't want the kids to worry."

"They'll worry a lot more if they hear from a stranger that their momma is tangled up in a homicide."

Morgan's cell phone buzzed.

"It's Bernie," she told Del. "Are you here?" she said into the phone. "Okay, I'll be right out." Morgan grabbed her coat and the olive-green camouflage fanny pack. "I've got to go."

"I'd be happy to stick around until you get back," Del said. "If it would make you feel safer."

"I'll be okay," Morgan said. "I'm getting used to the raccoons."

"You got the pepper spray?" Del asked.

Morgan unzipped the pack and pulled out the small device. "The pepper spray I don't know how to aim in the right direction? Check."

"Flashlight?"

"Check."

Del started to say something else, but Morgan interrupted him.

"I have enough gear to survive a week in the woods. I'll be fine for a walk through the city."

When Morgan climbed into the SUV, Bernie lifted one of her feet.

"New socks," she said. "New shoes."

"I've got mine on, too," Morgan said. "I can't believe how much I paid just for the socks."

"If I get so much as one blister, I'm going to demand a refund."

Morgan enjoyed the easy chatter all the way to O'Reily's. She liked having a friend who knew her as an individual and not as half of a couple or one component of a family unit.

Lucy spotted them when they arrived at the pub and checked their names off the running club's roster.

"Two races down," Bernie said. "Eight to go."

"See?" Lucy said. "You're getting there. I told you it would be fun." Lucy kept up the conversation while she signed in people. "Name?" She traced her finger down the list and checked a box next to the person's name on the roster. "We had a great response to the Run for Amanda five K," Lucy said to

Morgan and Bernie. "Over a hundred people have registered already. Thanks for helping on such short notice."

A throng of runners crowded closer. "Name?" Lucy asked.

"We'd better get out of the way," Bernie said.

Lucy waved. "See you later."

Morgan and Bernie squeezed through the crowd in front of O'Reily's, finding a space to stand farther down the sidewalk.

"This sure got popular," Bernie said.

"What's not to like about beer and running?" Morgan said.

"Well, what's not to like about beer, anyway," Bernie said. "Hey, look, it's Barton."

The shaggy-bearded runner jogged up the sidewalk. Morgan steeled herself.

"Hi, Barton," Bernie called.

He stopped abruptly. "Good evening, Bernie." Barton glanced at Morgan, but didn't greet her. "If you'll excuse me, Bernie." He pushed his way through the crowd at the entrance of O'Reily's.

"What brought that on?" Bernie asked. "Barton's usually such a nice guy, but he totally snubbed you."

"I might have sort of accused him of murder," Morgan whispered.

"This ought to be good."

"I'll tell you about it when there's less of a crowd," Morgan said.

The run started. Runners rushed down the sidewalk. Morgan and Bernie settled into a brisk walk. When the crowd thinned, Bernie returned to the painful topic.

"Now what's this about you accusing Barton of murder?"

"I was trying to make some connections about Dawn's death," Morgan said, "and I guess I jumped to conclusions."

They turned off the sidewalk and onto the gravel path through the park.

"He spends a lot of time in the woods," Morgan said. "I told you about running into him, literally, on the trail where I found Dawn. So when he came to the shop to sell some antique junk, I asked him where he was on the day Dawn died."

"Morgan, you did not!"

"I hadn't had much sleep the night before," Morgan said. "I wasn't thinking clearly. But still, how can I count him out? He didn't have a plausible alibi."

"She might have died of natural causes, right?" Bernie asked. "Or a drug overdose? They don't know yet."

"Beatrice came by the shop this morning," Morgan said. "She told us not to talk about it."

" 'Us' who?"

"Me, Del, and Cindy."

"Well, it's all over town by now, I'm sure."

"You're right," Morgan said, "but you have to keep this to yourself."

"I promise," Bernie said, "I won't repeat what you tell me, at least until it comes out in the *Golden Springs Gazetteer.*"

Morgan glanced around in the dark. They were in back of the pack again.

"Beatrice's nephew works in the crime lab," Morgan said. "He told her it was murder. Beatrice called it ligature strangulation."

"Ew."

"Barton had opportunity," Morgan continued.

"What about motivation?" Bernie asked. "Pastor Filbury had an obvious motivation and you don't suspect him."

"Pastor Filbury has an alibi, and hundreds of witnesses." Morgan told Bernie about the pastor's appearance at the well-attended conference.

"I'm happy for your pastor," Bernie said, "but I still don't think Barton is capable of murder."

"He's a hunter. He kills animals."

"Yes," Bernie said. "Animals. Not people. Lots of folks here hunt. If you're considering suspects, why isn't Piers on your list?"

"Oh, come on," Morgan said. "I know you don't like Piers, but he's a vegetarian."

"So was Hitler."

The bridge over the creek loomed in the darkness. Through the trees Morgan could see the street light marking their cutoff to head back to O'Reily's.

"Did I mention," Morgan said, "Piers asked me out to dinner?"

Bernie skidded to an abrupt halt. "You did not just say what I thought I heard you say."

"Why not?"

"Because." Bernie threw her hands in the air. "Because!" She stomped toward the bridge. "Because he could be a killer for all you know."

"At this point, anyone in Golden Springs could be a killer. Only Pastor Filbury has been crossed off the list."

Bernie stopped, throwing her arm in front of Morgan.

"Wait," she whispered.

The footbridge stood in the shadows to their left, a stand of cottonwood trees across the trail to their right.

"What?" Morgan whispered.

"Shh! I heard something."

Bushes grew thick on the far bank of the creek. Morgan could hear branches cracking as something large mowed a path up the bank.

"It's heading for the bridge," Bernie said.

"Should we turn back?" Morgan asked. "Or try to outrun it?"

A dark form climbed onto the bridge, rising from a crouch to full height. The sound of unsteady steps echoed on the wooden bridge.

Morgan unzipped her fanny pack, feeling for the flashlight. The creature ambled toward them, canting slightly to the left.

A drunken bear?

"Let's run," Bernie said, clutching Morgan's arm.

"You can't outrun a bear."

Morgan's fingers closed around the pepper spray. She jerked it out of the pack and held it at arm's length, ready to fire.

"Can you ladies spare a—"

"Stop or I'll—"

Bernie screamed. The man yelled and spun around, stumbling and falling to his knees. He scrambled to his feet and lumbered across the bridge.

Bernie grabbed Morgan's arm. They clung to each other for a moment, trembling.

"Well," Bernie said. "I would say this will make a great story to share at O'Reily's, but I'm not sure I'm ready to admit to anyone that we nearly assaulted a homeless man."

"He should have known better than to approach women in the dark. What did he expect?"

"A dollar?"

Morgan was still shaking when they reached the street.

"Here comes Lucy." Bernie sounded relieved.

There was only so much comfort in the company of people. Morgan found herself studying the back of every runner that passed them on the way back to the pub, debating whether they were capable of murder.

The homeless man looking for a handout might have seemed as frightened of Morgan and Bernie as they had been of him. But suppose he had been after something more than pocket change. And suppose, instead of two grown women, he had run across one lone teenager.

If Dawn had been killed in a chance encounter with a stranger, the list of potential suspects was endless.

CHAPTER NINETEEN

The dawn light softened the barn around the edges, as though time had worn down all the sharp angles. Shades of brown and gray blended with the surrounding earth and bare trees. Morgan crossed the gravel parking lot and entered the barn through the smaller door to the right of the double doors. She paused, letting her eyes adjust to the dark interior.

Houdini and Adelaide trotted into an open stall from the fenced paddock. Breath puffed from their flared nostrils in clouds of steam. The barn smelled of hay, manure, and livestock, an earthy odor that Morgan found pleasant. She unlatched the door to the tack room, and unhooked the metal band holding the lid on a fifty-gallon drum. She measured out a coffee can of oats.

Leaning over the low wall of Houdini and Adelaide's stall, she poured oats into the wooden trough. Adelaide nudged Houdini out of the way and began greedily munching.

"Sorry, fella."

Morgan reached over the wall to scratch Houdini's ragged mohawk of a mane.

"How about you eat over here, since your wife won't share?"

Morgan retrieved a half can of oats from the tack room, rattled the can to encourage Houdini to move to the next stall, and poured oats into the trough. Kendall and Allie had left strict instructions not to overfeed the donkeys, but Adelaide couldn't seem to get enough to eat.

Morgan's cell phone rang.

"I guess we get service today," she told Houdini. She checked the caller ID, then flipped open the small phone. "Hi, Sarah. How are you feeling?"

"I tried some ginger tea for my morning sickness, and it seems to be helping. Other than domestic bliss, not much is happening here. What's the scoop on Golden Springs?"

"Oh, nothing much. I just fed Houdini and Adelaide." Morgan latched the tack room door and headed across the pasture to the back of the shop. "I finally heard from Kendall."

"Are they in the jungle? What's it like?"

"I didn't get much information. We mostly talked about the shop. Or argued, I should say."

"What's going on?" Sarah asked.

Morgan opened the back door and walked inside the kitchen.

"Business is slow," Morgan said. "If I can't get customers to drive up the hill, we could lose the shop. It may not be a moneymaker, but the land is worth a lot. I suggested we need to consider selling the place, but Kendall disagreed. Rather strongly."

The coffee had finished brewing. She poured herself a mug full, doctoring it with cream and sugar.

"I agree with Uncle Kendall," Sarah said. "I want to bring my children to Colorado someday, just like you and Dad did. Don't rush into a decision, Mom. The baby's not due for months."

"If I can get Internet service, staying longer might not be too bad."

"I'll send your laptop, and we can email."

Then Morgan remembered Del's warning. The local media was already having a field day with the potential church scandal. Now that murder was involved, Golden Springs might hit the national news.

165

"Sarah, I don't want to upset you, but I need to tell you something else." Morgan related a condensed version of the story about finding Dawn Smith, leaving out as much emotion and detail as she could.

"I don't know if you remember Beatrice," Morgan said.

"I was a teenager the last time I spent summer vacation in Golden Springs," Sarah said. "I knew who the hub of the gossip wheel was."

"Beatrice has a nephew who works in the Granite Junction crime lab. He told Beatrice the girl was murdered."

"One more reason for you to stay," Sarah said. "You're mixed up in this. Leaving town might make you look suspicious."

Del was already sipping his coffee by the time Morgan entered the shop.

"I saw this deal on a kitchen remodeling show." He showed Morgan a rough sketch of a wagon wheel with hooks attached. "They used a copper hoop, but we have lots of wagon wheels. Instead of pots and pans, we'd hang up stuff we want customers to notice."

"Great idea," Morgan said.

"I'm going to work on the sign," Del said. "We'd better get it put up before Gerda changes her mind, or Piers figures out some way to throw a monkey wrench into things. Then I'll work on this."

"I'll be in the office." Morgan sighed. "Entering data on a spreadsheet."

It was close to noon when Del stuck his head in the office.

"I got the sign and the donkey cart painted," he said. "First coat, anyway. Now I need a hand with this wagon-wheel idea."

"Gladly." Morgan stretched her arms and shoulders as she followed Del into the shop.

"I think it would work here." Del pointed to a space at the

intersection of two aisles.

Morgan helped Del lift the wagon wheel to the top of the ladder. He climbed onto the rungs and fastened baling wire to the spokes, pulling the wheel nearly flush to the low ceiling.

The cowbell clanged as the front door of the shop opened.

"Anybody home?" a male voice called.

"We're back here," Morgan yelled.

Kurt Willard, in his 1940s reporter costume, came around the end of the aisle. Morgan clenched her hands into tight fists, fighting the inclination to give him a piece of her mind, or maybe a pop in the nose.

"Nice touch." Kurt shoved his hands in the pockets of his trench coat and looked up. "Very western."

"We're trying to broaden our customer base from serious rock hounds to tourists," Del said.

"Come by the newspaper office when it's convenient," Kurt said with a smile. "I can offer you a special winter price for advertising. I also publish a directory to local businesses, with maps and coupons."

"I'm not interested in discussing business with you," Morgan said.

She snatched a ball of twine and a knife from a table.

"I need some more wire from the barn." Del climbed off the ladder. "Will you be okay for a few minutes?"

"I can handle things," Morgan told him, gripping the knife in her fist.

"No doubt about that," Del mumbled.

Kurt watched the old cowboy exit the shop, then turned his attention back to Morgan.

"I wear many hats at the *Gazetteer*. I didn't come today to discuss business. I'm here in my capacity as a reporter."

Morgan suspected she knew what was coming next. She decided to head Kurt off at the pass. "You already seem to have a source. One who apparently provides more information than I can. I read your special edition."

Morgan reeled out a length of twine and cut it with the knife. She reached into the cardboard box full of old coffee pots and tied twine to the handle of one.

"When I asked you before about the body on the trail," Kurt said, his pencil poised above a spiral-bound notepad, "you implied that you might have imagined it."

"Search and rescue couldn't find the body, so I had to assume it might have been a figment of my imagination."

"And then the body was discovered in a different location."

"That's a matter of record." Morgan reached for another coffee pot, this one marred with a rusted bullet hole.

"Part of that record is that the pastor of a church that you attend was accused by that same young woman of inappropriate actions." Kurt tipped his fedora back with the end of his pencil. "She was going to press charges against him, but coincidentally she was murdered before she got the chance. There are no secrets in Golden Springs. Why not take this opportunity to clear the air about your involvement in this incident?"

Morgan slammed the coffee pot down on the wooden display table. "Did your source make up that lie, too?"

"Lie?"

"Pastor Filbury was at a conference in Denver the day Dawn Smith died," Morgan said. "There are hundreds of witnesses."

Kurt scribbled furiously on his notepad as he spoke. "Nothing in my special edition said your beloved pastor was guilty. A man doesn't have to pull the trigger himself to commit murder."

"She wasn't shot—" Morgan stopped abruptly. Kurt had managed to wring a tidbit of information out of her.

"I have a source who says the cause of death was ligature strangulation," Kurt said. "Is that what you saw?"

"I told you, I didn't witness anything," Morgan said.

"Are you sure you have no statement for the press?" Kurt tapped his pencil on his notepad, waiting. "When I examine the timeline of events, it's clear to me that your path may have crossed that of the killer's."

Beatrice had warned her that if the killer suspected she had witnessed the murder, Morgan would be in danger. Kurt had already plastered the front page of the *Golden Springs Gazetteer* with a story that implied she had seen the whole thing.

"Kurt, I told you, I did not witness a murder."

It was the one thing Morgan said that he didn't record on his notepad.

"The Golden Springs Community Church is a tight-knit group. Maybe you can't share information because you saw something that would implicate a fellow church member."

Morgan set the knife in the cardboard box. "You've got to be kidding me. Is that the best you can come up with? That the church cobbled together some conspiracy to cover up for Pastor Filbury?"

Morgan turned away from Kurt, her heart pounding as she recalled Herb's face, contorted with rage, and the fistfight in the church hall. There might be people willing to kill in defense of their pastor.

"I've said all I'm going to say, Kurt. Now, if you don't mind, I have work to do."

Kurt frowned, frustration obvious in his expression. He jammed his fedora onto his head and stomped out the door. Morgan watched him through the front window as he climbed into his antique car and tore out of the Rock of Ages parking lot.

Del walked in, shaking his head. "Willard was in a hurry. What did you do to him this time?"

"He wanted to know more than I would tell him."

"I suppose that could be enough to upset a newspaperman,"

Del said. "Can you hold the ladder while I climb up?"

Morgan grasped the rails of the ladder.

"For all I know," she said, "Kurt Willard could be the murderer. He certainly wanted to know whether I witnessed the murder. What if his interest wasn't merely as a reporter? One more name for a growing list."

CHAPTER TWENTY

As soon as the Granite Junction Police Department's spokesperson announced that Dawn had been murdered, the rock shop phone started ringing. Reporters seeking the dirt on the Dawn Smith and Pastor Filbury scandal were as persistent as velociraptors on a stegosaurus carcass.

Morgan unplugged the office phone and shut the door, where it was easier to ignore the constant ringing of the phone by the cash register. When she found a property tax assessment in the piles of papers scattered around the office, she spent the morning estimating how much profit would be required to pay the tax bill, breaking it down by week.

"If we could just sell the triceratops horn, all our problems would be solved." She sighed. "Or at least a portion of them."

She left the office and leaned against the display case, studying the horn.

Del walked in the front door. "I thought I'd drop by and see how things are going. The phone still ringing off the hook?"

"I quit answering it, and the calls slowed down. But we can't run a business without a phone."

"It doesn't work half the time." Del lifted the receiver and held it to his ear. "Yup. We've got a connection."

"I should get the Internet hooked up," Morgan said. "And start an eBay auction for that."

She pointed at the case.

"Everybody's going Internet these days," Del said. "I suppose it's just a matter of time for the Rock of Ages to be computerized."

"A website wouldn't be a bad idea."

Morgan pulled out the "idea" notepad and added "website" to the growing list.

Their connection to the outside world didn't last long. Later in the day, the landline was full of static, and Morgan's cell phone didn't have signal.

"It's spitting snow," Del said. "The phone usually doesn't work during a snowstorm."

"I need to call the people from church who volunteered for the Run for Amanda five K," Morgan said. "I'm going to Bernie's to use her phone."

When Morgan arrived at the bakery, Bernie ushered her upstairs to her living room.

"There's more privacy here," Bernie said. "Mr. Whiskers can keep you company. Let me know when you're finished, and we can have a bowl of soup together."

Morgan read her scripted message to several answering machines.

"Hello, this is Morgan Iverson from Golden Springs Community Church calling to remind you about the Run for Amanda five K this Saturday. The church team will meet at the corner of Oak and Fourth Street. If you've already registered, I'll have your bib number. Call Beatrice at five-five-five-one-zero-seven-nine if you have any questions. Remember to dress warm!"

Her next call reached an angry woman who declared she was no longer a member of the church. She went on a tirade about the embarrassment of being associated with a group that tolerated a pastor who would molest children. Morgan ended the conversation by explaining that there were no refunds for the charity event.

"You don't have to walk with the church group," Morgan said. "You can go by yourself—"

Click.

"She hung up on me!" Morgan told Mr. Whiskers.

He looked up from his comfortable perch on a soft wool afghan and yawned.

"Are you bored?" Morgan asked. "I'm almost done."

She finished her calls, reaching two more people who told her they were leaving the church. Morgan gathered her sign-up sheets and clipboard, and went downstairs to the bakery. Bernie delivered a tray of food to a table, then ducked into the kitchen. She returned with two steaming bowls on a tray.

"I saved some vegetable beef soup. My customers were raving about it."

Morgan followed Bernie to a window table.

"Thanks for letting me use your phone," Morgan said. "I called around, and I might be able to have more reliable phone service, and the Internet, hooked up at the shop. Whether I stay or leave, the shop needs a phone."

"I'd rather hear that you're planning to stay permanently."

Morgan shook her head. "I don't know yet. Kendall left too big a mess for me to straighten out in two weeks. Or maybe ever."

The rock shop was quiet, as usual. Morgan had time to slip through the door dividing the shop from the living area and start a load of laundry. Blue jeans hadn't been the mainstay of her wardrobe in Sioux Falls. If she didn't do laundry, Morgan would have to resort to office attire soon.

She emptied the pockets of her jeans onto the kitchen table. From the rear pocket of one pair, Morgan extracted the folded orange flier Sparrow had given her.

"Interfaith Potluck: the temples of Thailand. Wednesday, 6:00 p.m., town hall public meeting room."

Morgan knew Kendall's crowd, most of whom attended the Golden Springs Community Church. Maybe it was time to meet members of the community with a different worldview. She didn't need her mind opened, as Sparrow had suggested. But meeting more citizens would increase the likelihood she would run into whoever was capable of ligature strangulation.

City Hall was a traditional structure modeled after the state capitol building, but on a modest scale. Unlike the Denver capitol's dome of gold, Golden Springs's dome was covered with wood shingles.

The public meeting room shared the lower level of the two-story building with city offices, and the police department. Crooked rows of metal folding chairs faced a podium flanked by two scarred wooden tables.

Sparrow Plinkton fussed with a laptop computer and projector. She wore hippie attire of a fluorescent tie-dyed T-shirt and a floor-length denim skirt, but her short green hair stood in punk-style spikes.

"I don't understand," she whined in her raspy smoker's voice. "It was working earlier."

Morgan placed her pan of brownies on the potluck table and stepped around the podium to the projector. "I know a little about hooking up projectors."

"A little." A smirk creased Sparrow's doughy cheeks. "We'd better hope that's enough."

Morgan reconnected the cords to the correct ports. "Which file are you trying to view?"

In seconds, she had the Temples of Thailand slideshow projected onto the white movie screen behind the podium.

A man with a stringy brown ponytail nodded at Morgan.

"Sparrow, who's your new friend?"

"This is Morgan," Sparrow said. "She took over the rock shop. She's Kendall's sister, believe it or not."

The man pressed his palms together and bowed slightly at the waist in a vaguely Eastern gesture. "Elrond, at your service. Welcome to Golden Springs."

Another character in costume, Morgan thought. Elrond appeared to have borrowed his clothing from the movie set for the Lord of the Rings. Morgan was certain he had borrowed the elvish name, too. She felt overdressed in her black slacks and jacket.

"Nice to meet—" Morgan began, but Sparrow interrupted.

"Morgan's not staying."

"I had to extend my visit," Morgan said, her voice firm. She did not appreciate other people speaking for her, least of all the antagonistic, green-haired hippie. "My brother and I don't know yet what we're going to do with the Rock of Ages."

Elrond cocked his head to one side. His long, thin ponytail slipped over the shoulder of his brown homespun tunic, reminding Morgan of a rat's tail.

"May I be so bold as to inquire what your asking price may be, for the shop and the land?"

"Take a number and get in line," Sparrow said, a hint of a threat in her raspy tone. "Someone else is interested in the place."

Elrond just nodded, his brow creased with an annoyed look.

Morgan guessed that "someone else" was Piers, and that Sparrow was looking out for his interests, although Piers's business interests did not seem to need protecting.

Other people arrived with potluck dishes, most dressed in jeans and sweaters. Half the crowd of thirty seemed to be from the liberal arts college in Granite Junction.

When everyone was seated, Elrond stood behind the podium.

"Will someone please turn off the lights?"

Morgan glanced behind her as a young man flipped the light switch by the door. Piers slipped in at the last minute, easing onto a chair at the back of the room. He met Morgan's eyes and smiled briefly.

The audience was attentive during Elrond's slideshow. Morgan's head swam with the names of exotic gods and goddesses and their stories. Her mind wandered to the potluck table. She wished she'd eaten a snack before the meeting.

Finally the slideshow ended. The potluck foods were unfamiliar to Morgan, consisting of dark, heavy breads, casseroles of grains and vegetables, and more varieties of tofu than she had imagined possible. There was not a molded gelatin salad or green-bean dish to be found. Her homemade brownies were greeted with either horror or delight by people dedicated to a healthy lifestyle.

"Did you enjoy the slideshow?" Piers asked Morgan.

She noticed he didn't have a brownie on his plate.

"The photographs were beautiful." Morgan picked at something green and lumpy with a plastic fork.

Sparrow lumbered up to Piers, grabbing his arm. "We have business to discuss." She dragged him to the front corner of the meeting room where Elrond waited beside a young woman with a pinched face.

Morgan mingled, meeting people, struggling to memorize names and faces. It was difficult to learn much about people when conversation stayed on topics like colon-cleansing regimes. She stood at the edge of a group discussing how under-consumption of calories could extend a person's lifespan.

"The benefits are clear," a rail-thin woman said.

"Food is one of the last pleasures I have left," a chubby man in a tweed jacket said. "I've given up everything else."

The group chuckled at his comment. Morgan plunged in.

"You have to have balance," she said. "Even if you starve yourself to live a few days longer, you could die in an accident. Or be murdered, like that teenage girl."

"What girl?" the man asked.

"Please don't tell me," the thin woman said, holding a manicured hand up and turning slightly away from Morgan. "I don't want to hear anything negative."

"It's been on the news," Morgan said.

"Yes." The chubby man snapped his fingers. "I did hear about that. A tragedy. So young. So young." He shook his head.

"I never watch the news," the thin woman said. "Stress can weaken your immune system."

"That's true," another woman said. "But wouldn't half-starving yourself all the time cause stress?"

No one seemed interested in the abbreviated life of an unimportant girl. Morgan tried to turn conversations to the murder, but couldn't stir up anything more than brief comments about karma, the fleeting nature of life, or the effects of vitamin therapy on mental disorders. While the crowd seemed eager to avoid the topic of murder, Morgan did not detect any reactions that suggested guilt or complicity.

When the first cluster of people gathered their dishes and coats to leave, Morgan was ready to go also. In spite of the uniform condemnation of refined sugars and animal fats, only crumbs remained of Morgan's brownies. She tapped the heavy stainless-steel pan against the trash can to knock the larger crumbs out, then tucked it under her arm.

Piers stopped her on her way out the door.

"I apologize for abandoning you," Piers said. "May I walk you to your car?"

Sparrow materialized at his elbow. "Can you help me with something?" She glanced at Morgan. "Oh, am I interrupting?"

Sparrow placed a proprietary hand on Piers's arm and shot a

superior look at Morgan.

"You're not interrupting," Morgan said.

"I'll be right back," Piers told Sparrow.

"But I need—" Sparrow started.

"In a moment," Piers said, his tone firm, like a parent cautioning a child.

"It's okay," Morgan said to Piers. "We'll talk another time."

Sparrow's cheeks flushed a blotchy red, and deep lines creased between her eyes and around her mouth. She was a woman who frowned a lot.

Morgan attempted a sincere smile. "Thanks for inviting me, Sparrow. It was an interesting evening."

As Morgan walked across the deserted park to a stone pedestrian bridge, she mused about Sparrow's reaction. Piers seemed oblivious to Sparrow's interest in him, while she was wildly jealous of any imagined competition. Her persona must not have included the free-love attitude of the older generation of hippies. She wanted Piers all to herself.

Morgan kept to the middle of the bridge. Chunks of ice drifted in the dark water far below, congealing against boulders momentarily before breaking apart and continuing their journey downstream. She shivered, clutching her collar tight with one hand, and grasping her purse and the heavy stainless-steel brownie pan with the other.

The smell of cigarette smoke cut through the crisp night air. Morgan glanced around for the source. Other than the faint sound of music coming from a Main Street bar, she seemed to be alone. Dense winter-dead bushes crowded the far end of the bridge. Morgan studied the shadows as she neared them, relieved when she stepped off the bridge and onto the walkway.

Beyond the bushes, between Morgan and the parking lot, a man lounged against a tree, dim in the light of a distant street lamp. A black garment draped his broad shoulders. Like Dawn Smith's cloak, it looked too thin for the cold night air.

Piers had offered to escort her to her car. She wished she'd taken him up on it. She wished she'd brought Del's pepper spray. All that wishing wouldn't get her safely to her car, and besides, her judgment concerning danger had been proven wrong more than once.

Morgan's dress shoes clicked against the paving stones. She tried to keep her steps steady and slow, while her heart raced out of control. The dark-cloaked person flicked a cigarette onto the ground, the glowing red tip dying in a pile of slush. He tugged a ski mask over his face, covering a bushy mustache and goatee, and slouched toward her.

Veering to the left, Morgan planned to stay out of reach when she neared him. He sped up, his steps matching hers, his route angling toward her side of the walkway. She stopped. He stopped. Certain that his intentions were not good, Morgan spun around. Her chances had to be better returning to City Hall, where people might be lingering after the meeting, rather than facing the strange man head on.

She heard his loping strides behind her on the bridge. Morgan started to run, but he grabbed her arm, jolting her to a halt. The heavy brownie pan dropped with a clatter. Morgan pawed at the stranger's hand with her mitten. She tried to scream, but only a whimper pushed past her lips. He gripped both her arms, pushing her steadily to the edge of the bridge. One dress shoe slipped off Morgan's foot and splashed into the slushy creek.

"What do you want?" she gasped. "My purse fell over there."

He didn't seem interested in robbery. And if he had sexual assault in mind, why was he pushing her away? Her fear turned to anger.

"Are you crazy?" It was a rhetorical question. "Let me go!"

If he did, Morgan realized, she would plunge into the icy

water below the bridge. Switching tactics, she hung on to his arm, and wrapped one leg around him like a monkey. He stumbled, and for a moment Morgan feared they would both plunge into the water. Instead, he threw himself toward the bridge, pulling Morgan down with him. The landing was hard, and seemed to stun the stranger for a moment. The collar of his black cloak gapped open, revealing a gargoyle tattoo.

Morgan grabbed for the heavy brownie pan, clutching it tight with her mitten. Her first blow hit the stranger on the side of his head. She jumped up and grasped the pan with both hands, swinging it repeatedly at his face. The man curled up in a ball, his arms cradling his head.

"Hey," a voice called. "What's going on?"

Piers and Elrond ran across the park. The stranger jumped to his feet and sprinted toward the parking lot. Morgan lobbed the brownie pan at him. It bounced off the back of his head, hitting the bridge with a clatter.

CHAPTER TWENTY-ONE

After Golden Springs Police Chief Bill Sharp responded to Piers's cell phone call, Morgan had to convince him that she didn't need to go to the emergency room.

"If anyone needs an ambulance," Piers chuckled, "it's the man who attempted to assault Morgan."

"What happened to Mrs. Iverson was no joke," Chief Sharp said. "I'll need statements from all of you."

"I really have very little to report," Elrond said, "other than witnessing the flight of Morgan's assailant. Would tomorrow afternoon be a suitable time?"

"No," Chief Sharp said. "I want to talk to you tonight. Right now. Follow me to the station."

"I'll drive you, Morgan," Piers said.

The man on the bridge shared the same gargoyle tattoo Dawn Smith wore. The gargoyle that nested in a bed of velvet in a display case at Faerie Tales.

"I'll ride with Chief Sharp," she said.

Morgan spent the next hour at the small police department inside City Hall, telling her story several times over.

Knowing how fast news traveled in Golden Springs, Morgan told Del about her incident on the stone bridge as soon as he arrived at the shop Thursday morning. Then she had to convince him that she needed the Rock of Ages sign worse than she needed a bodyguard. Del reluctantly loaded the finished sign

181

into the car and drove to Gerda's.

When the phone rang, catching her in the middle of sweeping the floor, she grabbed the receiver. "Hello," she said, in a tone that was definitely not customer friendly.

"Nice to hear from you, too," Kendall said. "I'm glad I caught you before you headed home."

"You caught me in the middle of trying to straighten out your mess. Excuse me if I don't sound happy." Morgan paced up and down the empty aisles. "I can't leave until I get my car repaired. Look, Kendall, Sarah asked me to do what I can to hang on to the land, but I don't see how we can. Unless things turn around soon, we need to seriously consider selling the place."

"That's not an option."

"Tell that to the IRS. When were you going to let me in on your tax evasion scheme?"

"When were you going to tell me about Pastor Filbury and the murder, and the fact that you're right in the middle of it all?"

"You're in the jungle." Morgan stopped beside a table and grasped a geode with her free hand. "I didn't think you'd hear news from home."

"You're not the only family member I talk to."

Morgan set the geode down. She had shared the story with Sarah, but hadn't told Dave anything. Morgan's son was too busy studying to return her calls. Or maybe he was avoiding her. She couldn't tell Sarah about the stone bridge assault, at least until the murderer was captured.

"When were you going to tell me about Piers Townsend and his campaign to put us out of business?" she asked. "You could have warned me I was walking into a bear trap."

There was a pause, and for a moment Morgan thought they had lost connection. Then she heard Kendall exhale slowly.

"Okay, maybe that wasn't fair of me. I was desperate to get away, but I didn't want to give up the land. I figured you wouldn't want to run the place if you knew how hard it was going to be. Allie and I just got so weary of it all."

"Weary of what? Working for a living?"

"No, Morgan. Weary of the unending uphill battle to make the Rock of Ages survive."

"Excuse me, but it doesn't look like you were working all that hard."

"We were, in the beginning. That was when things were good. Then all the other crap started. The constant bickering and maneuvering, the petty politics. I was on City Council for one term. We went to meetings. Allie deserves a law degree for all the work she's done deciphering proposed ordinance and zoning changes. Maybe I thought you'd have a fresh take on things, or maybe I thought you'd get along with people better than Allie and me. Or maybe we just gave up."

Morgan sat on the aspen bench. "After all that effort? The place is a mess, the books are an invitation for an IRS audit, and nobody knows we exist."

"I had a sign ready to put up."

"Del found it."

"I was digging the post holes when Piers bought out the shop on the corner of Hill and Main. That was the end of that."

"I'm sorry, Kendall. For yelling. I know how difficult Piers can be. I tried to get permission from him to put the sign on that very corner, but I guess you know how that went."

"It'll only get worse now that Pastor Filbury's influence on City Council is diminished. Piers will get his zoning proposal pushed right through."

"That explains why he's so eager to buy the rock shop," Morgan said. "With the zoning change, he'd make a fortune off our land. I have good news, though. Del is putting up a sign, as we speak."

"You're kidding," Kendall said. "I can't believe he convinced Piers—"

"Not Piers," Morgan said. "Gerda Kruger. She told Del to put a sign for the rock shop on her lot."

"That's so far from the turnoff," Kendall said.

"It's worth a try, don't you think?"

"I suppose so."

Morgan heard a jungle bird in the background. Their connection was tenuous. She didn't want to waste a phone call. She couldn't be certain there would be another.

"Kendall, if you really want to keep the land, why did you spend the tax money?"

"Money's not the important thing now. We'll come up with a way to pay the taxes. I'm worried about you. Have you talked to anyone? I mean besides the police."

"People won't leave me alone. Del makes me carry a stuffed survival pack. Beatrice has me on her gossip speed dial—"

"That's not what I mean," Kendall said. "Have you spoken to anyone about how the trauma of the event affected you? There are people at the church who are very good at listening."

"They're kind of in a state of turmoil right now."

"Morgan. You know Pastor Filbury didn't do anything to that girl. I'm not just calming your parental fears because Dave and Sarah were in the summer camp. I have no doubts about this whatsoever. Pastor Filbury is innocent."

"Thanks." Morgan took a deep breath and released it slowly. She wiped her sweatshirt sleeve across her eyes. "You don't know how much I needed to hear you say that."

Kendall spoke in Spanish, then said, "I have to get off the phone. Do I need to come home?"

"No," Morgan said. "I can take care of myself. And if I can't, there are a dozen people standing in line for the job. Anyway, I would think you and Allie are in more danger than I am."

"It's a tight community here," Kendall said. "People are watching out for us." He laughed. "The local ladies have taken Allie under their care. They're trying every home remedy they know to cure her infertility. Allie's just humoring them. I mean, what are the chances, at our age?"

Morgan thought she detected a trace of bitterness in her brother's voice. Her heart ached for him.

"I really have to go now. This is the only phone in town. I'll call back as soon as I can. Give our love to everyone."

"Wait. When are you coming back? I need to know—"

Kendall began speaking in Spanish and hung up.

Morgan replaced the receiver slowly. The shop was empty. She didn't feel like doing any more data entry. But if she didn't keep busy, her mind would continue spinning over the same territory. Taxes and finances and small-town politics.

And murder.

She looked out the window at the empty parking lot. Heavy flakes began to drift from the gray clouds.

A delivery truck pulled into the Rock of Ages parking lot Friday morning. Morgan unpacked her laptop computer, while Del left to finish installing the sign at Gerda's place. Cindy had just arrived for her shift when Del threw the front door open and marched in like a conquering hero.

"Where are all the customers?" he asked with mock drama. "Haven't they seen the big sign for the Rock of Ages?"

Morgan laughed. "Not yet. But I'm guessing they will."

"The sign is up?" Cindy asked. "Yee-haw!"

She climbed onto her stool. In apparent anticipation of bad weather, Cindy wore maternity jeans, snow boots, and a down vest.

"I finished right before it started snowing," Del said. "I think we'll end up replacing the concrete this spring. But it looks pretty good for now."

"Kendall called," Morgan said.

"How are they?" Cindy asked.

"He and Allie send their love. Kendall was very happy to hear that his sign was going up."

"So are they coming back?" Cindy asked.

"I couldn't keep him on the phone long enough to have that discussion," Morgan said.

Del tugged at his mustache. "What about the shop?"

"I can't head back to Sioux Falls until I get the car fixed." Morgan made the decision that had been building for the past two days. "It's more complicated than I thought it would be. I'll stick around another week or two."

"That's good news," Cindy said.

Morgan couldn't give her false hope.

"If I sell the place, there's a lot of work to do to get it ready to put on the market."

The cowbell clanged as the front door opened. Four snow-dusted people crowded inside and stomped snow off their feet. A teenage girl made a beeline for Lucy's jewelry display, while a younger boy found the shark teeth. Cindy caught Morgan's eye and gave her a thumbs-up sign.

"Hurry up, kids," the father called. "We don't want to get caught in the storm."

The mother approached the checkout counter. She, along with the rest of the family, had the affluent attire and the fit physique of skiers. "Do you know how long this weather is supposed to last?"

"And how are the roads?" the father asked.

"I'll call the road condition hotline." Cindy pulled a pen out of her bun of red hair and punched buttons on the phone.

The man peered into the display case.

"You're kidding, right?"

"What?" Morgan asked.

"That bone, or rock, or whatever it is. Are you really asking over three thousand dollars for that?"

"It's a triceratops brow horn," Morgan said.

The boy materialized in front of his father and pressed his face against the glass. "Awesome!"

"It's seventy million years old," Morgan continued, "and in remarkable condition."

"Who would buy something like that?" the man asked.

"Some people collect coins," Morgan said. "Some buy fine art. Other people collect fossils."

"The roads are wet," Cindy said. "Driving conditions are good, for now. Where are you folks headed?"

"Monarch Ski Resort," the woman said.

"If it was me," Cindy said, "I'd try to get some miles put down before it gets dark."

"Thanks," the woman said. "Come on kids. Hurry up!"

Morgan respected Cindy's truthfulness, but she would have preferred the tourist family linger. She was sure she'd never convince the dad to purchase the triceratops horn, but the family seemed to have money to blow on impulse purchases. They gathered a pile of rocks, crystals, trilobites, coprolite, and shark's teeth. The teenage girl selected a string of beads from Lucy's jewelry display that Morgan had been admiring.

The mother glanced nervously out the window while Cindy rang up the items.

"It's coming down harder," she said.

"You'll make it," Cindy said. "No problem. And this snow will put a fresh layer of powder on the slopes."

"Don't worry, Mom," the boy said. "If it gets bad, I can drive."

"You don't even have a driver's license," the teenage girl said.

"Grandpa lets me drive the tractor every time we visit him."

"It's a lawn mower, you dweeb," the girl said.

"I drove it all the way to town last summer," the boy said.

The girl placed her fists on her narrow hips and leaned her face close to the boy's. "It's three miles from Grandpa's house to town. No way you drove the lawn mower that far."

Dad rumpled the boy's hair and gave Morgan an apologetic smile. "Kids. What an imagination."

"The total is sixty-eight twenty-two," Cindy said.

The first significant sale since Morgan had started managing the Rock of Ages.

"I'm doing a little survey," Morgan said. "How did you folks find out about our shop?"

"That sign in town," the father said. "Robby here is a nut about rock shops."

They watched the family pile into their SUV.

"That boy was quite the character," Del said. "I could just imagine the little guy driving a lawn tractor down the road."

"Oh, he was a taleteller," Cindy said. "That never happened, I'm sure."

Morgan stared out the window at the falling snow.

"Why make up something like that?" Morgan asked.

"Little boys want to do the same things big boys do," Cindy said. "Or sound like they can."

"Enough to lie?" Morgan asked.

"He was just being a kid," Del said.

Morgan turned from the window to face Del and Cindy. "I'm not thinking about that boy. Consider this. What if a person was put up to telling a tall tale?"

"I don't follow you," Del said.

"The girl who was murdered," Morgan said. "Suppose someone told her to accuse Pastor Filbury, or paid her to."

"Or forced her to," Cindy said.

"Now you've opened up a whole new can of worms," Del said. "Who put her up to it and why?"

"Maybe she had to say horrible things about our pastor as part of her initiation into a coven," Cindy said.

"Piers has been trying to push through his zoning changes for years," Morgan said. "He might have gotten impatient with Pastor Filbury, and figured out a way to end his influence on City Council."

"As much as I want to buy that scenario," Del said, tugging the end of his mustache, "there could be other people who would stand to gain from the deal besides Piers."

Morgan suspected Del was thinking of the man on the stone bridge.

"That still doesn't solve the murder." Morgan brushed a hand through her shoulder-length curls. "If anything, it would give Piers a stronger reason to keep Dawn alive."

The phone rang. Cindy picked it up.

"Rock of Ages. Oh, hi, Beatrice. Yup, she's here." Cindy put her hand over the receiver. "It's Beatrice. It's for you." She handed the phone to Morgan.

"Did you call the Run for Amanda team?" Beatrice asked.

"Yes," Morgan said into the phone. "I told everyone to gather at Oak and Fourth." Morgan walked to the office. "Those who are still going, anyway." She consulted the clipboard on the desk. "Three people who signed up told me they aren't attending Golden Springs Community Church anymore, so we shouldn't expect them to participate with us."

"I'm not surprised," Beatrice said. "Some folks fall away quickly."

"You have to admit, it's a touchy issue." Morgan sat at the desk. "Child molestation is one of those concerns where people are entitled to overreact."

"It's ridiculous to end a relationship with a church based on rumor and speculation," Beatrice said. "Pastor Filbury did not do the horrible things that girl accused him of."

"I agree," Morgan said. "Although some people may never be convinced one way or the other, now that the girl is dead."

"Dawn Smith was a drug addict. She would have lied to get her next fix."

"Are the toxicology results in?" Morgan asked.

"Not yet," Beatrice said, "but I am confident they will prove me right."

"Why would she lie about Pastor Filbury?" Morgan asked.

"I've heard that her boyfriend was a hard character. Maybe he put her up to it. They were probably high on drugs."

"That still doesn't answer the main question," Morgan asked. "Who killed her?"

"That gang they hung around with might have forced her to accuse the pastor," Beatrice said, "and then killed her."

Beatrice's theory didn't make any sense to Morgan. She steered the conversation back to the race. They settled the final details, and Beatrice hung up.

Morgan leaned back in the chair.

While it seemed plausible that the drug-addict boyfriend might have killed the girl, and dumped her body on the trail, that didn't answer why she had accused the pastor, or whether the two issues were related. Morgan shook her head.

"Great. One more suspect."

CHAPTER TWENTY-TWO

Morgan woke to the phone ringing. Wondering what emergency could cause a person to call at six o'clock on a Saturday, she dragged herself out of the soft, warm bed and into the chilly kitchen.

"Good morning?"

"This is Lucy." The line crackled. "I can barely hear you."

"The phone doesn't work well when it snows."

"It's not snowing now, and it didn't snow enough last night to cancel the race. If any of your church people call, it's still on."

"How much did it snow?"

"You haven't been outside yet?" Lucy asked. "It's just a dusting. I'll see you at the park."

Peeking through the curtain on the back door, Morgan saw more than what she considered a dusting. She dressed in layers. So many layers that it was difficult to squeeze behind the steering wheel. She moved the driver's seat back a notch.

Morgan turned the key several times before the engine started. Hill Street was slippery under the worn tires. She hoped she could make it back up the road after the race.

Bernie waited outside the back door of the bakery.

"I think we should drive to the park," she said as she climbed in. "Considering the snow and all."

Morgan didn't argue.

"I was worried you'd be late." Bernie stuck a to-go cup of

coffee into Morgan's cup holder. "Here, this is yours."

"Bless you!" Morgan sipped the steaming brew when she stopped at a stop sign. "I didn't have time to get breakfast."

Bernie lifted a white paper bag and opened the top. "I brought blueberry scones, too."

"That's the kind of survival gear I want." Morgan reached into the bag. She ate and drove while Bernie scanned for a parking spot close to the park.

"There," Bernie said. "In front of Sparrow's store."

Morgan started to pull in, but an orange cone squatted dead center in the parking space. Sparrow's battered van sat on one side of the space. On the other was a motor scooter. Before Morgan could put the car in reverse, Sparrow ran outside. Her cheap flip-flops slid on the snow-packed sidewalk. Morgan rolled her window down.

"These spaces are taken!" Sparrow screamed.

The odor of unwashed clothes and marijuana smoke rolled off Sparrow's sloppy thrift-store ensemble.

"I was just backing out," Morgan said.

Sparrow shook her meaty fist. "You out-of-towners think you can just show up and take whatever you want!"

Morgan backed out and rolled up her window to avoid the rest of Sparrow's tirade.

"Yeesh," Bernie muttered. "Somebody got up on the wrong side of the futon."

"Let's try the other side of the park." Morgan drove down Fourth Street to Pine Avenue.

"There's one," Bernie said. "Oh, no, it's a handicapped space. Quick. Over there. We can't miss the start."

Morgan squeezed her car into a parking space. "Why not?"

"They record your time at the finish."

Morgan groaned. "Is it too late to back out?"

"You'll have to tell Lucy. We'd never hear the end of it."

"I guess we're committed, then."

Morgan climbed out of the car. She lengthened the waist strap on Del's pack and fastened it on over her layers.

"The more I think about it," Bernie said, her eyes on the pack, "maybe you shouldn't be wandering through the woods carrying nothing but a Buck knife and duct tape. If I'd just been assaulted, I'm sure I wouldn't leave my house for a month."

"Over a hundred people are going on this run. Isn't there a saying about safety in numbers?" Morgan patted the heavy pack. "I'll be safe."

Six volunteers sat on metal folding chairs behind two utility tables. A banner that read "registration" had been taped to the front of the tables.

Morgan handed her church-team list to the woman sitting behind a "teams" sign. Just a glimpse of honey-brown skin, flushed from the cold, peeked out from layers of a fuzzy green neck scarf.

"Here are your bib numbers," the woman said.

She handed Morgan a stack of square sheets of heavy-duty paper printed with "Run for Amanda" and sequential numbers.

"You'll need these," the woman said, and poured a handful of safety pins into Morgan's mitten-covered palm.

Morgan must have looked confused, because the woman added, "You pin the bib to the front of your shirt. Don't tear off the strip at the bottom. They'll need that at the finish line."

"Thanks."

Morgan turned to leave.

"Don't forget your shirts!" the woman called.

"Shirts?" Morgan asked.

The volunteer shoved a dozen clear plastic drawstring bags into Morgan's arms.

"Morgan, look." Bernie held up a T-shirt. "Run for Amanda" was printed on the white cotton, arching above a bouquet of columbine flowers that bloomed in front of a palm tree.

"We get shirts!" Bernie squealed.

"What's the palm tree for?" Morgan asked.

"Amanda Palmquist, of course. And columbines are the state flower."

Bernie helped Morgan carry the bags with the team's shirts to the picnic table where church members were waiting. Three lean youngsters dressed in running clothes stomped the snow-covered ground like impatient racehorses. The rest of the team was heavier, older, and dressed for the cold, although none wore winter coats like Morgan and Bernie. The oldest team member was Beatrice, but she opted to guard everyone's coats and hats.

"I'm not going to walk," she said. "It's too slippery."

One young man shivered in shorts and a mesh T-shirt. Morgan might have appeared overdressed in her blue jeans and winter coat, but she was warm.

"You must be freezing," Bernie said to the young man.

"I won't be when I start running."

He pinned his bib number to the front of his shirt. Morgan followed suit, starting to pin her number to her coat.

"You're not wearing that." Anna looked lean and mean in gray fleece running slacks and a lightweight fleece jacket with the Granite Junction Zoo logo covering the back.

"It's cold," Morgan said. "And I'm not running."

"You might feel cold right now," Anna said, "but once you get moving, you'll start sweating."

"Lucy told us the same thing at O'Reily's," Bernie said. "And she was right."

Bernie shed her coat, handing it to Beatrice. Morgan unstrapped the fanny pack, removed her coat, and readjusted the pack's straps.

"You won't need that, either." Anna pointed at Morgan's pack.

"This goes with me," Morgan said.

"Morgan's paranoid," Bernie said, "and I don't blame her, after what your boss printed in his scandal rag of a newspaper."

"Kurt didn't let me proofread his special edition," Anna said. "Morgan, I'm sorry for the things he said. If I had known, I would have tried to stop him."

"I don't blame you, Anna. Do you know who gave him the information?"

"His source? No."

"Does Kurt hang around with any people with tattoos? Specifically, a gargoyle tattoo?"

"Not that I'm aware."

The tinny sound of a voice on a loudspeaker interrupted.

"They're lining up," Beatrice said. "Let's pray."

"Okay team," Morgan said. "Gather round."

The dozen members of Golden Springs Community Church formed a semicircle facing Beatrice. When she had everyone's attention, Beatrice spoke, bowing her head and closing her eyes.

"Lord, please keep us safe. As we enjoy this event, keep us mindful of our purpose, to help a family in need. We pray for Amanda's continued healing." She paused for a beat. "Amen." Beatrice looked up at Morgan.

"We're all starting together," Morgan said, "but I'm sure we'll be moving at different speeds. We've already achieved our goal, which was showing our support for Amanda Palmquist. Now go out there and have fun!"

The group broke up, moving to different spots in front of the start line. Morgan had envisioned something more elaborate than the blue chalk line across the sidewalk. A digital timer mounted on a tripod counted backwards. Someone made announcements on a squawking loudspeaker that Morgan couldn't understand.

"There's Barton," Bernie said.

Morgan looked around. Barton had on a few more clothes than the young man on the church team, but not by much. His shirt had long sleeves, and he wore running pants. Runners crowded close to the starting line, but Morgan worked her way through to Barton.

"Hey," she said.

"Kind of busy right now," he said, stretching one leg behind him.

"Barton, about the other day, at the rock shop, I've been kind of jumpy, with all that's happened."

"Understandable."

"Del told me he trusts you, and I trust Del."

Barton glanced at Morgan, then continued stretching.

"I apologize for asking those questions," Morgan said. "Baseless accusations are not usually my style."

Barton stood. He studied Morgan for a moment, then held out his hand.

"Apology accepted."

An obnoxious air horn sounded. The mass of runners surged forward. People funneled from the park onto the sidewalk. Morgan found Bernie toward the back of the pack.

"I saw you shake hands with Barton," Bernie said. "I'm glad that's resolved. This town is too small to have enemies."

They walked briskly, covering two blocks of paved sidewalk in just a few minutes. It had been plowed, and the icy spots sprinkled with sand.

"If it's like this the whole way," Morgan said, "Beatrice will wish she'd come along."

The sidewalk ended at a dirt parking lot. Morgan watched the walkers ahead of them funnel through a narrow gap in a split-rail fence and disappear into the woods.

They followed through the fence and found a wide, snow-packed dirt trail. Although it branched in three directions, it was easy to follow the correct path. Over a hundred runners had stomped it into mud and slush.

"Great," Bernie said. "Our new shoes will be filthy."

Behind them came the sound of rapid splashing. They stopped and turned.

"Lucy!"

"I was helping with registration," Lucy said, "but I'm running, too. How are you gals doing?"

"Piece of cake." Bernie laughed.

Morgan pointed down the trail. "Look. We're not last."

An older couple walked behind them. They might have been casual hikers at the pace they were moving, except for the distinctive bib numbers pinned to their windbreakers.

"Those are sweepers," Lucy said.

"They clean up the trail after people?" Bernie asked.

"No," Lucy said, "they make sure no one is left behind. They'll follow you the whole way. And Pine County Search and Rescue will be driving an ATV around with a first-aid kit. I'm going to run. Have fun!" She took off, making fresh footprints in the slush. "Oh," she called over her shoulder, "it's an out-and-back. You can't get lost."

"What did she say?" Bernie asked.

"Something like outback."

"I wonder what that means."

"No idea."

"My feet are cold," Bernie said. "And wet."

"We just got started."

The trail had been relatively level, following a frozen creek. Now it curved toward the hillside to the right. Morgan struggled to keep her footing on the slippery trail. Her lungs burned as she gulped in cold air, her breath coming out in clouds. The trail crested at the top of the hill. The trampled path stretched across a wide, flat hilltop thinly populated with pine trees.

"There they go." Bernie pointed.

Runners disappeared over the far side of the hill.

Morgan tugged back the sleeve of her sweatshirt. "We've been walking at least fifteen minutes. We can't have far to go."

"I don't know," Bernie said. "It takes us twenty minutes at O'Reily's, and we only walk half of that 5K."

The loud rumble of an ATV engine sounded behind them. The driver slowed as he pulled alongside. In his puffy down jacket, Rolf made the oversized search and rescue ATV appear small.

"Hi, Morgan." He spoke loudly, to be heard over the idling engine. Exhaust fumes spewed into the crisp air. "You gals doing okay?"

"So far, so good," Bernie answered, "but ask me in another mile."

"Another?" Rolf said. "You haven't hit the first mile marker yet."

Bernie groaned.

He stuck out his glove-covered hand. "I'm Rolf."

Bernie grasped his hand. "Bernie Belmont."

"Of Bibi's Bakery?"

Bernie's green eyes sparkled. "The same!"

"I love your banana bread." Rolf patted the passenger seat. "You can ride with me."

"This is my first race ever," Bernie said. "I want to keep going."

"You're doing better than me," Rolf said. "I agreed to drive the ATV, but no way I'm running."

Morgan clamped her arms around her torso and shivered. "We'd better keep moving."

"See you at the finish line." Rolf sped ahead, the tires kicking up slushy snow.

They trudged across the hilltop, nearing the end of the flat area. Bernie told Morgan that she remembered seeing Rolf at the bakery, buying banana bread.

"He's such a nice guy," Bernie said. "One of the last true gentlemen."

While Bernie talked, Morgan watched the forest. Every movement put her on high alert, until she identified the culprit as a fluttering bird or scampering squirrel. Then she noticed something that didn't fit into the natural scenery and felt her jittery nerves justified. The chilly breeze whipped the tails of a long black coat against the tree trunk.

"Bernie, someone's hiding behind that tree."

"Don't point. It must be a guy who couldn't wait for the porta potty."

The cloak disappeared from view.

"I can't see him now." Morgan held on to Bernie's sleeve. "Slow down. I think he's watching us."

She unzipped the pack at her waist and fumbled for the pepper spray with mitten-covered hands.

"You think it's the man who attacked you on the bridge?" Bernie whispered.

"He's wearing the same kind of coat. I'm not taking any chances."

Morgan pulled off one mitten and held the spray canister in front of her. As she and Bernie crept closer to the tree, the sweepers caught up to them.

"You're doing great," the woman said in a cheery voice.

"We think there's a stalker behind that tree," Bernie said. "But don't worry. Morgan has pepper spray."

The man in the black coat stepped onto the trail. Morgan aimed the canister's nozzle toward him.

"Stop, or I'll shoot!"

The man jerked his hands up, letting his camera drop against his chest, where it dangled from a wide strap. Morgan realized he was wearing a full-length heavy black canvas western duster, not a cloak. If the short-haired, clean-shaven man had a tattoo, it would probably be something from his days in military service. He was definitely not the gargoyle type.

"Criminently, lady. Just tell me if you don't want your picture taken!"

Adrenaline abruptly drained from Morgan's body as she realized what she had nearly done. The sweepers each grabbed Morgan's arms. She sagged against the elderly couple. The man tugged the pepper spray gently out of her hand.

"It's just Harry, the race photographer," he said. "He's relatively harmless."

"Morgan's a little jumpy," Bernie said. "She was assaulted Thursday night."

The elderly woman wrapped an arm around Morgan's shoulders.

"You poor thing. Are you okay?"

"Morgan," Harry the photographer said. "You're the gal who found the Smith girl's body. I read about it in the newspaper. No wonder you're twitchy."

"I see runners," the elderly man said, pointing down the hill.

"We'd better get moving," the woman said, "before we cool off."

They started walking again, the sweepers hanging back, but following a little closer than they had before. The trail wound down the hill in tight switchbacks. The new running shoes did not grip the compacted snow as well as Morgan would have liked. She worked her way slowly down steep sections of trail.

She heard the runner an instant before she saw him. He raced around a curve, churning up a flurry of snow in his wake. Bernie squealed. Morgan jumped to the side of the trail, into powdery snow. The runner, a lean young man, flew past.

They watched him dash to the top of the hill in considerably less time than it had taken them to climb down. Another runner, this one older but just as fit, bolted around the curve. Then another.

"Oh," Morgan said. "Out-and-back. We go out, then turn around and come back."

"Then we must not have far to go, if they're coming back already."

Morgan and Bernie kept to the right side of the trail, walking single file when clusters of runners approached.

"One mile."

Bernie pointed to a hinged wooden sign that reminded Morgan of a "wet floor" placard. Propped up in the snow, bright yellow with red lettering, it announced Mile One.

"Only one mile?" Morgan checked her watch. "It took us twenty minutes to get this far?"

"Hills," Bernie said. "And snow. It's like wading through sand. I'll never complain about O'Reily's again."

Bright orange traffic cones guided runners to a folding table straddling the middle of the trail, blocking further travel. Rolf's ATV idled while he dumped a ten-gallon plastic container of water into the snow.

Warmly dressed volunteers held out paper cups with mitten-clad hands. Gerda appeared to be in charge, as usual. An enormous white quilted down coat enveloped her round figure.

"Great job," the volunteers yelled. "You're halfway. Water or sports drink?"

Discarded paper cups littered both sides of the trail.

Morgan accepted a half cup of yellow sports drink. She chugged down the syrupy liquid.

"You must drink something," Gerda told Bernie. "You will get dehydrated."

Apparently Gerda had been following her own advice, but it wasn't water or sports drink on her breath.

Bernie braced herself against the table. "I don't suppose you have a toilet?"

"Pee over there," Gerda said. "We won't look."

"None of those trees is wide enough to hide my backside."

Gerda rolled her eyes.

"We'd better keep moving," Morgan said.

"You made it to the aid station," one of the volunteers cried. "Halfway! You're gonna make it."

Their enthusiasm was annoying. When she and Bernie circled around the last orange cone and headed back, Morgan could overhear them.

"Were those the last ones?"

"Finally. I'm freezing. Let's pack up and get out of here."

The sweepers smiled as Morgan and Bernie passed.

"Good job," the woman said.

Heading back uphill, Morgan needed every breath just to keep placing one foot in front of the other.

They heard the ATV long before it appeared. Rolf had managed to load the table, water container, and Gerda onto the ATV. The two younger volunteers jogged behind. Rolf offered them a lift, and Morgan thought Bernie might take him up on it. She bravely turned him down, but Morgan could see the longing in her friend's eyes as the ATV rolled out of sight.

"You could have gone with Rolf," Morgan said. "I've still got the sweepers."

"I want to earn my T-shirt," Bernie said. "It took Amanda two months to be able to walk without assistance. I've got to do it for her."

The sweepers kept a respectful distance behind. Morgan was convinced the athletic seniors were holding back, not wanting to humiliate the slow ladies. She would have preferred that they stay in sight.

The walking became mindless for Morgan. One foot in front of the other. One more step, one more step, one more step.

"This looks familiar," Bernie said.

"It should all look familiar," Morgan said. "We're going back the same way we came."

"Well, of course. I meant I think we're getting close to the end."

The split-rail fence appeared through the trees and brush. Then the dirt parking lot. Then sidewalk, which felt heavenly under Morgan's tired feet. Finally they saw the park and the big digital timer.

"If we hurry, we can finish in under an hour," Morgan said.

"I can't move any faster," Bernie said. "I've given it all I've got. You go on without me."

"We started together. We're finishing together."

Volunteers and spectators cheered as they entered the park. Beatrice trotted alongside them.

"You made it! Good job!"

They had to walk single file across the finish line. Morgan and Bernie lost a few seconds arguing about who should go first, both insisting the other should have the honor. Bernie pushed Morgan ahead. Waist-high plastic poles strung with orange nylon rope funneled them through a narrow chute where volunteers tore off their bib tags.

"How was it?" Beatrice asked.

"Fantastic!" All the struggle and pain seemed to vanish in an instant as Bernie gushed about the experience.

"We came in last," Morgan said.

"That doesn't matter," Bernie said. "We finished!"

CHAPTER TWENTY-THREE

The next morning, Morgan was not as sore as she anticipated. What hurt the most were her inner thighs. She had worn blue jeans to the race, but they had caused serious chafing.

First running shoes and socks. Now she needed special running pants. Her accidental sport was becoming more expensive by the day.

Morgan didn't want to get out of bed, but she knew people would want a report on the Run for Amanda. After feeding the donkeys, Morgan showered and changed into going-to-church clothes.

New snow glistened on the church lawn. The sidewalks and parking lot had been cleared. Morgan parked close to the rear door in the half-empty lot. She entered through the kitchen, walking into the middle of a conversation about the murder. Beatrice was stuck on her theory about Dawn's drug problem.

"She was mixed up with druggies. Her boyfriend was a known addict. He might have been upset that she spoke to the police."

"But why kill her?" Anna asked. "Wouldn't it be better to be arrested for drugs than for murder?"

"Drug people aren't logical," Beatrice said with great authority. "They probably weren't thinking straight to begin with. Good morning, Morgan."

Morgan pulled off her coat and hung it over the back of a kitchen chair. "Good morning, everyone."

"Did you enjoy your race?" Teruko asked.

"It was hard," Morgan said. "But fun, too."

While she and Anna described the challenges of the slushy trail to the other ladies, the introit music began. The kitchen ladies headed for the sanctuary. Morgan was stunned by all the empty pews.

The distinctive red hair of Cindy and her family caught Morgan's eye. They took up most of a pew. Cindy and the girls wore denim jumpers over blue and white checked blouses. Herb and the boys had on western shirts in the same blue and white gingham.

Cindy waved when she saw Morgan.

"I'm going to sit with Cindy's family," she whispered to Beatrice. "I'll see you in the kitchen after the service."

She settled next to Cindy and grabbed a hymnal.

"Do you believe all these people?" Cindy waved a hand around at the empty seats, presumably indicating the people who weren't there. "They're so quick to believe a lie."

"Maybe people overreacted," Morgan said. "But not everyone knows the pastor like you do."

"Whatever happened to 'innocent until proven guilty'?" Herb grumbled.

The choir stood. The first hymn invoked faith in the face of adversity. Morgan suspected that would be the theme of Golden Springs Community Church for many months to come.

When the guest pastor took his place behind the podium, a new situation occurred to Morgan: A jealous younger preacher seeks to discredit Pastor Filbury, who seems to have no intention of retiring, in order to assume the position as leader of the congregation.

Then there was the enraged congregant theory. Someone caught wind of Dawn's accusation, and decided to eliminate the accuser. That implied a certain amount of doubt that the pastor would be able to beat the charges.

What if Dawn's accusation and her murder were unrelated events? Suppose Beatrice was right, and someone put Dawn up to accusing the pastor, but her druggie friends didn't appreciate her involvement with the police, resulting in her death?

Morgan ran through her other theories. She had crossed off the stranger-in-the-park from her list because the autopsy had revealed no signs of sexual assault. Of course, Morgan might have walked up on them before the assault could be accomplished. Barton could have caught the girl digging in his topaz mine. He as much as admitted that he would shoot anyone trespassing on his claim. Except the girl hadn't been shot. Finally, she considered that Piers might have put Dawn up to accusing the pastor so he could pass his zoning ordinance. If anything, that would eliminate him as a murder suspect. He would have wanted Dawn alive and pressing her case against Pastor Filbury.

It seemed a dark curtain was drawn across the entire situation. But the more she considered the possibilities, the more she thought Beatrice might be right.

Morgan needed more information about Dawn's boyfriend.

The opportunity to question Beatrice didn't arise until after the coffee cups were loaded in the dishwasher, and Anna left to drive Teruko home.

"Beatrice, when I came in this morning, you were talking about Dawn Smith's boyfriend."

"Oh, yes. The young man Dawn was living with was involved with drugs." Beatrice sorted the pile of clean silverware on the counter. The utensils chimed musically as she dropped them in their proper drawers. "So was she."

"Did the boyfriend have an alibi?"

"The police haven't been able to find him."

Morgan sat down hard on a kitchen chair.

"She had a boyfriend," Morgan asked, "and he's missing?"

"The police rounded up all the known members of that group of druggies. They claimed they didn't know where the boy was. That he disappeared the same time she did."

"So he might have killed her," Morgan said.

"Could be." Beatrice closed the spoon drawer.

"Or the gang might have killed him and Dawn." Morgan clasped her hands in her lap. "Are they from Golden Springs?"

"Oh, no," Beatrice said with assurance. "People here wouldn't put up with that kind of thing for long. They congregate at General Minton Park. You know, in downtown Granite Junction?"

"I know where that is," Morgan said.

She walked past it every Tuesday night.

People had been driving since the snowstorm, marking their comings and goings in the gravel road. Morgan followed tire tracks up Hill Street. One set of tracks continued to the houses farther up the road. Another turned into the Rock of Ages parking lot. Her tracks led to the carriage house garage. A new set of tire tracks had made a loop, passing close to the short, scrubby trees on the north side of the Rock of Ages parking lot. The vehicle was gone now.

Someone lost, Morgan thought. They had used the rock shop parking lot to turn around.

The melting snow made a mess of the parking lot. Her dress shoes would not survive mushing across the mud from the garage, and she only had one pair left. The left shoe from the other pair she had brought to Golden Springs had been lost in the creek the night she had been attacked. Morgan parked in front of the shop. She dug in her purse for the key.

She wouldn't need it. The door was ajar. Cindy had the day off, and Del wasn't due until later. Morgan felt her heart pounding as she pushed the door open and looked inside.

"Hello?"

Her dress shoes echoed on the pine floor. Morgan slipped out of them and held them in one hand. She tiptoed, creeping down the aisles. She doubted the effectiveness of her low-heeled shoes as weapons, and pulled Del's pepper spray out of her purse.

The door to the living quarters stood open. Morgan peeked inside. Del blocked the kitchen door. Cold air flowed across the open threshold.

"What are you doing?" Morgan asked.

Del spun around, his hand going to the holster strapped under his vest. Morgan dropped her shoes with a clatter and ducked back behind the door to the shop.

"Morgan, you scared the crap out of me."

"How do you think I feel?" She peered around the door. "What's going on?"

Del stepped away from the kitchen door. The pane of glass nearest the doorknob was broken. Shards of glass lay on the linoleum.

"Someone broke in?" Morgan slipped her shoes on and walked closer.

"I heard Houdini and Adelaide braying," Del said. "I thought maybe you'd forgotten to feed them before you went to church. I walked down to the barn, and saw a strange vehicle in the parking lot. But it was off to the side, like they didn't want anyone to see them. I might not have seen it if it was spring and there were leaves on the trees."

"Did you see who it was?" Morgan grabbed the empty coffee carafe.

"No. They took off when they saw me coming."

"What kind of car was it?"

"A black SUV. Never saw anything like it before. If I'm not

mistaken, it had the Mercedes logo, but I didn't think Mercedes was in the SUV business."

"It sounds like the car that almost ran over me last week."

Morgan's hand shook as she filled the carafe. Water spilled down its sides.

"Why would someone in a Mercedes break into the rock shop?" Morgan poured water in the coffeemaker and set the carafe on its stand. "Unless they were after the triceratops horn!"

Morgan ran through the shop. The display case was secure, the horn resting in its nest of southwest-patterned cloth.

She returned to the kitchen, where Del was tapping short nails through a rectangle of plywood over the hole.

"I'll fix this right when I get to town for a pane of glass," he said.

"I'm not so sure I want a glass window in the door," Morgan said.

Del closed the door and locked it.

"We'll talk security later," he said.

"Did you call the police?"

Del accepted a mug of coffee from Morgan. She opened the refrigerator.

"I didn't have time during the incident," Del said, "but I did call afterwards."

Morgan paused, a bag of bagels in her hand. "Incident?"

"I caught the burglar in the act," Del said proudly.

"Del, you could have been hurt." Morgan turned, clutching the cream cheese in one hand. "Or killed."

"Houdini got to the burglar first. That donkey is better than a watch dog." Del pointed to a scrap of black cloth lying on the kitchen table. "He got a mouthful of the guy's coat. I gave half to Chief Sharp, but I saved some for you."

"What is it?" Morgan sat at the table.

"Evidence. But I'll get to that part. When I came in to the

kitchen, the son of a gun had broken out the glass and had his arm stuck through the empty pane. I grabbed his arm and pulled the door open."

"He could have had a gun."

"I admit, I wasn't thinking clearly," Del said. "I just couldn't see the point of turning and running when he was at a disadvantage like that. Plus he had Houdini at his backside, with a mouthful of coat." Del picked up the scrap of cloth and tossed it to Morgan. "You'd think we had him hemmed up enough. But he got away."

Morgan touched the cloth. The girl had worn a black coat. It had made an impression on Morgan of being too thin to provide protection against the cold. Like this material.

"As I recall, the girl had a tattoo on her neck," Del said. "Do you remember what it looked like?"

"You saw it, too."

"Tell me again."

Morgan spread cream cheese on a bagel. "It looked like a gargoyle. A monster with wings."

Del nodded. "The intruder had a tattoo on his forearm. It looked the same as the one on the girl."

"Beatrice said the girl had a boyfriend. Maybe that was him. What did he look like?"

Del took a bite of his bagel. "Oh, no." He wiped his mustache with a paper napkin. "I don't want you going out there looking for the guy. He might be the killer."

"I just want to ask Beatrice," Morgan said. "See if it's the same guy."

"I'll probably regret this." Del shook his head. "He was dark skinned, but not real dark." Del pointed at Morgan's coffee, heavily dosed with cream. "About like that."

"Was he African-American?" Morgan asked. "Hispanic?"

"African-American," Del said. "He was medium build,

medium height. What stood out was the tattoo and his hair. He had long ropes of hair. Looked like snakes."

"Dreadlocks?" Morgan asked.

Del nodded. "If that's what you call them."

"Beatrice said Dawn and her boyfriend were involved with drugs," Morgan said. "He might have been trying to rob us."

"With a Mercedes for a getaway car?" Del asked. "And why not go rob one of the houses farther up the hill? Why us?"

"I don't know."

"Maybe he thinks you saw the murder," Del said.

Morgan tried to swallow, but the bagel seemed caught in her throat. She gulped coffee.

"I'm moving in to the guest room for a few nights," Del said. "And you need to start carrying this."

He pulled his handgun out of its holster and pushed it across the table toward Morgan.

"Del, I can't carry a gun. I haven't fired one in ten years." Morgan pushed the gun back toward Del. It was heavy, and the metal was cold. "But you're welcome to stay in the guest room."

She wasn't ready to admit how comforting it would be to share the small house with another person.

The bell above the shop door sounded.

"Maybe it's the police," Del said. "They might have caught the guy already."

It was only a customer.

The sign at Gerda's worked better than any of them had anticipated. On Monday, Morgan called Cindy and asked her to come to work. Most of the customers were locals, checking out the new management and prying for details about the murder. They were far from making the kind of profit that would enable Morgan to pay the property taxes, but she decided Del and Cindy deserved a reward for their enthusiasm and hard work.

"I'm getting lunch from Bibi's," she said, when they had a lull. "What do you want?"

After calling in the order, Morgan grabbed her coat.

"You should take the car," Del said. "After that attack Wednesday night, and then that kid trying to break into the shop Sunday, I don't think it's safe for you to walk by yourself."

"Did I miss something?" Cindy asked.

"I'll fill you in later," Del said.

"I'll take Houdini," Morgan said. "You told me he's better than a watchdog."

"Then let me hitch them both to the wagon."

Del followed Morgan to the barn. The donkeys trotted into their stall, probably hoping for oats. They seemed just as pleased when Del hitched them to the cart. He unhooked a buckle, lengthening a strap on Adelaide's harness.

"I think we need to get the vet out here," he said. "If she wasn't so old, I'd suspect this girl was carrying a foal."

"Pregnant?" Morgan asked. "What are the chances of that?"

Del patted Adelaide's side. "You're probably right. It's just a case of too many oats." He opened the barn door. "Be careful, Morgan."

"I'll be fine with my trusty steeds at my side."

Hill Street was not nearly as wet as the previous day. Roads dried out fast after a snow, especially when the sun shone bright and clear. Adelaide was lively enough going downhill.

Morgan kept alert for gargoyles, magpies, and a black Mercedes, but nothing more threatening than a flock of finches disturbed their walk. Morgan wondered if life would ever return to normal.

When they reached the corner of Hill and Main, a car stopped. The window of the green Subaru lowered, and a man wearing a wool ski cap leaned out.

"Can I take a picture of your donkeys?"

Houdini and Adelaide were happy to pose. Two more carloads of skiers stopped Morgan for photos. When the tourists left, Piers stepped outside his shop. Morgan held up a plastic trash bag and shovel.

"I promise I'll clean up after them," she said.

"Your donkeys are quite the attention getter. And the cart. You couldn't do better with a billboard."

The sides and back end of the colorful cart were emblazoned with "Rock of Ages fossils, rocks, and curios"—the phone number, and directions—"north on Hill Street."

"I think they're enjoying the attention."

Piers walked down the wooden steps. He rubbed Adelaide's neck with skilled fingers. Apparently he didn't fear contamination from a donkey's aura.

"You are a beautiful creature," he whispered in Adelaide's ear. "When you're not eating my flowers."

Morgan wondered how she could have imagined the gentle healer would maliciously release the donkeys to run wild in the streets. He clearly loved animals. Unless this was just a ploy to get to Morgan, and her land, through the donkeys. After all, he had convinced City Council to pass an ordinance banning livestock.

"After your encounter in the park," Piers said, "I recommend therapeutic massage."

"I'm okay," Morgan said.

"Your very being exudes tension." He returned his attention to Adelaide, whose blissful expression seemed a good advertisement for Piers's skills as a masseur. "Have you considered my dinner invitation?"

"I don't think they serve hay in any of the local restaurants," Morgan said.

Piers laughed. "Although this gentle creature might prove to be a delightful dinner companion, especially for a vegan vegetarian like myself, I was referring to the invitation I extended to you several days ago."

Piers turned the full intensity of his blue eyes on Morgan. She wanted her reply to be casual, but she feared she would stammer and make a fool of herself. Again.

"Oh. Um. What day were you thinking?"

"Would this Friday be agreeable?" Piers asked.

"I think Friday is open," Morgan said.

Piers pressed the palms of his hands together and bowed. "Excellent. May I pick you up at the rock shop? Perhaps six-ish?"

Morgan was not about to climb into the car of anyone on her suspect list until the murder was solved. Even going to a public restaurant was probably foolish.

"Can I meet you in town?" Morgan asked. "I might be running errands anyway."

"Certainly. Let's meet at the Hot Tomato at six-thirty. They serve vegan dishes as well as more traditional fare."

"Okay." Morgan shook the donkeys' reins. "I'll see you then."

The cart rolled up Main Street. Morgan felt quite pleased with herself. She tried not to think about Piers's plan to run the Rock of Ages out of business and rezone the hill. Maybe she wasn't destined to spend the rest of her life alone. The twinge of guilt she felt at betraying Sam's memory subsided with the realization that she wouldn't have wanted him to remain alone if the situation were reversed.

The sun was shining. The air was crisp and clear, the sky a stunning shade of cornflower blue. Morgan clung to the soaring optimism filling her spirit. Until reality intruded on her carefully constructed fantasy.

She was going on a date with a man who might be a murderer.

CHAPTER TWENTY-FOUR

Morgan looped the donkeys' reins around the hitching post outside Bibi's Bakery and went inside. Bernie's jaunty pink and white striped chef's hat bobbed above the pastry display case. Morgan waited in line, happy to see her friend so busy.

Finally it was her turn at the counter. "We're here to pick up our order," Morgan said.

"We?" Bernie looked around the bakery.

"Me and the donkeys," Morgan said. "I thought I'd better leave them outside."

Bernie laughed. "Yes, that was probably a good idea."

"Call me later," Morgan said. "I want to run something by you."

Morgan paid for her order and left. She told herself there had been no time to tell Bernie about her dinner date with Piers.

Adelaide plodded slowly back uphill. Morgan climbed out of the cart and tugged on the reins.

"Come on, girl. Lunch will be stale by the time we get home."

When they reached the Rock of Ages, two cars sat in the parking lot. More customers. One of them had stopped to take photos of the donkeys in town earlier.

"I guess you're not totally worthless," Morgan told the donkeys.

★ ★ ★ ★ ★

Bernie called late in the afternoon.

"Hang on." Morgan carried the cordless phone into the office and closed the door. She didn't want Del to catch wind of her plan.

"What's up?" Bernie asked.

"Beatrice told me yesterday that the murdered girl had a boyfriend. The police have been looking for him so they can question him, but he's nowhere to be found."

"Interesting," Bernie said.

"Then yesterday, when I got home from church, Del was repairing the back door. Someone tried to break in."

"Who would be silly enough to break into the rock shop?" Bernie asked. "Especially with Del around?"

"Del said the man had a tattoo on his forearm. It sounded like the same tattoo the girl had on her neck."

"Uh-oh."

"Beatrice said the boyfriend's buddies hang around downtown Granite Junction, in General Minton Park."

"That's where all the teenage druggies hang out," Bernie said.

"I'm thinking of going there tonight—"

"What?" Bernie asked, disapproval thick in the one word.

"I want to see if Dawn's boyfriend is hanging around the park. Or someone who knows him."

"Morgan, are you crazy?"

"I'm going to be crazy if the police don't solve the murder soon."

"If you and Del are right, the guy tried to break into the rock shop. He might have committed murder. What are you planning to do? Make a citizen's arrest?"

"If he's there, I'll call the police." Morgan hesitated. "I can't tell Del about this, but I wanted somebody to know what I'm doing, in case, you know, I don't make it back."

Bernie was silent for so long, Morgan thought she'd lost the connection.

"Hello?"

"I volunteer at the soup kitchen," Bernie said. "I know some of the street people. I don't think you have a clue what kind of people hang around the park. I have to go with you."

"I'm not asking you to go—"

"Stop. I'm not trying to talk you out of this, so don't you try to talk me out of coming with you."

"Thanks, Bernie. I really appreciate this."

Bernie sighed. "I must be as crazy as you."

Bernie insisted on driving. Her SUV would be more reliable if they had to make a quick escape.

"Before we go to the park," Bernie said, "I want to talk to Mrs. Calloway."

Morgan walked beside Bernie through the streets of Granite Junction. Some were familiar from their Tuesday night O'Reily's outings.

"I hope she's around," Bernie said. "Some of the homeless people migrate to warmer climates in the winter."

Bernie boldly walked into a dimly lighted alley that was surprisingly tidy and clear of trash. An elderly lady leaned over the edge of a dumpster, lifting out plastic trash bags and placing them on the ground.

"Hello, Mrs. Calloway."

The lady looked up, startled. She smiled as she recognized Bernie. "Hello, honey!" She lifted a to-go container out of the dumpster. "They know me here. They leave me some special treats." She opened the container, revealing an untouched sandwich. "I don't tell nobody, but I trust you, Miss Bernie."

The lady shuffled toward them. Morgan could smell unwashed body and cheap liquor over the rotted food stench of the dumpster. Mrs. Calloway wore a remarkably clean men's tweed jacket, several sizes too large, over soiled pink sweatpants. Filthy gloves covered her hands. A tangle of matted gray hair spilled out from under a baby-blue wool cap decorated with the remnants of iridescent white spangles. She had the ruddy complexion of a longtime alcoholic.

Mrs. Calloway glared at Morgan. Bernie rested a hand on Morgan's arm.

"This is my friend. She won't take your food."

Mrs. Calloway smiled. She was missing four front teeth.

Morgan was anxious for information, but Bernie took her time, engaging the old woman in conversation. Mrs. Calloway perched on the edge of a concrete step and devoured her meal.

Finally, Bernie got down to business.

"You know a lot of people."

"Yes." Mrs. Calloway rocked back and forth. "Lots of people. I got lots of friends."

"Do any of them have tattoos?"

"Lots of people have them tattoos nowadays. It's the thing now. Like people don't think they're pretty, so they want pretty pictures on their skin."

"And sometimes not so pretty," Bernie said.

"Like maybe a monster?" Morgan asked. "With wings?"

Mrs. Calloway frowned at Morgan. "Birds have wings," she said slowly. "People like birds on them. All kind of birds. Eagles, mostly." She threw her arms in the air, releasing a cloud of funk that nearly knocked Morgan down. "A firebird! All in flames!"

"We're looking for a man," Morgan said.

"They make them tattoos with needles, you know."

"I know," Bernie said. "That's why I won't get one. But some people like tattoos. They get birds tattooed on their arms, or even their necks."

"I know some people say I'm not quite right in the head." Mrs. Calloway cackled. "But sticking a needle in your neck for no good reason, now that's crazy!"

"Have you ever seen a man with wings on his arm, and a girl with the same kind of wings on her neck?"

Mrs. Calloway looked away. "People with wings on them, they get flighty, like a bird." She glanced at Bernie. "You know how a flock of pigeons does when they're on the sidewalk and you walk through them?" Mrs. Calloway raised both arms again. "Whoosh! A lots of feathers! And they all fly away at once!"

"Sure," Bernie said. "I've seen them do that."

"That's the way those people with the wings are. Jumpy. Flying off at the least little thing. You got to be careful around those kind of people. You understand?"

"I'll be extra careful around the people with the wings," Bernie said.

"You never know what they'll do. Peck your eyes out if you give them the chance." She grabbed Bernie's coat sleeve with her filthy gloves. "Don't give them a chance, Miss Bernie," she wailed. "You're one of the only folks around here who treats me right. I'd hate myself forever if anything bad happened to you."

"I don't want to run into them by accident." Bernie paused. "Can you tell me where they are?"

"They come out at night," Mrs. Calloway whispered. "They like those benches in the park. The ones under the trees." She continued in a louder voice. "I like those benches in the summertime. The trees are shady when it's hot. But this time of year, you don't want shade, because it's just cold everywhere."

"Why aren't you in the shelter tonight?" Bernie asked.

"They won't let you in if you smell of liquor." Mrs. Calloway looked sheepish. "I didn't even have hardly any at all. The bottle spilled, see." She pointed to a grease stain on her pink sweatpants. "So they won't give me a bed."

Bernie extended a hand to Mrs. Calloway and helped the old woman stand.

"A cup of coffee might warm you up," Bernie said.

Mrs. Calloway shook her head. "They won't let me in those fancy coffee shops."

"I'll get you something," Bernie said.

Morgan's patience was stretched thin while she waited outside the coffee shop with Mrs. Calloway. Bernie purchased a huge to-go cup of coffee with lots of milk and sugar. Morgan could see her selecting what looked like one of everything from the pastry display. Bernie made certain Mrs. Calloway drank half the coffee and ate a pastry before they left her.

They crossed a street and stood at the edge of General Minton Park. Bernie leaned her backside against a low concrete wall.

"If your burglar is here, he's with those people."

The group huddled on the benches under bare tree branches, just as Mrs. Calloway had said they would.

"I don't know, Bernie. There are quite a few of them."

One of the dark-clothed figures stood and drifted across the dead grass.

"He's coming toward us," Morgan whispered.

"He probably thinks we came here to buy drugs," Bernie whispered back.

"Us?" Morgan hissed.

"Sure. This is where people come to find a drug connection."

The tall, thin young man looked like a wraith, his face pale. His black cloak fanned out behind him, reminding Morgan of the wings she'd seen fluttering over Dawn's body. Silver rings protruded from his eyebrows, nose, and lips. He shoved his hands deep in the pockets of his worn jeans and drifted past.

"Hey," he said.

Bernie nudged Morgan with her elbow.

"Hello," Morgan said.

He walked past them. Morgan turned to watch. Other young people mingled with the street people, sitting on the cold ground, bundled in blankets on park benches, or drifting about like ships that had slipped their moorings.

"It's a garden of lost souls," Morgan whispered.

The wraith made a loop around the park, then returned. When he passed them this time, Morgan lifted her hand and gave a quick, discreet wave. He wandered close, looking across the park, not directly at her.

"Need something?" he asked.

"Yes," Morgan said. "I'm looking for someone."

"Can't help you. We don't hunt down runaways."

"She's not looking for her kid," Bernie said. "We're looking for a guy."

"Do you know someone with a tattoo of a gargoyle on his forearm?" Morgan asked. "He has dreadlocks. I need to talk to him."

"I'll see what I can do."

The spectral young man returned to the park benches under the bare tree branches. He spoke to the others. One by one, two by two, they drifted away from the bench and out of the park.

"They're leaving," Bernie said. "I'll bet your burglar was with them."

"Should we call the police?" Morgan asked.

"No. If he was here, he's gone now." Bernie sighed. "And he knows we're looking for him. We might as well go home."

As they left the park, Morgan felt defeated.

"Every time I think I'm getting close to finding answers," Morgan said, "I find more questions instead."

They walked the rest of the way to the parking lot in silence. When they were inside the SUV, with the doors locked, Bernie turned to Morgan.

221

"The kids in the park," she said, "they're not the typical troubled teens, you know. They think they have nothing to lose. Until we know who broke in and why, I'd feel better if you moved in with me and Mr. Whiskers."

"Thanks for the offer," Morgan said. "Del is already staying in the guest room for just that reason."

"Good."

Bernie started the SUV and headed away from downtown.

"We can skip O'Reily's tomorrow if you want to," Bernie said.

"I can't let a little thing like murder stop me from having a pint with my friends."

CHAPTER TWENTY-FIVE

Morgan was relieved that Del didn't wait up for her. His steady snoring was muffled by the closed guest-room door. She had dreaded the questions she was sure he would ask about her evening out. By morning, she had invented a story that was mostly not a lie. If a half-truth would save the old cowboy some anxiety, Morgan was willing to fudge the facts.

Business was slow Tuesday. Del went to his trailer to watch TV. Morgan worked on the books. As she entered data, questions kept coming to mind about motivation.

Everyone believed that Piers was buying up local businesses. He was accused of manipulating City Council to pass zoning ordinances to facilitate his plan. Were the complaints a case of sour grapes, because Piers had the drive to achieve his goals and the resultant success? Or was there an actual conspiracy and corruption, possibly resulting in murder? Morgan only knew the story circulating through the gossip grapevine. She needed to get to the source.

When Cindy arrived, Morgan grabbed her coat and gloves.

"I'm going to town," Morgan said. "Do you need me to pick up anything for you?"

"No, thanks." Cindy grabbed a catalog and hiked herself onto the stool behind the cash register.

"You've got my cell number," Morgan said.

"Sure, cowgirl, assuming the phone works."

★ ★ ★ ★ ★

The offices of the *Golden Springs Gazetteer* were as quirky as Morgan had expected. Old typesetting trays hung from the walls. Yellowed front pages framed in rustic styles announced major historical events.

Anna sat at the receptionist's desk, her fingers dancing rapidly across the keyboard of her computer. Her sophisticated look, complete with power suit, seemed more at home in a Fortune 500 company than a small-town newspaper.

"Hi, Anna. Is Kurt around?"

"He's in his office." She pointed the way. "I'll let him know you're coming."

The top half of the Dutch door to Kurt's office was open. Kurt sat at an impressive oak desk scarred with use. His brown leather trench coat and fedora hung on a wooden coat rack. The sleeves of his white cotton shirt were rolled up to his elbows. An antique typewriter occupied his attention.

Morgan knocked on the doorframe. "Hello."

Kurt set down a screwdriver and stood. "Welcome. Come on in." He opened the bottom half of the door. "Make yourself at home."

Seeing him in his natural environment made the 1940s reporter persona seem not quite so ridiculous.

"We're putting together our annual business directory. It's distributed free to local hotels and—"

"I'm not here to discuss advertising." Morgan perched on a leather upholstered chair. "I need to know who gave you the information in your special edition."

Kurt leaned back in his chair, the old leather creaking.

"I can't reveal a confidential source."

"What if your source tried to kill me?"

"The man on the bridge?"

"So you've heard what happened?"

"I would have attempted an interview," Kurt said, "but you seem to have an aversion to the press."

"Maybe if I thought you were more interested in digging up the truth than in selling advertising, I might have more reason to talk to you."

"I'm sensing some hostility."

"Someone might be trying to kill me, Kurt."

She told him about the assault, not caring whether he printed the details in his newspaper. When she described the man, with his goatee and gargoyle tattoo, Kurt frowned, tapping his pencil against his notepad.

"Is he your source?" Morgan asked. "You know the guy, don't you?"

Kurt met her eyes. "I spoke to my source on the phone. I don't know what he looks like."

Morgan slumped back in her seat.

"You could have told me that," she said.

"You didn't ask."

Kurt picked up the screwdriver and fiddled with the side of the clunky black typewriter. Morgan was convinced he knew more, but it was obvious the topic was closed. For now.

"To change subjects," Morgan said, "do you keep copies of the City Council meeting minutes?"

"Yes, and my own notes. But the official minutes are filed at City Hall."

"I went there first," Morgan said. "I don't have a specific date in mind, and the clerk wasn't going to let me browse. I just want to familiarize myself with the issues."

Kurt looked up and smiled. "Let me guess. You want to learn about the rezoning initiative."

"Of course I'm interested in the rezoning," Morgan said. "It would negatively affect the rock shop."

"I don't see it that way at all." Kurt picked up an oilcan and

225

applied drops of oil in strategic spots. "If anything, rezoning the hill would increase the value of your property."

"But making the area solely residential would put us out of business," Morgan said. "What use would an increase in the value of the land be if we couldn't make a living with it?"

"If you sold it—"

"That's the point," Morgan said. "Maybe I don't want to sell. What if you were in my position, and someone was trying to force you out of your newspaper business?"

"No one's forcing you to do anything." Kurt set down the oilcan and wiped his hands on a cloth. "Are they?"

"I've heard that Piers Townsend has bought up half of Main Street."

Kurt frowned. "I suppose he has the right."

"That's what I thought, too, until I realized he's after the rock shop."

"There are several businessmen interested in rezoning your property. But people in Golden Springs constantly seek rezoning, from residential to business and back again, to suit their interests of the moment. City Council is notoriously slow to make changes, unless the interested party can prove a need benefiting the community."

"Suppose someone had friends on City Council," Morgan said. "They might be swayed to vote to benefit him."

"Now wait a minute! One industrious businessman does not equal a conspiracy."

"I heard that Pastor Filbury led the opposition to Piers's plan," Morgan said. "Then he gets discredited by a girl who ends up dead. Am I the only one who sees a connection?"

Kurt picked up the screwdriver. He rolled the handle between his hands. "You've given me speculation and gossip, not facts."

"If you're not interested, can you help me get started on my own investigation?" Morgan asked.

"You're welcome to read anything that's public record."

"Can I make copies of the Council minutes?"

"Don't bother with that," Kurt said. "Save a tree or two. I can burn copies on a thumb drive."

"A what?"

"Thumb drive." Kurt unplugged a small metal rectangle from a port on his computer.

"Oh, a memory stick. I don't have one on me."

"I'll lend you one." Kurt rummaged around in a desk drawer. "Anna spends a lot of time converting paper files to electronic. Otherwise we'd be buried in paper." Kurt plugged the memory stick into a port. "Where did she put that folder?" He rolled his mouse across a pad decorated with letters in a variety of type fonts. "Here it is. City Council minutes. How many years back do you want to go?"

After an afternoon perusing dry Council minutes, Morgan was ready to have fun. Del double-checked the fanny pack to make sure she was prepared for any emergency.

"You need an upgrade before going to O'Reily's," he said.

He pushed his handgun across the kitchen table toward Morgan. She pulled her hands away to avoid touching the weapon.

"I can't take your gun," she said. "You might need it here."

"You're the one going walking in the dark," Del said. "In the city."

Morgan was glad she hadn't told Del the truth about her excursion with Bernie to downtown Granite Junction the previous night. He might have insisted they drive an armored car.

"The burglar broke into the shop," Morgan said. "Nothing has happened in Granite Junction."

Del tugged at his mustache. "Well, okay. You've got the pepper spray?"

"Got it."

Morgan was spared further fuss when Bernie pulled up.

Lucy and her family beat them back to the pub again. Morgan and Bernie worked their way through the crowd to Lucy's group. Chuck, Vonne, and another couple sat on benches at the long wooden table.

Before Morgan and Bernie could get seated, Lucy handed fliers to both of them.

"Oh, no," Bernie said. "I'm not racing again until I stop hurting from Saturday."

"No running," Lucy said. "No walking either. I need volunteers to run aid stations for the Hopping Bunny Snowshoe race."

"What exactly does that involve?" Bernie asked.

"Exactly freezing your buns off," Chuck said.

"It's hard enough getting volunteers for events without you making cracks." Vonne slapped him lightly on the arm. "You just hand out water to people as they run by," she told Bernie.

"Like Gerda did at the Run for Amanda?" Bernie asked. "It was cold Saturday."

"You dress for the weather," Lucy said. "It's a fundraiser, like the Run for Amanda. Proceeds go to Pine County Search and Rescue. And Morgan, since you know CPR, you'd be a great help."

Morgan had not been able to use CPR the one time she'd been in a situation requiring it.

"And we don't have to walk?" Bernie asked.

"Bernie," Chuck said, "don't you see what's happening? You're getting volunteered."

"That's the way it is with Lucy," Paul said. "You get sucked into her vortex. I ought to know. I'm the assistant volunteer coordinator. How'd that happen, you might ask?"

"You men stop it," Vonne said.

"You volunteered," Lucy said to Paul. "Don't lie. You wanted the shirt."

Paul shrugged. "It's a pretty nice shirt."

Bernie's green eyes sparkled. "We get a shirt?"

"A special volunteer shirt," Paul said, "with long sleeves."

"Sign me up!" Bernie bounced up and down on the bench. "I love my Run for Amanda shirt. Morgan, you'll go, won't you?"

"Can't you just buy a shirt?" Morgan asked.

"You have to earn it," Paul said.

"I've always seen people wearing race shirts," Bernie said. "It seemed like they were part of a special cool club. I've never been athletic. I didn't think I'd ever have a race shirt of my own."

"Oh, that's so sweet," Vonne said, dabbing at her eyes with a paper napkin.

Clothes did make a person part of a club. Morgan thought about the kids in the park. They wore the same dark clothing, tattoos, and piercings. Morgan imagined that badge of belonging had a lot of appeal to teenagers.

"So are you in, Morgan?" Lucy asked.

"That's a week and a half away. I don't know if I'll still be here."

Morgan looked around the table, at the expectant expressions on her new friends' faces.

"Okay. I'm in."

CHAPTER TWENTY-SIX

The next morning, Del accepted the car keys from Morgan. His mustache drooped.

"I'll get that old truck fixed soon," he said. "Or replace it. I can't keep borrowing your car."

"We have to look out for each other," Morgan said. "You'd do the same for me, I'm sure."

She lifted the lid of the slow cooker on the kitchen counter and stirred the chili.

"It's a wasted trip," Del said. "That's what makes me mad. Doc Drewmoore says I need tests with a specialist in Granite Junction."

"What does he think's wrong with you?" Morgan asked.

Del thumped a fist against his chest. "Heart. Blood pressure. Cholesterol. You name it. He wants me to take a bunch of pills, but I feel fine."

Morgan tasted the chili. She stirred in more chili powder, then placed the lid back on the slow cooker. "You need to follow your doctor's orders," she said. "I want to keep you around. You're my bodyguard."

"That's another thing. I don't want to be gone too long. What if the burglar comes back?" Del unbuckled the shoulder holster under his leather vest. "I'm leaving this with you."

He pulled the revolver out of its holster and placed it on the kitchen table.

"Del, don't leave that here."

"You'll be defenseless if that burglar comes back." He pointed at the wood patch on the kitchen door. "He almost got in once. He might make it next time."

"I haven't handled a gun in years," Morgan said. "I probably wouldn't remember how to shoot."

"You don't need to shoot," Del said. "Just convince the burglar that you will if you need to."

Morgan picked up the handgun, feeling a little rush of adrenalin at the feel of the textured grip in her hand. It was smaller than she expected, but heavier, too.

"Is it loaded?"

"Do you remember how to check?" Del asked.

"Not really."

"Here's how it works."

Del gave Morgan a quick review of handgun safety. He left before she could change her mind. Morgan placed the gun in the towel drawer near the kitchen sink and went into the shop. Perched on the stool behind the cash register, she thumbed through the western goods catalog.

When she got Internet service, she would place the order online. Morgan circled items with an oversized green highlighter.

Something caught the periphery of Morgan's vision. Movement outside the shop windows. She looked up. There were no cars in the parking lot. Maybe Del hadn't latched the gate correctly. It had to be Houdini and Adelaide, running loose.

Sliding off the stool, she moved to the front door and stared through the glass panes. The donkeys trotted along the far side of the pasture fence. They were secure. Moving in a hurry toward the garage, but on the correct side of the fence.

She opened the door and looked around.

"You're being silly," she told herself.

Morgan headed to the office, determined to do something

constructive.

A loud cracking noise stopped her in her tracks. She knew the sound in an instant. Splintering wood.

One part of Morgan's brain insisted she run out the front door of the shop. The nearest neighbor was a half mile up the road, and there was no guarantee they were home.

Fighting the instinct to put distance between herself and the noise, Morgan ran to the kitchen and yanked open the towel drawer. She grasped the handgun with both hands.

The wood patch dangled from one twisted nail. Morgan watched the hole, expecting a hand to reach through to unlatch the door. She picked up the phone. The line was dead. Had it been cut, or was it the usual unreliable service?

An unholy racket erupted outside the door. The donkeys brayed like they were being skinned alive. A trash can crashed across the paving stones.

Morgan threw open the door, ready to defend Houdini and Adelaide from whatever horror they faced.

A man crouched beside the wall of the house. He raised his hands in front of his face, protecting himself from Houdini's wrath. Morgan was certain he was the burglar Del had described. Ropes of matted brown hair hung over brown hands. He wasn't dressed for the weather, his lean frame covered in black jeans and motorcycle boots, and a long-sleeved black turtleneck sweater. Classic cat burglar costume, Morgan thought.

Houdini turned his backside to the burglar and kicked. Adelaide continued braying, either in alarm, or cheering Houdini on. Morgan wasn't sure which. The donkey's hooves made contact with the wall, knocking loose a wood shingle. The next kick hit the young man in the side.

"Uff!"

The man fell to his hands and knees. Morgan could see his

face now. He was young, his handsome face marred slightly by acne scars. One silver ring decorated his right eyebrow. Brown hoof marks clearly stamped his black sweater. If Houdini repeated his effort, he might kick the burglar in the head.

"Houdini!" Morgan called. "Back off!"

The donkey raised one back leg and threatened, then planted his hoof on the ground with a thump. He snorted.

"Good boy." Morgan's hands shook as she aimed the gun at the burglar. "Get up."

He looked at Morgan, his brown eyes growing large as he focused on the gun in her hand.

"Stand up." Morgan wished her voice would stop trembling. "Raise your hands."

Houdini turned around and faced the young man. He pulled his lips back in a donkey snarl, baring his long yellow teeth.

"Your donkey has rabies," the burglar said.

"He remembers you. This isn't the first time you've been here."

The young man glanced from Morgan to Houdini.

"Yeah. That was me."

Morgan was terrified she might pull the trigger by accident, even though her finger was alongside the gun, the way Del had showed her, and not inside the trigger guard.

"What do you want?" Morgan asked.

"I was told to get something," the burglar said. "When that didn't work—"

" 'Told'? By whom?"

"I can't say."

"Why not?" Morgan waited for a response. When there was none, she added, "Or would you rather tell the police?"

The young man groaned and slumped against the wall. He looked very tired. "I'm almost ready for that. But, no." He drew his arms close to his body and clenched his hands into fists. "I

233

know what would happen. I'd get blamed."

"I caught you red-handed!" Morgan cried. "I've got witnesses." She nodded her head toward the donkeys.

"Breaking and entering?" The young man gestured toward the broken door. "I didn't even get inside, so it's not technically entering. That's nothing. The police want me for murder."

Morgan gripped the gun tighter, her knuckles white. "Dawn Smith?"

Pain creased his young face. "If they throw me in jail, I'll never find out who killed her."

Morgan didn't have a lot of experience with drug addicts, but the young man's eyes were clear. He was upset, yet seemed rational. His speech was coherent. She was certain he wasn't high or drunk.

"Before I call the police," she said, "let's talk."

"About what?"

"You're afraid no one's going to listen to your side of the story?" Morgan asked.

"Why should they? The police like to solve crimes quick, even if they accuse the innocent."

"I need to know two things," Morgan said. "Who sent you, and what they sent you for. That's pretty simple."

The young man spat out a laugh. "If I knew the answers to your questions, I wouldn't be here."

He shivered and wrapped his arms around himself.

"What happened to your coat?"

"I—I—lost it when I escaped."

Morgan debated what to do. She had control of the situation for now, but the young man was shivering convulsively. He might be going into shock. Maybe Houdini had broken his ribs or damaged an internal organ. Both the unreliable landline and her cell phone were inside. Morgan had to call the police, but if she went inside, the young man would just run away.

"Let's go in," Morgan said.

The young man hesitated.

"Inside." She waved the gun in the direction of the house. "Now!"

He edged ahead of Morgan, walking sideways, keeping one eye on the door, one eye on her. Adelaide nuzzled Morgan's arm. She was tempted to invite the donkeys inside. Instead she closed the door behind her and leaned against it. The slow cooker scented the warm air with the savory smell of chili.

"Sit at the table," Morgan said.

The young man slumped onto a chair. He clasped his hands together and pressed them between his knees. Trembling wracked his body. His hair, in matted dreadlocks, danced against his face and shoulders.

"What's your name?" Morgan asked.

"T—trevin Pike."

"Trevin?"

"R—rhymes with K—kevin, but with a T. My m—mother was creative."

A plate of Bernie's chocolate chip cookies caught Trevin's attention.

"Hungry?" Morgan asked. "Have a cookie."

He grabbed for the plate, then stopped, glancing up at Morgan. "I h—haven't eaten in a while."

"Want some tea?" Morgan asked. "Hot cocoa?"

She reached into the cupboard, keeping one eye and the gun aimed on Trevin while she pulled out the selections. The good hostess holding her guest at gunpoint.

"Will you put th—that thing down?"

"I'm not letting go of the gun," Morgan said. "You're taller, younger, and faster than me. I need an equalizer."

"You sure it's not 'cause I'm b—black?"

"Oh come on," Morgan exclaimed. "You tried to break into my house!"

Trevin looked down at his hands. "Okay. That was lame." He looked up at Morgan. "But th—things happen, you know. You mean it to go one way, and then it g—goes the opposite of what you intended. I just don't want to get shot by accident."

Morgan hesitated, then lowered the gun. "Is that better?"

"A little." He ate another cookie. Between the food and the warmth of the kitchen, he gradually stopped trembling.

"You must be new at this," Morgan said.

"New at what?"

"Being a burglar. You escaped the first time. And breaking in when someone's home—not too professional."

"I saw the car leave. I thought you were gone."

Morgan used her free hand to set the drink choices on the table one by one. "Two kinds of tea, hot cider, instant cocoa."

"Hey." He grabbed the box of tea Morgan had purchased at Faerie Tales. "Where'd you get this?"

His swift movement startled Morgan. She gripped the gun, but didn't raise it. Trevin's sleeve rose slightly as he held up the box of tea, revealing the edge of a gargoyle tattoo on his forearm.

"It's from Faerie Tales." Morgan placed a mug of water in the microwave.

"You hang out there?" Trevin opened the box.

"I've been in there a couple times. I wouldn't call it hanging out. I'm not really a New Age type."

Trevin emptied the tea bags onto the kitchen table and shook the box, He peered inside. "So you're not taking classes there?"

"No. Do you want tea?"

"Anything but tea."

The microwave timer rang. Morgan dumped a packet of cocoa mix into the mug and stirred. She set the steaming mug on the table, careful not to place it close enough that Trevin could grab her arm. He stood slightly and reached for the mug.

"So you know my name," Trevin said, settling back in his chair. "What's yours?"

"Morgan Iverson. I'm managing the rock shop."

Trevin gulped down the cocoa and ate another cookie.

"You want some chili?" Morgan asked.

"That would be great. It's kinda weird, though. I mean, you've got a gun aimed at me, and you're feeding me."

Morgan had to set the gun on the counter to ladle out a bowl of chili. She picked up the gun and set the chili on the far side of the table. She stepped back and leaned against the counter.

"Spoon?" he asked.

Morgan grabbed a clean spoon out of the dish drainer on the counter. She handed it to Trevin. Morgan realized she had made a mistake as he took it from her hand, his fingers brushing hers. Maybe he thought she would shoot if he tried to grab her. In any event, he didn't take advantage of her lapse.

"So why did you break my door?" Morgan asked. "What are you after?"

"I don't know."

Morgan pulled a chair away from the table and sat.

"You tried to break into my house twice, and you don't know why? Am I supposed to believe that?"

"It sounds stupid, I know. They think you found something on Dawn."

"First off, who are 'they'?" Morgan asked.

Trevin scraped his spoon across the bottom of the bowl, going for every last bite of chili.

"I could tell you who brought me the first time," he said. "But they're just passing on orders from someone higher up. That's who I'm after. I thought that if I could find what they sent me for, I could figure it out. After I escaped—"

"Slow down," Morgan said. "You told me outside that you

escaped. From whom? Hand me your bowl." She gave Trevin a generous refill. "What do you mean 'escaped'? From the police?"

"No, I've been a prisoner. They had me locked up in a basement. I broke out a window—"

"You're good at that."

"Somebody was looking for me and spooked them pretty good. I thought they might decide to get rid of me. You know, like kill me."

"I'm sorry," Morgan said. "That was probably me. I went to General Minton Park and asked around about you."

"Maybe that was a good thing. I was more scared of staying than escaping, so I did. I've been hiding for two days, trying to figure out what to do."

It was either the most incredible story Morgan had ever heard, or the biggest load of donkey manure.

"I got so cold and hungry, I considered turning myself in. But the police—"

"Look," Morgan said, "you're dancing all around the edges of this story, and you're not giving me any details that could actually help. I want to find Dawn's killer, too, and so far only one suspect has been crossed off my list."

"Who was that?"

"Pastor Filbury."

"Why was he a suspect?"

"You're kidding me," Morgan said. But the confusion in Trevin's face seemed genuine. "It's been in the news. Pastor Filbury was questioned about Dawn's death. He has an alibi and witnesses, so the police are certain he's not the killer."

"Man." Trevin shook his head. "That's crazy."

"Did 'they' drive you here in a black SUV?" Morgan asked, thinking of the Mercedes.

"You've seen it?"

"Someone in that black SUV almost ran me down last week,"

Morgan said.

Trevin nodded. "Slice was probably driving. It's not his car, I can tell you that."

"Did he steal it?"

"No, he was running errands for someone, but I can't tell you who. Only that I think they're involved in Dawn's death."

Morgan shook her head. "It sounds like you're mixed up with a rough crowd. But you seem like a guy who should be in college. As I've heard it, Dawn didn't exactly come from a nice family."

"I'd like to try college someday," Trevin said. "If all this ends without me going to prison. I guess that depends on whether I can get anyone to believe me."

"I'm trying, Trevin. But you're not giving me much."

"Okay. Maybe if I explain a little about Dawn, it'll start to make sense." Trevin set down his spoon. "We went to the same high school. She was popular, even though everyone knew about her messed-up family. She wouldn't look twice at me back then. Do you have any more cookies?"

"I've got something better. Keep talking."

Morgan set the gun on the counter while she made a pot of coffee. When it was going, she set out a plate of blueberry bagels and a tub of cream cheese. She was starting to believe Trevin. He certainly acted like he hadn't eaten in two days.

Trevin told a story that wouldn't have been unusual, had it not ended in murder.

Dawn was the pretty girl from the wrong side of the tracks. She had fallen for a wealthy young man in her senior year of high school in Granite Junction. Right before graduation, he broke up with Dawn, declaring, in what Trevin deemed a heartless manner, that he was going to college out east, and wouldn't be back. She had been counting on marriage to be her ticket out of the squalid trailer park.

Trevin ate two bagels while he described his role as Mr. Rebound. His parents refused to pay for college if he chose to shack up with trailer park trash. White trailer park trash, at that. So he got a job in one of the few factories in Granite Junction.

"Did Dawn work?" Morgan asked.

"She had trouble holding down a job. But Dawn was good with computers. She was a real genius about some things."

Morgan refilled Trevin's coffee cup.

"She wasn't smart about people," Trevin continued. "Maybe if I'd been better at convincing her, she'd still be alive. Maybe if I'd just said, 'we're moving,' and taken her to Denver or somewhere else, away from that crowd."

Morgan wanted to say something about the importance of personal responsibility, but she held her tongue.

"My grandma used to make a big deal about Harry Potter," Trevin said. "She said things like Ouija boards and tarot cards opened the door to the devil. I used to laugh at her. That was until I met these people."

Dawn was lured in by the thrill of belonging to a secret world. She adopted the clothes, the tattoos, the piercings, and soon the drugs.

"At first there weren't any drugs around," Trevin said, "and then it was all about the drugs. I'll admit that I did it, too."

Trevin lost his job, and became even more estranged from his family.

"Excuse me," Morgan said, "but if you were using drugs, how do you know you didn't kill Dawn?"

"Because I quit. I could see what was happening, what drugs were doing to me and Dawn. I was losing her. I quit the drugs. And I almost had Dawn convinced to quit, too. She was ready to get out. And then she disappeared."

Chapter Twenty-Seven

Morgan kept one hand on the gun in her lap.

"You really didn't know that Dawn had accused Pastor Filbury of molesting her?" she asked.

"No," Trevin said. "She never told me anything about it."

"Do you think the molestation really happened?" Morgan asked. "Or could she have made it up?"

Trevin shrugged. "That doesn't seem like the kind of thing Dawn would lie about." He leaned back in his chair and folded his arms across his chest. "She told me everything. Stuff I wish I'd never known. It seems strange she'd leave that out."

Morgan pushed a shopping list and a pen across the table.

"Trevin, I want to help you, but I need names."

"I gave you one. Slice. Nobody uses their real name. I can tell you this. The clue they think you took from Dawn has something to do with a fairy tale."

"A fairy tale?" Morgan asked. "Is Piers part of this?"

"I don't know. Dawn started hanging around Faerie Tales before she disappeared."

Morgan could imagine a young woman falling for Piers, and his icy blue eyes.

"You have the gargoyle tattoo," Morgan said. "You must have been there, too."

"Piers stole that idea from us," Trevin said. "That dude doesn't have an original idea—"

The cowbell clanged as the front door of the shop opened.

Trevin jumped up.

"It's just one of my employees," Morgan said. "Or maybe a customer."

"I've got to go."

Morgan stood. "No! You haven't answered my questions."

Trevin placed his hand on the doorknob. Morgan aimed the gun at him. He met her eyes with a look of calm determination.

"The only way I'll find Dawn's killer is if I'm out there," he said. "I can't do anything sitting in a jail cell."

Morgan lowered the gun. Trevin opened the door.

"Take that jacket." Morgan pointed at Del's well-worn insulated work jacket, hanging from a peg by the back door.

Trevin pulled on the jacket and zipped it up. He paused, then reached for a bagel, stuffing it in a pocket.

"Be careful," Morgan whispered.

And he was gone.

Morgan sat at the kitchen table and watched the back door, her hand on the gun, for several minutes before Del wandered in.

"I made it back," Del said. "I thought that doctor—Hey, what's going on?"

"The burglar came back."

"While you were eating lunch?" Del examined the mess on the kitchen table.

"No, I fixed him lunch."

Del sat down next to Morgan. "You what?"

Morgan pushed the gun toward Del. "He was hungry, so I fed him."

"That sounds like something Kendall would do. Feed a thief." Del placed his hand over Morgan's and gave it a gentle squeeze. "Are you okay?"

"I'm fine. A little shook up, of course. But Trevin got the worst of it when—"

"You got his name?"

"After Houdini kicked him in the ribs—"

"Wait," Del said. "This is not a story for an empty stomach. Is there any chili left, or is that just for thieves?"

Del fixed bowls of chili for himself and for Morgan, when she told him she had not eaten anything. It would have made for poor digestion to eat with one hand holding a gun on an intruder.

She recited her conversation with Trevin. When she finished, Del glanced at his watch.

"Seems like the police should have gotten here by now."

"Police?" Morgan asked.

Del rested his forearms on the edge of the table and leaned toward Morgan. "You did call the police?"

"No." Morgan looked down at her coffee mug, stirring the spoon around. "The phone wasn't working. I'm getting the new phone service, and Internet. I don't care what it costs, or how long I'm here to enjoy it. I want a phone that works."

Del stood. "I'll call them now."

"No!" Morgan looked up. "Del, I don't see any reason to call the police. Not this time."

"What makes this attempted break-in different than the last attempted break-in?"

"Trevin's trying to figure out who killed Dawn. If the police pick him up, he won't be able to continue looking for the murderer."

"It's a good thing I showed up when I did," Del said. "The burglar might have sold you the Royal Gorge Bridge before it was all over. He didn't give you any answers."

"You interrupted him before he could tell me everything he knew."

"Give me one good reason I shouldn't call the police right now."

"Because no damage was done," Morgan said. "Because he could file charges against us for Houdini attacking him. Because I held him at gunpoint, and I don't want to have to explain that. And because I need to talk to him again."

"Apparently if you wait long enough," Del said, "he'll be back to steal the fairy tale thingy."

"This is serious."

"Darn right it's serious," Del said. "I leave for a couple hours, and you let in a thief and a drug addict, and serve him lunch, no less."

"He has more pieces to the puzzle." Morgan tapped the table with her index finger.

Del released a big sigh.

"What?" Morgan asked.

"I won't feel right letting you out of my sight until this whole deal is cleared up."

"I did okay," Morgan said. "Now if you're done scolding me, let's see if we can figure out the clue Trevin was looking for."

In between waiting on customers, Morgan and Del spent the afternoon brainstorming. Morgan finally gave up.

"I didn't remove anything from Dawn's body," Morgan said. "I didn't see anything that made me think of fairy tales, or even Piers's store."

"Ask Beatrice," Del said. "She might have heard something. And don't forget, the kid could have been lying."

"I'm sure Trevin was telling me what he thought was the truth. Maybe he was sent to break in to the shop because they wanted him to get caught."

"And take the blame for the girl's murder?" Del tugged at his mustache. "Could be."

When they closed the shop at the end of the day, Morgan was grateful that Del offered to accompany her to the barn to tend to the donkeys. Even knowing Del was in the next room that night, she slept restlessly, waking at every noise. Coyotes yipped. The wind gusted, bumping pine branches against the roof.

What-ifs churned through her mind, dozens of conflicting theories, unanswered questions, and possible suspects. Among the thoughts keeping her awake were: What if the clue meant Faerie Tales? What if Trevin was the murderer, and she had let him walk away free? And most disturbing, what if Dawn might have lived if Morgan had stayed with her instead of running away?

Then none of this would matter.

Morgan was certain she slept for stretches of time, but when she woke, she felt exhausted.

"You should have let me call the police," Del said. "You look like you didn't sleep a wink."

"I keep thinking about Trevin's clue. Maybe I missed something on the trail after I found Dawn's body."

When Cindy arrived for her afternoon shift, she took one look at Morgan, and shook her head.

"Cowgirl, you look terrible," Cindy said.

"She didn't sleep last night," Del said. "The burglar came back."

Morgan had to tell Cindy a condensed version of the story, along with a request to keep it to herself.

"Del, that means you, too." Morgan yawned.

"We can manage the shop," Cindy said. "You should go take a nap."

"I wouldn't be able to sleep," Morgan said. "What I need is a walk to calm my nerves. I'm calling Bernie."

"Before you go walking again," Del said, "I'm going to have to insist you take that upgrade with you."

★ ★ ★ ★ ★

When Morgan entered the bakery, Bernie sat at a table reading a novel.

"Slow afternoon?"

Bernie looked up. "In a fit of optimism, I called Darlene in to work, but it looks like I don't even need to be here."

"Can you take off for an hour or so?" Morgan asked.

"Gladly. What's up?" Bernie placed a hand on her hip and raised her eyebrows. "Or should I ask, 'What's up this time?' "

"I need to look for something."

On the drive to the Columbine Trail parking lot, Morgan told Bernie about Trevin's attempted break-in, and the fairy tale clue.

"You're sure you want to do this?" Bernie asked.

"Yes," Morgan said. "Are you sure you want to go with me?"

"I'm in."

The parking lot was empty. They climbed out of Bernie's SUV. Morgan strapped on Del's olive-green camouflage fanny pack.

"I haven't walked since O'Reily's." Bernie zipped up her jacket.

They headed up and down the gently rolling hills, chatting about the upcoming race, business, and the weather forecast. Their running shoes crunched rhythmically on the gravel. Clouds skittered across the sky, teasing them with glimpses of the sun.

Morgan slowed when they approached the grove of cotton-woods where she had first seen Dawn. Damp, rotting leaves muffled the sound of their shoes on the trail.

"Is this the place?" Bernie asked.

"Yes."

Bernie wrapped her arms around herself and shivered. "It's gloomy. Where was she?"

The brush where Dawn had lain was thoroughly trampled.

"Here." Morgan stopped. "And then across the meadow, the police found her the second time."

Bernie followed Morgan as she circled around the area, lifting branches, kicking over rocks, and digging through matted leaves and snow.

"I don't see so much as a gum wrapper," Bernie said.

"If the donkeys hadn't escaped that day," Morgan said, "or Adelaide hadn't chosen this trail, or if it'd been an hour earlier, or an hour later . . ." Morgan shrugged. "It just seems like I was supposed to find her. But I feel like I failed her. I ran away."

"You did what your CPR training told you to," Bernie said.

"Not knowing," Morgan said. "That's what really bothers me. Did I do the right thing or not?"

They followed the trail to the meadow.

"The burglar came back."

"What!"

Morgan told Bernie the story while they walked.

"You held a potential murderer at gunpoint?" Bernie asked. "And fed him lunch at the same time?"

"I'm convinced he's not the killer," Morgan said.

"And you let him go, instead of letting the police decide whether he was a killer or not." Bernie walked slowly uphill, stopping at the crest of the hill. "He could be out here. We should turn around. It sounds like you could be a target."

"Del upgraded my pack." Morgan patted the fanny pack.

Bernie stared at the camouflage pack, then at Morgan. "Upgraded? What do you mean? Do you have the gun with you?"

"He made me bring it."

Bernie grabbed Morgan's arms. "This isn't the Wild West, and you aren't Annie Oakley," Bernie exclaimed. "You can't just walk around with a gun in your pocket. You need a permit to carry a concealed weapon."

"Del didn't mention a permit." Morgan heard rustling in the dried leaves clinging to the scrubby bushes. "Shh! What's that?"

"Probably a squirrel. You also need a license to shoot them."

They continued to walk, and Bernie continued to scold. Morgan kept one ear on the conversation, and the other on the bushes. Then a louder noise competed with the rustling leaves. Morgan heard the familiar whine of an ATV engine in the distance. It faded, then came within range again, growing louder.

Bernie pulled the cuff of her jacket sleeve back and checked her watch. "We've been out for thirty minutes," she said. "We'd better turn around."

"Not yet," Morgan whispered. "I think there's something behind us."

"It's just the wind," Bernie said, but she kept walking. "What are we going to do?"

"I hear an ATV, too," Morgan said. "We keep walking until we run into the ATV, then ask them for help."

"What if the ATV isn't on this trail?" Bernie asked. "What if we don't run into them? What if the murderer drives an ATV?"

Morgan hadn't considered all the worst-case scenarios.

"I can hear it now," Bernie whispered. "Not on the trail. In the bushes. Let's stop, and see if it stops."

Bernie grasped Morgan's coat sleeve. They stood still, listening.

"Nothing," Morgan whispered. "Now start walking again."

After a few paces, the rustling resumed.

Morgan unzipped the fanny pack slowly. She reached inside. Her fingers folded around the textured grip of the handgun.

"Slow down," Morgan whispered. "Maybe they'll show themselves."

"Is that what we want?" Bernie asked. "I'd rather they—"

A magpie burst out of the brush, flapping its wings and

squawking furiously. It skimmed just above Morgan's head. She threw her arms up to protect her face, dropping the gun on the trail.

Bernie screamed. Morgan lowered her arms and caught a glimpse of long ropes of matted brown hair disappearing across the trail.

"Trevin!" Morgan called.

He crashed through the brush. Morgan crouched down. Her hand shook as she grasped the gun.

"I can't believe I dropped it," Morgan said. "I feel like such an idiot."

The ATV roared into view. It skidded to a stop, sending a shower of dust and gravel into the air. The rider wore a full-face helmet, but Morgan recognized the tall, lean form.

"Stand back, ladies." Del flung his helmet off, grabbed his shotgun, and waded into the brush.

Morgan followed. Branches clawed at her jeans. They climbed a steep hillside. Del sent showers of gravel and dirt into her face, then plunged down the other side. Morgan stopped at the top of the hill. At the bottom, Trevin stood with his hands raised. The old cowboy struggled to breathe as he aimed his shotgun at Trevin's chest.

"I caught him," Del gasped. "And wearing my jacket."

CHAPTER TWENTY-EIGHT

"Trevin," Morgan asked. "Why were you following us?"

"I wasn't following you," Trevin said. "I was following the guy who was following you. I might have caught him, too, if the geezer patrol hadn't stopped me."

"Was there someone else?" Del asked Morgan.

"I didn't see anyone," Morgan said, "but maybe Bernie did."

"You left that girl alone?" Del asked.

Morgan had assumed Bernie had joined the chase, but her friend was not in sight. It wouldn't be the first time Morgan had left a woman unattended on the trail. She spun around without answering Del and scrambled down the hill on her backside. Morgan burst onto the trail, adrenalin pounding through her veins.

Bernie perched astride the ATV, grasping the handgrips. "I've always wanted to ride one of these."

Morgan doubled over, her hands on her knees, struggling to catch her breath.

"I thought"—wheeze—"you might"—gasp—"be in trouble."

"I was just fine, knowing the guns were on the other side of the hill." Bernie swung her leg over the ATV and slid off.

Trevin pushed his way through the brush and onto the trail. Del struggled to keep up with the young man.

"Is this the fella who was following you?" Del asked Bernie.

"I saw you run across the road," Bernie said to Trevin, "but you were chasing someone."

"See?" Trevin said. "Always picking on the black man."

"Get over yourself, Trevin," Morgan said. "Who were you following?"

"And why?" Bernie asked.

"I don't know," Trevin said. "I was hanging out in the coin laundry last night, trying to warm up, and I read an old newspaper that told where Dawn was found." He paused. "I wanted to see where—"

He stopped.

"So you came out to the trail," Morgan said. "Then what?"

"I was looking for the clue," Trevin said. "I thought maybe it was still where you found Dawn."

"Did you find it?" Del asked.

"No," Trevin said. "But I did remember what Dawn told me. Thumbelina was her favorite fairy tale when she was a kid."

"You're looking for a fairy?" Bernie asked.

"He's getting you sidetracked," Del said. "Get back to the part where you were following the two ladies."

"I saw you hiking," Trevin continued. "Then I noticed someone following you. So I started following him."

"It was a man?" Del asked.

"I never got a good look at him," Trevin said. "I guess it could have been a woman."

"One of your drug buddies?" Del asked.

"I don't think so," Trevin said. "Can you aim that thing somewhere else?"

"Del, let him go," Morgan said.

"You believe him?" Del asked. "After we catch him sneaking around the woods, following you?"

"Apparently, you were following me, too," Morgan said. "Or did you just happen to be riding the ATV on this trail at this particular time?"

"You took off for a walk after telling me you missed a clue on the trail," Del said. "It didn't take Sherlock Holmes to figure

251

that one out."

"Would you put the shotgun down?" Morgan said.

"What if he's the murderer?" Bernie asked.

"Put your hands behind your back," Del said.

"Why?" Trevin asked.

"Morgan wants me to quit pointing my gun at you," Del said. "That requires that you put your hands behind your back."

Trevin complied. Del handed his shotgun to Bernie, apparently not trusting Morgan to keep it trained on Trevin. Bernie stood with her legs wide apart, both trembling hands gripping the shotgun, the barrels aimed in the general direction of Trevin. Del pulled zip ties out of his back jeans pocket and bound Trevin's hands. He took the gun from Bernie.

"Get on the ATV." Del waved the gun at Trevin. "Back seat."

It wasn't easy for Trevin to climb on to the ATV without the use of his hands.

"Bernie," Del said, "do you know how to drive?"

"I'm sure I can manage." Bernie climbed into the driver's seat, a smile on her face.

Morgan turned to Del. "You're making a mistake."

"I'm going to have to override you on this one," Del said. "We have to turn this kid in."

He called the police on Morgan's phone when they got in cell phone range.

The police cruiser arrived at the trailhead parking lot at the same time they did. Officers Sanchez and MacKenzie were only too happy to take custody of Trevin. Sanchez asked Morgan and Bernie to drive to the police station right away. Del could ride his ATV back to the rock shop, and come in to give a detailed statement later.

Bernie started the SUV. Morgan opened the passenger door, then turned to Del.

"I hope you're happy," she spat out.

"No, I'm not, but I'm not willing to take chances with your

safety. If that young man comes back to the shop again, there's no telling what could happen."

"You've made a terrible mistake," Morgan said. "He didn't kill Dawn."

Del nodded his head with a swift jerking movement. "Mistake, huh? I can see you don't appreciate me saving your royal keister twice."

"Twice?" Morgan yelled. "Where do you get twice?"

"Today was number two," Del said. "Yesterday was number one. If I hadn't—"

"I don't need protecting," Morgan interrupted. "Nothing happened yesterday that—"

"Nothing happened because I made sure you were prepared," Del said. "You're too trusting. If Trevin's innocent—"

"He is innocent," Morgan said. "You just sent an innocent man to jail."

"I guess we'll just have to wait and see about that."

Del pulled his helmet on, mounted the ATV, and gunned the engine. He headed up the trail, spraying gravel behind him.

Morgan climbed in the SUV and slammed the door.

"Well," Bernie said. "That was interesting."

"You're going to tell the police Trevin was chasing a man, aren't you?" Morgan asked.

"I'll tell them what I saw," Bernie said.

"Trevin wasn't after us."

"I know," Bernie said. "That doesn't make him innocent of Dawn's murder. But maybe we'd better not talk about it until we get to the police station."

"You're right. We might influence each other's eyewitness accounts."

"I was more concerned that if we talk, you might start yelling at me."

★ ★ ★ ★ ★

After an hour, Officer Sanchez finally put down her pencil.

"You've been remarkably uncooperative," Sanchez said, "especially considering this man tried to break into your house twice."

"He's innocent of killing Dawn Smith," Morgan said one last time. "I'm convinced you've got the wrong man."

"We're going to hold him for attempted breaking and entering—"

"He never actually entered the house," Morgan said for the third time. "And I refuse to press charges."

She wasn't certain she felt that strongly about Trevin's harmlessness, even if she did believe he was innocent of murder. But the more Del and the police tried to paint Trevin as a killer, the more resistant Morgan became.

"Mr. Addison also resides at thirty-five Hill Street," Sanchez said, reading from the police report. "He's willing to press charges."

"Mr. Addison is my guest," Morgan said. "He's only at thirty-five Hill Street at my invitation, to protect me from intruders." Morgan folded her arms across her chest. "He didn't do a very good job."

Officer Sanchez lowered the papers and studied Morgan across the desk. "Look, we're just trying to get the full story. We might be doing the young man a favor locking him up."

"How can you possibly say that?" Morgan asked.

"Supposing he's innocent," Sanchez said, "and he finds the killer before we do? He could end up dead. Or in prison if he decides to enforce his own vigilante justice."

"So if he was chasing Dawn's killer," Morgan said, "then the murderer is still out there."

Sanchez nodded. "That's a possibility."

"Don't stop looking just because Trevin's behind bars."

"This case isn't closed yet," Sanchez said. "As far as I'm concerned, there could still be a killer on the loose."

Morgan and Del managed to avoid each other the rest of the day. That was no small feat, considering the size of the rock shop and its living quarters. Every time Morgan thought about asking Del to move back to his trailer, she remembered Officer Sanchez's words.

That evening, Del sat in the easy chair, reading an outdoors magazine and feeding logs into the wood stove. Morgan rocked back and forth, trying to concentrate on a romance novel.

She set the book aside, took a deep breath, and turned toward Del.

"I do appreciate how you've looked out for me."

Del closed his magazine. He rolled it up into a tube and clutched it with both hands. "I know you can take care of yourself. You proved that Wednesday."

"You insisted on leaving the gun with me," Morgan said. "I don't believe Trevin would have tried to hurt me—"

Del started to speak, but Morgan held up her hand to stop him.

"Time will tell which of us is right about him," Morgan continued. "But I'm willing to admit that things would have turned out entirely different if I hadn't forced him to stay and talk."

"You're welcome to borrow my revolver any time."

"I don't plan to," Morgan said. "Not after dropping it on the trail. I'm not capable of handling a gun safely."

"You just need practice," Del said. "You're gonna need the gun again before this is all over with, mark my words."

In the morning, Del switched back and forth between three local news stations. Each predicted snow of varying intensity. Del had his opinions about which forecaster had the best track record. Finally, he made his decision.

"It could be a good one," he declared. "We'd better get ready."

Morgan had learned that his "good" snowstorm met her criteria for bad. Del wrote up a detailed shopping list.

"We need to stock up, in case we get snowed in."

Morgan drove to Granite Junction to shop. After yesterday's events, she hoped for a reprieve from stress. Instead, she was plunged into the tension of a community preparing for an impending blizzard. The aisles were jammed with carts, and the checkout line seemed endless.

The bread shelves were nearly bare. In addition to her distaste for cheap white bread, Morgan had been spoiled by Bernie's baked goods. She stopped at the bakery on her way home and stood in another line. Emma manned the cash register.

When Morgan finally reached the counter, Bernie motioned for her to step behind the counter. Morgan followed Bernie into the kitchen.

"I saved you a loaf," Bernie said. "I'm almost out of bread."

"Thanks." Morgan accepted the loaf. "This is Del's favorite."

"You two are on speaking terms again?" Bernie asked.

"I couldn't stay mad at Del for long," Morgan said. "He's just trying to protect me. Like you and half of Golden Springs."

"Speaking of half of Golden Springs, that would describe the population of the bakery right now. I need to help Emma."

Bernie walked Morgan to the backside of the pastry counter. "I'm just glad this is all over."

"You and Del may think so," Morgan said, "but Trevin did not kill Dawn."

The words came out of Morgan's mouth a little too loud. Kurt Willard's head popped up above the pastry display. His eyes grew wide.

"Did I hear that the murder has been solved?" he asked.

"No," Morgan said.

"It's okay, Morgan," Bernie said. "I'm sure everyone's heard that the police have a suspect in custody. But you'll have to get the details yourself, Kurt."

"Who is it?"

"Obviously not you," Morgan said.

Kurt smiled his most charming smile. "I wasn't aware that I was a suspect." He bowed toward Morgan. "I am truly flattered."

Morgan rolled her eyes. She pushed her way past Kurt and onto the boardwalk.

A magpie stood on top of her car.

"You," Morgan yelled. "Bird. Off my car. Now!"

The bird ruffled its black and white feathers and paced across the top of the Buick. Morgan stooped to pick up a rock. She pulled her arm back and prepared to throw.

A hand grabbed her sleeve. Morgan spun around, and was face to face with Piers.

"Don't harm the bird," Piers said.

"It's scratching up my paint," Morgan said.

Piers released her arm. She let the rock fall to the ground.

"You're stressed," Piers said. "And you're striking out at a defenseless creature."

"I'd hardly call a magpie defenseless. I'm a bad aim, anyway. I couldn't hit it if I tried."

"Perhaps we can discuss whatever it is that's troubling you tonight," Piers said.

"Tonight?"

"Dinner," Piers said. "Had you forgotten?"

Completely, Morgan thought.

"I heard there's going to be a blizzard," she said.

"Regardless of the intensity of the storm, I'll be able to walk to the restaurant," Piers said, "but the drive could be difficult for you. Would you prefer to postpone dinner?"

"I'll call you if I can't make it," Morgan said.

"Then I may expect to see you tonight?"

"Yes. I'll be there, weather permitting."

The magpie flew off the car when Morgan opened the driver's side door. Birds dropped a couple notches on her list of worries.

A new one looming before her was, what did one wear to dinner with a sensitive New Age type who might be a murderer?

Chapter Twenty-Nine

When Del asked to borrow the car, Morgan was more than happy to get him out of the house. She rummaged through the wardrobe. Her clothing ran from muck-out-the-barn, to going-to-church, to business casual. Nothing seemed right.

That set her on another train of thought. Heels were definitely out. She might need to run.

Just when Morgan was considering camouflage and Army boots, she found an Indian tunic Sarah had given her for Mother's Day. It wasn't exactly Morgan's style, but it would be perfect for tonight. A nice pair of jeans and boots, a turtleneck sweater, and the blue tunic over everything.

By the time Del returned, Morgan was ready for her date.

"What did you get?" Morgan asked. "I don't see any bags."

Del took off his jacket and hung it on a peg.

"Gas for the chain saw," he said. "We might go through some wood this weekend, if it snows like I think it will." He grabbed his mug and headed for the coffee maker. The glass carafe was empty. Del went about the business of brewing a fresh pot. "I also got a couple bales of straw. The donkeys will be stuck in the barn for a few days. The straw will keep them more comfortable."

"You really think it's going to get that bad?"

Del opened the wood-burning stove and stirred the coals. "Maybe I'm hoping. I enjoy a good storm. It forces a person to relax."

He put a log in the stove, then settled in the rocking chair. The smell of wood smoke and coffee filled the kitchen.

"Say," Del said, "you're kinda dressed up."

"I have a dinner engagement," Morgan said.

"You're not going through with that date with Piers? I don't trust that guy. Plus it could start snowing any minute."

"I'll keep an eye on the weather."

Del stood abruptly and walked to the guest bedroom, returning with the handgun.

"You'll need this."

"Oh, no," Morgan said. "Not this time."

"After all that's happened, you still want to argue with me about carrying protection?" Del let his shoulders slump. "Okay. You win." He looked Morgan in the eye. "If you can tell me that Piers Townsend is innocent with the same conviction you claim Trevin is."

Morgan wanted to argue with the old cowboy, but she knew she couldn't. Not with confidence.

"How can I carry it?" Morgan asked. "And I am not wearing the camo fanny pack on a date."

"How about in between layers? Under that blouse, on top of your sweater."

Morgan pulled off the tunic and let Del adjust his shoulder holster to fit her smaller frame. She had to admit, when she pulled the tunic over the turtleneck sweater, the gun was not obvious. She wondered how many people walked around Golden Springs with loaded weapons tucked in their underarms.

Snowflakes drifted to earth as Morgan pulled out of the Rock of Ages parking lot. Main Street was nearly abandoned. She parked in front of the Hot Tomato restaurant.

Piers sat by a large window. One arm rested across the table. He gazed at the snow with a look of contentment. In his poet shirt, his blond hair curling at his shoulders, he could have stepped out of an earlier century.

Morgan passed two occupied tables on her way to the window. A young couple dressed in outdoorsy attire sat at one. A group of seven shared the other table with a balloon bouquet, wishing someone a happy birthday.

Piers stood as Morgan approached his table.

"I was hoping you wouldn't let the weather deter you from our dinner date." Piers pulled out a chair opposite his and held it for Morgan.

"I'll have to head back if the snow comes down any harder."

The waitress breezed up to their table immediately. She was probably anxious to feed people and go home, before she got snowed'in. She'd dressed for the possibility of bad weather, in snow boots, blue jeans, and a Nordic sweater that matched her blue eyes.

The menu listed typical restaurant choices of soup, salad, and sandwiches, but there were some items she was not sure about. Hummus dip, roasted tempeh, and cold pumpkin soup sounded interesting, but she ordered a spinach-walnut-cranberry salad that came with a mini loaf of dark bread. Piers ordered a salad, too, but with modifications.

"I would like the Greek salad without onions," he said.

"Of course," the waitress began, but he was not finished.

"And no feta. I'm vegan."

"We do have vegan salads on the menu," the waitress said.

"I prefer the Greek salad with no feta. If you have a good vegan parmesan, the cook may use that instead. Don't put any croutons on my salad. I would prefer the dark bread instead of the sourdough. And I believe that is it." He handed the menu to the waitress with a smug smile.

Morgan gave the waitress credit for not rolling her eyes. She was probably too busy scribbling notes on her order pad.

"Can you make those separate checks?" Morgan asked.

Piers did not protest.

"You got it." The waitress nodded.

When she left, Piers turned his attention to Morgan.

"You are lovely tonight."

"Thank you." Morgan tugged self-consciously at the sleeve of her tunic. She hoped he didn't look closely enough to notice the bulge of the shoulder holster.

They chatted about the weather until the waitress brought their drinks.

"Merlot." The waitress placed a glass of wine in front of Piers. "And herb tea." She set a pot of steaming water, a selection of teas in a basket, and a mug on Morgan's side of the table.

Morgan wanted a clear head. At the very least, she was dealing with a business adversary. At the worst, a murderer.

"I do enjoy this time of year," Piers said. "The pace of life slows down. It's almost a form of hibernation."

"Slow would describe it." Morgan shook her head. "I can see why so many businesses fail every year."

"It's a struggle to survive until the spring influx of tourists." Piers sipped wine the color of blood. "I don't know why people put themselves through the stress."

"But you just said you enjoy the slower pace of life. I'm sure it's the same for other business owners."

"Some of us are in a better position to endure the vagaries of the business world." Piers smiled. "In so many ways it's less stressful to work for another person, rather than attempting to manage your own business."

"I worked for a corporation before moving here," Morgan said. "I'd say the stress is different, but it's there in either situation."

"Yet there must be an appeal to the security of a regular paycheck."

"It's a false security," Morgan said. "You work at the whim of economic forces over which you have no control. Here one day. Gone the next."

"Not unlike the many shops that go out of business each winter," Piers said.

The waitress brought salads and bread to the table, balanced on a large round tray.

"The spinach, walnut, cranberry." She set a generous platter of greens in front of Morgan. "A Greek salad, hold the onions and croutons, with vegan parmesan instead of feta." She set it in front of Piers with a look of triumph. "And two loaves of dark bread. Can I get you anything else?"

"That will be all for now," Piers said, not giving Morgan a chance to speak.

The waitress glanced at Morgan and raised one eyebrow.

"Everything looks wonderful," Morgan said with a smile.

Piers poked his fork delicately around his salad, as though searching for an errant crouton or bit of onion. Morgan dug into hers. It had been a busy day. She was starved.

The conversation had been strained so far. Morgan supposed that was the way first dates were. Although on her first date with Sam, canoeing on a river, there had been little of the awkwardness she felt with Piers. She and Sam had known each other through church and friends for several months before they started dating. It probably wasn't fair to hold Piers up to the standard of a man like Sam. And why was she even making the comparison? Her intention in accepting Piers's dinner invitation wasn't to become romantically involved. It was to evaluate his potential as a murder suspect.

Piers broke the silence, startling Morgan.

"I am so pleased that you moved to Golden Springs."

"Oh?" Morgan said.

"You're a good fit for our community of diverse people,"

Piers said. "We gather the peacemakers, the artists and poets, the gentle souls striving to make our world a healthier environment, not just physically, but socially and emotionally."

Morgan was sure she didn't belong in a group of such elevated talents.

"We've made progress in recent years," Piers said, "but there are still too many people in Golden Springs dedicated to thwarting our vision."

"I've heard that Pastor Filbury opposed your rezoning initiative," Morgan said.

The birthday party people stood, their chairs scraping across the wood floor. They pulled on coats and mittens, preparing to go out in the storm. Morgan would have to leave soon if she hoped to make it back to the rock shop.

"Oh, yes," Piers said, "Filbury is certainly one of the forces seeking to stop the winds of change."

"I suspect you consider my brother, Kendall, to be one of those forces, too."

Piers nodded, a sad smile on his lips. "And yet, the winds will blow in spite of their efforts."

"And one of those changes is rezoning the rock shop," Morgan said. "Surely you can understand why Kendall and I would be opposed to that?"

"You would benefit," Piers said. "The property would be much more valuable if it were zoned residential."

"I wouldn't be able to make a living," Morgan said. "I'd lose the land."

"If your property were to go on the market, I am prepared to make a very generous offer."

"You don't understand. I might decide to keep my family's land." Morgan speared a forkful of greens. "Pastor Filbury opposes the rezoning proposal, too. That made someone angry enough to try to ruin his reputation."

Morgan tried to meet Piers's eyes, but he looked away, pushing his salad aside.

"I hardly think the pastor needed any assistance in that endeavor."

"Do you believe what that young woman said about him?"

"Whether I believe it or not is irrelevant," Piers said. "Reputation is a delicate creature. It is unfortunate the pastor became embroiled in this tawdry business, but now City Council can make forward progress, free of impediment."

Morgan's heart beat faster. She hadn't expected Piers to confirm her theory. The gun poking her in the ribs now felt comforting.

"It seems terribly convenient that the young woman accusing the pastor was killed," Morgan said. "Now we may never know the truth."

"While we may not learn beyond a doubt whether or not the pastor assaulted the young woman, we may soon know who killed her," Piers said. "I understand the police have detained a suspect."

"If they have the right person."

The young couple exited the restaurant. They paused in front of the window to zip up their ski jackets. The young man kissed a snowflake off the young woman's nose. Their journey was as fresh as the clean white flakes covering their hair and shoulders. Morgan could feel the wintry air pressing against the window. She felt old, tired, and alone.

And tired of fighting.

Piers reached across the table and placed his hand over Morgan's.

"I thought you didn't touch people," Morgan said.

"I have no clients until tomorrow," Piers said. "And if the blizzard hits as predicted, we may all have the day off. Perhaps you would accept my offer of a massage? You are very tense."

Piers's hand was smooth and warm. A part of Morgan wanted to jerk her hand out of his grasp, but another part of her melted at his touch.

"I don't know," she stammered. "The snow—"

"It's what you need," Piers said. "Soft music, candles, scented oil. Perhaps a glass of wine."

"It sounds heavenly," Morgan said.

"I can assure you, it will be."

Piers's smug confidence in his abilities brought Morgan back to earth. The man wanted her land, she reminded herself. He might have been willing to commit murder to get it. Seducing an overweight middle-aged widow might be one more unsavory step in his march to victory.

"I need to go."

Piers smiled. "I understand. My powers of persuasion are not strong enough to override your concerns about the storm." He lifted Morgan's hand to his lips. "Perhaps next time."

Morgan pulled her hand away, hoping her expression more closely resembled a smile than the grimace she felt.

There would be no next time.

CHAPTER THIRTY

Morgan opened the back door a crack and peeked inside. Del slept in the easy chair, his long legs propped up on the padded footstool. The plaid wool blanket draped across his lap, but it wasn't long enough to cover his gray socks. Morgan thought she would make a clean escape across the kitchen to the hallway when Del woke.

"Made it back okay, I see." He yawned.

"Hill Street was slippery, but I made it," Morgan said. "The snow is coming down hard now."

Del stood and stretched. "I'd better check on Houdini and Adelaide before I turn in."

"I already did," Morgan said. "They have plenty of hay and water. Thanks for putting them in the barn."

"So how was your date?" Del asked.

"Strange."

Del opened the wood stove and stirred the coals with a fireplace poker. "I would have expected that from Mr. Faerie Tales."

Morgan sat on the rocker next to the easy chair. "Did you ever date after your wife passed away?"

"I tried it once or twice." Del placed two pieces of wood inside the stove. "But it just didn't feel right. I guess I'd rather be alone than marry the wrong woman, you know?"

"I do know."

"You can have the chair," Del said. "I'm turning in."

Morgan wrapped the wool blanket around her shoulders. She dozed off in the easy chair to the smell of wood smoke and the sound of pinesap popping. A loud cracking woke her. Morgan jumped out of the easy chair. She ran to the back door in her sock feet and peered through the glass. A branch had broken off a tree near the back door under the weight of the wet snow.

No monster, no Trevin, no murderer. Morgan went to bed.

When she walked into the kitchen the next morning, Del seemed ecstatic about being snowed in. He bundled up and stomped his way through knee-high snow to the woodpile. The sound of the chain saw broke the peace of the morning. Morgan started a batch of pancakes from a box mix. Turkey sausage links sizzled in the cast-iron skillet.

While she cooked, she watched a sparrow land on the window sill and puff out its feathers. Snowflakes dusted the little bird and covered the openings on the feeder. Morgan stepped outside to knock the snow off the feeder. The sparrow attacked the feeder the minute Morgan retreated indoors.

She couldn't imagine surviving the winter with only a thin layer of feathers to keep her warm. Maybe the sparrow had a nest to huddle in.

The day she had found Dawn, the magpie had flown to a nest, carrying something in its beak. Wintertime bird nests. Morgan would be able to look it up on the Internet soon, when the new service was installed. Phone service would be more consistent, too. Morgan checked her cell phone.

No signal.

"Great."

The pancakes and sausage were done. Morgan started to fry eggs to go with the rest of the meal. It occurred to her that she hadn't heard the chain saw in a while.

She leaned out the back door. "Del! Breakfast is ready."

No answer.

Morgan sat on a kitchen chair to pull on her snow boots. She grabbed her coat and scarf and walked outside. Heavy snow-flakes splatted against her face.

"Del?"

His knee-deep boot prints were half buried with fresh snow. Morgan followed his trail around the side of the house to the woodpile.

"Del!"

The old cowboy leaned against the stack of firewood. His shoulders quaked as he shivered. Then Morgan saw the red staining the white snow.

"I had a little accident with the chain saw," Del said through chattering teeth. He attempted a smile.

Morgan ran to the woodpile. Del pressed one gloved hand to his left forearm. Blood soaked the jagged edges of his coat sleeve. Red drops oozed down his glove and plopped onto the snow.

Morgan knew the correct response to emergencies. She was determined she wouldn't panic this time.

"We've got to get that bleeding stopped, and get you to the hospital."

Del tried to walk, but he was shivering so hard, his body didn't seem to cooperate.

"Put your arm around my shoulder."

Morgan had to get Del inside, by the fire. He was either freezing, or going into shock, or both. Somehow she managed to half carry and half drag the tall cowboy into the kitchen. Morgan helped him lower himself into the easy chair. She stacked pillows on the arm of the chair and rested his forearm on top, to elevate the wound. She stirred the fire and threw on two more logs.

Morgan flipped open her phone. No signal. She resisted the urge to throw the useless phone against the wall, and stuck it in her jeans pocket instead. She picked up the receiver for the landline phone. No ring tone.

"Del, I need to see your arm. I'll try not to hurt you."

He nodded his head. He had stopped shivering, but his normally ruddy face was pale.

"I think pulling your coat off will cause too much movement. I'm going to cut off the sleeve."

She got scissors and sawed at the sleeve from his wrist to above his elbow. Morgan gently pulled it open.

Nausea nearly overwhelmed her when she realized the extent of the injury. The bloody gash revealed bone and tendon. Blood pumped out of his arm in a steady rhythm.

"I need to put a compress on your wound."

She pulled clean dishtowels out of a drawer and placed them on Del's forearm. Morgan held them to the wound, pressing firmly. The towels soaked through with blood.

If the blood clotted, removing the compress might cause the clot to dislodge, and the bleeding to resume. Morgan wondered how she could tell whether the blood had stopped pumping out of Del's arm.

She tried both phones again.

Nothing.

Del closed his eyes.

"Stay with me, Del."

The pillows under his arm dripped blood onto the floor, already soaked through.

"Del, I can't get the bleeding stopped."

"Damn doctor," Del whispered.

"What?"

"Doctor's orders." Del opened his eyes. "Blood thinner. Must be making me bleed out."

Morgan looked out the window. Huge flakes smacked against the glass. Maybe one of the neighbors had phone service. Morgan debated leaving Del for the chance that someone further up the hill might be able to call for an ambulance.

That was what she had done for Dawn. Left her alone to go call for help.

Del rested his head against the back of the easy chair.

"I'm not leaving you," Morgan said.

She grabbed the car keys and ran to the garage. Falling snow obscured the path to the garage. Morgan remembered Del's warning about people freezing in blizzards, and not being found until spring. A snowdrift piled against the door waist-high. Morgan grabbed the door handle and pulled as hard as she could.

"Shovel," she said.

She struggled through knee-high snow back to the house and grabbed a snow shovel. Back to the garage. Morgan shoveled furiously. The faster she dug, the harder the snow seemed to blow back in. She got one side of the double doors open wide enough for her to slip inside.

Maybe she could push the garage doors open with the car.

Morgan jumped into the driver's seat and turned the key. The engine made a reluctant effort to turn over. Morgan tried again. And again. Until the engine did not respond at all. She turned the key one last time. Click click click.

The battery was dead.

Morgan let her head fall onto the steering wheel.

A battery wouldn't have broken her budget. And now Del might die due to her negligence. Morgan brushed away tears with her gloves. There had to be something she could do to save Del.

The keys were in the ATVs. Morgan fired up one, and drove it to the garage door. She gunned the engine. The tires spun on the garage floor. The door wouldn't budge.

"I'm wasting time."

Morgan slid out the door and hurried to the house. She rested her wrist against Del's forehead. He felt cool and clammy.

They were so close to town, and yet they might as well have been a hundred miles away. Or in another century. How did people survive without phones and cars in the horse and buggy days?

Or donkey and cart days.

Morgan headed for the barn. The doors faced south. The snow was only a foot deep against the front of the barn. She ducked inside the small side door and pushed the double doors open from inside.

"Time to earn your feed," Morgan told the donkeys.

They cooperated as Morgan fumbled with the bridles, harness, and cart. She was certain she had not fastened all the buckles and straps correctly, but when she drove the cart through the open barn doors, everything held together.

The sturdy little animals strained against their harness, plowing through deep snow. They negotiated two gates and stopped near the back door. Morgan ran inside. She strapped on the survival pack, then grabbed the comforters off both beds.

"Del, we're going to the hospital," Morgan said. "Houdini and Adelaide are taking you."

She was able to rouse Del enough to get him out the door and onto the cart. After bundling him up, she walked beside the cart. The donkeys knew the way to town. She let them set their own pace, even though her heart was racing. It was like walking inside a snow globe.

Hill Street was devoid of traffic. The snow muffled every sound except for clinking buckles on the donkeys' harness. Their hooves punched holes in fresh snow. Morgan's breath came out in steaming clouds. Sweat soaked through her wool cap and trickled into her eyes.

When they reached the bottom of Hill Street, Morgan pulled back on the reins. She hadn't thought beyond getting Del to town. She fumbled for her cell phone. No signal. No tire tracks marred the snow.

She didn't expect anyone to be out in the blizzard, but surely people were holed up in their above-the-shop apartments. Morgan turned in a circle, searching for signs of life in the shops. She could barely see across Main Street. A neon fairy danced in Piers's shop window, but the "closed" sign faced the street.

Morgan drove the cart into the rear parking lot of Faerie Tales.

"Piers! We need help!" She pounded her fist against the back door. "Help!"

She had assumed he went home after dinner. But no one answered. Morgan took a step backward and looked up at the second-floor windows. She bent down to form a snowball, and aimed it at a window. It splattered against the glass.

The curtain gapped open slightly. Morgan caught a glimpse of a person through the cream-colored sheers. Just enough to see it wasn't Piers looking at her.

"Hey!" she yelled. "Call nine-one-one! Del is hurt!"

The figure turned slightly, and Morgan thought she detected a heavy, but definitely womanly, shape. The sheers and the falling snow obscured her vision.

"Sparrow?" Morgan whispered to herself.

Piers certainly hadn't wasted any time when Morgan spurned his advances just hours ago. The curtain fluttered closed.

Morgan's injured ego would have to wait.

CHAPTER THIRTY-ONE

It might have been seconds, but it seemed that she waited in the falling snow behind the closed rear door of Faerie Tales for an hour. She pounded on the door again. No answer.

"Front door," she told the donkeys.

They plowed their way toward the front of the shop. The cart jerked to a stop. They had run against some snow-covered obstacle. Morgan pulled, and the donkeys strained against their harness, but the cart's wheels wouldn't budge. Morgan abandoned them at the side of the shop. She ran to the front door and beat her fist against the glass.

"Piers! Help!"

Morgan pulled her cell phone out. She tried dialing nine-one-one, even though her phone didn't have signal. She turned, scanning Main Street for any open shops. Golden Springs was a ghost town.

She checked Del. His eyes were closed. If he was breathing, Morgan couldn't tell through the layers of comforters.

"Del, I'm sorry!" Morgan wiped her glove across her eyes. The tears threatened to freeze to her cheeks. She didn't want to leave Del, but she had no choice. She had to get help. "I've got to run to Bernie's. I'll be right back."

"Morgan!" Kurt Willard post-holed through knee-deep snow across Main Street, a still camera bouncing against his chest. "What's wrong?"

"Del tore up his arm with a chain saw."

"Follow me."

Kurt helped dislodge the cart, then plowed back across Main Street. Morgan followed. The donkeys struggled to drag the cart across the slick pavement. Kurt led them to a Victorian-style house on a side street. He clambered up the snow-covered steps onto the porch and hammered his fist on the door.

A woman with soft gray hair opened the door. She clutched the neck of her pink fleece bathrobe. A huge black Labrador pushed past her legs, sniffing the air and eyeing the donkeys.

"What's going on?"

"Mrs. Drewmoore," Kurt gasped. "We have an emergency. We've got to see Doc."

Kurt lifted Del off the donkey cart, and struggled up the slippery front steps. Morgan looped the donkeys' reins around the porch railing and followed Kurt inside.

Doctor Drewmoore ushered them into an examining room. He pulled a lab coat on over his sweatshirt and pants, and slid his sock feet into rubber heelless shoes.

The men lifted Del onto an examining table.

"Is he alive?" Morgan asked.

Del moaned as the doctor unwrapped the comforters.

Morgan burst into relieved sobs. Mrs. Drewmoore put an arm around Morgan's shoulders.

"Come with me," she told Morgan. "We'll have a cup of tea while we wait for the ambulance."

It was a long wait.

Patty Drewmoore distracted Morgan with small talk. She and the doctor were semi-retired. They maintained a small clinic that took up one side of the ground level of their home. They were well equipped for minor emergencies. The doctor often administered first aid, keeping people stable until the ambulance could take them to the hospital in Granite Junction.

"We weren't supposed to be here today," Patty said.

Morgan rubbed the Labrador's blocky head. "What do you mean?"

"Henry and I were going to meet our son and his family at Monarch Ski Resort last night. When we heard the weather forecast, we debated whether to try outrunning the storm, but we decided to stay home. For Del's sake, I'm glad we did."

Kurt stuck his head into the kitchen.

"Del wants you."

Morgan rushed to the examining room. Del lay flat on the table, still pale, but awake. An IV snaked from his good arm. The doctor had bandaged the wounded arm.

"We've got to get him to the hospital," the doctor said, "but once he's down the hill, I'm sure they'll get him patched up."

"Thank God!" Morgan pressed her hands to her face as the tears started to flow again.

"I'm a tough old buzzard," Del whispered. "Don't worry about me."

"Thank you, Doctor," Morgan said.

The doctor shook his head. "You got him here. You saved his life."

The Granite Junction ambulance couldn't get up the pass to Golden Springs. The blizzard had dumped too much snow for ordinary vehicles to navigate. Instead, a search and rescue snow-cat rumbled up to the doctor's house.

Morgan ran onto the porch with Mrs. Drewmoore and waved at the snowcat. The donkeys stood with their reins looped around the porch railing, falling snow covering their backs. They eyed the boxy orange contraption with suspicion, but seemed too worn out to run from the noisy vehicle.

Four triangular rubber snow tracks, modeled after the continuous track of a military tank, gripped the snow-packed street. A paramedic jumped out of the cab and ran up the porch steps.

Mrs. Drewmoore led the woman into the house. Morgan paced across the porch, wearing a path through the snow. Finally, the doctor and Kurt carried Del out of the house on a stretcher and down the steps to the snowcat.

Morgan started to climb into the cab of the snowcat with the paramedic.

"No," Del whispered. "Houdini and Adelaide."

"I'll go with Del," Kurt said. "I'd offer to take care of the donkeys, but I don't know anything about livestock. I'll call you when we get to the hospital. Where will you be?"

"I don't know," Morgan said.

She pulled the cell phone out of her pocket. The signal was strong. It figured.

"Call my number." Kurt recited his cell phone number. Morgan dialed it. Kurt's ringtone was a big band song. "Now we're connected!" Kurt flashed one of his charming smiles, and for once Morgan wasn't annoyed by it.

The snowcat rolled slowly out of sight.

Morgan turned to Houdini and Adelaide. She threw her arm around Adelaide and buried her face in the donkey's neck.

"You are the best donkeys. The best!"

Patty Drewmoore stepped onto the porch, Buddy the Labrador at her side. "Have they got a place to stay tonight?"

"We'll head back up the hill," Morgan said. "If we made it down, surely we can make it up."

"Oh, no!" Patty said. "It's still snowing, and it'll be dark soon. They must be exhausted from their adventure. Our garage was a carriage house once upon a time. Bring them around back."

Patty backed an SUV out of the converted carriage house. Her neighbors helped clear space while Morgan unharnessed the donkeys. News spread quickly about the donkeys who had saved Del Addison's life. The riding stable near Mineral Springs Park sent two bales of straw and a bag of oats to the Drewmoores', pulled by a horse-drawn sleigh.

"What exactly happened to old Del?" the Drewmoores' neighbor Abe, as old as Del, asked.

"He cut his arm with a chain saw," Morgan said.

Abe snorted. "I've done that myself."

"No, Abe, not this bad you haven't," Patty said. "Plus Del was taking blood thinners. His blood wasn't clotting fast enough. Henry said Del could have died if he hadn't made it to the clinic when he did."

"Could have," Abe said, but without the snort this time.

"Why are people so ready to dismiss the miraculous?" Patty asked.

"You're calling this a miracle?" Abe asked.

Patty and Morgan met eyes.

"It was a miracle," Patty declared.

"I don't know about that," Morgan said. "There were so many things that had to happen just right in order for Del to make it to Doctor Drewmoore in time. But still, 'miracle' might be too big a word for it."

Patty rubbed Houdini's forehead. "It was an everyday miracle. The kind that go unnoticed by people who don't see the miraculous in life."

Morgan nodded her head. "An everyday miracle," she agreed. "Courtesy of ordinary donkeys."

Houdini snorted and nodded his head.

Morgan's cell phone chimed.

"Hello?"

"Kurt here. We made it. What a trip!"

"How's Del?"

"The doctors aren't sure whether they can save his arm,"

Kurt said, "but they're making every effort."

Morgan's stomach churned. "Was it anything I did? Or didn't do?"

"No. The doctors say you did the right thing. Del wants to know how the donkeys are."

Morgan laughed. "I'm happy to report that the donkeys have never had it so good. They're spending the night in Doctor Drewmoore's heated carriage house on a bed of the softest straw available. They might never want to go home."

"How about you?" Kurt asked. "Have you got a place to stay tonight?"

"Patty offered me their guest room, but I'm going to call Bernie—"

Morgan stopped. In all the excitement, she had forgotten that there was a murderer on the loose. Kurt Willard didn't need to know her whereabouts. Whether or not she suspected him now, he couldn't keep his mouth shut. Her location might end up as front-page news before the streets were plowed.

"I'll stay at the hospital," Kurt said. "The roads are still terrible, and I think Del appreciates having someone he knows here, even if we aren't exactly the best of friends. Do you have his son's phone number?"

Surely she could cross Kurt off her list of suspects now. If he hadn't been photographing the blizzard, she might not have gotten Del to the doctor in time. And now he was going out of his way to take care of the old cowboy.

"I'll have to call Cindy," Morgan said. "She might know."

It was dark by the time the donkeys were situated. Morgan got Del's son's number from Cindy, and relayed it to Kurt.

Finally, she called Bernie.

Bernie threw open the bakery's front door before Morgan had a chance to knock.

"Are you okay?" Bernie asked.

"I'm exhausted," Morgan said. "It's been a long day."

"Come upstairs! Here, carry this."

Bernie handed Morgan a loaf of lemon poppy-seed bread. When she opened the door to her upstairs living quarters, Morgan could smell soup and freshly baked bread.

"I wish the circumstances were different," Bernie said, "but this will be fun. Like a slumber party."

"Only I think I really need the slumber part more than the party," Morgan said.

"Mew," Mr. Whiskers said.

She was revived by good food and a hot shower. When Bernie opened a bottle of wine, Morgan finally started to relax. It took a long time to tell Bernie the events of the past twenty-four hours. Morgan couldn't keep it in chronological order. Her dinner with Piers the previous night, Del's accident, the trip down the hill, being ignored by Piers when she beat on his door; it all came out in a jumble.

Bernie was ready to march over to Faerie Tales in the dark, through the snow, in order to give Piers a piece of her mind.

"I don't know if Piers heard me knock," Morgan said.

"Don't defend him," Bernie said. "He had to have heard you."

Morgan sipped her wine. "I'm not sure he was there. I saw someone peek out the curtain. It wasn't him."

"Who was it?" Bernie asked, her green eyes growing large.

Morgan shook her head. "I only caught a glimpse of the person. If I had to say, I would guess it was Sparrow."

Bernie pressed her hands to the sides of her face. "Get out of here!" She laughed. "Sparrow? It's obvious she has a crush on Piers, but I never guessed he was interested in her."

"Maybe she was consoling him because I wouldn't go home with him. What I don't understand is why she wouldn't open the door, or call nine-one-one."

"I wonder if Piers knew you were out there."

Bernie refilled Morgan's wine glass.

"The person who really surprised me was Kurt Willard," Morgan said. "He jumped right in to help, even though neither Del nor I have been particularly nice to him."

"He did what you're supposed to do," Bernie said. "What anybody would do."

"Not anybody," Morgan reminded her. "He saved Del's life."

It was still dark when Morgan heard roaring and clanking in the street. She climbed off the fold-out sofa bed and stood at Bernie's apartment window in borrowed pajamas several sizes too large. The snow had stopped falling. The first snowplow worked its way up Main Street.

Bernie shuffled out of her bedroom and mechanically started coffee brewing. She joined Morgan at the window.

"Today will be like a holiday," Bernie yawned. "Most of the shops won't open."

"Then we should go back to bed," Morgan said.

"Oh, no," Bernie said. "Everyone will want coffee and pastries. This is the kind of day than helps me make it through the winter." She pulled a medallion on a heavy chain from under her nightgown. "Saint Elizabeth brings me days like this. She's the patron saint of bakers."

Saint Elizabeth worked overtime as a festive mood seized Golden Springs. The bakery filled with people unable to drive on the snow-blocked roads. Morgan helped Bernie bus tables, wash dishes, and mop melted snow off the floor. The crowd didn't thin out until after an unprecedented off-season lunch rush.

Kurt and Doctor Drewmoore made it back to town as the sun sank behind the mountains. The doctor stomped the snow off his boots, and Kurt off his shoes, before entering the bakery.

"The highway's clear," Kurt announced.

"Just dropping by to give you a report," the doctor told Morgan. "The physicians taking care of Del think they'll be able to save his arm."

Morgan sat down. "Thank God!"

"He'll be in the hospital several more days, but he's doing remarkably well for a man his age."

"Del's son made it to the hospital," Kurt said. "He followed the snowplows all the way from Denver to Granite Junction."

"I'm heading home," Doctor Drewmoore said. "It's been a long day and a half."

Morgan jumped up. "I can't thank you and Patty enough."

Doctor Drewmoore clasped Morgan's hand. "If you hadn't gotten Del to me in time, he wouldn't have had a chance."

Morgan sank back onto her chair. Kurt sat across the small table from her as the doctor left.

"Kurt, you're as responsible as I am, or the doctor, or the donkeys, for saving Del's life."

"I've been thinking about that all day," Kurt said. "Why didn't Piers answer his door? You were yelling to raise the dead."

Morgan hesitated a moment too long. "I don't know."

Kurt tapped his nose and smiled. "Yes, you do. I've got a nose for news."

Bernie sat next to Morgan. "Tell him. I think people should know."

"But I don't—" Morgan began.

"That slimeball Piers was home," Bernie said. "Sparrow Plinkton wouldn't open the door or call for help. I know Piers had to hear what happened. He was going to let Del bleed to death in the street."

"Bernie, we don't know all that."

Kurt pulled his leather gloves off and set them on the small table. "Sparrow Plinkton and Piers Townsend, eh?"

He started to pull out his notepad and pencil. Morgan placed her hand on his arm.

"I thought this was a private conversation," Morgan said.

Kurt left his reporter's tools in his pocket.

"Fair enough. I'd be delighted to file this under 'conversation between friends.' "

"But you can print the miracle of the donkeys," Bernie said.

"Miracle?" Kurt's eyes opened wide.

"Kurt," Morgan said, "you were there. You saw how the donkeys pulled Del to the doctor. Well, the story has grown a little with the retelling."

Kurt pulled out his notepad and pencil.

"I've already got the photos," he said. "Let's hear the story."

CHAPTER THIRTY-TWO

When Morgan retrieved the donkeys the next morning from the Drewmoores' carriage house garage, Adelaide had her head plunged into a bucket of oats.

"Kendall and Allie told me not to feed the donkeys too much," Morgan said. "Adelaide's getting fat."

Patty Drewmoore patted Adelaide's back. "I asked the vet to drop by. It's official. Adelaide's pregnant."

Houdini snorted and nodded his head. The Drewmoores' Labrador lay down and rested his head on his paws.

"That's great news!" Morgan rubbed Adelaide's forehead. "What do I owe you for the vet visit?" She dreaded the answer.

"The doctors trade consultations," Patty said. "You don't owe a dime. And I have a sheet of instructions for you. Adelaide needs special attention, considering her age."

"These two aren't going to want to go home," Morgan said. "But I'd better take them back up the hill, if it's okay for Adelaide to pull the cart."

Adelaide carried precious cargo. Offspring meant the legal continuation of donkey residency at the Rock of Ages, according to the city ordinance.

"Donkeys have a long gestation," Patty said. "It might be months before she's due."

Patty helped Morgan harness the donkeys. Morgan was getting proficient at the task. She led them up freshly plowed Main Street, heading for the auto shop. Regardless of the cost, Morgan was purchasing a new car battery.

Gerda waited in the doorway of the auto shop, wearing black snow boots over the pant legs of her eggplant-colored jumpsuit.

"You see now, when I tell you the battery needs replacing, I was not going for a profit."

"I wish I'd listened to you."

Morgan didn't mention her doubts that the Buick could have made it downhill in the blizzard. Only donkey instinct had kept them from landing in the ditch. But then, Gerda might lecture her about the need for snow tires.

Gerda directed Morgan's purchase of a battery with a martial air and a few more I-told-you-so comments. She gave detailed instructions on its proper installation, then opened the office door to get a receipt pad.

Morgan tried not to notice the half-empty bottle of bourbon sitting on the desk blotter.

People shoveling sidewalks greeted the miracle donkeys as they passed, some running inside to retrieve cameras. When she reached Hill Street, Morgan watched the windows of Faerie Tales. The lights were off.

By the time Morgan had the donkeys unharnessed, fed, and bedded down in the barn, the sun had gone down. She unlocked the front door of the shop. The last of the setting sun cast an orange glow through the windows. Morgan flipped on the lights.

Melting snow dripped off the roof, plopping onto the gravel. The old building creaked as chill night air wrapped around it. Morgan strained to hear anything out of the ordinary. She had left the door between the shop and the living quarters open. Morgan peered into the kitchen. The overhead light was still on. The back door was closed, but she remembered she had not locked it.

A pile of bloody pillows lay strewn half on the easy chair and half on the floor. Everything was the way she had left it, including the stack of dry pancakes and shriveled sausage on the table. Mice had nibbled on both, and left the evidence of their feasting. Morgan cleaned up the mess, then checked the phone. It had a dial tone.

"Of course."

She played her messages.

The first was from the satellite dish company. "We're still planning to come out to install your dish and set up your Internet. Please call if you need to reschedule."

Message two was her brother.

"This is the third time I've called," Kendall's voice boomed. "I'm starting to get worried." Pause. Morgan could hear a tropical bird singing in the background. When Kendall spoke again, his voice was softer. "I'll call back the next chance I get."

If he and his cult weren't so determined to live "off the grid," she'd have a number to call him back. He deserved to worry.

Morgan shivered. The fire had died long ago. She stirred the ashes with an iron poker. Amazingly, there were still smoldering coals. Morgan stuffed the smallest bits of kindling into the stove. They ignited, burning quickly. She placed twigs, then larger pieces in the stove. Before long, she had a real fire going.

"Del would be proud of me."

The cowbell clanged. Cindy stepped inside, stomping snow off her boots.

"We haven't had a storm like this in three years," she said. "Have you heard anything more from Del?"

"Doctor Drewmoore said he'd be in the hospital another few days."

"What's that?" Cindy pointed at the car battery sitting on the counter.

"Part of the miracle donkey story," Morgan said. "My car battery went dead when I was trying to get Del to the hospital.

That's the replacement."

Cindy rushed to the door and waved at the car backing out of the Rock of Ages parking lot. "Hey, Herb! Hold up!" She turned to Morgan. "Herb can put that battery in for you."

"Gerda gave me instructions."

"It'll take you an hour to change out your car battery. Herb can do it in ten minutes."

A white van pulled up beside Herb, the tire chains churning up the snow-packed parking lot.

"Customers already?" Cindy asked.

"No, it's the satellite dish company," Morgan said. "I'm getting the Internet hooked up. I'm surprised they made it up the hill."

The installation technician hooked up the dish, and then made sure Morgan's Internet service and television worked.

"Cindy, come here!" Morgan called from the office.

Cindy crowded in around the satellite dish technician. "What is it?"

"An ultrasound of my grandchild," Morgan said.

"If I'm not mistaken," Cindy said, "you've got a grandson."

"I'll bet that picture alone made the satellite dish worthwhile," the installation technician said.

"Yes," Morgan said. "I feel like I'm back in the twenty-first century again."

The cowbell clanged, signaling the start of a steady stream of customers. People braved the treacherous roads to see the miracle donkeys.

Houdini and Adelaide stood at the fence closest to the parking lot, posing for photos and snacking on cookies, until Morgan posted a "Do not feed the donkeys" sign.

"Cookies will make the donkeys sick," Morgan explained to a little boy and his sister, standing knee-deep in the snow.

"Set your toys down," a man told the kids. "Daddy wants to

take your picture."

The kids set their shiny trinkets, prizes from a fast-food meal, on a fence post. A magpie swooped onto the fence as Dad snapped a photo.

"My car!" the little girl screamed.

The magpie flew off in a rush of white and black feathers, the cheap plastic car clutched in its claws. The girl burst into tears.

"My toy!" she wailed.

"I'm so sorry," Morgan said. "Let me see if I've got something I can replace that with."

The father stifled a laugh. "It was just one of those things." He patted his daughter on the back as she clung to him. "There's nothing you could have done. I just wish I'd had my video camera. That would be great on YouTube."

"I insist." Morgan dashed inside the shop. "Cindy, a magpie stole a little girl's toy."

"Oh, yeah," Cindy said. "Magpies are like crows. They like to steal things and take them to their nests."

Morgan looked around frantically for something to give the girl, finally grabbing a pink polished stone carved in the shape of a cat, strung on a red satin string.

The girl was more than happy with the trade.

When Morgan returned, Cindy was on the phone. She clamped her hand over the receiver.

"It's Kendall," Cindy whispered loudly. She uncovered the receiver. "Your sister's back. She has to tell you about the miracle of the donkeys."

"I'll take it in the office." Morgan rushed to her desk and picked up the phone. "The sign is working," she told Kendall. "We have customers."

"Are Houdini and Adelaide okay?" Kendall asked.

"More than okay. Adelaide is pregnant."

"Unbelievable!" Kendall boomed. "Are you sure?"

"Confirmed by a veterinarian," Morgan said. "We don't know when she's due."

"That's fantastic! I can't wait to tell Allie. Is that the miracle Cindy mentioned?"

"That's only part of it." Morgan told a condensed version of Del's accident, and his rescue by donkey cart.

"Don't let Del move back into his trailer until he's fully healed," Kendall said. "It's not the safest place."

"I haven't seen his trailer up close. What's wrong with it?"

"The steps to the front door are rotting out. The trailer needs a lot of repairs. Keep him at the shop if you can."

Morgan knew Kendall might end their conversation abruptly. She cut to the chase.

"Kendall, someone tried to push me off a bridge." She gave a quick rundown of the stone bridge incident. "Do you know if anyone wants the rock shop badly enough to kill for it?"

"Morgan, I'm so sorry you got mixed up in all this."

"What haven't you been telling me?" Morgan asked. "Or maybe the question is, what have you ever told me? The rock shop is half mine. You could have let me know if you were having problems this serious."

"Sam was sick when this all started. Do you really think you could have handled more stress during that time?"

Morgan didn't have an answer.

There was a pause, and when Kendall spoke again, he sounded bone tired. "It was after Sam got sick. Allie and I had given up all hope of having children. We were caught up in the legal issues surrounding the rezoning proposals when Allie realized something was different. She thought she was going through menopause."

Kendall spoke to someone in Spanish, then returned to the conversation with Morgan.

"People need the phone," he said. "I'll have to rush this. Allie found out she was pregnant."

Another miscarriage, Morgan thought.

"Oh, Kendall. I'm so sorry."

"Let me finish," Kendall paused. "Just let me get through this. She wasn't very far along when she was driving home from a City Council meeting one evening. It had been a particularly passionate meeting. Allie got into it with Sparrow Plinkton—"

"Sparrow!"

"Allie crashed into the irrigation ditch. She thought a car ran her off the road, but it happened so fast, she only remembered headlights, then waking up in the hospital. If Del hadn't happened by, Allie might have died. She wished she had, when she lost the baby." There was another pause. "Maybe she would have lost the baby anyway. She'd had miscarriages before, you know. But she just didn't want to be there after that."

"You never told me," Morgan said. "I'm so sorry."

"I am too," Kendall said. "About a lot of things. But not about moving. I know it was the right decision."

Kendall spoke in Spanish again. Morgan was going to lose him.

"Wait," she said. "Does 'Thumbelina' mean anything to you?"

"The fairy tale?" Kendall asked.

"It has something to do with the murder," Morgan said.

"Doesn't ring a bell," Kendall said. "I have to go."

Kendall hung up before Morgan could ask more questions.

Sales were nearing what Morgan estimated were necessary for the shop's survival. It had taken a "miracle" to draw that many customers. Rather than making her optimistic, Morgan realized the dim likelihood of sustaining that level of sales. She was musing over the possibility of joining Kendall's cult in the jungle when Bernie called.

"Morgan, can you come to town?" Bernie asked. "You have

to see this."

"I've actually got customers today," Morgan said. "I don't think Cindy can manage without me."

"Did you get the Internet hooked up?" Bernie asked.

"Yes. Just this morning."

"Then I'll scan it and send it to you," Bernie said. "Give me your address."

Morgan recited her email address.

"Call me when you get my email," Bernie said, and hung up.

By the time Morgan had her computer on and her email up, Bernie's message hit her inbox. She opened the attachment.

Someone had photo-shopped a picture of Houdini and Adelaide, placing wings on their backs and haloes over their heads. Morgan called Bernie.

"Where did that come from?" Morgan asked. "It's adorable!"

"Kurt Willard, of all people," Bernie said. "He said he's going to run it on the front page of a special edition of the *Gazetteer*, coming out tomorrow morning."

Make hay while the sun shines, Cindy had said.

"I've got to call Kurt," Morgan said. "I have an idea. Are we on for tonight?"

"You bet!" Bernie said.

When she called Kurt, he was more than happy to let Morgan use the image of the donkeys for a T-shirt.

"I'll want credit for the photo, of course," Kurt said. "And the name of the paper somewhere on the shirt."

"That's fair," Morgan said. "I was planning to have the name of the rock shop printed above the picture of the donkeys."

"Why don't you let me work up a design?" Kurt asked. "I know Mike and Hannah at the T-shirt shop. I'm sure I can negotiate a good deal, and we can split the cost of the shirts."

"I'd like to see the design before you take it to be printed,"

Morgan said. "And I want to get some shirts made as soon as possible."

"Absolutely. Do you have email?"

"I do now," Morgan said.

"Give me your address. I'll email you when I have something ready."

When Morgan hung up the phone, Cindy pointed to the window. Another carload of donkey fans pulled into the parking lot.

"I wish Del were here," Cindy said. "He'd love to see this."

Morgan was happy to let Kurt take charge of the T-shirt project. She had enough to do, dealing with the celebrity donkeys. Besides, she was changing her opinion of Kurt Willard. As annoying as the newspaperman could be, when faced with an emergency, Kurt had jumped into action without hesitation.

Unlike Piers.

It only took Kurt a couple of hours to design the T-shirt. Despite her growing respect for him, she had feared the design might turn into a glorified advertisement for the *Gazetteer*. Morgan was pleasantly surprised that the newspaper logo was the same size font as the rock shop's name.

Cindy studied the image on the laptop screen over Morgan's shoulder. "I'll need seven."

The cowbell clanged.

"I'll get that," Cindy said.

Morgan called Kurt.

"I like it," Morgan said. "Could I get some shirts printed right away? I don't know how long Houdini and Adelaide will be attracting this attention."

"Can you come to town?" Kurt asked. "I think we should both be there to order the shirts, plus I have something interesting to show you."

★ ★ ★ ★ ★

Morgan parked the Buick in front of the *Gazetteer.* Anna sat at the receptionist's desk.

"I heard about Del," Anna said, "and your adventure with the donkeys."

"Kurt saved Del's life," Morgan said.

"Oh?" Anna arched her brows in surprise.

"He didn't tell you?" Morgan asked. "When I got Del and the donkeys to town, Kurt was photographing Main Street. He led us to Doctor Drewmoore just in time."

Kurt came to the door of his office. "Come on in, Morgan. I want to show you what Anna and I have been working on."

Kurt pointed to a map of Golden Springs pinned to the wall of his office.

"I decided to investigate what you said about Piers Townsend buying up property," Kurt said. "Small-town rumors become fact with the retelling, but Anna spent a day in City Hall pouring over real-estate sales records since Piers moved here."

"It was dull work," Anna said. "Kurt owes me a steak dinner. But when I started to see the pattern, then it became exciting."

The half city block taken up by the retirement home was outlined in blue. The rest of Main Street was a checkerboard of colors.

"What do the colors mean?" Morgan asked.

"Ownership," Anna said. "But that was a little trickier to determine than it seemed. Notice the yellow?"

Anna pointed to rectangles of yellow highlighter.

"Those belong to Piers Townsend."

"Only four," Morgan said. "So it's not true?"

"That's what I thought," Kurt said. "But see the pink?"

Rectangles of pink marked every third building in downtown Golden Springs.

"Those are owned by Sparrow Plinkton."

"Sparrow!" Morgan said. "She owns all that property? How?"

"She's hiding behind a development company," Kurt said, "but she's the owner of the company, and therefore, the properties."

"I wouldn't have guessed Sparrow had the resources to buy a third of Main Street," Morgan said.

"When you told me that Sparrow was in Piers's apartment Saturday morning," Kurt said, "it occurred to me that they might have some business connection, as well as a personal relationship."

"Do you think Piers is bankrolling her acquisitions?" Morgan asked. "Hiding behind her?"

"There's nothing wrong with buying property that's for sale," Kurt said. "I don't understand why he'd think he needed to cover up his real-estate acquisitions."

"Notice something else?" Anna asked.

She pointed to the newspaper office on the map. Except for Kurt's newspaper, the entire block was marked with pink.

"Sparrow's development company owns everything on this block?" Morgan asked.

"This is hitting a little close to home for my comfort." Kurt picked up a printout. "We'd better head to the T-shirt shop before it gets any later."

Morgan walked beside Kurt down the boardwalk.

"I want to thank you," Kurt said.

"For what?" Morgan asked.

"I was so busy playing small-town reporter," Kurt said, "I forgot what it meant to actually be one. There's more to being a newspaperman than sticking a press card in your hat band."

CHAPTER THIRTY-THREE

Mike and Hannah were delighted to receive business during the off season. They waived the charge for rush orders. Printing miracle donkey T-shirts would be a pleasure, Mike assured them.

On her way back to the rock shop, Morgan passed Faerie Tales. She slowed the Buick, then pulled into a parking space. When she walked in, it was apparent that the metaphysical shop was enjoying spillover from the miracle donkey crowds.

Morgan wound her way through the bookcases and clothing racks until she found Piers.

"Hello, Morgan," Piers said. "How may I help you?"

Morgan hesitated. She didn't want to embarrass Piers in front of his customers when she didn't have all the facts about Saturday morning.

"Can I talk to you?" she asked, her voice strained.

"I sense you are troubled—"

Morgan grabbed Piers's tunic sleeve and dragged him past the seating area. Sparrow hunched over a cup of tea, having an animated conversation with the older lady who had wanted to buy a gargoyle necklace. Morgan hauled Piers to a quiet corner of the shop.

"Damn right I'm troubled," she said in a harsh whisper. "Why didn't you come to your door Saturday? Del nearly died!"

Morgan gave Piers credit for looking genuinely surprised.

"I don't understand."

"Don't try to tell me you haven't heard about Del's accident,

295

and the miracle of the donkeys."

"Yes," Piers said. "What has that got to do with me?"

"I beat on your back door that morning," Morgan said. "I yelled for help." Morgan's lip trembled. She fought back angry tears. "Del almost died, and you wouldn't even call nine-one-one. Is that part of your philosophy? Was it Del's karma?"

Piers shoved his hands inside his tunic sleeves. "This was the morning of the blizzard?"

"Yes."

He turned toward the seating area. Sparrow glanced their way, shooting daggers with her eyes at Morgan.

"I was occupied," Piers started to say, watching Sparrow. He turned to Morgan. "I didn't hear the door."

Morgan looked from Piers to Sparrow and back.

"Too busy to call nine-one-one?" Morgan asked. "What really makes me angry is that you're enjoying business because my donkeys have more of a sense of humanity than you."

Morgan stormed out, assured that she had disrupted the auras of every patron in Faerie Tales.

That evening Morgan drove Bernie to O'Reily's pub, confident her new battery would not leave them stranded.

"I'm so happy to have a break," Morgan said. "It's been crazy at the shop all day."

"Isn't that what you wanted?" Bernie asked. "Customers?"

"I wish Del were there," Morgan said. "We need help."

"I could see if Emma or Darlene needs extra work," Bernie said. "As long as you don't steal them from me."

"I have no idea how long donkey mania will last. I'll manage a little longer."

O'Reily's Runners was becoming a comfortable routine. When Lucy announced the Hopping Bunny Snowshoe race to the crowd of runners, Morgan and Bernie helped hand out fliers. Barton approached, holding out his hand to Morgan.

"I would like a flier," he said.

"Do you snowshoe?" Bernie asked.

"When need be," Barton said. "I like to support Pine County Search and Rescue any chance I get. You never know when you'll need them."

"They took Del to the hospital in Granite Junction when no one else could get through."

"When is Del going home?" Barton asked.

"He wants to come home now," Morgan said, "but the doctors have convinced him to stay another day or two."

"I'll visit him."

The run started, and Barton sprinted off.

Kurt's special edition of the *Golden Springs Gazetteer* hit the streets Wednesday morning. Carloads of people drove up the hill to see the miracle donkeys. Most wandered in to the shop to warm up, use the restroom, and, quite often, to make a purchase.

Morgan called Cindy and asked her to come to work. Cindy arrived with two of her older children, and two teenagers.

"You remember my Matthew and Ruth," she said. "And I brought Robin and Martin. They need credit for their home-school life skills class."

"I made this." Robin had taped the photo-shopped image of the donkeys from the newspaper to a sun-tea jar, with a handwritten sign, "Donate to Search & Rescue."

"That's a great idea," Morgan said. "You can put it on the counter next to the cash register. What do you two know about working in a shop?"

"Nothing," Robin said. "I've only ever babysat."

"And I've mowed lawns," Martin said. "I'll do anything, if you'll sign my sheet saying I learned a life skill."

"I'm sure I can keep you busy," Morgan said.

The donkey celebrities needed a bodyguard to protect them from the paparazzi. Morgan put Martin on first shift supervising Houdini and Adelaide's photo ops. The rush order of tourist trinkets arrived. As quickly as Morgan could enter them into inventory, Matthew and Ruth placed them out for sale, while Cindy and Robin rang them up on the cash register.

Morgan was halfway through the box of trinkets when Cindy rapped on the office door.

"I can't keep up with you," Morgan laughed.

"Someone wants to talk to you, cowgirl," Cindy said. "You'd better come here."

Trevin stood in the shop doorway. Morgan recognized the dreadlocks immediately. His clothing had changed dramatically, though. In place of the goth black, he wore baggy blue jeans and a baby-blue T-shirt under a clean fleece jacket. The ring was missing from his eyebrow.

"I came to fix the back door," Trevin said. "Think of it as my community service, to pay back all the trouble I caused. If Del hasn't done it already."

"Did you hear about Del?" Morgan asked.

"Yeah," Trevin said. "I was hoping he'd be here."

"He's still in the hospital. He'll be home in a few more days."

Trevin held the door for a family equipped with cameras.

"I heard about the donkeys, too," Trevin said. "Something about a miracle?"

"Come on in. I'll tell you all about it, but then you have to tell me what happened to you."

"Okay," Trevin said, "but I need to tell my ride I'm staying."

Morgan watched through the window as Trevin dashed to a passenger car and spoke to the driver. It had to be Trevin's father, judging from the family resemblance. When he came back inside, Morgan led Trevin through the door to the living quarters. She told him the details of Del's accident and rescue while Trevin took measurements for a new pane of glass.

"It does sound like a miracle," Trevin said. "I'm glad Del made it, even though he turned me over to the police."

"I tried to stop them from keeping you," Morgan said.

"It turned out okay. My folks picked me up when I got released. They let me move home for a while. It's kind of like jail, but with better food."

"I'm glad to hear that," Morgan said. "The part about moving home, not the jail part. Since the police let you out, I'm guessing you were cooperative?"

"Officer Sanchez convinced me I wasn't getting anywhere on my own, and that I might as well tell them what I know. It didn't help them much."

"You said your old friends held you prisoner. Couldn't the police stake out the house?"

"That was the one thing Sanchez got excited about," Trevin said. "But it was just an old abandoned house, and somebody torched it."

"Good way to get rid of evidence," Morgan said. "What about the car? You said they drove you here in the black SUV."

Trevin shrugged. "I didn't get the license number. And Slice, the guy behind the wheel, didn't own it. He sure enjoyed driving it, though."

Someone rapped on the door dividing the living quarters from the shop.

"Mrs. Iverson," Robin called. "Telephone."

Trevin followed Morgan back into the shop.

"It's Hannah from the T-shirt shop," Cindy said, handing her the phone.

Trevin's parents seemed to find reasons to call or text-message their son several times as he ran errands with Morgan, but Tre-

299

vin didn't complain. The hardware store in Golden Springs had the window repair supplies they needed, as well as plenty of free advice. Next they picked up the T-shirts. Morgan took a half-dozen shirts to the *Golden Springs Gazetteer*. Trevin studied the old newspapers framed on the wall while she spoke to Kurt in his office.

"These look great." Kurt held a shirt against his chest. "I might have to make a temporary wardrobe change."

"Hannah assures me they can do a better job with a little more time," Morgan said. "Add color. Improve the print quality. But I think I like this simple black and white image."

"Is there any way you could bring the donkeys to the snowshoe race?" Kurt asked.

"Bernie and I are volunteering. We're in charge of an aid station. I don't think we'd be able to watch the donkeys, too."

"I'll talk to Del. Maybe I can work out a way."

Kurt walked out of his office and arranged a shirt in the front window of the newspaper office. He watched Trevin for a moment.

"Is your friend who I think he is?" Kurt whispered to Morgan.

"Dawn's boyfriend?" Morgan whispered back. "That's him." Louder she said, "Trevin, this is Kurt Willard. He owns the newspaper."

The two shook hands.

"I'm looking for a job," Trevin said. "If you hear of anything."

"Give me your number, and I'll call if something comes up."

Like a request for an exclusive interview, Morgan thought. She would warn Trevin later.

"Before I forget," Morgan said, "here's your thumb drive." She pulled the memory stick out of her jeans pocket.

Trevin snatched it from Morgan's hand.

"Hey," Morgan said.

"What did you call that?" Trevin asked.

"It's a thumb drive, and it belongs to Kurt."

Trevin held the computer memory stick at arm's length. "Dawn used these all the time. How could I be so stupid?" He tossed the thumb drive to Kurt. "Gotta go!"

Morgan grabbed the sleeve of his fleece jacket. "Wait a minute. You're supposed to repair my window."

Trevin turned, his hands clenched into fists. "Thumb drive! Thumbelina? That's what Dawn was trying to tell me."

"Where are you going?" Morgan asked.

"To find Thumbelina," Trevin said.

"Do you know where it is?" Kurt asked.

Trevin's shoulders slumped. "No. But maybe if I search the places I looked before, I might see it this time."

"Before you go running off," Kurt said, "chasing after this needle in a haystack, I think you need a plan."

Morgan grabbed both men's arms.

"We don't need a plan," she said. "I know where it is."

Kurt followed Morgan and Trevin to the rock shop. Cindy was thrilled to get the T-shirts.

"We're taking the ATVs out," Morgan said.

"Right now?" Cindy asked. "I could use some help."

"I think there's a clue to the murder out on the trail."

"Then you'd better put the chains on," Cindy said.

"Chains?" Kurt asked.

"Like tire chains for cars," Cindy said. "There's a lot of snow on the hill."

They managed to locate the ATV tire chains, and fasten them around the fat tires. Trevin climbed on behind Morgan, and they drove through the pasture to the back gate. The chains dug into the snow, leaving a distinctive trail behind them.

Morgan pushed her machine as fast as she could. The sun

had nearly dropped behind the mountains by the time they reached the spot where Morgan had first seen Dawn. She slowed the ATV to a stop and turned off the engine.

"That's where I saw the magpie fly with the chain." Morgan pointed to a nest in a cottonwood tree.

"That's pretty high," Trevin said. "We should have brought a ladder."

They walked across the meadow.

"Kurt," Morgan said, "you really need to get some boots."

His scuffed dress shoes filled with snow, and his pant legs were soaked.

"I wasn't expecting to go hiking." Kurt stopped at the base of the tree and looked up. He pulled the digital camera from his coat pocket and snapped a picture. "Anyone good at climbing trees?"

"Give me a boost," Trevin said.

Trevin managed to clamber onto the lower branches of the tree with Kurt's help. He worked his way up to the nest. Kurt snapped photos.

"I'll feel awful if nothing's up there," Morgan said.

Trevin reached the nest.

"Nobody's home," he called.

"That's good," Kurt said. "Do you see anything?"

"A foil gum wrapper," Trevin said. "A quarter. Something that looks like it came off a bike. A chain—"

"That's it!" Morgan yelled. "I saw a chain."

Trevin stuck his hand inside the nest.

"Uh-oh." Kurt pointed out a magpie, wheeling across the sky.

"Hurry, Trevin," Morgan called.

"The chain's stuck on the nest."

The magpie spied the intruder, and soared into the cottonwood branches. Trevin threw an arm across his face.

"Ah!"

"Hang on!" Morgan yelled.

The bird cawed and beat its wings against Trevin.

"Got it."

Trevin threw a fistful of leaves and twigs to the ground. Kurt pawed through the snow. Morgan watched Trevin's retreat. The magpie flapped its wings and screamed at Trevin all the way. Trevin scrambled down the tree trunk until he was low enough to jump. He dropped to the ground and rolled in the snow.

Morgan ran to Trevin. "Are you okay?"

"I'm fine. Did you get it?"

"This is it?" Kurt asked. He held out his hand. A black leather pouch the length of a finger hung from a silver chain. Piers's gargoyle was sewn to the smooth leather with heavy black thread.

"I think that's what I saw," Morgan said. "The chain must have been what glittered. Maybe there's a thumb drive in the pouch?"

Trevin reached for it. Kurt wrapped his fingers around it.

"You're a suspect," Kurt said. "If you open this, the police might accuse you of tampering with evidence."

"I just want to see if it's Thumbelina," Trevin said.

"There's no sense taking it to the police if it's empty," Morgan said.

Kurt photographed the unopened pouch. He took a close-up of the drawstring closure. When he had worked open the pouch, he took another photo.

"Would you hurry up?" Trevin asked.

Kurt frowned at Trevin. "I'm doing this for your benefit. You should be thanking me."

"Sorry," Trevin said in a sullen tone.

Finally, Kurt tipped the pouch upside down, spilling its contents into his gloved hand.

"A crystal," Kurt said. "Bits of dried leaves. The tiniest address book I've ever seen. And a thumb drive."

Morgan clasped her gloved hands together. "Yes!"

"Do you have a computer?" Trevin asked Morgan. "When we get back to the rock shop—"

"No," Kurt said. "This goes straight to the police."

CHAPTER THIRTY-FOUR

If business hadn't kept her occupied, Morgan would have camped out at the police station, waiting to learn what was on the thumb drive. She had the happy distraction of crowds of customers anxious to see the Angel Donkeys.

When the phone rang Thursday morning, Morgan was prepared to give directions to the shop for the hundredth time.

"Good morning. Rock of Ages. How may I help you?"

"I'm coming home."

"Del, the doctor wanted to keep you another day, at least," Morgan said. "I'm not picking you up."

"You don't need to get me," Del said. "I've got a ride. See you in an hour or so."

"Del, I don't think this is a good idea," Morgan began, but Del hung up.

After noon, Barton's rugged old truck pulled up in the parking lot and drove around the side of the rock shop. Morgan ran to the kitchen and unlocked the back door.

A man in a suit helped Del out of the passenger seat. Morgan would not have recognized him if not for the bushy beard. Barton carried a plastic personal items bag with the hospital logo in one hand, and a large paper sack from a fast-food place in the other.

Del struggled to free himself from the seat belt, and hobbled to Morgan on unsteady feet.

"I'm back!"

Barton followed Del inside.

"If you so much as sneeze," Morgan scolded, "I'm sending you right back to the hospital. Barton, I can't believe you let Del talk you into bringing him home."

Del's arm was in an elevated cast that looked too complicated to wear home. Morgan imagined Del and Barton sneaking out the back door of the hospital, fleeing watchful nurses.

"The doctor said it was okay," Barton said, "if Del promised he wasn't staying alone at his place."

"I hope you don't mind." Del seated himself at the table and opened the fast-food sack with one hand. "It's just until I get this thing off my arm."

Morgan was curious to see how Del would manage eating a taco.

"Of course you can stay here," Morgan said. "You won't be much use as a bodyguard, though."

"Sure I will. This thing's hard as a rock!" Del swung his arm back and forth. "Ow."

"See what I mean?" Morgan said.

"Mrs. Iverson?" Robin rapped on the door and stuck her head inside the kitchen. "Someone wants to write a check."

"I'll be right there."

Morgan watched Barton unwrap a taco and place it in Del's free hand.

"Barton?"

He looked up at Morgan.

"Do you know anything about memory sticks? Ones used for personal computers?"

Del snorted. "If it has something to do with computers, Barton probably invented it." Del bit into his taco. It broke in half, spilling its contents on the kitchen table and floor. The mice would be happy.

"I wish I'd invented them," Barton said.

"How sturdy are they?" Morgan asked.

"They're pretty tough," Barton said, "but not indestructible. I've washed them in my clothes before, and they still worked. Why?"

"Mrs. Iverson?" Robin rapped on the door again.

"I'll tell you later," Morgan said to Barton.

Too many people knew about the thumb drive already. She couldn't let every murder suspect in town know she'd found it.

Friday was a blur involving T-shirts, customers, and preparation for the Hopping Bunny Snowshoe race. Kurt arranged for the stable to transport the donkeys to the race the next day, after Morgan confirmed with the vet that Adelaide could travel. She put in a call to the church ladies to provide something in between a babysitter and an armed guard to make sure Del stayed off his feet, per doctor's orders. Beatrice promised to be there at six to fix Del breakfast.

The morning of the race came too early. Morgan woke at four to help Bernie make pastries and coffee to feed the volunteers. She sneaked out of the house without waking Del and drove to the back of the bakery.

"Look, Morgan." Bernie held up a long-sleeved purple T-shirt. "I'm on the shirt."

Bibi's Bakery was printed in white letters on the back of the race T-shirt, along with other sponsors.

"Nice!" Morgan said.

"We'd better get busy. I did a lot of prep work yesterday, but we only have a couple hours to get things cooked and to the park."

It was still dark when they loaded Bernie's SUV with trays of pastries and insulated boxes of coffee.

"Did you remember a flashlight?" Bernie asked.

"Del made sure I packed the entire sporting goods store,"

Morgan said. "I have a backpack this time. But I drew the line at the gun. I don't feel confident handling it, especially after that day we ran into Trevin on the trail."

Bernie put her vehicle in gear and headed to the park. They had no trouble finding the staging area. Cars, trucks, and vans crowded the small parking lot. Spotlights on poles illuminated the tables set up on trampled snow.

Lucy, clipboard in hand, talked to search and rescue volunteers astride ATVs.

"Hi, Bernie." Rolf smiled and waved. "Hi, Morgan."

Lucy consulted her clipboard. "They're running aid station number six."

"I'll take them," Rolf said.

"First I need to know where to put the coffee," Bernie said.

The volunteers cheered.

By the time they headed to their aid station, the sky was growing light.

"Who wants to go first?" Rolf patted the seat of the ATV.

"We don't have to walk?" Bernie asked.

"I have to haul in the water and sports drink," Rolf said. "I have room for one passenger at a time."

"I'll walk," Morgan said. "We'll be standing all day. Walking might help me warm up."

"Maybe I should walk, too." Bernie looked at Morgan with an expression that was crystal clear.

Morgan waved a hand. "No, you should ride."

Rolf's smile was as delighted as Bernie's. Morgan had guessed right.

"But if you have room," Morgan said, "could you take my backpack?"

She handed Rolf the supersized survival pack.

"Yow!" he exclaimed. "What's in this thing?"

"Pretty much everything," Morgan said.

Bernie hopped onto the ATV with Rolf. Morgan lagged behind so they could chatter without including her. The trail following the creek was level, and the snow was packed. Morgan checked her watch. She was certain she could walk the mile to the aid station in less than twenty minutes.

The course looped through the woods in a circular route. They were the last aid station before the end of the race.

The ATV disappeared around a curve. The sound of the engine grew faint. She supposed it was a good sign that Bernie and Rolf were so interested in each other that they had forgotten all about her.

Pine trees thick with green needles and heavy with snow blocked out the dim rays of the morning sun. One lazy white flake floated out of the gray clouds. Morgan shivered.

All of her survival gear was on the ATV. If she got lost, she wouldn't last long. Morgan tried to shake off rising panic. The last time she had let fear get the better of her, she had nearly slipped off a trail. She had almost pepper-sprayed Barton. She'd been ready to pepper-spray a photographer, also presumed innocent. And yet she had been unprepared for the tattooed man on the bridge. The problem was, until Morgan knew who the killer was, she had to assume everyone was potentially a murderer.

Snowflakes wove through tree branches, increasing in quantity and intensity with every step Morgan took. She was all alone in the dark woods.

Morgan shook her head. "Don't be ridiculous," she told herself.

The police had Thumbelina. For all she knew, they might have already made an arrest. She could hear ATVs, shouts, and laughter. There were hundreds of people in the woods today.

Including, quite possibly, one murderer.

★ ★ ★ ★ ★

Rolf set up a folding table. He lifted the five-gallon containers of water and sports drink onto the table.

"Here's your walkie-talkie." Rolf handed Bernie the device. "Every aid station gets one. You probably don't have cell service out here, so use it if you need help. I have to go now, but I'll be back to check on you." Rolf seemed to remember Morgan. "Both."

Morgan felt like an afterthought. Rolf hopped on the ATV and roared off in the direction of the park. She and Bernie unpacked the paper drinking cups and trash bags. Bernie hummed an airy tune as she filled cups halfway with water or sports drink.

"You're remarkably cheerful, considering it's snowing," Morgan said.

"It must be the new ultra-light thermal underwear I bought. Not to mention the wool socks."

"Are you sure it doesn't have anything to do with Prince Charming and his noble metallic steed?"

"I have to admit," Bernie said, "it's nice feeling you have the undivided interest of a handsome gentleman."

Her cheeks were pink with emotion as well as the chill air. Snowflakes settled on Bernie's eyelashes.

"I'm afraid the water's going to freeze," Morgan said.

"I can't imagine wanting to drink water in this cold weather, but Lucy insists people get dehydrated as fast in the snow as in the heat."

Morgan checked her watch. "The race should have started by now."

"I wonder when we'll see our first runner?"

They heard the ATV several minutes before it roared into sight. Bernie looked disappointed when the driver wasn't Rolf. The woman pulled the ATV to a stop and killed the engine.

"Hi. I'm Sharon, with search and rescue. There's a storm heading this way, so we're taking some extra precautions." She climbed off the ATV and handed Bernie a clipboard. "Please mark off runners as they go through your aid station."

Morgan looked over Bernie's shoulder at the printout of bib numbers and names.

"I suggest one of you be the spotter," Sharon said, "and one of you check names off."

"Okay," Bernie said. "We can do that."

"We're going to keep search and rescue personnel on the course until every runner and volunteer is accounted for," Sharon said.

"How will we know when the last person goes by?" Morgan asked.

"We'll send someone around," Sharon said. "We won't leave you out here."

"When will the first runner be here?" Bernie asked.

"It'll be at least another hour."

The snow stopped, then started again. Morgan dug the pepper spray out of her backpack and tucked it in her jacket pocket.

"In case I run into a raccoon," she told Bernie. "I'm going to find the little girls' room."

Morgan made a trip behind a pile of boulders to relieve herself. When she rejoined Bernie, the baker had rearranged the half-filled cups of water and sports drink.

"My feet are cold," Morgan said.

"Mine, too," Bernie agreed.

"I thought your wool socks were working."

"They must have a time limit. This is kind of boring."

"Barton said he was going to run today," Morgan said. "Is his name on the list?"

They found Barton, Lucy and Paul, and Chuck and Vonne

from the running club. The sun struggled through the pine trees for a brief time, warming the aid station.

Finally, they heard the peculiar sound of snowshoes on the trail. The first runner charged past at an amazing speed, considering the aluminum and web contraptions he wore on both feet. He ignored their offer of refreshments.

"Did you get his number?" Bernie asked.

"Two forty-two," Morgan said.

"Joey McCormick. I wonder if he's any relation to Teruko?"

Two minutes passed before the next runner went by. He was followed closely by two more. The rest of the runners seemed to travel in groups of three or more. Most accepted a half cup of water or sports drink, gulping down part of it, and tossing the rest, with the cup, on the side of the trail.

In between clusters of runners, Morgan and Bernie picked up the cups.

"Look!" Bernie cried. "I think it's Barton."

There had been more than a few full beards run through the aid station, but this one's bib number matched Barton Potts's.

"Hi, Barton," Bernie called.

"Good morning, ladies." Barton slowed to a brisk walk. "Water, please."

Morgan handed him a cup. He gulped it down while walking, then tossed it aside. "Gotta go!"

Rolf checked on them, as promised, riding up on his ATV an hour and a half into the race.

"How are you doing?" he asked. "Everything okay?"

Bernie consulted the clipboard. "About half the runners have gone by."

"Do you need anything?" Rolf asked.

"A fireplace, an easy chair, and a hot toddy," Bernie said.

Rolf laughed. "Maybe we can arrange that later."

A cluster of runners approached as he drove away.

"Hi, Lucy," Morgan said. "Hi, Paul. You're doing great."

"Better than we thought we would," Lucy said.

"We got a late start." Paul gulped down a half cup of sports drink, then grabbed a half cup of water. "About ten minutes after the race started."

"That's the price of being a volunteer," Lucy said.

"Wow!" Bernie said. "Then you're doing fantastic."

"Gotta keep moving." Paul tossed his paper cup in Bernie's trash bag.

"See you at the end," Lucy called.

Morgan watched Lucy and Paul disappear down the trail. Bernie held out her hand.

"It's snowing again."

Morgan looked up. Fluffy flakes spiraled down through the branches of the pine trees.

"Is it me," Morgan asked, "or is it getting colder?"

"It's getting colder." Bernie wrapped her arms around herself and shivered. "I'm freezing."

The snowshoe racers stomping past the aid station traveled at slower speeds as the morning wore on. There were still twenty-three names on the checklist when Rolf returned, followed by Sharon. Her ATV was loaded down with a table, five-gallon beverage containers, backpacks, and a volunteer. Another volunteer trotted behind the ATV on snowshoes. Sharon didn't stop, but Rolf pulled off the trail and parked.

"Hi, ladies." He climbed off his ATV. "How are you doing? Staying warm?"

Bernie's green eyes sparkled. "We're doing fine. How much longer do you think we have?"

"I can take you back now," Rolf said. "We're packing out the aid stations that are finished. I'm sure we can get someone to run your aid station if you want to call it a day."

"Don't tempt me," Morgan said. "We know how it feels to be

last. I want to be here for every runner."

"But seriously," Bernie said, "what do you think, Rolf? Another thirty minutes?"

"Last year," Rolf said, consulting his clipboard, "the last runner crossed the finish line at twelve forty-five." He looked up at Bernie. "It's almost noon now." Rolf climbed onto the ATV. "Last chance!"

"We're fine," Bernie said. "Go ahead."

Before I change my mind, Morgan thought.

"I'll be back to pick you up," Rolf said.

He roared down the trail.

"Forty-five minutes," Bernie exclaimed. "I need to use the restroom."

"You could have left with Rolf," Morgan said. "I'm glad you stayed, though."

"I didn't want to look like a quitter," Bernie said. "Do you have any TP in your survival bag?"

Morgan dug out a roll of toilet paper and handed it to Bernie.

"And you'd better take this." Morgan handed Bernie the walkie-talkie.

"In case I need to make an important call?" Bernie asked with a smile.

"I'll be at the table," Morgan said. "Search and rescue can find me."

"Good point." Bernie stuck the walkie-talkie in her jacket pocket. She marched off toward the boulders Morgan had used as a restroom earlier.

Three more runners straggled past the aid station. Morgan had no trouble reading their bib numbers. After checking them off the list, Morgan looked toward the boulders. Bernie was certainly taking her time. Morgan wondered whether she should check on her friend, but didn't want to bother her at an inconvenient time. Morgan pulled her cell phone out of her pocket. No signal.

A chill wind blew cups of water and sports drink over. Morgan attempted to mop up the mess with paper towels, but the liquid froze to the table.

After the next runner, Morgan decided she had better check on Bernie. She watched a person laboring up the trail with the grace and speed of a box turtle. No bib number. The runner's bulky coat must have been buttoned up over it. And no snowshoes, either. Maybe he or she was a volunteer, trying to beat the storm by leaving their aid station early.

Then Morgan saw her face.

CHAPTER THIRTY-FIVE

"Sparrow." Morgan flipped through her clipboard, pretending to study the sheets. She knew Sparrow wasn't a participant or a volunteer. "I don't see your name on the list."

"There's a blizzard coming." Sparrow's raspy smoker's voice was harsh. "They sent me to warn people. I'm taking you back to town."

"I can't leave yet," Morgan said. "There are still runners out there. And Rolf is coming with an ATV—"

"Ralph sent me," Sparrow pronounced his name incorrectly, convincing Morgan she didn't know Rolf. "Come on!"

Sparrow was dressed like a thrift-store lumberjack, in a plaid wool jacket, a cap with earflaps, and baggy olive-green insulated pants. Trevin hadn't been able to tell whether a man or a woman was following Morgan and Bernie on the Columbine Trail. Now Morgan knew why.

"But I can't—" Morgan started to say she couldn't leave without Bernie, but reconsidered. "I have to get my backpack." She walked toward the table. Morgan needed to think fast, but she could feel her brain congealing like the spilled sports drink.

Sparrow trudged across the snow, following Morgan. "Ralph will get your backpack."

Morgan stepped behind the table, keeping it between her and Sparrow.

"I have to wait for search and rescue." Morgan spoke loudly, hoping Bernie could hear. "I can't leave with you."

"You don't have a choice." Sparrow tried to reach across the table, but Morgan stepped back.

Sparrow hadn't made it onto Morgan's suspect list. She doubted the hemp-store owner had been considered by the police, either. If not for Kurt and Anna's research, Morgan probably wouldn't be making the connection now. Sparrow had as much motivation as Piers to push through the zoning changes. Maybe more.

"You killed Dawn," Morgan said.

"That girl was on a path of self-destruction. She wasn't long for this world."

"So that gave you the right to take her out?"

"What's this? A Sunday-school lesson in morality?" Sparrow angled left, then right, but Morgan stayed a step ahead of her.

"Are you the one who talked her into making that false charge against Pastor Filbury?"

"Who said it was false?" Sparrow asked.

Morgan concentrated on goading Sparrow into a confession, while playing keep-away around the small folding table.

"If you coerced Dawn into making a statement against the pastor," Morgan said, "then the only reason you'd kill her is if she backed out. Dawn knew the truth would come out in court."

"That brainless boyfriend of hers is the reason Dawn is dead," Sparrow said. "If he'd left her alone, she'd still be among the living."

"So you did kill her."

"Did I say that?" Sparrow grinned. "Ha. You really take me for a fool, don't you?"

"Then it must have been Piers."

Fury flashed in Sparrow's small gray eyes. "Don't drag him into this."

"Dawn had a gargoyle necklace," Morgan said. "She had to be his student. Or maybe something more?"

"It wasn't like that," Sparrow growled. "She was just a trampy kid. Piers doesn't go for that type."

Sparrow bobbed left, then right. Morgan could anticipate the larger woman's slow movements. If Sparrow got her hands on Morgan, it would be a different matter. Morgan reached into her jacket pocket for the pepper spray.

"I had you pegged from day one," Sparrow ranted. "You're just as bad as your crazy brother. In case you haven't figured it out, Piers isn't interested in you. He's only after your land."

Sparrow grabbed the table and flung it aside. The water and sports drink containers crashed to the ground. Paper cups scattered across the snow. Morgan ran behind a pine tree. She grasped the pepper spray, concealing it with her glove. Del had assured her there was plenty of spray left, even after her ill-fated encounter with Barton. Morgan figured she had one good shot. If she missed, Sparrow might go berserk. It had to be dead on.

"Golden Springs could be the perfect New Age retreat if it weren't for people like you."

"You killed a girl over a failed business plan?"

"Everything would have worked out," Sparrow wheezed, "but you had to play the Good Samaritan."

"I saw a person lying on the trail. Some of us don't turn away when people need help."

"Who are you kidding?" Sparrow asked. "You ran away."

Morgan realized the crashing in the brush that day had not been a deer. Sparrow had been watching her.

"So you were there. You could have helped."

"You were too late," Sparrow said. "All this mess, for nothing."

"Dawn was already dead?"

"You were as good as dead the minute you chose to meddle in something that was none of your business. What's the problem with you? With your whole damn family? Can't leave well enough alone until somebody makes you stop."

"Like Allie? You ran her into the ditch, didn't you? Just like your pal Slice nearly ran over me. But it's all over, Sparrow. Dawn left a clue. The police have it."

"You're bluffing." But doubt creased Sparrow's brow. "Quit wasting my time. We've got to get out of here—" Sparrow stopped. "What the—" She looked past Morgan, toward the boulders.

Bernie ran across the snow, waving the walkie-talkie in the air.

"I called search and rescue," Bernie yelled. "Whoops!"

She slipped and fell. The walkie-talkie flew from her hand, disappearing from sight as it sank into the snow.

"Bernie," Morgan yelled, and ran toward her friend.

For the first time, Sparrow moved swiftly. She grabbed the back of Morgan's coat and yanked hard. Morgan fell on her backside.

Sparrow jerked Morgan to her feet and grabbed the collar of Morgan's coat, attempting to get her hands around Morgan's throat. Morgan wrestled with her, struggling to aim the pepper spray in Sparrow's face. Sparrow grabbed Morgan's arm, slamming her right wrist against the trunk of a tree.

Morgan yelped in pain and anger as the pepper spray flew out of her hand. Bernie grabbed Sparrow's arm. When Sparrow released her grip, Morgan fell on her side, cradling her wounded wrist against her body.

Morgan watched as Sparrow elbowed Bernie in the gut. Bernie doubled over. Sparrow grappled with Bernie, finally getting her fingers around the heavy chain of Bernie's religious medallion.

Ligature strangulation.

Bernie thrust her mitten-covered hand under the medallion, grasping Saint Elizabeth and a fistful of chain. Sparrow jerked hard on the chain, squeezing Bernie's hand against her throat.

Morgan struggled to her feet. She beat her left fist against Sparrow's back, but it was as effective as punching a boulder. She threw her good arm around Sparrow's neck and yanked back as hard as she could. Sparrow reached around with one hand and pushed Morgan away.

Morgan stumbled backward. She threw her hands down to break her fall. Pain shot through her wrist. Stars danced before her eyes, and ringing filled her ears.

"Bernie," she gasped, and forced herself to sit up.

Enraged inhuman sounds erupted from Sparrow's throat. Purple splotches colored her cheeks as she throttled Bernie. With one hand, she twisted and jerked the chain, and with the other she tore at Bernie's protective hand. Bernie went limp in Sparrow's grip, her grasp on the medallion weakening.

Morgan rose to her hands and knees. Her right arm buckled and she rolled in the snow, hitting something hard with her shoulder. Morgan groped for the object, hoping for a sharp, heavy rock. She wrapped her mitten around it and struggled to her feet.

The pepper-spray canister.

Staggering like a drunk, Morgan stumbled toward Sparrow. She held the canister in front of Sparrow's face and hit the trigger. The spray seemed to have no effect. Sparrow gripped the chain of Bernie's medallion tighter. Bernie slumped to the ground.

Awareness penetrated Sparrow's rage. She shrieked, the sound echoing through the snowy hills. Pressing her gloves to her face, she careened blindly, slamming into trees and stumbling over rocks. Sparrow fell to her knees, wailing and cursing as she rubbed handfuls of snow in her face.

The forest had been silent all day except for bird song, the wind sighing through the trees, the crunching and squeaking noises of snowshoes, and her conversations with Bernie. Now the discordant sounds of Sparrow's pain cut though the crisp air.

That, and the engine of an ATV. Bernie's walkie-talkie call to search and rescue must have gone through. Morgan struggled through the snow to her friend's side, dropping to her knees. Bernie rolled to face Morgan.

"Help is coming," Morgan told her. "Hang on."

Across the trail, snow cascaded off bushes. Muffled curses erupted, as a man thrashed his way through the thick branches. He stumbled onto the trail, shaking snow off his black cloak.

The man from the stone bridge glared at Morgan.

"We have unfinished business."

He took a step toward her. Sparrow wailed, drawing his attention away from Morgan. The man spun around, pointing a gloved finger at Morgan.

"Did you hurt my cousin?"

"Sparrow is a murderer," Morgan said. "And you tried to kill me."

"If Piers hadn't stuck his nose into things, I might have finished the job." The man tried to help Sparrow up. "This whole mess is his fault."

"Piers killed Dawn Smith?" Morgan asked.

"Yeah, sure. It was Piers." He didn't speak the words with conviction.

"Nooooo!" Sparrow wailed. "Not Piers."

"Shut up, cousin."

He managed to get Sparrow to her feet. The sound of the ATV grew louder. Maybe there was more than one.

"We gotta get out of here," the man said.

"Can't see," Sparrow muttered. "I can't see."

She tripped over a snow-covered rock and went down, taking her cousin with her.

Rolf's ATV went airborne as he raced over the hill. He skidded to a stop, sending up a shower of snow, then hopped off his ATV and raced toward Sparrow and her cousin.

"Not them," Morgan yelled. She looked down at her friend, who was clutching her throat with a mitten-covered hand and gasping for breath. "Sparrow tried to kill Bernie!"

"Oh, God." Rolf ran to Bernie's side and knelt in the snow. "Bernie!"

He looked panicked for an instant, then switched emotional gears as he unzipped a large fanny pack.

Another ATV roared into the aid station and headed toward Morgan.

"Stop them." She waved her good hand toward Sparrow and her cousin, who were struggling their way across the trail. "Don't let them get away."

CHAPTER THIRTY-SIX

It was past midnight when Lucy brought Morgan home from the emergency room, but the lights were still on at the Rock of Ages. The comforting smells of wood fire and coffee wrapped around Morgan as they entered the kitchen. Beatrice set her playing cards face down on the table and hurried to Morgan's side, grasping her good arm.

"I was beginning to think they were going to keep you overnight," she said.

"Well, look at you." Del laughed. "We're a matched set!" He raised his cast. "Ow."

Beatrice led Morgan to the easy chair. Lucy placed a pillow on the wide arm of the chair and rested Morgan's splinted arm on top of it.

"How bad is it?" Beatrice asked.

"It's a closed fracture," Lucy said. "Definitely broken, but she probably won't need surgery. Just a splint and ice for now."

"I have to go to the doctor on Monday," Morgan said. "Unless it swells, and then it's back to the emergency room."

"Here are the instructions." Lucy handed Beatrice a sheet of paper. "And the pain medicine."

Beatrice examined the bottle. "Over the counter?" She looked dismayed. "Is that all they gave you?"

"You'd think a broken arm would warrant something more than ibuprofen," Morgan said, "but that's all I get."

"So we heard the *Reader's Digest* version of the story when you called," Del said. "How about we hear the whole thing now?"

Morgan retold the story she had already related to Chief Sharp, Officers Sanchez and MacKenzie, and Detective Parker.

"Are you ready to get your concealed weapons license?" Del asked. "You could have saved yourself a lot of trouble if you'd been packing."

"I'll think about it," Morgan said.

"How's Bernie?" Beatrice asked.

"Strangulation is a tricky injury," Lucy said. "They're keeping her overnight as a precaution, but she should be okay."

"If she hadn't been gripping her Saint Elizabeth medallion," Morgan said, "Sparrow might have gotten enough pressure on Bernie's carotid artery to kill her."

"If you hadn't pepper-sprayed Sparrow," Lucy said, "she might have finished the job."

"I don't see how she figured to get away with it," Del said. "The woods had to be crawling with people."

"Sure, at the beginning," Morgan said. "Bernie and I didn't see people for long stretches toward the end."

"How'd she get there?" Del asked. "Sparrow's not exactly the athletic type."

"They found her car," Lucy said. "Sparrow's cousin Slice had driven it up a jeep road just behind the hill where Morgan and Bernie's aid station was situated."

"That dilapidated old hippie van?" Del asked.

"No, a black Mercedes Benz SUV," Lucy said.

"She's the one who let the donkeys out," Del exclaimed.

"Maybe not," Morgan said. "Slice drove Trevin up here for the first break-in. Trevin never met Sparrow. Slice had his own little gang of teenage followers."

"I have to admit," Del said, "that woman really had me fooled. I believed she was poor as a church mouse."

"It was just a disguise," Morgan said. "Sparrow had enough money to buy up a third of downtown Golden Springs."

"I've got to run home," Lucy said, "but don't hesitate to call if you need anything."

"Don't worry," Beatrice said. "We've got things covered. I'm staying until these two can take care of themselves."

"Thanks so much for waiting in the emergency room with me," Morgan said to Lucy. "And I'm sorry."

"Sorry?" Lucy asked. "That's what friends are for."

"But you missed the awards ceremony."

"They postponed it," Lucy said. "With the police and all the excitement at the end, the race committee decided to move the ceremony to tomorrow night. You have to come."

"We're not exactly mobile," Del said, wiggling his fingers from the end of his cast.

"You don't want to miss it," Lucy said. "The ceremony is going to be really special."

Beatrice went to church Sunday morning, returning to the rock shop with a chicken dinner.

"Who gave the message today?" Morgan asked.

"Some young pastor from Cañon City." Beatrice reached into the kitchen cupboard for plates. "He was very excitable. I didn't care for him too much."

"Any word on whether Pastor Filbury is coming back?"

"I expect he'll be back soon," Beatrice said.

"Why is that?" Morgan shifted in the rocking chair. "Do you have some news?"

"Have they wrung a confession out of that Plinkton woman yet?" Del asked.

"They don't need to." Beatrice placed three plates on the kitchen table. "My nephew heard that the computer memory thing Morgan found contains a statement from Dawn Smith. It absolves Pastor Filbury of any wrongdoing. Dawn said she was put up to the whole thing by Sparrow. She even recorded her conversation with Sparrow using a camera on a computer. That's on the computer memory, too. Sparrow said she'd kill Dawn if she backed out of the case against Pastor Filbury. My nephew thinks the police will have a strong case, in spite of any high-dollar attorneys she may hire."

Del nodded. "That'll be a tough one to fight, especially when she tried to kill Bernie the same exact way. I have to admit, though, I'm kinda disappointed they couldn't pin it on Piers Townsend."

"That man will face his own reckoning," Beatrice said. "His finances are so tangled up with Sparrow's, he could lose everything. Apparently, she wove quite the elaborate web in her attempt to buy his affection."

"But she had enough money to buy a third of Main Street," Morgan said. "She'll just buy her way out of the murder charge and bail Piers out of his problems, too."

Beatrice shook her head, a satisfied smile on her lips. "Her wealth was a house of cards, built with creative financing and shady business deals. It's all about to crumble now."

That evening, Beatrice drove Morgan and Del to City Hall. Rows of utility tables covered with white plastic tablecloths filled the community room. The aroma of the catered spaghetti dinner scented the room with garlic. Beatrice placed her oatmeal cookies on the potluck dessert table while Morgan and Del settled at a table with Lucy and her family.

"Is this seat taken?" Barton asked.

"Squeeze in," Del said. "I'm taking up more than my fair share of room with this contraption."

Bernie arrived, causing a scramble to set up a small table to accommodate her enormous tray of petits fours. Kurt took photos of the desserts, the trophies, and the audience. Bernie sat next to Morgan, across from Del.

"How do you feel?" Bernie croaked.

"How do *you* feel?" Morgan asked. "You sound like you have a bad case of laryngitis."

A thin band of purple bruise wrapped around Bernie's neck. She adjusted a silk scarf in an attempt to cover it.

"I'll heal before you do." Bernie's voice was painfully raspy. "I'm so glad you both made it to the ceremony."

"I'm not feeling glad right now," Morgan said. "I'd rather be sitting in my rocking chair."

"It'll be worth it," Barton said. "Trust me."

"I'm glad we had a late lunch," Morgan said. "Spaghetti might possibly be the worst food to eat with a broken arm."

"No," Barton said. "That would be tacos."

Beatrice led Morgan and Del through the buffet line. Spaghetti was as difficult to manage as Morgan had expected. She spilled more food on the table and floor than she got in her mouth. As they finished eating, a lean young man in a black fleece jacket with reflective silver piping stood at the podium.

"Welcome to the annual Hopping Bunny Snowshoe race awards ceremony."

Instead of handing out awards, he introduced the guest speaker. Then a sponsor spoke. Then a high school coach.

Morgan was already tired. Somehow she thought that races had three winners—first, second, third. Maybe six, if men and women were awarded prizes separately. She soon learned about age categories. For men and women. The table loaded with over two dozen trophies slowly emptied, while Morgan's arm throbbed and her head ached. Neither she nor Del could clap when Barton took second place for men aged forty-five to forty-nine. After accepting his trophy, Barton slipped out the side door. Morgan envied him.

She debated asking Beatrice to drive her home when Rolf

walked to the podium. He thumped the microphone with his finger.

"Is this on?"

"It's been on through the whole thing, Rolf!" someone yelled.

"Ha. Okay." Rolf rattled a sheet of paper. "We've come to the end of the awards ceremony, but before we leave, search and rescue has a special award to give."

The double doors opened. Houdini and Adelaide clopped across the wood floor, led by Barton and Kurt.

"What are the donkeys doing in City Hall?" Morgan whispered to Del.

"There are so many possible answers to that question." Del chuckled. "I can't even begin."

"You've all read the story in the *Golden Springs Gazetteer*," Rolf said, "or heard it firsthand. Houdini and Adelaide saved Del Addison's life by pulling him down the hill in the middle of the blizzard."

People turned toward their table. Del raised his good arm and gave a little wave.

"In honor of heroism above and beyond the call of duty, the mayor has stricken the anti-donkey ordinance from city code."

When the audience clapped, Houdini showed the whites of his eyes and bared his yellow teeth. Morgan hoped he wouldn't go into attack-donkey mode.

"And in appreciation for the money they raised for our volunteer Pine County Search and Rescue crew, we request that Houdini and Adelaide serve as our official mascots." Rolf looked toward Morgan's table. "If that's okay with you, Morgan."

She stood, her splinted arm cradled in a sling. "I accept, on behalf of Houdini and Adelaide."

Houdini tried to eat the medal Rolf hung around his neck. Adelaide accepted hers with more poise. Kurt's camera flashed. The donkeys posed. They were used to paparazzi.

"That concludes this year's Hopping Bunny Snowshoe Race awards ceremony," Rolf said. "We'll see you all again next year."

As Barton led the donkeys out of the community room, Kurt headed for their table.

"Uh-oh," Del said. "We're next."

"Let's go," Morgan said.

They couldn't move fast enough to avoid the intrepid reporter. Kurt squeezed in between Bernie and Morgan, and pulled out his spiral-bound notepad and stubby pencil.

"You've had a lot of excitement during your first few weeks in Golden Springs," Kurt said.

"Hold on, Kurt," Beatrice said. "Can't you give being a newspaperman a rest for one night? Morgan and Del are exhausted."

Morgan started to agree with Beatrice, until she remembered how much she and Del owed Kurt.

"It's okay," Morgan said. "I can spare a few minutes for a friend."

Kurt smiled.

"Keep it quick," Del said. "My pain meds are wearing off."

"Do you have any thoughts about recent events you'd like to share with the *Golden Springs Gazetteer*?" Kurt asked.

"I don't know how interesting my thoughts would be," Morgan said, "but you were right when you told me I didn't understand small towns. I thought I was moving to a sleepy Old West tourist town, but Golden Springs isn't what it appears to be."

"You can say that again," Lucy said. "A poor hippie girl is really a ruthless business tycoon and murderess."

"The burglar is a sleuth," Bernie croaked.

"Our scruffy old donkeys turn into angels," Del added.

"What about you?" Kurt asked. "Big city girl moves to Golden Springs and becomes a hero?"

Morgan raised her hand, fending off Kurt's praise. "I failed Dawn."

"That's been settled," Del said. "You couldn't have saved her."

"And you did save Del," Lucy said.

"And me," Bernie rasped.

"I'd say that makes you a hero," Kurt said.

Morgan looked around the circle of new friends, and their encouraging smiles. Del sat on a folding chair. He was fading fast.

"We need to get home," Morgan said.

"Just one more question," Kurt said. "Are you staying in Golden Springs?"

"I can't drive back to Sioux Falls yet. Not until I get this splint off my arm."

"Good," Del said. "That'll give me time."

"Time for what?" Morgan asked.

She expected Del to announce his plan to create a travel survival kit, complete with parachute.

"Time to convince you to stay."

Morgan didn't have a clue how she would handle being a long-distance grandmother, or where the money would come from to pay the rock shop property taxes, but she finally knew one thing with certainty. The shop, like a geode, might be rough and homely on the outside, but it concealed hidden treasures whose worth couldn't be measured in dollars. Treasures she meant to preserve for her family.

ABOUT THE AUTHOR

To **Catherine Dilts,** rock shops are like geodes—both contain amazing treasures hidden inside their plain-as-dirt exteriors. Catherine caught mountain fever after a childhood vacation in Rocky Mountain National Park. Determined to give up her flatlander ways, she moved to Colorado. Her husband, a Colorado native, proposed to her as they hiked Barr Trail on Pikes Peak. Catherine works as an environmental scientist, and plays at heirloom vegetable gardening, camping, and fishing. She has published short fiction in *Alfred Hitchcock Mystery Magazine.* In her spare time, she attempts to lure wild donkeys to her property in the mountains.

Visit her website at http://www.catherinedilts.com.